THE BIRTHING HOUSE

THE BIRTHING HOUSE

Christopher Ransom

WINDSOR
PARAGON

First published 2008
by Sphere
This Large Print edition published 2009
by BBC Audiobooks Ltd
by arrangement with
Little, Brown Book Group

Hardcover ISBN: 978 1 408 42951 8
Softcover   ISBN: 978 1 408 42952 5

British Library Cataloguing in Publication Data available

Printed and bound in Great Britain by
CPI Antony Rowe, Chippenham and Eastbourne

X000 000 046 9448

This tale, concerning mothers and wives
and the men who drive them to darkness,
is for the two strongest women I know . . .

Sandra Ransom

Who told me every day that I could

&

Pia Gandt

Who was there every day while I did

Death borders upon our birth, and our cradle stands in the grave.

Joseph Hall, English bishop and satirist

1

Conrad Harrison found the last home he would ever know by driving the wrong way out of Chicago with a ghost in his car. When he crossed the Wisconsin line he was lost, too tired to care, and what traveled with him remained invisible and unknown. The wide green medians and fields of plowed fertile soil were relaxing. The road was black and smooth, free of those brain-jarring seams found on concrete highways. The spring thunder and rain moved over him from the side, pummeling the rented gray Dodge in bursts as brief and intense as a car wash. He could have gone on this way until he reached Canada, but an hour or two later there was some traffic and the sign for the Perkins in Janesville, so he exited.

He might have been tired and lost, but he was suddenly hungry, ravenous. Filled with the kind of animal appetite that shuts out all else and goes to work like it needs to prove something. He ordered the country fried steak with three over easy, and when the girl came to take the plate away he said, You know what? Let's do it again.

In between dinners, he picked up the paper the last guest had left in the booth. He liked to read the classifieds, to see what scraps people were offering, what hope they sought. He fell into the local real estate listings. The photo was black and white, all grainy and pixelated newsprint.

140 yr old Victorian in Black Earth. 4 bdr, 2 bath on 1 acre. 3500 sq. feet. Front parlor,

library, orig. woodwork, maple floors, fireplace. Cornish stone foundation. Det 2-car garage. Historic turn-of-the-century birthing house restored to mint. Perfect for family! $225,000. Seller motivated. Call Roddy—608-574-8911.

Now lightheaded from all the hash browns and gravy, he swallowed the last of his third cup of coffee and carried his meal ticket to the front counter. He paid with cash and left the girl a twenty for no real reason other than he felt, for the first time in his life, burdened by money. He juggled the page he'd torn from the *Wisconsin State Journal* and powered up his mobile. There were no messages, or maybe they had not come through the regional carrier's towers yet. Or maybe Jo was too busy to call.

The man who answered was polite. Sure, he could show the house as early as nine o'clock tomorrow morning. And did he know how to get to Black Earth?

Conrad said he was pretty sure he'd remember the directions, all the while thinking, What a name for a town. Don't worry, Dad. I'm not far behind.

So maybe he knew there was a ghost traveling with him after all.

2

From the front it appeared modest, a simple vanilla bean Victorian on a street of pleasant others. But later, when he would find himself walking the long slope of backyard alone at night, Conrad Harrison would come to see that its humble if charming façade masked ingenious depths and a height that seemed to grow at night, like Jack's beanstalk. The needle-helmeted dormers, covered front porch, chocolate pillars and squat front door brought to mind a fairy-tale house made for trolls or elves, not city people.

It was not love at first sight, but she made his heart beat faster.

Conrad tried to mask his excitement, if only because that was what you were supposed to do when considering a major purchase. He tried for a moment to imagine Jo's reaction if she were standing here beside him. It looked like the kind of house she was always talking about. Something old, something to redecorate when she was ready to settle down. But she wasn't here beside him now and the realization that he didn't much care what she thought gave him a deviant thrill. The house was like another woman in that way. Looking was just looking, and there was no harm in looking unless looking turned to touching. Or buying.

'Got kids?' Roderick 'call me Roddy' Tabor said, smiling like a man in a milk commercial. Instead of a dairy moustache, Roddy had a badass seventies cop 'stache and wooly sideburns, sans irony. The realtor was tall, very slim and balding. The brown suit and wide, brown tie were priceless. Conrad liked the realtor the minute he'd spotted him behind the desk at the crummy, wood-paneled real estate office down on Decatur Street. Roddy had grown up in Chicago, and they'd talked about city life vs country life for all of the ten or fifteen minutes it took to walk from 'downtown' Black

3

Earth up the broken sidewalk hill to 818 Heritage Street. 'Perfect place to raise some kids. Property taxes are steep, but the schools here are top-notch.'

Conrad cleared his throat. 'No. No kids. Just the two dogs. Both rescues from a shelter in Los Angeles. But they're like our children.' Conrad thought about mentioning the other pets he liked to keep from time to time, the animals that weren't really pets at all, but didn't. You never knew how people were going to react.

'Sure. Young couple. What's the hurry, right?' Roddy turned the key. 'Oh, door's unlocked. Pretty common 'round here.'

Conrad stepped past the realtor and laid his eyes on the first of several living rooms. Actually, he knew they weren't all living rooms. In these Victorians it was parlor-this and sitting room-that. Whatever you called them, they amounted to a lot of space to spread out, play cards, eat, watch TV and entertain friends. They would need new friends.

'I don't go for the song and dance myself,' Roddy said, dropping the keys on the ceramic tile and oak mantle. 'Figure adults know what they like when they see it. Holler if you have any questions.'

'Will do.'

Roddy ambled into the kitchen, helped himself to a glass of water, and stepped out back for a smoke.

Conrad found himself in the dining room, paced off the long maple floorboards, ran his fingers over the pinstriped wallpaper. Not a crack in the plaster walls or a splintering window sill in sight. The doorframes were straight. In the kitchen, the

4

original wooden shelves and pantry drawers were nicked black in many places, aged smooth and full of character. The trim was a clean, buttery shade of toffee. The lines of the house were immaculate. The house felt solid.

But confusing.

Conrad started in the front parlor, then exited through the French doors that opened into the main foyer, making a U-turn back into the dining room and living room. From there he backtracked and took a left into the family room and deeper into the kitchen. Once inside the kitchen, he forgot where the living room was, even though it was just on the other side of the wall. He went up the rear stairs from the kitchen, over one landing, through the library, and down the front stairs (which, despite the beauty of the black maple banister, seemed somehow formal and forbidding, though he couldn't say why), winding through the main floor clueless as to what he had already seen and what was new.

'You'll get used to it,' Roddy said, startling him. 'Ever seen a house with servants' stairs?'

'No, not really.' Conrad followed Roddy through the family room.

Roddy pointed to the faded hinge patterns on the doorframe at the base of the stairs and mouth of the kitchen. 'See that?'

'There was a door.'

'Yep. And another one here.' Roddy tapped the doorframe at the kitchen's front entrance. 'This way, you have two doors here, the help stays in the kitchen, out of sight from the proper company while you're warming your feet by the fire. When dinner has been served and the good doctor is sipping his brandy, the maidens duck up the servants' stairs here—'

Before Conrad could pursue the doctor reference, Roddy dashed up the servants' stairs. Conrad followed at a less eager pace. When he hit the landing, Roddy made a sweeping gesture into the smallest bedroom.

'Goodnight, you princes of Maine, you kings of New England,' Roddy said. 'And *voilà*. Servants are out of sight for the night. Let the party continue.'

'*Cider House Rules*. Nice.'

'That's right,' Roddy beamed. 'You're a movie guy.'

'Not really.' Conrad had mentioned Los Angeles and the screenwriting thing, as if that still mattered to him or ever had. 'I was in sales. Did some consulting from home. We had friends in the business. The writing was just something to do.'

'Oh? You cash in your chips?'

'Ha, yeah, no.' He'd never admit as much in Los Angeles, but out here, standing next to this stranger, Conrad decided to skip the embellishment for a change. 'A guy I knew used to hire me for cheap rewrites, but I never sold any material. Nothing original. I was laid off from a software firm. Been working in a bookstore until my wife gets another promotion. I don't really know what I'm doing, actually.'

Was Conrad imagining it, or did Roddy's smile slacken a bit on that one? Maybe not too smart, mentioning the layoff—probably just raised a red flag on the financing.

'Uh-huh, and what does your wife do?'

Conrad hesitated. 'You know, Roddy, I don't

6

know what she does any more. I mean, I know she works for a company that sells pharmaceuticals, or consults with pharmaceutical companies. Or medical supplies. I think she's something between a sales manager and a project manager. She travels a lot, that I do know.'

'Sounds promising.' The realtor seemed sorry he'd asked.

The bedroom was perhaps eight feet by six, with two small windows. Small enough for a child's twin bed and a trunk full of clothes, no more. It seemed cruel.

Conrad nodded. 'Where's the master?'

They continued through the library and around the black maple banister in a sort of zigzagging shuffle that led into a T-shaped hall branching to three bedrooms. The master was just a regular bedroom, not much larger than the other two spare rooms, but three times the size of Tiny Tim's room in the back.

'This is the master,' Conrad said, failing to conceal his disappointment.

'Old houses, my friend,' Roddy said. 'Back then people didn't use their bedroom for a whole lot. Not like now where you got your flat screen, your Jacuzzi, your orbital whattya call it, one of them gerbil wheels.'

'Not very LA,' Conrad offered.

'Bingo.'

'Besides,' Conrad said, taking over the pitch. 'We have a library. What do we need a TV for?'

'There you go. I'll give you some time up here, then we should grab some lunch before the saloon closes.'

'No problem. I'll be down in a few.'

'We're gonna feed you some fine Wisconsin cuisine, Mr Harrison.' Roddy clomped down the front stairs.

Conrad poked his nose into the first of the remaining two bedrooms. Unremarkable, but a perfect size for Jo's office, with a small window overlooking the rolling backyard.

He turned to the bedroom nearest the master. The knob wiggled loosely but he had to knee the wooden door from the frame to pop it free. Before it could swing all the way in, a short girl-woman with white hair scurried out, bumping his shoulder as she slipped by. Before he could get a bead on her, she swooped around the banister and trotted down the front stairs.

'Whoa, hey.' Conrad tasted a wash of adrenaline like a nine-volt battery pressed to his tongue.

'Sorry 'bout that,' she said in a flat, nasal tone, her face lowered even as she hit the foyer and exited through the front door.

White jeans or painter's pants. A blue pocket tee over a pudgy midriff. Small feet shod with chunky black skate shoes bearing a single pink stripe. Didn't get a look at her face, but her arm skin was white with white hairs standing up in a line to her wrist—he'd noticed that much. The scent of vanilla filled his nostrils, reminded him of a birthday cake shaped and decorated as a snowman, the one his mother had baked for his third birthday.

'It's okay,' he said to the empty foyer.

Another buyer? A lingering daughter sent to pick up the rest of her things after the move? But she hadn't been carrying anything on the way out, had she? No box of sweaters. No lamp or framed

8

art left behind by the movers. Huh. Must be just one of those chance encounters made possible by a house between occupants.

He turned back to the bedroom she'd just exited. It was decent size, maybe fourteen by sixteen. Two windows with bright red shades and black beaded tassels like something out of a western whorehouse. Deep pile the color of moist moss, didn't match. No furniture. But the same scent of vanilla was here, stronger, with something herbal hanging beneath it. From the girl, or just the smell of the house? He felt a pang of regret like walking in on someone in the bathroom. Like if he'd been here a minute earlier he would have caught her in the middle of . . . what?

Conrad backed out of the room and left the door open. He wondered if Roddy had seen her go. He'd ask about her later, after he'd studied the library.

The library. The house had a library.

'Hell, yeah,' he said, entering a patch of sun pouring through a street-facing picture window. But even while he ran his fingers over the ornately carved fronts of the pine shelves, his mind returned to the girl. She reminded him of someone, but he couldn't put his finger on whom. That didn't make sense, though, did it? He hadn't really seen her face. Maybe the shape of her body, something about the way she'd trotted down the stairs. Like a girl trying to get out before her parents could call her back and remind her of her curfew.

The house was nice, if somewhat anti-climactic. What makes this house a birthing house? What makes any house a birthing house, besides the fact

9

that probably a lot of babies had been born under her roof? It didn't feel like some sort of makeshift hospital ward or shelter where you'd have one large room with a bunch of beds, their occupants coughing on top of each other. It was just a house. So what if a doctor used to live here. Birth was life, life was good. Right?

Children. The relentless question childless married couples are bombarded with pretty much non-stop after age thirty.

Is that what this was about? The way Roddy looked at you when he realized you were eyeballing a four-bedroom house with nothing but a wife and a couple of pound mutts in tow. If not to start a family, what exactly are you hoping to do here? Do you really want to move to the middle of nowhere? Sure, Los Angeles is crowded, traffic makes you homicidal, the air is a fucking smokestack, you never use the ocean, and Jo's job is shit. But at least there's stuff to do there. Movies, hiking, gallery parties, the best tacos in the world. Women. Ungodly women everywhere you turned. Enough to make you groan just walking down the street. A city was a space to live tightly, then stretch out your career, your lunches. A place to play around, get involved with strangers, make deals behind your employer's back, hide.

It was killing them, the City of Angels. He knew it was only a matter of time. It was too easy to watch five years of your life go by. People thirty, forty years old still living in apartments and driving leased BMWs, trying to hit something big. Too many casual friendships, too much need. Maybe just too many choices.

Jo's parents were retired—mom in Phoenix, the old man splitting time between Roxbury and London. She wasn't any closer to them emotionally than geographically. Flying back to Connecticut for Christmas every year had become every other year, and then every third or fourth. Jo was a Wi-Fi wife, always working from home, hotels, airports. She was too busy for family. What did she care where they lived?

Conrad's family was Jo and the dogs. Simpler now.

This was doable.

The house was warm. The smell was in him. Conrad's blood churned and his pulse escalated. The library seemed somehow familiar and foreign, a place he'd come back to after a decade of forgetting. A draft brought the clean, wild scents of nettle and lavender, overpowering the vanilla scent from the girl—*forget about the girl, there was no girl*—and he was not aware of the erection forming under his black Lucky Brand dungarees, only of the titillating possibility of a new environment, of new hope. Maybe even a whole new life.

Call Jo, talk things over. Stay a few days, kick around the town.

He dialed her mobile, got only silence. He looked at his phone. There were no signal bars. Maybe the house or the big tree out front. Or maybe the whole town was a black spot.

Didn't matter. That was just fear trying to slow him down. And there was another, deeper voice drowning out the fear. He did not recognize it, and it did not have a name, though in time both of those things would change. It came from the house

11

as much as it came from his head or his heart. It was buried beneath years of stone, and it had been buried on purpose.

This is a new beginning, it said. *This is your only hope. To save the family. It is our birthing house, and we deserve to be born.*

He had no idea what the words meant, but they felt true.

When he turned, Roddy was standing at the library's rear entrance.

Conrad nodded. 'We'll take it.'

'You wanna call your wife, talk it over?'

'She trusts me,' he said. 'And this feels like home.'

'Boy, I guess she must. You have some financing arranged? I can throw you a name if you want someone local. Real honest guy down at Farmer's—'

'Not necessary.' Conrad pulled out his wallet, removed and unfolded the little slip of paper. 'No loans, Roddy. Just point me to a bank, give me a couple days to clear this.'

Conrad held the check out, displaying the insurance company's logo in some sort of hope that he wouldn't have to explain the rest.

Roddy took a step closer and frowned. 'Jesus, son. That's a big check.'

'Is it?' Conrad guessed five hundred thousand dollars was a lot. Not specific, though. Not a sum calculated by tables and software. This was the kind of round figure that suggested payoff. Considering the source it seemed insignificant.

'Your last house burn down or something?'

Conrad looked at Roddy. He hadn't told anybody since he'd gotten the call a week ago. Jo

12

had been in Atlanta. He told her what had happened, of course, but he hadn't known how it would end. She offered to go with him, cancel her trip. He said no, he'd be fine. The man from Builder's Trust Nationwide had been there at St Anthony's, anxious to close the matter and avoid litigation, which Conrad had no interest in pursuing. He hadn't even recognized the man in the bed until the very end, when it was like watching the man fall asleep the way he had more than twenty years ago. Even recognizing that didn't change anything.

'Construction accident,' Conrad said.

Roddy reared back and looked Conrad over as if he'd missed something obvious, perhaps a limp or a facial tic that would bespeak brain trauma.

'My father was an electrician.'

'Oh. Oh, jeez.' Roddy was nodding. Then he stopped and ran one palm over his mouth. Conrad could see him putting it together. Living in Los Angeles. Insurance money. Got lost on the way back from Chicago. Erratic behavior, jumping into a new deal. When he spoke again, the realtor's voice was quiet. 'Was it . . . recent?'

'Seven days ago.'

Roddy visibly twitched at that. 'I'm very sorry, Conrad. You must be—'

'Don't worry about it.' Conrad crossed the room and patted Roddy on the shoulder as he went by, suddenly wishing to be out of the library, out of town, back on the road.

Roddy caught his arm and held him back. The big realtor's grip was gentle, but it stopped Conrad and made him look up.

'Hey. Nothing would make me happier than to

13

sell you a house today. But I wouldn't be doing my job unless I asked. I can sit on the property. You want to maybe take some time on this?'

'I appreciate that.' Conrad looked out the picture window facing the street and the enormous tree blocking the view. 'Dad traveled a lot for work. Sometimes out of state. Then one time he didn't come back. Haven't seen him since I was six.' He turned back to Roddy. 'Hey, what say we just pretend I won the lottery or something, huh?'

Roddy did not respond.

The moment stretched out and Conrad imagined Roddy suddenly grabbing him by the arm and paddling him over one knee. He burst into uneasy titters. That seemed to help. Roddy grinned and offered his hand. Conrad shook it and held it longer than usual.

'This is a fine town full of nice people, Conrad. You and your wife are gonna make a good life here.'

'Thanks, Roddy. Thank you for your help.' Shit. Now Conrad did feel like crying, but that was just gratitude, not grief. He swallowed it down.

'You hungry?'

'Starving. You?'

Roddy slapped his belly. 'My man, I love to eat.'

They went to a lunch of the locally renowned Cornish pasty stuffed with cubed beef, potatoes, onions, and rutabaga. The miners' dish was hard and salty, even with the cocktail sauce you were supposed to splash all over it. But Conrad was so hungry after knocking back the first three bottles of Spotted Cow he gobbled his lunch down and forgot to ask Roddy about the doctor, the girl or any other player concerning the history of the birthing house.

14

3

With its tiled roof, yellow stucco façade and rainbow of bricks that went up over the porch, the house Joanna Harrison had rented three years earlier should have been easy to love. It was a 1940s bungalow on a quiet street in Culver City, three blocks from industrial compounds, three blocks from the Sony lot and only one block from Washington Boulevard's diners, art galleries and coffee shops. Conrad's windfall notwithstanding, they'd be priced out of the rent in another six months and forget about qualifying for the mortgage—they'd already tried, but the landlord was asking $670,000 and 20 per cent cash down. She'd decorated the house as if they had bought it, but to Conrad it had never felt like home. Just another temporary stop until they found the next thing.

In the backyard was a tall avocado tree that never produced edible fruit. He could always see them up there, ripening in the sun, until one day they dried out and fell, too young and hard or desiccated beyond consumption. He knew it was the landlord's job, but he took the tree's ill health personally. He felt he should be up on a ladder, pruning or doing something more so that it might yield real fruit, but he never got around to learning exactly what.

It was just past 9 a.m. on a Tuesday when he dropped off the rental and the taxi delivered him from LAX. Her silver Volvo wagon was sitting in the driveway. So, sick or just running late, Jo was

15

home. Good. Maybe she'd take the entire day off. He could make her her favorite omelet (red peppers and Swiss, with a dash of olive oil) and they could roll around in bed all day, open the windows and fuck the stress away the way they used to cure their hangovers.

He moved through the living room and saw the wine bottles on the coffee table. Cigarette butts mashed into the congealed cheese on the pizza box. Candles burned down. Allison must have come over, Jo's divorced friend with the augmented breasts and the little travel agency over in the Marina specializing in Japan. They liked to get into the wine and talk about their relationships, a once or twice a month habit Conrad dreaded not so much for the mess they always left but because he didn't think Jo had much to learn from a woman who needed plastic tits to feel wanted.

Alice and Luther *click-click-clicked* in from the bedroom, all sleepy and stiff-jointed, yawning their greetings while their tails wagged with no real enthusiasm. Alice was the brindle, her coat like that of a chocolate tiger. Luther was splotched black and white like a cow. Fifty pounds apiece, rescue muscle turned chubby and about as scary as your average golden retriever. He bent and petted them and murmured in their ears.

He shuffled into the bedroom. Jo was sleeping on top of the spread, wearing his favorite vintage Sebadoh tee and her black lace panties, her bare feet a little dirty, her mouth open.

Ah, beautiful wife. Even in her morning state. She was a heavy sleeper, a heavy lot of things. Worker, drinker, emoter, lover. During periods of

16

stress, she was always moist. Her eyes, nose, mouth and loins watered up with her moods. She had irritable bowel syndrome from the work anxiety and rushed dietary choices. If she didn't have a cold, she had allergies. If she wasn't seething, she was lusting, and not always for sex, not always for him. In truth, she frightened him. He liked this about her; felt she kept him from becoming a snail in the great lawn of Los Angeles. If he was the snail, she was the nautilus. Curled around herself on the bed, even now, waiting for him to crawl inside.

There was a click of door and creak of hinge in the hall behind him. Conrad turned and saw his friend, their friend, Jake Adams, standing there in those great shredded surfer-boy jeans Jake always seemed to wear, unbuttoned at the navel. Jake was an actor who'd been bumming around Los Angeles for a decade, taking bit parts in indies and the occasional episode of one failing sitcom or another, always treading water and never really making it. He was not wearing shoes, socks or shirt, and Conrad thought of telling him *No Service.*

'Whoa, hey, 'Rad,' Jake said, scratching his unshaven neck.

Jo sat up as if he'd yelled her name.

Conrad looked at Jo and then back at Jake. His next thought was, *If this motherfucker came on my Sebadoh, I'll break his head open.*

Jake wiped one corner of his mouth and bit his pinky nail. Jake's lips were chapped raw. His eyes were red, alert.

Are we up to coke now, Jo?

'Go.'

17

Jake pointed and leaned toward the bedroom as if asking permission to retrieve the rest of his clothes, but Conrad just shook his head, once. Jake blew air from his cheeks and then padded through the living room. Conrad kept his nose turned up and eyes closed until he heard the front door shut, and it was almost inaudible when it did.

When he turned back to Jo she was staring at him, flushed, her lower lip quivering.

'It's over,' he said.

The color drained away. She didn't know the lyrics, but she knew the tune.

He patted around for it, reached into his pocket. He handed her the MLS printout Roddy had given him. There were six photos, in color. The house from the front, the sprawling backyard, the front parlor, master, full bath and library.

She unfolded the paper, turned it sideways. She looked up, her whole face a question mark.

'I signed the papers two days ago. Offer accepted.'

She was trying to understand what was left for her to negotiate, to explain.

'My father bought that for us.'

Her expression crumpled and she coughed. He almost asked her if she was okay, but she started to cry and he was glad for that.

'I called you.' A heaving breath. 'You should have let me come.' A ghastly inhalation. 'Conrad, I'm so-so-so—'

'No. No going back. Not so much as one fucking minute. Start packing if you want to come. Otherwise leave the dogs and get out.'

He went to the kitchen and grabbed a trash bag from under the sink. His fingers ripped through

18

the plastic and he shook it open like a parachute. He grabbed the nearest thing—the toaster, fuck the toaster, they hadn't made toast in years—and threw it in the bag so that it clanged deafeningly on the floor. You had to start by throwing a lot out. It made the packing go faster, the move a clean getaway.

4

They were in the house a week before it came for him.

Joanna Harrison was dozing on the couch in the TV room while her husband stood on the deck, breathing through a sweet clove cigarette that burned his throat and floated a candy cloud above his empty thoughts. The cigarette was the kind found on the back covers of men's magazines, the smoke of wannabes. What Conrad wanted to be this night was content, and, for a few more minutes of this vanishing sunset hour, he was.

Content equally with himself and his lot: a full acre of sloping lawn, century-old maple and black walnut trees, and a garden as large as a swimming pool, its aged gray gate roped with grape vines. Raspberry and clover grew thick in the shade of the shaggy pines still moist with the day's sweet rain.

He heard running water and looked through the window into the kitchen. Her blurry, sleepy-slouched shape hovered for a moment, probably filling a glass to take to bed. He waved to her. She either did not see him or was too tired to wave

19

back. The shape faded . . . back into the house.

He wanted to follow her, but he waited. Let her brush and floss, finish with a shot of the orange Listerine before she turned back the freshly laundered Egyptian cotton. You can't rush these things. These are delicate times. Eyes closed, he could almost see her stretched out in one of her tank tops and cotton boy-cut underwear, a big girl-woman reading another marketing book he always said were made for people on planes. She must be happy here. Otherwise, she would be cleaning and planning and avoiding bedtime.

Summer had arrived early. The house was muggy. He wondered if she would be warm enough to go without covers, but cool enough to allow his touch.

He had been shocked to discover that he wanted her more now. He was still madder than hell about the entire stupid scene and all its implications, its mysteries. But he knew the balance of things and how he'd not been holding up his share of them was half the problem. Maybe more than half. She'd almost slipped away. Even before that nasty little homecoming it had been months, and since the fresh start (that was how he thought of it, but never named it as such, not aloud) he'd been watching for signs. If Luther and Alice were in their crates, that was one sign. If she had showered that was yet another, though never a binding one. None of the signs were binding, which added suspense to the marriage and kept his hopes in a perpetual swing from boyish curiosity on one side to blood-stewing resentment on the other.

He walked up the deck steps to the wooden walkway, into the mudroom. He climbed stairs (the servants' stairs off the kitchen, not the front stairs with the black maple banister, which for some reason he had been avoiding since the move) and felt the weight of the day in his bones.

By the time he finished brushing his teeth he was tired the way only people who have unpacked 90 per cent of their possessions in a single day can be tired. His mind was empty, his muscles what his mom said his father used to call labor-fucked, the old man's way of suggesting that work is its own reward.

I'm sorry, Dad—

Work. He knew his hands still worked for her. He thought she liked his hands better than just about every other part of him. He no longer relied on his appearance as the catalyst, didn't know many men married more than a few years who did. He knew he wasn't a Jake. At thirty he was what divorced female bartenders had from time to time called cute, no longer handsome, if he ever had been. He felt remarkably average. He had acquired a belly, but the move had already burned that down from a 36 to a 34. With the yard work he'd be down to a 32—his high-school Levi's size—by the end of June. Jo always said she liked his laugh lines, the spokes radiating from what his mother used to call his wily eyes. Wily used to be enough, but now he was just grateful for a second chance. He could live with average—so long as he could still seduce her.

Conrad wound his way through the back hall, making the S-turn through the library, into the front hallway. The creaking floorboards were a new sound, allowing him to birth one final clear thought for the day.

21

This is a healing place. This is home.

Conrad waded into the moonlight pooling on the new queen-sized bed—another purchase, this one more deserved—he'd made without her input. The ceiling fan was whirring, the dogs were curled into their crates on the floor, and Jo was waiting for him on top of the new sheets. She was without a top, wearing only loose fitting boxers (his), which were somehow better than if she were naked. That she had gone halfway without prematurely forfeiting the under garment was a gesture that made him feel understood. The arc of her hips rose off the bed like the fender of a Jaguar and his blood awakened.

With his blood, his hopes.

No longer content, Conrad stretched out, not caring what funny tent shape his penis made as it unfolded like a miniature welcome banner. He rolled to one side, facing her. She smelled of earth and lavender and something otherwise herbal—new scents for her in this new place. Her belly was nearly flat except for the smallest of rolls just above the waistband, and he loved this, too. He called it her little *chile relleno* and she would slap him, but it didn't bother her, not really. Her hips were womanly wide, but with her height she remained sleek, especially when prone, like now. She stood a little over six feet to his five-nine. His fingers grazed her fine brown navel hairs. Her eyes gleamed under heavy lids, glassy and black as mountain ponds at midnight.

It was a beginning, and he was a man who loved beginnings more than middles or endings.

'Come,' Jo said. Or maybe *Con*, half of his name.

'Hm?'

'. . . not ready.'

'Not what?' His hand found the elastic rim of her waistband, then moved into the open front of his boxer shorts on her.

'. . . about behbee,' she murmured.

'What, Baby?'

Not baby. Upper case, Baby. A nickname he used.

'. . . owin me the behbee . . . be-ah-eye,' she mumbled, which sounded like *was going to be all right.*

'Of course,' he said, like it was his idea too. He had no idea.

'. . . bee woul' go a father.'

We should go farther.

He pushed one, then two fingers lower to her mound, but her legs were crossed and he swerved off course, touching only her thigh. Just her thigh, but soft was soft and his excitement ratcheted up another notch.

'—not ready,' she squeaked, rolling away.

Shit. Might not have been sleeping before, but was now. Snoring, too. Weird, he thought. Had she done this before? With the eyes open and the talking?

Should he let her sleep or try one more time?

Yes . . . no. He kissed her goodnight and rolled on his back, allowing the fan to push warm summer air over his fading, obedient hard-on. His mind dropped into that lower gear, the one that is not yet sleep but somehow dreaming already.

In the half-dream he was in the house, beside her, finding the wetness and sliding in not for the first time but as if they had been moving this way

23

for minutes or an hour. He was all corded muscle and arched away, feeling her soak him in her own undulations. The movement was soothing, almost non-sexual, like being rocked in a crib.

Her grip on him strengthened and clenched, pushing back with legs and ass, drawing his ejaculate out in a sudden burst that ended too quickly, leaving him weak and sleepy all over again.

Drifting . . .

Until the dream, the same one or some new post-coital version, was split by the sound of crying. His body twitched itself awake, and he knew these were not Jo's tears. This was the noise a newborn makes after sucking in its first violent breath as it enters this violent world. It was a sound that had skipped mewling and launched straight into wailing, and it was coming from behind a wall or far away.

Faintly, under the baby's hacking shriek, there arose another sound. This one *did* sound like a woman, and he imagined the infant's mother, or the midwife, perhaps. This older cry in the dark was a trailing scream, as if something was pulling her away from her child and down a long corridor that narrowed to nothing.

Panicked, he rolled over to shake Jo—*why hasn't she woken up and grabbed me?*—and felt the cool stirring of air as she lifted off the bed. He could see only blackness, and with the drone of the fan he could not hear her feet padding on the wood floor. A flash of her silhouette in the doorway left a retinal echo, but the room was too dark to grasp any details. If he saw her at all, she was gone now.

24

To the bathroom, he thought. There she goes, carrying my seed. The semi-sleep-molestation and abrupt ending made him wince with guilt, but he did not seek her out in the ensuing silence. Exhausted from the day of unpacking (and tossed dream sex), Conrad decided the crying was but a fragment of the dream, a lingering audible planted by her words.

'. . . the behbee, the behbee . . .'

The crying returned once, quieter and farther away, until like a passing thunderstorm it faded to nothing.

He hovered on the edge of sleep.

Something's wrong.

He sat up and rubbed his eyes. She had not returned.

'Jo?'

She did not answer.

'Jo,' he said, louder. 'Baby, you okay?'

His eyes adjusted to the dark. The dogs were standing at the master bedroom door facing the hall, whining, tails stiff like the hairs on their shoulders. Conrad flattened his body and counted to ten. It's rational, he told himself. When something so unexplainable and real (the dogs made it real) as a crying baby in your childless home wakes you, it is normal to ignore it and go back to sleep. So back he went, as deep as a man can go, until he forgot all about the crying sounds and her cold departure, her absolute absence. He did not think again about the sleep-slouched shape he'd glimpsed through the window, fading into the house.

Even when, in the morning, waking to a half-empty bed, he padded downstairs and found her

25

where he'd left her before he stepped out for a smoke at dusk, sleeping on the sofa.

Alone.

5

Well, not really alone. The dogs looked up at him but did not abandon their mistress. Jo was curled around a body pillow, arms above her head, eyes open but unmoving.

'Morning, kids,' he said. 'Morning, Mommy.'

Jo blinked and her mantis arms folded down. 'Coffee?'

After waiting for the pot to fill, Conrad brought her a cup the way she liked it—strong, with milk and a heap of non-dairy creamer. Had to have it both ways, did his wife.

She sat up and accepted the mug, leering at him over the steaming brew. 'Are you mad at me?'

'Why would I be?' He was thinking he should have made iced tea.

'I fell asleep on the couch.'

Conrad shrugged. 'Waiting makes it better, right?'

'We've been waiting a long time. You must be going out of your mind.'

'Yeah, it's funny. I think the move sort of tapped me out. All this work. It's good for us. I feel good.'

Jo sipped her coffee, unable or unwilling to pursue the topic of what was good for them now. He guessed she was going to do the safe thing and wait for him to bring it up, and that was fine. He could postpone that forever.

26

'So.' He heard a wet lapping sound and looked at the dogs. Luther was licking the small flap of skin where his balls used to be. 'What's on deck today?'

'I thought I'd do the unthinkable and go to Wal-Mart. We need trashcans, sponges. House stuff.'

'I have a little project going in the garage. Mind if I stay here?'

'Oh, yeah. I keep forgetting we have a garage.'

'The doors don't work. It's a mess.'

'Are you turning over a new leaf, becoming a handyman?'

'Not really,' he said. 'It's kind of a surprise, something I wanted to do with a little of the money left over. So don't go in there for a few days, 'kay?'

'Ooh, a surprise.' Jo studied him a bit, then lost interest. 'When I get back I think I'll tackle the garden, get my hands dirty.'

'Save some energy for me.' He offered a lame and hopeful smile.

'Not so tapped out, after all.' She slapped him on the ass and went up to change.

* * *

He had knocked down all but two book boxes forming the massive pyramid in the library when the phone rang. Her voice echoed up the servants' stairs, excited.

'Oh, hi! Yes, we're great. Everything is just beautiful.' A long pause ensued. Jo punctuated the beats with a series of 'Uh-huhs'. His stomach lurched when he heard her say, 'Donna! Sudden is right.' And then in a lower voice, 'Of course I'm interested.'

27

Donna was Donna Tangelo, Jo's headhunter. Calling from LA, already.

Conrad folded up more boxes and continued his eavesdropping for another five minutes.

'Yes, Donna, we'll talk it over and I'll call you back tomorrow, I promise. Thanks for thinking of me.'

Before he could ask what the hell that was all about, Jo bounded up the stairs and announced, 'I'm hopping in the shower, honey.'

He flexed his mouth for another thirty seconds, turned away from the closed bathroom door and went to the kitchen for a beer to celebrate the completion of the unpacking. It was the time a cold beer tasted best, especially a Coors Light on a hot day.

Upstairs the shower stopped hissing. He thought about her up there, covered with nothing more than water droplets in the humid afternoon. She would apply lotion to every inch of her skin and then dress quickly, throwing her hair into a ponytail before it could dry. The window to spontaneous post-shower sex narrowed with the age of the marriage. He did not want to lose her to another job that made her a basket of stress, but running up there with a boner wasn't going to change that.

Ah well, there was the cold beer.

*   *   *

They were eating pizza over the little two-top, a rusted wrought-iron thing they had purchased at the Rose Bowl Flea Market for twenty dollars and decided to call quaint. After a month of pretending school was out for the summer, the prospect of yet more change lent the meal a first-date feel. He was alarmed by how difficult it was to read his wife as she set her pizza slice down, eyeing him cautiously.

And they're off!

'So, you think I should take it?'

'It's very flattering.' He could tell she wanted to take it, so he spoke slowly, carefully. 'Maybe a little soon? Like maybe you want to keep your options open before you jump back in?'

'Yeah, no, I love it here, sweetie,' she said. 'I really do.'

'So?'

'Well, if I took this, we wouldn't have to touch our new little nest egg.'

'So it's purely a money thing?' The old sales routine: ask questions, put them in a box. Yes or no. Shut down and close.

'No, but there's less than we thought,' she said, her face tightening. 'Of my share, anyway. I took what you gave me and paid off the rest of our debts.'

Conrad set his pizza slice down on the paper plate and patted his lips with a paper towel. 'And?'

Up until the insurance from the accident, Conrad's income from the bookstore and various dubious writing assignments had been so small Jo had handled all of their finances except for pocket money and a few small bills: DirectTV, his cell phone, the lone credit card in his name only with its laughable $700 credit limit. After he paid cash for the new house, he'd given Jo half of the remaining two hundred and change to pay off her MBA ($43,000) and told her to 'Set up some IRAs or something.'

'And we have to be careful now.'

Then she explained exactly how fragile their new little nest egg was.

Another twelve thousand went to her father, who'd loaned them the moving and deposit money on the LA property. Somehow Conrad had managed to forget about this. Another four thousand for the movers to get out. It had only cost sixteen hundred to move from Denver to Los Angeles, but that had been metro to metro. LA to the middle of Buttfuck, Egypt, or at least Black Earth, Wisconsin, cost a lot more because 'there aren't a lot of Cheeseheads heading west,' she said, and Conrad laughed. In pain.

'There were other debts,' she said.

'*Other* other debts?' He really had no idea. He'd always assumed the bulk of their lifestyle, furnishings and vacations had come straight from Jo's income, which had been north of eighty thousand last time he'd asked.

'The credit cards were pretty bad.' She winced.

'How bad?'

'Thirty-four thousand.'

He winced back. 'We had thirty-four thousand dollars in credit card debt?' He could not keep his voice from rising. 'For what?'

She sighed. 'Conrad, I was pretty much paying for everything. Rent was twenty-two hundred alone. Utilities, the cars.'

'I sold my Maxima a year ago.'

'I know, honey, but you were upside down on the equity by almost three thousand.'

'Still, thirty-four thousand? Jo, Baby, c'mon! Maybe ten thousand went to furniture and stuff, but—'

'I wanted to have nice things, okay? I wasn't working my ass off to live in an empty house. Your TV was two thousand.'

'Jesus! If I had known—'

'Conrad, stop. I wanted to get you something special for your birthday. Don't be difficult.'

'Is that—' He tilted his beer and suckled. 'Shit.'

'Need another beer, honey?'

'Yes, please.'

She fetched him one. She knew this was harder for him than it was for her.

'Thanks, Baby.'

'Where were we?'

'I was about to ask, is that all?'

She patted his hand. 'And I was about to say in a hesitant tone, well, not exactly. I took a pay cut a year ago.'

'A year ago.'

Jesus, wasn't this something you talked about with your husband, even when you kept separate checkbooks?

'David sat me down and asked me if I liked my job. I lied and said yes.' David Donaldson was the VP of Sales at her former company, PrimaPro Pharmaceuticals. Jo'd called it mind-destroyingly boring work for a merciless boss, but it paid well. Or had paid well. 'He said I was talented and worked hard, but he couldn't really afford a director of marketing and another for sales, that whole bullshit spiel. "We're a sales firm, not a marketing firm." Like it was my fault he hired me before the class action bullshit tanked the stock.'

'Jo, why didn't you tell me?'

'Oh, you didn't really want to hear about it. I

31

don't blame you.'

'I did too want to hear about it.'

'Conrad Harrison. You'd just gotten laid off. I was scared. And you were never home. Nights at the bookstore while I worked days. We hardly ever saw each other. That was the deal we made until something better came up. I understood that. Now we have to pay for it. Can we leave it at that?'

He stared at her, unsure who was to blame.

'We carved that whole life out and it wasn't easy to cut back. I loved that house. I wanted to buy it—'

'We never could have afforded it. Or did you really want to stay in LA for another five years?' He loaded that question to the hilt.

'No. *No*. This is a great house. I'm just trying to adapt. Think about the next move. My next move. Job, I mean.'

Conrad sighed. 'I'm sorry. Cutting your salary down. You shouldn't have had to deal with that blow by yourself. That must have been horrible.'

'It wasn't. But I might've gone shopping a few times to ease the pain.'

Her forced laughter made him sad. They had lost control of a lot more than their finances in the past year. They had lost even the normal day-to-day verbal tennis ball going back and forth across the net. The financial shit was the same as the thing with That Fucker Jake. And not so different from Conrad's thing. The thing with the girl, Rachel. Not that he'd done anything, but still. It had been close. Bad choices they wouldn't have made if they'd kept each other in the loop. The money was like that—it came from the same place, anyway. Worst of all, here they were talking in a

32

healthy way and it sucked, yes, but it was honest. He didn't want it to end. He wanted to sit here in their new old kitchen until they were discussing holes in their Medicare coverage.

And it was pretty clear that, since his father's death, money was not the real issue. She needed something to do, he'd rushed her, and now here they were.

'I just want you to be happy,' he said.

'It's eight weeks,' she said. 'And the next training class starts day after tomorrow.'

He wouldn't taste another beer this good until she came home.

*　　　*　　　*

Jo did not cry as they said their goodbyes inside the Dane County Airport. Surrender had been reached; neither husband nor wife had the energy to continue the debate. Conrad shuffled aside to make room for three generations huddled around a tall girl in a University of Wisconsin sweatshirt, the whole fam-damly seeing off their pride and joy for the summer.

Conrad squeezed Jo's hand. 'I can stay a while.'

'You're sweet,' she said, releasing his grip. 'I trusted you about moving here. Trust me on this one, for a little while?'

Trust was still a loaded word—he could make a list of loaded words now—and he let the comment slide. He kissed her scar for comfort. The thin line ran from the left arch of her top lip to the exact middle-bottom of her nose, one of childhood's accidental fissures he'd always found sexy, the snarl of a *femme fatale*.

33

He passed another Perkins and looped around Madison on the Beltline at a steady sixty miles per, stealing glimpses of the Capitol dome at the top of State Street. Then he was winding his way on to Highway 151, which split off Madison and went south to Black Earth and then another fifty miles to Iowa. Suburbs gave way to box stores and furniture outlets.

After that, farmland. The familiar rolling greens. Dense mini-forests gathered around the streams. The silent sweet manure field of nothingness, tranquil as the sea. Just as it had been when he discovered it the first time, it was a lonely patch of country, but soothing, almost hypnotic. Made him glad they'd left California.

Conrad saw the sign for *Black Earth, Pop. 2713*, and switched off the cruise control. Riding the business loop, he passed a farm equipment dealership and a graveyard full of enormous granite headstones. Apparently, these small towns liked to keep their dead front and center, on Main Street if possible. Would they live here long enough to raise a family, a family that would bury him in yonder graveyard? How soon would it come? Another thirty years, or forty? Fifty was not out of the question, but even that seemed too short a time. Look at Dad. One day you're working and joking around with the boys with your hand on the box and ZAP—you're fucking fried, end of story. No more time to apologize to your son.

He nosed the Volvo alongside the curb and stared through the windshield, up at his house.

Again, that nagging question:

If not for to have children, what are we here for?

He sat in the Volvo and listened to the tick of the engine and creak of the upholstery. The idea that she might not come back pressed down on him like a seatbelt possessed. Perversely, his mind tightened the belt further by reminding him of the last one who'd left him.

Holly.

Why was he thinking about her now? Holly was more than twelve years ago. What could a high school romance hold to his life now? To Jo? To this beautiful new home?

Don't think about Holly. She's old news.

Her tears. She cried for what we did.

'Enough of this shit.' He exited the car, bidding Holly to stay buried.

He was on the porch with one hand on the door when the man started yelling.

'Harrison! Conrad Harrison!'

For a second, Conrad was sure the voice belonged to his father, that the whole thing had been a strange dream and now he really was dead and the old man was coming to lead him away for good. He turned around slowly.

But it was only Leon Laski, the former owner of 818 Heritage Street. They'd not met, mainly because Laski had groused about the closing dates and Roddy had kept them out of it. 'Believe me, it's better this way,' Roddy had said. 'You don't want to meet the S-O-B.'

Too late—here came the S-O-B, barreling up the sidewalk and across Conrad's lawn. In his hands, a heavy wooden soda crate, stiff-armed away from his body as if it were full of dirty

35

diapers.

'Excuse me?'

Laski dropped the crate on the porch. 'This all belongs to you now.'

'Is that right?' Conrad said, a skeptical grandfather.

Laski was shorter than Conrad by six inches, but he was clearly the larger man. He had the hard-packed muscle, ruddy cheeks and battered hands only middle-aged mechanics and sailors seem to acquire. His gray-blond beard and scraggily locks were more frayed rope than actual hair. He wore blue workman's pants and a plain brown shirt with a name patch that read LEON stitched to the tit.

'Wife packed her up on accident . . . crazy bitch.' Laski's accent was aggressively northern Wisconsin.

The dogs went off like fireworks.

'Quiet down,' Conrad yelled at the door, though he was glad he had Alice and Luther if things turned nasty. 'Sorry, dogs aren't used to the place yet. I'm Conrad Harrison.'

'Ya say.' Laski ignored the proffered mitt, removed a moist, splintered toothpick from behind his ear, and began to gnaw at it like a beaver, his tongue darting over his callused thumb and forefinger as if they were next. 'Anycase, don't need more'n I already got to unpack, so dare ya go.'

'Fine. Thanks, I think.' The crate was covered with a sheet of black felt tucked into the sides, obscuring the contents. 'Something for the house?'

'Could say that, ya sure could.'

'Uh-huh. Well, looks like you cleaned out pretty good. I'll call Roddy if I find anything.'

36

Laski whistled through his toothpick. The end flapped wetly like a ruined party favor. 'Cleaned out all right, all right, but I wouldn't call it pretty anything. You two woulda taken another week getting your shit together, we'd a lost the deal on the new farm. But you go ahead and tell 'at big buck Roddy anything you want. I got what I need. We're clear.'

Conrad managed to smile. 'Anything else I can do for you today, Leon? No? Good.' He grabbed the crate and turned for the door.

Laski spoke in a low, slithering voice. 'You got kids, boy?'

'What was that?'

'I hear dem mutts tearing up your floors in dare, but I don't see no kids. Appears you don't got none yet, but what I mean is, you plan on having any?'

'No, we—why would you ask that?'

'Just curious.' Laski pointed one thick finger at Conrad's front door. 'You have yourself a nice life in 'at old house.'

Before Conrad could reply, Laski wheeled on his dirty boots and knuckled down the walk, flicking his toothpick in a high arc as he disappeared around the corner, his vehicle out of sight or non-existent.

Conrad slipped inside and summoned his courage to open the crate.

6

Alice and Luther pogoed at him as if he'd abandoned them for weeks instead of hours. He set the crate on the coffee table and rolled around with them, letting them slobber on his face. There wasn't a pill on the market that cured mild depression—or just a shitty day—as fast as these two dogs.

Then he quit stalling and went to the crate. The covering was indeed felt, but thick as a shroud. As he lifted one corner he was overcome by an irrational thought: what if it's a trap? Like the kind used to catch badgers or snap my hand off at the wrist? But that was ridiculous. Nothing more than his imagination blowing off steam.

Wedged inside the crate was a large portfolio or scrapbook. It was heavy. Maybe five, six pounds. Why in the hell would Laski think this belonged to him?

Conrad examined the cracked spine and yellowed paper edges. It wasn't a book. It was an album, but photo albums had ten, maybe twenty cardboard pages. This thing had fifty or more, some thin, others not.

The first page had pinpoints of black mold in the crease, but he could see the rest well enough. It was a charcoal sketch. Bare land, the lines done over and over, mostly grass and a few shrubs and a single sapling with no leaves. The plot of land stretched back over a rolling slope, narrowing on the page to give depth to the short horizon. Deeper, 'over' the rise of the land he could just make out two slashes of the artist's pen. At first he thought it might be another tree, but no, upon closer inspection, his nose almost touching the musty paper, he could see the clean lines, one shorter and horizontal over the taller vertical.

A cross.

And why not? Black Earth, like a lot of Middle America, was full of devout Christians and probably had been more so a century ago.

But why did the rest of the sketch seem familiar?

'Hey—shit.'

He backed out the front door and up the cracked sidewalk to the street. He looked at the book and then back up at his house. His house and the lot. Standing next to him, almost exactly one third of the distance from the western property line, was a tree that topped out at least twenty feet higher than Conrad's roof, its trunk as thick as three men. The house was two and a half stories with the attic—the tree was pushing fifty feet. He looked back at the drawing, then back up at the tree. The huge tree stood where the sapling in the drawing stood, and the slope of the land in the sketch matched Conrad's yard.

'How 'bout that,' Conrad said, smiling for the first time all day. It wasn't quite like discovering buried treasure, but it still gave him a child's satisfaction. If the MLS printout had been accurate, this tree was, like his house, over one hundred and forty years old. 'The house's birthday tree.'

The next page wasn't a sketch. Pasted to the stiff yellow paper was a photo of unusual size, roughly seven inches high and nine inches wide.

The light looked rusty, the photo developed in sepia. The framing and scale matched the sketch, but that was where the similarities ended.

The people gathered in front of the completed house looked cold, arms crossed, angry that they had been called out for this impromptu Kodak moment. All were women, late teens to geriatric and everything in between, garbed in the frumpy black dresses and white bonnets of maids or nurses. *Little Midwife on the Prairie.* Maybe a family . . . no. They all wore such dour expressions and pale countenances, he was unable to imagine them as anything other than employees. He didn't think more than a few of the women were relations; their size, shape and facial features were too diverse to be of the same stock.

Relations, stock.

My God, he thought, I'm musing in the vernacular of their time just looking at them, and it feels right. No, it feels *proper*. And what is, what was, the purpose of this gathering? If they were marking some special day, why the pug chins and hunched backs? The tired boredom in their sunken black eyes? Some of them were looking away from the lens, as if someone or something on the street had captured their attention. Or maybe they had simply refused to look into the camera. This made more sense because they were looking in different directions, not focused on any one point of interest. The women had no shape except bulky, even the one with the breasts.

'No, they were bosoms back then,' Conrad said to the book. 'Bosoms or teats, depending on the company you ladies kept.'

Another woman, this one in her twenties or

40

thirties (it was hard to tell; for all he knew women had aged twice as fast at the turn of the century), was holding her skirts above the ground as if preparing to step over a puddle. Another stood ramrod straight with a broom clutched in her thick fists.

Wrapping up his inspection, Conrad found only two common details uniting these women. They all wore black boots that rose above the ankles, mannish in their thick soles and metal eyelets and pointed toes. The other was that none was smiling. Not all were sour or angry. It was simply that happiness, even a forced smile, seemed a foreign thing to them.

His thoughts turned to the unseen photographer. Would he have been their employer, the owner of the house? A doctor? Or a hired man, a local with the equipment and a knack for taking pictures? Conrad guessed the latter, for it was clear even to his untrained eye that, grim as its subjects were, the photo itself was quite good. Nothing you'd want to hang on your staircase wall (it might give someone cause to fall down the stairs), but a strong piece of work nonetheless. In its own droll way, it was almost lovely.

Who said the owner was a man? Maybe the house had been full of women, and only women.

Midwives, wet nurses.

Mothers, daughters, granddaughters.

What if some of them are still here?

He went over them again one by one, his nose close enough to the warped paper that he caught the scent of a sun-dried milk carton.

Roaming, searching . . .

His eyes locked on the one he had missed, the

41

one standing behind the first row, elevated in her stance on the porch step so that only her face was visible between the shoulders of the other women. He saw her clearly then, recognized her open mouth, the teeth exposed as if preparing to bite.

No. Not possible.

But there she was, hollow-eyed and waxen like the others. The tall raven-haired woman in the photo stared back at him with something akin to hatred, and he recognized her, of course he recognized her, for hers was a face he had come to know intimately. She of the compressed lightning bolt of a scar, the lovely fissure running from under her nose to her lip.

An involuntary cry escaped his throat as he ran into the house, leaving splayed on the sidewalk the album containing a century-old photo of his wife.

7

Conrad stood in the front sitting room, looking out the window to the album on the ground. Twenty minutes had elapsed since he'd fled the scene. What if the neighbors had seen that little show? What were they thinking of the nice young couple from California now, 'Rad?

He must have been mistaken.

Feeling foolish, he put his hand on the doorknob and stopped. If he went back for the album, he would have to bring it back inside the house or throw it away in one of the new Rubbermaid cans out front. Either way, he knew he would have to look one more time. How could he not? His wife was in there, with teeth that wanted to bite.

Even if it turned out to be a coincidence, a striking resemblance and nothing more, he did not want to see that woman again. She had those black eyes. That starved look only women who've suffered and absorbed evil can project. And if it was a coincidence, what did that say about his state of mind, his wife gone only a few hours?

Just before he turned the knob there was a quick, pitter-pat rapping at his door. Conrad's heart jumped. A woman was standing on his porch, a shadow shifting behind the gauze curtain Jo had installed last week.

Christ! Who the fuck was this? Was she coming out of the photo to ask for her supper?

'Conrad, everything all right?' The voice was country-sweet and tinged with humor. Ah, yes— Gail Grum, his new next-door neighbor. Conrad and Jo had met Gail and her humongous husband three minutes after staggering out of the car, foggy from the drive from California. He remembered feeling overwhelmed by Gail's politeness. 'You left your book on the sidewalk, do you want me to put it on the porch?'

Conrad opened the door and smiled. 'Sorry about that. Phone was ringing. Thank you, Gail.'

He accepted the album and tucked it under one arm while she plowed on.

'I hate to bother you—I'm sure you're still unpacking. Do you two need anything to help you get settled in?'

'Oh, no, you're not a Hobbit—bother, I mean. Sorry.'

He didn't mean to say it. Most people would

43

have found it rude. Gail laughed like he'd told a terrific joke.

'A Hobbit! Maybe I am!'

Gail was five feet tall when standing on a phone book, a fifty-year-old in better shape than Conrad at seventeen. Her smile was warm and toothy. As she spoke her hands never stopped moving, waving like three fawning members of a welcome committee. He found it impossible to be abrupt with her. She was wearing the same gear as when they'd first met four weeks ago: a tank top that revealed her strong, tanned arms, green cargo shorts with a pair of cotton gloves hanging from one pocket, and yellow rubber gardening clogs with no socks.

The dogs broke out and clobbered Gail with affection.

'Okay, Luther, Alice, stop that.'

Gail only encouraged them. 'Look at them go. Upsy-daisy! Oh, how sweet! They're beautiful. Oh, they must be so happy in their new home! Joanna said you rescued them—they must love you soooo much.'

It was this immediate taking to his dogs that warmed Conrad to Gail Grum. 'I'm sorry, you're just standing there. Would you like to come in? I have iced tea.'

Gail flapped her hands. 'Oh, no. Listen, I saw you run inside and I just wanted to make sure everything was all right.'

'I was up late unpacking and didn't sleep well, been a mess all morning, and . . .' he trailed off, taken by the motherly look in her eyes. She wasn't just listening to him; she was hanging on every word. Without meaning to, he blurted it out. 'Jo

44

left me.'

'Oh no!'

'Oh, not like that,' he said. 'She took a job. She's in Detroit for eight weeks of something they call intensive consultative sales training.'

'But you just got here. Eight weeks? What are you going to do? I'd just go crazy if John left me!'

'Ah, yeah, well,' he said. 'It's a great job. Just kind of sudden.'

He stood there in the doorway for another ten minutes, filling Gail in on all the details. He told her how he was already looking forward to Jo's first trip home at the three-week break, and added, 'but hey, at least I have the dogs'.

'We're having the Bartholomews over for roast beef, even though it's summer, I know, we like our hearty meals, ha-ha-ha. Have you met the Bartholomews, across the street?'

'I haven't met anybody.'

'Oh, you have to come over, Conrad. It'll be so much fun!'

'That sounds great, but don't wait for me. I might have to finish this . . . thing.' He didn't have a thing, but he wanted an out. 'You're very kind.'

She slapped his hands. 'I'm not kind. This is what we do. You don't know it yet, but you now live next to some of the best people you'll ever know. Anytime after seven is fine. See you tonight, Conrad!'

Conrad watched her goofy garden clogs flapping across the yard. When she had popped back into her house, he closed the door and dropped the album on the coffee table.

It's not that I'm afraid of it, he told himself, heading up the stairs to check his email. *It's simply that there is no possible way the woman in the photo could be my wife and I've got better things to do than stare at a bunch of memories that belong to someone else. So fuck that, okay?*

Right.

* * *

It was after seven when the phone rang. That made it past eight in Detroit, but she was still all kinds of excited from her big first day, which irritated him.

'Is Detroit everything you dreamed it would be?'

'Actually, it's nice. The offices are in Troy, not really Detroit, and it's pleasant in a Midwest corporate way. Sort of like the Long Beach of Detroit, without the ocean. My suite is a dump, but kinda cozy.'

'The Residence thing?'

'It's like going back to school. Everyone eats at the buffet in the clubhouse every night and there's a sand volleyball court and a pool. I met a nice girl named Shirley. She's twenty-three, two kids. She was crying all day because she misses them so much. But then I was thinking, well, if little Shirley from Akron can make it here, then I can definitely make it, right?'

'Of course, Baby. You're brilliant. You'll do fine.'

But what about me? What am I going to do?

'What have you been up to?'

'I've been invited to dinner.'

'Really?' The way she perked up, he knew she had been hoping for this.

46

'Gail came by earlier.'

'Oh, sweetie, please go. I don't want them thinking we're rude.'

'Well, she knows you're gone, so she can't think you're rude. But I told her I was tired, and I am.' He was inching toward the album on the coffee table.

'We need to get off on the right foot.'

'I can see them rolling out the Pictionary now.'

Jo sighed. 'Conrad.'

'I know.'

They said goodbye. Then, before he could chicken out, he flipped the cover open and stared at the photo of the women in black. It was night and the lighting was dim in the living room. He had to squint to make out their faces. At first he couldn't find her and he was sure he had imagined the whole thing. His eyes darted and then he locked on her, saw her teeth and her scar—

'Fuck you!' Conrad threw the album across the room. He had not imagined seeing her the first time. He had not imagined seeing her now.

It was Jo.

The dogs darted to the couch, swerving wide of his path. He felt like an asshole for losing it like that. But he couldn't ignore her now whether he tossed the album in the garbage or set it on fire and danced on the ashes.

What if there are more? What if she's in a whole bunch of them? What will you do then, 'Rad? What if she's on every page staring back at you with those glossy black eyes, smiling into the camera so close you can see into her soul?

No, impossible. With six billion people on the planet (not even counting the dead) there had to be an explanation. It simply could not be his wife.

And he was not crazy. Lonely, yes. Recovering from a very stressful exit from the City of Angels, yes. But not insane. He needed to investigate the house's history, these women, but where would he begin? Who else besides Leon Laski would know about the house? People who lived here. People who—

'The neighbors.'

He hopped off the couch and ran upstairs to get ready for dinner. A few laughs, some human company. Jo would be pleased with the effort.

8

The House of Grum was another Victorian, barn-red with crème and robin's egg trim, pillars slim as dancers, with bursts of filigree on top. The front porch was narrow, wrapping around and widening on one side. Inside, the décor was somewhere between antiquarian and mid-twentieth-century frugal farmer's wife. The dinner table would seat twelve, but tonight was attended by only two couples—Gail and John Grum, and the neighbors, Steve and Bailey Bartholomew—plus Conrad. Both couples were comfortably attired in Lands' End (worldwide headquarters was just two towns over, people kept telling him): cargo shorts, untucked shirts with button-down collars, slip-on shoes. Canvas shades of ecru, loden, heather abound.

This is us in ten years, Conrad thought. But if this was the Game of Life, he was missing his pink

48

peg. If Jo were here, she would do all the talking, knowing what to reveal and what to hold back. As it stood, he felt like a fraud and kept waiting for one of them to call him out on it. What do you do? Is it true you paid cash for that house? What the hell are you doing in Wisconsin, Conrad?

Hiding? Or running?

But they didn't call him on anything. Instead, they fed him and watched him like the polite stranger he was, and spoke kindly, even when he began to pry.

'So what's the story with the guy used to live in my new house,' Conrad said, pushing his roast beef aside to dig into Gail's peach cobbler.

'What about Leon Laski is it you want to know?' Gail Grum said, a spoonful of vanilla ice cream hovering under her nose.

'Oh, I dunno,' he lied, reminding himself these people might very well still be friends with the man who once owned his house. 'He came by earlier today and, well, it was weird. Some issues with the closing, I guess.'

Gail pulled the spoon from her mouth slowly. 'Leon can be a touch abrasive at times, but they're good people.'

Big John Grum turned to his wife, 'How long were dey in dare? Ten, twelve years?' At six-six and pushing two hundred and fifty pounds, Big John towered over his little garden gnome of a wife. He was a carpenter and a mason, with the hands to show for it. The gentle giant was also a haggard giant.

'Oh, nooo. More like sixteen,' Gail corrected.

Big John shook his head. 'Leon's just upset he's overextended himself on that farmette. He was

49

probably all in a rush to get the money out of your deal, and now that you're here he doesn't know where to put his family. Don't even have plumbing's what I hear. Be another three months yet.'

'Poor Leon's going to be shitting in the woods all summer long,' Steve Bartholomew added. Steve had the tidy presence of a financial manager, but his voice filled the room. He strode around with his belly out, red in the face, his gray-flecked black hair shorn military tight enough that Conrad could see the shiny sunburn on his scalp. As with many men of his disposition, Steve's wife was his opposite. Bailey Bartholomew was so quiet she seemed to disappear, popping back into the conversation only to temper her husband.

'In the woods, huh?' Conrad said. 'Do we have poison ivy around these parts?'

'Yes, we do!' Gail said, laughing with the others.

Steve drained half his wine and fixed on Conrad. 'A man raises his family in a house, I don't care how well he does in the transaction—and that house was worth a lot less when Leon bought it—it's never easy leaving your home.'

'Of course not,' Conrad said, feigning sympathy. 'I'm sure Leon's a decent guy.'

Gail touched Conrad's arm. 'Greer—that's his wife—was probably just worried about the kids. Four is a lot to carry around, with or without plumbing.'

'Three,' Steve corrected. 'But she's preggo again.'

'Actually, Steve,' Big John put in. 'Wasn't it two plus the pregnancy?'

'Oh, that's right,' Gail said. 'I can't keep track.'

50

Steve scoffed. 'Don't even try. It's like ten little Indians over there.'

'Okay, everybody,' Big John said, heading to the back porch for a post-meal smoke.

A mutually regrettable silence ensued.

'How old are his kids?' Conrad waited, but suddenly no one wanted to crunch the numbers. All eyes around the table had drifted away or downward.

Steve nudged Conrad in the ribs. 'Our Leon's a regular Johnny Appleseed. Shoots more bullseyes than Robin Hood.'

'Steeeeve!' Bailey wailed. 'You are terrible.'

Steve winked at Conrad—*aren't I a piece of work?*—and Conrad smiled, realizing he liked Steve and his cruel humor. Suddenly Conrad imagined spending long summer evenings on his porch with Steve, the two of them getting red in the face over the state of the world. He realized he was making a new friend, or could be.

Bailey turned to Conrad. 'They lost their first two. Years ago. So sad. Gail, did Greer ever—'

'No one knows,' Gail said. 'Could have been something rare. Just . . . one of those things.'

'They should have called the doctors sooner,' Steve said. 'There's just no excuse.'

When no one added to that, Conrad decided to let the topic go for now. But two kids 'lost'? Something bad had happened, oh yes.

'I'll kill you, you asshole!' the girl screamed. 'How dare you fucking touch me. No, no! Come back here, Eddie! Eddie, you piece of shit!'

Her voice was an octave shy of a shriek and it was coming from outside. A car door slammed, the engine revved to the moon and tires barked.

Conrad jerked in his chair, certain the car was coming through the walls.

The front door banged open and a teen girl crying her eyes out barged in, colliding with her mother. Everyone turned to witness the drama.

'Liebschen!' Gail grabbed her daughter by the elbow.

'Don't touch me!' The girl clawed back like it was her mother that had been hitting her, if hitting was part of it. Conrad glimpsed tears and blood near her mouth, but not much, and it was hard to be sure with the long hair tangled over her features.

Before Gail could corral all five feet nothing of her daughter's whirling madness, the girl turned on them, aware she was making a scene. Face gone red, blue corduroy jacket flapping, exposing the bulges, her awkwardly large breasts like twin summits over the earth orb that was her belly peeking from under her skin-tight tee. Her entire life on display, daughter Grum glared across the table and locked on Conrad with eyes as large and green as turtles.

'Who the fuck is that?' she said. 'What's he looking at?'

All he thought was, *Damn, that girl's pregnant.*

And she was the one hiding in my house the day I toured it with Roddy.

'Nadia, out.' Gail pointed like a hunter for her setter.

Conrad felt a snap of embarrassment for her, followed by shame, like he was on some jury deliberating her guilt. All that was missing was the big red P on her chest. He turned away quickly and saw Steve shut his mouth, wisely offering no comment while Gail wrestled her into the adjacent room, applying a mantra. 'Nadia, calm down, Nadia, calm down . . .'

He owed her one, in a way. The girl had taken the attention off of him. He felt relieved and run over. She had that effect on him from the first. Even in her tears, her corded neck mottled with angry red patches, her white hair flying, little Nadia Grum was, to a wounding degree, gorgeous.

*   *   *

His birthing house was a sauna. Hoping to cool down and stave off the inevitable wine hangover, Conrad took a beer from the fridge and returned to the album. The whole notion that his wife was trapped in there now seemed absurd. He plopped down on the couch and flipped the pages idly, skipping the first photo of the women, the ones he had begun to think of as the Heritage Street Gals. He didn't really want to know if Jo was still with them, waiting for him to look again into her dead black eyes.

The next few pages were sketches of the house under construction and he skimmed them without much interest. Then the book seemed to fall open to a gatefold containing another photo. The perspective was from garden level, inside and looking out one of the basement windows. The photo was a close-up and it required some effort for him to make out its true subject. Around the window frame were the nubs of the natural rock foundation. In one small gap in the mortar was a large brown spider—Conrad, who knew something about reptiles, amphibians and arachnids, guessed

53

it was a brown recluse—perched with the weight of its thorax tilted back, one needle-like foreleg extended. A woman testing the temperature in a body of water. Her web had been spun out in every direction, and desiccated insect carcasses remained stuck within the spokes. Her fat body— no, wait. It wasn't her body bulging this way. It was her egg sac the photographer had been after.

She was nearly bursting.

Conrad stared at the spider, imagining her offspring. Hundreds of tiny brown spiders scurrying beneath him, crawling in the foundation, in the walls, in the soil all around, descendants of this old girl.

The spider connected his thoughts to the Heritage Street Gals and, without reflection, to talk of the Laskis' lost children and even the pregnant Nadia Grum. And then his mouth went dry.

The album was all about the house. A history he wanted no part of.

There were fifty or more pages remaining.

Head pounding, Conrad carried the album to the fireplace, rolled three balls of newspaper into the grate, wedged the album in and set the entire works ablaze.

9

The routine was comfort. The routine was habit. The routine was boring.

The routine lasted two weeks.

He kept telling himself if he could stay positive

until Jo's first planned visit home, all would be reconciled, or at least renegotiated.

He was wrong.

Hot, jobless, wifeless, he roamed in a fugue from one hour to the next. The days passed so slowly Conrad found himself staring at the kitchen clock (a plastic hen happily handing eggs to a farmer), wishing for a gun to blast it to pieces.

And he was trying, at least in the beginning. Conrad forced himself to rise and shower before eight, to dress as if he had a job. Clean-shaven, freshly polo-ed and khakied, his navy and lemon-striped Adidas kicks (his one concession to acting the man of leisure) laced neatly, he would walk the two blocks to the Kwik-Trip and pick up the *Wisconsin State Journal*, a watery coffee and maybe a banana or plain cake donut for breakfast. After reading the paper during his meditative and open-door toilet time, Conrad would walk the dogs around town. He became familiar with the houses, many of them old like theirs. Most were smaller. Some were twice as large, but these looked tired, thirsty for paint. He told himself 818 Heritage Street was the best in the entire town. That it was a special place.

After walking the dogs, Conrad would work the yard, pruning here and there, never making much of a dent in the wild grapevines and pine trees. It had been a wet spring, and so far June had delivered heat in the morning, rain almost every afternoon and sometimes again at night. The result was a gardener's dream climate of steamy, lush growth. He would weed the gardens until his back spasmed and his arms trembled. By noon he always found himself back inside the house, panting, guzzling iced tea, spitting and wheezing from the humidity or some allergy he could not classify.

To combat the afternoon malaise, he took to drinking iced tea by the gallon. It poured through him while he wasted hours checking email, surfing the web, reading scandalous DrudgeReport and PerezHilton headlines: This Little Starlet Went to Rehab, This Little Starlet Forgot to Wear Panties When She Pumped Gas. This Little Terrorist Had Roast Beef, This Little Husband Had None.

Left to fend for himself, he cooked four-course meals and shared them with the dogs. He looked out the windows and tried to time his trips to the mailbox with the neighbors' comings and goings. Steve Bartholomew worked from home— architecting databases with co-workers in Bangladesh—and always asked about Jo, which only angered Conrad. He talked with Gail Grum when he saw her in one of her six or seven gardens that grew in her backyard and between their homes. Sometimes Big John would wave to his junior neighbor as he unloaded diamond-blade saws and scrap rock from his truck at the end of stone-dusty days.

He thought about Holly, his one that got away. Every guy had one. Eventually you forgot her and moved on, and he had, but she was coming back. He fought the indulgence, however, and in her place turned his imaginings on Nadia Grum. The expectant girl next door. A little blonde ball of blustery ignorance. Did she live at home? Did she have bruises from her fight with what's his name, the boyfriend? Teddy? Davie? What did she do with her days? Was she a student? A dropout? Was

Teddy preparing to be the father?

Was he still fucking her?

He spoke with Jo every night. Their conversations were short and depressing. She was always too tired to discuss the job and her routine in any detail. As they talked, Conrad would lie on the couch and imagine her lying on the bed in her pajamas in her suite, both of them flicking channels as the conversation dwindled to static sighs and half-hearted miss-yous, neither willing to admit they were stuck in a rut, separated by a lot more than Lake Michigan. He mentioned how excited he was to have her home for the weekend, floated the idea of a special night out in Madison—drinks on Monona Terrace, some live music, maybe.

'Ugh,' she said. 'All I can think about is sleeping in my own bed, cuddling with the dogs and taking a long, hot bath. The tub in my room is tiny and I just want to sleep for days.'

'Yeah, you sound tense,' he said, angling for the common thread. He imagined her long body folded up in the suite's tub, a washcloth draped over her eyes. 'We could always, you know . . . like we did that one time.'

She didn't remember 'that one time', back when they did all kinds of things. Undaunted, he hinted around it three or four times. She yawned. Finally he just said: 'Here's an idea. You're alone there. I'm alone here. Pour yourself a glass of wine, let's get crazy and have a hot and dirty conversation.'

He could hear her tense up and he immediately regretted the suggestion.

'No, not happening,' she said. 'Sorry.'

Maybe she was just tired. And maybe he was

57

being too sensitive, sounding weak, which she always despised. Either way, her answer felt cruel.

'I wish you'd never gone.'

'Conrad, please. We chose this.'

'But I didn't go away. You did.'

'Don't be mad.'

'I'm not mad.' *I'm fucking horny. Seventeen years old revved up and ready to go fifteen rounds!* 'It's been a long time.'

'I'll make it up to you, honey. No pouting.'

'Yeah, yeah.'

'Call me tomorrow.'

'I will.'

'I love you.'

'Love you, too.'

It didn't add up. Shouldn't she be the one trying to make it up to him? Shouldn't she be writhing at his feet for the way he forgave her? For the house he'd bought for her? For getting her out of the rut, no questions asked?

He couldn't recall the last time they'd had sex, but he remembered their last night together in this house all too well. He'd had the chance and somehow he'd blown it.

*　　　*　　　*

It had been late and they were in bed. They had been tired from chores, but it was a shared pain and therefore good.

Jo had leaned against his shoulder and whispered, 'I love it here.'

He'd been cranky on purpose. 'What kind of training makes you leave home for eight weeks?'

'Think of it like, I dunno, the down payment on

58

your own business. As soon as I'm done, I can telecommute—'

'—from anywhere in the world,' he finished for her. 'Is that what Donna said? Are you still selling me, now?'

'Maybe I am selling you. But if I do this, you can take all the time you need to figure out what you're going to do next. And I don't care, I really don't. Take as long as you want.'

'I thought this would be different. I thought it would be a relief for you.'

'What's to relieve?'

'I never liked being the man who depends on his wife. I'm supposed to be supporting you, and now I am.'

'I don't want you to support me.' She had said as much before and this always bitched him up. He had married a smart, capable woman, but he couldn't help feeling useless for the past couple of years. Maybe it was a man thing, not just a Conrad thing, but that didn't change the basic truth of it. 'It's six figures. One-fifty plus a bonus, to be precise.'

'Yeah. That's a lotta lettuce, Baby. But will you be happy?'

'With one-fifty? How can I not be?'

'Jo—'

'That's not what I meant. But this is a good thing. You know I never wanted to be the stay-at-home mommy. I have to do something.'

'Is that all this is about? Career fulfillment? Or is there something else going on?'

'Like what?'

'Jo. Okay.' He chose his next words like a man on a game show who's just realized this one's for

59

the trip to Maui. 'We never went into it. You might have thought I was avoiding it, or just too mad to deal. But I want you to know. I . . . I understand what happened.'

'What does that mean?' She wasn't looking at him. Just whispering, but he could feel her tighten under his hand.

'It means it happens. People who aren't full seek sustenance elsewhere.'

The minute that followed was a long, silent one.

'Maybe this job is my way of filling myself up,' she said.

'Is it?' *Yes, maybe I am willing to allow you that much. For a little while. And by the way, what am I filling myself up with?* 'If you're sure you want it, then you should go for it.'

She pushed him on to his back and began kissing his neck, his chest, pushing his shirt up. 'I'm not sure. I'm never sure about anything.'

'You're not?'

'No one is.'

'Oh.'

'It is kind of scary, but exciting, too.' She nibbled at his waist.

'You don't get scared.'

'Yes, I do.'

She was waiting for him to put her fears to rest, to explain what was eating him up. But he hadn't been able to find the words, not when she was preparing to leave. She rested her head on his stomach. He was immediately aroused. She noticed and popped him free. The unexpected movement and sheer heat of her tongue made him groan. A minute into it, she'd paused and looked up, speaking in a voice as faint as a radio transmission from Iowa.

'I need you to know something,' she said.

'Whuh?'

'What you walked in on. It wasn't what you thought. I admit it was very close, and wrong. But it wasn't sex.'

Amazing. A little three-letter word. Timed right, it was a sledgehammer.

'Please, don't,' he said.

Her grip remained firm but the stroking had ceased. Her eyebrows arched and she bored into him.

'Look at me,' she said. He sat up on his elbows. 'I've never been unfaithful, Conrad.'

He did not accept her words, but neither did he disbelieve them. They just hung there between them. He wanted to throw her off and throw her out. He wanted to roll her over and fuck her until she wept.

He fell back and covered his eyes.

She started to cry and he hated her for that. His balls were ready to explode and he hurt worse than that in worse places. But no, he wasn't going to comfort her. That Fucker Jake had been there. Whatever had or had not happened in the house, Jo had fallen asleep in her panties and his Sebadoh and That Fucker Jake had been there.

She pulled herself up and rested against his shoulder, releasing him when she felt him softening. Even if he wasn't so sure about the past, he believed she was being faithful now. What were dropping bad habits and moving away to start a new life together if not faith that your marriage would work out?

'I guess we're both a little freaked out here,' he

said.

'I'll make it up to you next time, okay?'

What if there is no next time? a nasty little voice shot back.

'I just want you to want this as much as I do,' he said. Meaning, in that male way, the sex and the love and the marriage and the house. They were inseparable to him.

'I do.'

*　　*　　*

It seemed a trade he'd failed to make—his comforting words for her sexual favor. A small thing, perhaps. A lost opportunity on both fronts.

And so, his wife rejecting his person-to-person potty mouth, Conrad's frustration deepened until he caved in and embarked on one last running attempt to get the job done by himself, if only to prove that he still could (and so that he might last more than thirty seconds when she returned). His tall and beautiful Jo was out of town, but there was a high-speed pipe and a portal of infinite titillation at his fingertips.

The overture to the main event arrived courtesy of Visa and a mega site that humbly billed itself as ShavedPussyEmpire.com. He searched in vain for something less Chesterish but the tamer domains like NiceYoungGirlsYourParentsWouldApprove Of.com and ArtfullyDepictedNakedLadies.com had been blown out of the water early in an Internet porn arms race toward mutually repulsed destruction.

Knowing this, he hesitantly Googled 'free sex movies' and got the universe of porn, none of it free. Settling upon a site that appeared somewhat legit (ho ho), he linked around until he had eliminated the most ghastly fetishes and entered, 'The World's #1 Destination for Shaved Pussy!' After failing to become aroused by the thirty-second free sample clips, he fumbled his credit card and tried to shoo the dogs out of the office, but the door wouldn't stay latched. Luther kept nosing in, and there was simply no way he was going to perform an act of onanism with his dogs staring at him.

He finally shouted loud enough to stop their scratching at the door and logged in, only to find himself staring at so many hairless girls in pigtails and academy plaid performing such unnatural acts of faked arousal, the 'director's' distracting and often mean-spirited verbal cues lobbed at the coke-addled nubiles, that he was overwhelmed (okay, nudged) by guilt and couldn't bring himself beyond a plumpie, let alone to climax.

After five minutes of frustrated tugging, he angrily logged off, waddled to the bathroom (the door latched, hallelujah), his pants sliding down around his knees and launched into act two, standing over (no, not the sink, you filthy pig) the bathtub, eyes closed, visions of Jo riding him reverse cowgirl style with the lights on (she had done it once and only once, on the living-room couch, pretending not to remember when he'd made the request several times since, which only made it more precious) dancing in his brain.

As he ramped up to the third act reveal, his mind performed a sort of miraculous shuffle function, a libido iPod playing every song in its pitiful six-soul library of ex-girlfriends, adding several *Hustler* Honey of the Months that had been burned into his memory from the teen years when you only had the one magazine and protected it like fire for the tribe, the iPenis playing them all at the same time at full volume, parading every girl and woman Conrad had ever bedded or seen naked before his mind's lubricated eye like a carnival wheel, round and round she goes and where he comes nobody knows, all of the breasts and hips and hair and necks and asses and lips and moans and grunts shuffling again and again until Jo slew them all and claimed her rightful spot on his lap, the ultimate authority who knows what her man needs to finish the job, the Tarot card that read simply The Wife, riding him with such hip-flexing force and the gleaming crystal reality that can only come from memory, never fantasy, that for a minute he forgot he was bent over the tub and alone in this strange small town in this huge strange house, a man with a past he desperately wanted to forget, and he lost himself in the backs of her thighs and the dimples and fine black hairs above her ass above him, her wetness wetting the length of him and he felt huge, enormous yet fully enveloped, just so fucking *owned* by this animal called woman, this being called Joanna, this entity that was physically larger and infinitely more complex than he would ever be and he slipped out ready to burst and she grabbed him and planted him back inside without missing a single stroke, she was so tuned-in, and best of all he was giving her this moment too, sending her fears away by making her come and she slowed, crunching down on him, squeezing him in contractions, her voice heavy, almost male in its animal need until she

64

came and he came with her, there inside her and here, now, in the bathroom, his fantasy and lonely reality coalescing so forcefully he felt her anger and weight clap into his body and her face—*her* face, the *other* face, the sepia woman in the photo staring at him from inside his head, her crooked smile exposing her sharp teeth—and he fought her back too late, crying out in repulsed terror as he began to ejaculate—

And an invisible lead weight slammed into his neck, dropping him to his knees, stopping the blood flow to his brain and sounding an alarm of pain that stretched from his shoulder to his forehead.

Pants around his knees, his orgasm interrupted but still surging, purging him of his life force, his seed, Conrad lost consciousness on the bathroom floor.

HOLLY

Once upon a time there was a boy, and this boy, he had something inside him. Hunger, curiosity, need. Older things without names. Things that got a hold of him at an age younger than most. Things that need to find a way out, things that need a home.

She arrived in a pink sweater and blue jeans faded almost white. She had bad new wave hair, thirty bracelets on one arm, and she carried a purple Mad Balls lunchbox instead of a purse. She was a true child of the eighties. Her sweater, her cheeks, and her lippy smile (when she did smile) were all shades of pink. She was a drug called Girl.

Just staring at her released endorphins and filled him with light.

I know what you're thinking. It's not that. Girl was not his first sexual encounter. But she was his first love. She was the girl no one could get to, which is what made him try harder. But he could not win her attentions. He was too young, too plain.

He studied her and made plans and two more years passed. Eventually she noticed him, the quiet kid who stared at her like she was made of golden candy. She knew who he was, of course. They had some classes together, but different circles of friends, and she was a circle of one. Holly Bauerman. There isn't anything in a name. But she was Holy. This was the time in which he wore her down with one simple act of courtship: staring.

He stared at Holly Bauerman in class, in the halls, and wherever he saw her around town, at parties and in the clothing store where she worked. She found him creepy at first, and then became curious. Once, on a Monday night, he spray-painted her name in ten-foot letters on the street in front of her house. No one knew it was him. But she knew.

She resisted, but what else has the power to melt us than the adoring eyes of another? If you have ever been adored this way, and by adore I mean with the perfect mixture of fear and craving, then you know. It is not something one can give to oneself. Only another's eyes have the power to show us how beautiful we can be. When his longing became obvious and overwhelming, her disgust turned to disinterest to a thing she missed when it was withheld, until finally the watching

66

became a form of ego food she could no longer live without. She went to the Last Day of School Picnic alone and he was there.

'Hello, Holly,' he said. 'Happy last day of school.'

'What do you want from me?' A kind of tough, quiet panic entered her voice. She stood there in her plaid shorts, her pink tee shirt and plastic bracelets, her lunchbox-purse swinging like a second grader.

'If I don't see you all summer,' he said, 'then what's the point?'

'There is no point. Point of what?'

'The best days of my life have been the first day of school,' he said. 'I just wish I had more than four of them.'

She didn't have to think back to know that this was true.

'So are you going to give me your summer, or should I get it over with and kill myself?'

She laughed, but later confessed it was the most romantic thing anyone had said to her. They spent the summer together. Once they started talking, she relaxed. He became a clown, a little brother she could abuse, a friend to cheer her up, a reliable jester in her not-so-funny world. The world that had given her things like divorce, eating disorders, rival cliques, a dented and rusting Volkswagen Rabbit—this world he washed away. Puppy love brought them together, but what bound them was divorce. They had that brokenness in common and he thanked his parents for that much, for making him into something resembling her. His new wave girl morphing into a little prep-hippie before his eyes.

67

The summer was slow and warm and full of nights sitting on the hood of her car at Flagstaff Mountain, looking over the town. They pretended they were in a 1950s movie and he bought her milkshakes. She showed him how to dip the fries in the shake. They stayed away from parties. It was better just to walk in the park, go to the movies, or stay at home and talk on the phone. One day they talked on the phone from ten in the morning until midnight.

She made him take long hikes with her. She told him how she loved wild flowers, herbs, iced tea. She brewed her own special concoctions on the deck in glass gallon jars. She said it was a healing art, preparing this sun tea. She said that tea was purifying, good for the soul. He had never felt so clean as when he was with her. She collected herbs from the mountains and brewed special batches for him and he believed her. Later, when she grew bold toward the end of that endless summer, she leaned back in one of her mother's chaises longues and poured iced tea down her chest and let him lap at her swimsuit. She filled her mouth and kissed him while he drank from her, a bird to her fountain statue.

Then school came, and it was news. People did not agree that it was a good fit. He was too strange. Wasn't he that kid who played with snakes? But they didn't care. They were in their own world and they laughed at everything. At the teachers, other kids. At their parents. At policemen who pulled them over for speeding. At people who cared, at people who tried.

Their physical courtship lasted six months and he was patient. They kissed for hours, sometimes all night. It became serious before the sex and after, deadly serious. They lost all shyness in bed and talked through every step of it. She taught him how to touch her and for how long until it worked better than it was supposed to work at age sixteen.

In the last semester of their senior year they were seventeen and, though they did not know it, afraid. They had been together for nearly two years and become one of those inseparable couples that cause teachers to cluck their tongues and parents to lie awake wondering how can it possibly be so serious at this age, having forgotten in their middle age that love at seventeen is deadly serious because nothing else matters, it is the first and purest and . . . because it's love at seventeen.

So the boy set out to become a man, at precisely the time when his tribe was most unwilling to let the girl become a woman.

10

When he regained his senses he had no idea how much time had passed. Daylight had faded somewhat. His shoulder throbbed and the bathroom seemed to be tilting in every direction at once. He raised himself on shaking legs and began to pull his pants up. What just happened here? How much time had he lost? Minutes . . . or hours? The last thing he recalled was experiencing a too realistic vision of Jo and the first strand of a mighty orgasm.

He patted the front of his boxer shorts and pants, then up higher to his tee shirt. He bent over, which made his headache sing, and scanned the floor, the tub, the sink. Where the hell did it go? He longed for an ultra-violet light, one of those scanners they used on *CSI*, the better to locate his discharged DNA.

Conrad cupped his package, shifting things around. He was sore in the way that suggested he had, in fact, climaxed. He felt it in the muscles of his loins, the need to urinate. But his chafed, limp penis was clean and dry. He held his hands up in front of his face, turning them in the light. For a moment he caught the scent of lavender, of summer spices. But it was faint, and then gone.

So, let's get this straight. It was so good I blacked out, but didn't come? Then why do my neck and shoulders feel like I've been playing catch with an anvil?

Someone knocked him down, there was no other explanation. And not the dogs. Couldn't have been the dogs. The door was still latched.

Someone knocked me down . . . and cleaned me up? Or was I out so long it dried, becoming invisible?

Hey, who knows, maybe the house swallowed it up!

'Jesus Christ.'

Swearing off masturbation for at least another week, Conrad undressed, climbed in the shower and let the cold water run. At age thirty, he was tired of his sex drive, frightened of where it was leading him.

*　　*　　*

Conrad was walking the dogs when he saw the car come to a stop at the four-way intersection, and by

70

then she was attempting to escape. The boyfriend—Teddy, Eddie, something always unsteady—braked hard. The passenger door swung all the way out and rebounded into her shin.

'Ow, you asshole!'

It was early in the afternoon, eighty-eight degrees, and no one came out when she started yelling. Eddie grabbed at her shirt to keep her from fleeing and Nadia's palm cracked against her boyfriend's cheek, causing him to blurt, 'Aw, fuck!'

'Aw, fuck, is right,' Conrad said to the dogs, stepping off the curb. 'Here we go.'

There were two types of kids here, he'd noticed. The almost unbelievably plain second- and third-generation farm kids and do-gooders who'd yet to be exposed to even the imagined horrors of teen angst. Coming from what appeared to be a loving home and despite the company she kept, Nadia seemed like this type.

The other type was Eddie's type. They used to be called townies, but now . . . whatever they were called, Eddie's car was not helping his case. It was one of those compact models Pontiac made for about three years. Teal-green with purple pinstriping down the side—just a little sexiness to make the buyer feel like this mass-produced hunk of shit would help him express something. The mortarboard tassel dangling from the rearview mirror suggested the best days of Eddie's life were behind him, and the thumping bass emanating from the sub-panel in the back was a white trash-y, effete disco—*uhn-tiss, uhn-tiss, uhn-tiss*—that nearly drowned out the yowling hole that was the muffler. The entire package had to be violating at least three noise ordinances.

71

At least until Eddie and his cruiser stalled out and began to roll down Heritage Street in reverse, when everything became quiet.

Conrad cleared his throat. 'Nadia?'

'What?' she said, tearing herself from Eddie's clutches.

'Sorry to bother you. You know where we can go swimming?'

Eddie peered over her shoulder. The boy's lacquered buzz cut and wispy thin sideburns reflected sunlight and made his acne gleam.

Conrad smiled. *You see me, you little fuck? Good, 'cause I'm on my way.* Alice and Luther crossed leashes and started whining to go for a ride.

Nadia blinked at him. 'You want to go swimming?'

'My dogs are just about to croak from this heat; thought we'd find a watering hole.' Luther and Alice pawed at the door. 'Conrad, your new neighbor? It's Nadia, right?'

Eddie continued to project his best thousand-yard stare through the windshield. It was nine hundred and ninety feet short. Conrad winked at Nadia—*work with me, girl.* Nadia smirked—she got it.

'They look like they could use a swim,' Nadia said. 'Hey, hot doggies, what's up?'

'By the way.' Conrad nudged the door open so the dogs could play their part. 'I'm Conrad Harrison, you must be Teddie, right?'

'Eddie,' Eddie said, scowling at Conrad's outstretched hand. Nadia was cooing at Luther and Alice as they nosed into her lap.

'These two are Luther and Alice, my sweet little baby bulls.' Conrad felt a pang of guilt for using

72

them this way, adding to the stereotype he and Jo had tried to prove undeserved ever since adopting the mutts. 'Oh, don't worry, though. Terrier mixes are no different than any other species of dog. In fact, they're a lot like people. Most are good, some are bad, and it all depends on who raises them.'

'Shit, I gotta go, Nads, get those dogs outta my car.'

'Sorry, Eddie. Let me just—hey, where was that watering hole, did you say?' Conrad made a show of trying to pull them out, leaning over Nadia. 'Darn it, they don't want to come out. Come on, Alice, let's get out of the nice man's car.'

'Here, let me.' Nadia hauled herself out and unwound Alice's leash from her legs.

Conrad pulled Luther from the front seat. 'There we go, all clear. Sorry.'

'Tssh,' Eddie said and turned to his girlfriend. 'We going or what?'

'Hold on.' Nadia turned to Conrad. 'You still need to know how to get to Governor Dodge?'

'The what?'

'The lake up the state park. Dogs are allowed.'

'Oh, yeah. Cool.' He stood there in the street, nodding at her.

'Tell you what,' she said, glancing back at Eddie, who was revving his engine. 'Why don't I draw you a map?'

'That'd be helpful.'

'Eddie, why don't you—'

Eddie squealed the tires and blew the stop sign near the Kwik-Trip, cranked his music and floored it around the corner.

Nadia watched the spot where Eddie had just been, then nodded and snapped her fingers.

73

'Thanks for that.'

'Oh, no, it wasn't—'

'Yes, it was. I needed rescuing and you rescued me.'

'If that's true, then I'm glad I was walking by. I should get them home. You going this way?'

'I live next door, don't I?'

'So, you do live at home?'

'Where else would I live?'

'I don't know. None of my business, actually.' *Dumbfuck.*

She walked beside him as the dogs careened, sniffing every inch of the sidewalk. He noticed her small feet, the retro Eastland mocs she wore with no socks, the laces done up in that preppy pretzel thing like two little boat fenders hanging over the sides—shoes Holly used to wear. She wore simple blue canvas shorts and her calves were muscled, a soccer player's legs. A plain white tee on top, snug over the soccer ball of her belly. He guessed she was five or six months along, but he was afraid to ask. The rest of her was shorter than he remembered. Compared to his nearly Amazonian wife, this was like walking a girl home from school. It felt like he was already courting her, and that couldn't be right, no matter how much benefit of the doubt he gave himself.

Nadia said, 'Oh, and don't tell my parents, okay?'

'About?'

'About Eddie,' she said.

He kept his eyes on the sidewalk. 'Of course.'

What else could she have meant, 'Rad?

'Hey, by the way,' she said. 'What's with the red light?'

74

'The red—oh, in the garage. Must seem pretty weird, huh? New neighbors and there's a spooky red glow emanating from the garage.'

'I wasn't spying.'

'No, I know. It's kind of neat, actually. Or at least I think so. Do you want to see them?'

'Them?'

'Yeah,' he said, tromping faster as the dogs pulled him through their little Eden of a backyard. 'I pretty much guarantee you haven't seen these before. Come on.'

Nadia followed him to the detached garage where the red light glowed night and day.

* * *

'There's nothing dangerous in here, you have my word. But before we go in, do you have any phobias?'

Nadia stepped back, crossed her arms and pursed her lips.

Conrad nodded. 'I guess I better just spit it out. I have snakes. Non-venomous, harmless snakes. In cages.'

This was the moment when they either turned and fled or got all bright-eyed and brave.

'Snakes. You have snakes, like for pets?'

'Ah, not so much pets as a hobby. Snakes aren't really pets, because they don't like or dislike people. Well, some of them are afraid of people, but most of them are indifferent.'

'Yikes.'

'If it's not your thing, we don't have to—'

'Show me.'

'You sure?'

She nodded quickly, tensed but excited.

'I knew you would be brave.'

They stepped inside. Conrad dropped the leashes and deactivated the ADT system as the dogs went on a sniffing spree along the indoor-outdoor carpet. The six hanging fixtures housed twin four-foot Vita-Life bulbs and the space was full of purple-tinted white light. A portable swamp cooler for dangerously hot days sat in the corner. The old workbench was clean, with towels, water bowls, plastic hide-ins and cleaning products stacked neatly to one side. Along the front of the bench hung three stainless-steel gaff hooks that looked like dental instruments made for an ogre.

Nadia noticed none of these things. Her attention was fixed on the fiberglass cages on the rolling iron racks against the south wall. The cages were four by two by two feet each, three to a tier, two tiers wide for a total of six. The front panels were sliding glass doors with keyed locks. Without the aid of a human hand, nothing was getting in or out of these cages.

In the corner of each cage and rigged to a series of digital thermostats, a lamp holding a one hundred and fifty watt infrared bulb glowed, ensuring that the thermometers read 86.5 degrees, twenty-four hours a day, year round.

'They can't get out. Have a closer look.' He waved her on.

Nadia stepped forward cautiously, looking back at him with huge eyes. 'Oh-my-gosh, this is so crazy. If my mom saw these she would die!'

'Yes, let's not surprise her then, shall we?'

Nadia stepped closer to the only cage with some activity. Inside, perhaps eighteen inches from the girl's face, his largest female was peering over a natural wooden branch siliconed to the wall. Half of her nearly six feet stretched up, her head raised as if in prayer to the invisible sun. She moved like a levitating wand, the muscles along her neck and mid-body holding her steady, exposing the cream-colored belly and vertical slashes that swept up and back like tiger stripes before fading into the iridescent black velvet scales that covered the rest of her fist-thick girth.

'That's Shadow, my largest female.'

Shadow's forked tongue waved lazily, testing the air as she moved closer to the heat-radiating patch of fuzziness that was the girl.

'Holy shit!' Nadia put a hand over her mouth. 'Is she going to bite me?'

'No, she's just checking out the action. Snakes have very poor vision, so what she's seeing now is just your general shape. They don't have ears, so when you see her tongue moving like that she's tasting the air, so to speak, sensing vibrations.'

'So she can hear my voice?'

'She might feel it. And in the wild, they sense vibration on the ground, approaching animals.'

'What are they, boa constrictors?'

'They are a type of constrictor, but not boas. A very rare species called Boelen's, or black pythons. They're found only in the mountains of Papua New Guinea.'

'Where's that?'

'Near Australia, at the end of the Indonesian Archipelago. They're heavily protected and somewhat illegal to export from their native country, and very illegal to import into the US.'

'What'd you do? Smuggle them?'

'One of the curators at the San Antonio Zoo is a friend of mine. Dr Hobarth sold me these wild-caught specimens at a reduced rate, off the books, so I could try to reproduce them. Captive-bred babies are more stable, free of the parasites you get with wild caught animals.'

'People buy these? How much?'

'Wild caught, not much. Too hard to keep. But assuming the babies are healthy and eating, which is the hardest part, to get them eating once they hatch, they'll go for eight to ten grand per head.'

Nadia gaped at him. 'Ten thousand dollars? For a snake?'

'And each female may produce six to twelve eggs. I'd have to split the proceeds with the zoo, of course.'

'That's . . . that's a lot of money,' she said. 'Why snakes? Is this like your job or something?'

'It used to be. When I turned sixteen, my first job was working in a tropical fish and reptile store—Dr Hobarth owned the shop while he was finishing his Ph.D. By the time I got out of high school, I had thirty-five or forty snakes in my bedroom. King snakes, milk snakes, rat snakes, boas, pythons, a couple of iguanas and a monitor lizard. My mother was very patient with me. I used to do shows for elementary schools, give talks at the Humane Society. I reproduced some of them, sold the babies for a few hundred dollars here and there. Sold off most of my collection to pay for college. I always wanted to keep Boelen's, but I could never afford them. Then I sort of came into a little money, and here they are. They are my favorite species.'

'How do they . . . you know . . . ?' Nadia

blushed.

'What?' He knew but he wanted to hear her say it.

'Do it.'

'Snakes aren't all that different from people. Once their primal needs are met—food, shelter, the right climate—they just hook up. It's survival, so they aren't too picky, as long as they are healthy. They cross paths, the decision is practically made for them. The actual physical part is a little different. With snakes, the boys have two.'

'Shut up!' Nadia said. 'Two? That's so gross!'

'Yeah, well, you do with what Mother Nature gives you, I guess.'

'Then what?'

'Then they wrap their tails around each other in a twist. Sometimes the male uses his mouth to hold the female by the neck. They sit like that for a few hours or a few days. Then they separate and move on.'

'What does your wife think?'

'She's not afraid of them, but I think she sees them as some juvenile part of me that won't grow up, you know? Like I should be too old for this kind of creepy-crawly kid stuff. Maybe she's right.'

'She won't be complaining when you buy her a new car with the money from the little kiddy snakes, right?'

'No, she won't. Do you want to hold one?'

'Do they have poison?'

'No, pythons are not venomous. They constrict their prey before swallowing them whole.'

'Is she going to constrict me?'

'No, she is very tame and she would never try to

eat you because you're much too large.'

'What does she eat?'

'Rodents, birds.'

'Like rats?'

'Or chickens. But I've got them on rats now.'

'Ew! Where do you get rats?'

'Pet stores.'

'Isn't that kind of mean?'

'Everybody's got to eat.'

She watched the snake. 'Are they slimy?'

'No, those are the amphibians. Snakes are smooth, not slimy.'

'She is sort of beautiful.'

'Here.' Conrad unlocked the door. Shadow did not flinch, even when he picked her up, supporting her body like a garden hose draped over his forearms. He went slowly, more for Nadia's benefit than the snake's.

Nadia screwed up her courage as the serpent stretched out and raised her head, her tongue flickering gently, moving toward his face. The snake rested her neck against his shoulder and began slithering over his back while her tail hung semi-loose over his arms and waist.

'I can't believe I'm doing this.' Nadia set her hand on the snake's back and did not recoil at the first touch. 'She's so smooth. Like velvet.'

'Boelen's have exceptionally smooth scales, very delicate skin. See the iridescence there, the way it makes little rainbows in the light?'

'Yeah.'

'Boelen's survive in the higher elevations because her black scales absorb heat.'

'What's that on her lips?'

Shadow had come around his other shoulder.

80

On her top lip, the vertical scales were thicker, the black grill of a sleek new car.

'Those are called pits. She senses heat with them. For hunting.'

Nadia let the snake slither forth, feeling the muscled length settle on her arms. Conrad stepped from under the snake's body and allowed the full weight to hang on her.

'Oh my God. She's amazing.'

'Yes, she is.' He could see that she was proud of her bravery.

'Thank you for showing me this, Conrad. This is really, really cool.'

'My pleasure.'

She was like the camp kids that came to the Humane Society. They started the hour crying and cowering in the corner. By the end they were fighting each other to be next in line while their parents stood stiffly at the back of the room, eyes accusing him. Except with Nadia there wasn't much fear to begin with.

'Hey, Conrad. What are those?'

'What?'

'There, in the box thingy.' She pointed. 'The white stuff? Is that her poop?'

'Uh, maybe.' Snakes defecated white calcified urates, like hardened marshmallows. 'Those are kinda big to be—hey, wait.'

He froze, trying to process what he was seeing.

'What is it?'

'My God.'

'What's wrong?' She had seen something in his eyes.

'Those are eggs.'

'And they're not supposed to be?'

81

'They can't . . . she's never—' He checked the locks on all the cages, opened Shadow's cage and searched under her hide-in, the water bowl, the paper substrate. Foolishly looking for what he knew wasn't there, a sign that another of the animals had gotten inside with her. 'She can't have eggs, not now.'

'Why not?'

'Because Shadow has never, never once been with a male. Hobarth documented everything meticulously. And she's not even mature. I wasn't planning on putting her with the others until next spring and, even then, that was a dream. I figured two years, but this, uh-uh. There's no way.'

'They don't just lay eggs like chickens or something?'

'No, they need to be fertilized. They must mate to become gravid. No mate, no eggs.'

'One of the others got to her, you think?'

'No. Not a chance. And if they did, what, they locked themselves back in? No. The crazy thing is, I was just thinking how she looked too slim.'

'It's a good thing, though, right? She's not sick?'

'No, she seems healthy,' he said, returning to the eggs. Eight or nine white orbs the size of a cue ball, all but two stuck together in a moist clutch. He was wide-eyed, giddy and a little frightened.

'That's like, what? A hundred thousand dollars?'

'Nadia, it's much more than that,' he said, stars in his eyes. 'This is a virgin birth.'

'Okay,' she said. She didn't understand he meant it literally.

'This is a miracle.' His eyes were full of a hunger that made her step back.

'Really? Wow. I . . . I guess I should be getting home.' She headed for the door. 'Thanks for everything.'

'No problem. Sorry, I'm a little out of it. I need to call someone. Dr Hobarth's going to freak.'

'Okay,' she said. 'Good luck.'

'Yes,' he said. 'You must be some kind of luck.'

He was still laughing when she shut the door behind her.

An untouched female. Nine Boelen's eggs.

'Holy shit.'

11

His hand was on the phone when he realized she still didn't know he'd bought the snakes. She would argue that he was being silly and juvenile. But this wasn't the same as the organic juice pyramid scheme, or the Pre-Paid Legal side business, or any other half-assed endeavor he'd thrown his hat in with over the past five years waiting for his real life to begin. These were different. They were an investment, one he knew would soon pay large dividends. She would understand. Once she laid her eyes on the offspring. But even with the good news about the eggs, he had to catch her in the right mood.

He set the phone down and it rang immediately, startling him to fumble the receiver.

'Hello?'

'Conrad!' A one-word accusation. 'Where have you been?'

He heard her crying and was seized by the idea

that she knew he had walked Nadia home and lured her into the garage.

'I was in the yard. What's wrong, Jo?'

'I'm not, I'm not feeling so good. I'm having a hard time staying in class. I keep telling myself it's just nerves but it won't go away. I keep thinking about it.'

'About what?'

'About what? Everything. This, us! I'm living in a hotel in a random city, I don't know anybody. You have *no idea* what this is like.'

'I'm sorry, Jo. Calm down. I do know what it's like. I'm living in a city where I don't know anyone, either.'

'It's not the same. You're home! You have the dogs.'

'They miss you. We do. A lot.'

She was still on the verge of shouting. 'Have you even thought about this? One week we're living in Los Angeles and now, what, we just decide to move to the middle of nowhere? I don't think this is what we thought it would be.'

'What did you think—? No, skip that,' he said. 'I know what we said it would be. What is it now?'

'I think you need to do some serious thinking.'

Some serious thinking! 'About?'

'About everything.' Her voice had resumed a normal pitch. This frightened him, that she could be nearly hysterical one minute and then go Dr Phil the next. 'For starters, why did we have to leave Los Angeles? No, don't answer me now. I want you to think about it because this is really important, are you listening?'

'Yes.' *Talk, don't talk. What do you want me to do, woman?*

84

'This isn't like us, it's too fast, the whole thing. It's like we woke up different people. I know you've been through a lot with your father dying, but I'm sorry. There's more to it. You're not being truthful with me. I know something . . . else . . . happened to you. Something bad. You've always been aloof, but you're different now. Darker. And I'm sorry if that sounds paranoid. But I'm not sorry because it's how I feel, so don't try to blame me.'

This, more than anything about his wife, made his blood jump. The way she dumped everything on him and, whether he deserved it or not, backed it all up by telling him that he could not, dared not, dispute it because this was the way she *felt*. He equated this sort of haired-out logic with fundamentalists who burned books because they were offended and pissed off at the world. She felt bad; it was his responsibility to change until she felt better.

'—and then there's your career. Because I can take care of myself, but I don't want to take care of you, too. And you shouldn't want me to.'

Wasn't that what married people were supposed to do, take care of each other? And, Christ, he'd just inherited five hundred thousand dollars. What the fuck was this about?

'I'm solvent now. We're ahead of the game here, Jo.'

'It's not about the money, Conrad. You have to do something real.'

'Something real? Like what? Selling more software I don't even understand? Like traveling around the country so much neither one of us is home to so much as feed the dogs, let alone a kid?'

'What has that got to do with anything?' It was an actual screech now. 'You don't think I will make a good mother?'

'No. Yes, of course you will. I'm just saying we're both still in transition here. I'm going to find something else. Just have some patience.' *And stop acting like you have it all figured out because obviously you do not.*

'Are you going to figure it out?'

'Yes—'

'Because I can't take another diversion.'

'Now wait a goddamned—'

'That's not what I meant. I'm sorry.'

He was fuming. A diversion? They'd moved to Los Angeles for her goddamn career, not his. And the staying home all the time. She said it was nice knowing he was home. She'd even started to call him Mr Mom, for fuck's sakes.

'If you thought the past few years were a diversion, you should have spoken up,' he said. 'Instead, you waited for me, and I changed. I was the one who pushed us to move. Before I came home to find That Fucker Jake standing in the hallway with his dong in his hand. Jesus!'

'Conrad, I don't want to fight.'

'You don't—hey, that's actually funny.'

'I can't. Not here.'

'Then don't.'

'Okay.'

'Okay.'

'But you should know . . .' she said in a condescending tone.

'What?'

'I'm not coming home this weekend.' This wasn't lobbing one over to see how it would play.

This was something she knew from the minute she called.

'Why not?' He made his voice cold.

'I don't feel like it.'

'You don't feel like it.'

'No.'

'Fine, then do whatever the fuck you feel like with whoever the fuck you feel like and leave me the fuck alone!'

There was a small tea saucer lying on the kitchen table, next to the cordless phone cradle. When the phone went down like a torpedo, it nicked the saucer and shattered the porcelain into a thousand white slivers, one of which embedded itself in the cheek meat just below his left eye. There was a ringing sound from the shattering and for a second he thought it was her calling back. He reached for the phone, heard silence and threw the phone at the wall and kicked the chair up in the air where it did a neat little somersault and landed almost perfectly straight again.

His breathing came in ragged gulps like he'd been punched in the balls.

And it was a lovely summer day.

She doesn't feel like coming home? And why should she? She's got Shirley from Akron to keep her company.

'Fuck Shirley, fuck Shirley's baby, and fuck you Jo, fucking Oscar-The-Grouch-cheating-ass-bitch.'

Easy. Deep breaths. He would go to Wal-Mart and buy a new phone, and maybe sign up for whatever shitpoke regional coverage worked out here, because his Verizon mobile still wasn't working in this house and he just wanted to put the stupid thing in the garbage disposal. Later. Right now he needed to calm down and figure out what to do with the next two weeks until his wife deigned to visit him in their new home. He needed to think about his freak-ass snake eggs, and the fucking hundred year-old photo album full of ugly fucking women he burned because he was too afraid to turn the page.

He poured himself an oceanic glass of iced tea and drank it in one go. God, he could never remember being so thirsty. The summer air was so thick you could drink by wagging your tongue in front of your face. He refilled, walked upstairs and thought about Los Angeles. Rachel, the girl from the bookstore. Oh, he should have given it to her upside down and from behind when he had the chance. He went to the bathroom and tweezed the saucer shrapnel from his face, squeezed the cut like a pimple, swabbed it with witch hazel.

Luther and Alice followed him from a safe distance. They were staring at him and he stared back, all three of them panting. He opened all the windows in the library and the master bedroom. He finished the second glass of iced tea. Properly brewed iced tea with no lemon or sugar was better than most water. He wished he had brought the whole pitcher with him so he could fucking bathe in it.

Conrad fell into bed with his dogs beside him, pulled one pillow over his eyes and thought about showering in a golden waterfall of iced tea, some Edenic setting with sprigs of mint growing from rocky walls, drinking and drowning in the pure wash of it. Ice cubes floating around his balls in the basin, tea seeping into his pores until his skin was stained brown, tea-swamped and purified. With his belly full of the stuff, Conrad drifted and cooled and soon fell into the deluded reprieve of an angry, deviant nap.

*   *   *

Later, he woke in darkness to the sound of the dogs stirring from their crate beds, the *click-click-click*ing of their nails on the hardwood floor. Abruptly they stopped. And he sat there waiting for the dogs to jump on to the bed.

'Come on, Alice,' he said, realizing he was about to pee the bed. Too much iced tea.

Silence.

When the clicking started again, the sound was different. Instead of going *click-click-click* in timed groups, now he heard them individually. Not the dogs, the clicks.

Click . . . silence . . . *click* . . . silence . . . *click*. He smiled at the image of Alice tiptoeing, stepping on a single claw at a time, but the smile vanished as the next *click* drew closer and he realized there was no weight behind the sound. This was not the sound of a dog at all. It was something else.

He found the lamp, twisted the knob, and crunched his eyes shut until his pupils adjusted to the flood of light. He blinked at the foot of the bed, waiting for the next click to offer a clue as to the dogs' whereabouts.

But it's not one of the dogs, and I think you know that now, don't you?

Conrad leaned over. Nothing on the hardwood floor.

Click.

There—on the other side of the bed. It was in

89

the room, whatever it was.

'This is ridiculous,' he said to the room. Before he could talk himself out of it, he jackknifed belly down over the covers to see into the blind spot on Jo's side.

Between the dog crates and the bed was a two-foot path of wood floor. A pair of Jo's panties collecting dust sat crumpled in one corner, the lavender Victoria's Secret ones he liked on her. Down this little wooden path, at the foot of the bed, there appeared to be twin Popsicle sticks jutting out from the post of the bed frame. For some unknowable reason, the flat sticks made him think of crude shoes, what you would see if you were to encounter a clown hiding behind a tree. As soon as this image came to him, as if reading his mind one of the feet jerked up perhaps two inches and stepped forward, and the rest of the doll pivoted around the post and tilted its head . . . up at him.

His heartbeat became violent even as his limbs and back seemed to fill with concrete. Blood rushed into his face, neck and scalp, making everything itch.

'Oh, for the love . . .' he moaned.

Less than twelve inches tall, the home-made doll looked like a finger puppet or some poor child's art project. The legs were thin sticks attached to the flat feet and the cloth stitched over the body was of faded pink flowers on white, frayed and yellowed with age. Just below the neckline the thing appeared jolly and fat, the stuffing wrapped inside coarse cotton, bulging in obscene contrast to the stick legs. The doll had no neck, but it had a head.

It did not have a face.

Under the dry and stiff black hair that sprouted from the crown, where there should have been button eyes and a cute cross-stitch of a nose there was only a blank pad. Most queer of all, while the little rag had the hair and dress of a female, he sensed the other sex in its posture. It felt mean and hard, a little male troll that would speak in a clipped, ugly voice if it had one. He really hoped it did not speak. A few seconds passed. He was starting to doubt that he had actually seen it move when the doll took another step—*click!*—and then another after that one, moving with renewed purpose, as if had just found what it was looking for.

But that's crazy, because it has no eyes.

Conrad was splayed crooked on the bed, immobilized as the absurd stick figure doll, no wider than a Scarecrow Barbie, came at him in rapid steps—*click-click-click-CLICK-CLICK-CLICK!*—and raised its pipe cleaner arms to attack.

It wants to put my eyes out, his mind cried, *damned if it doesn't!*

Conrad's bladder wrenched in pain as the thing trotted alongside the bed. He flung himself away and tangled himself in the bedding as he scrambled off the other side. His right foot hit the floor and he had the crazy, self-preserving presence of mind to yank his bare foot back up in case the thing had taken a shortcut and was now coming at him from under the bed.

What if it jumps up on to the bed? What then?

How can it jump? It's only a pile of sticks, no taller than a number two pencil. Hey, it fucking walked, didn't it? No, at the end there it had started

91

to run.

Get the fuck out of here!

His feet hovering over the floor, Conrad glanced over his shoulder—nope, not coming over the bed—and then back to the floor. He couldn't see the doll now, but he could hear it. *Click-click-click* . . . pause. It was pacing, maybe coming around the other side, taking the scenic route for Chrissake, but coming just the same.

Blood humming through his veins, eyes wide and snapping left to right, Conrad planted his feet, shot off the bed, and bee-lined for the open door. Approaching the threshold he (*Don't look back! No, fuck you, I have to!*) glanced down just in time to see the doll marching stiffly after him, swaying left and right, and the moment stretched into a vacuum of pre-car-crash clarity that seemed to last five minutes.

He saw the doorframe floating toward him; behind him the doll high-stepping like a Nutcracker reject. He saw the arms reaching up, but not *after* him this time, no, instead arcing out and back down until the tiny home-made fingers dug into the wiry black hair and proceeded to yank it out in clumps, shaking its dead growth at him with that blank pad of a face somehow conveying pure, untainted hatred.

Conrad's shoulder slammed into the doorframe, pinwheeling him sideways and down. His forehead bounced off the black maple banister (another two steps of uninterrupted momentum and he might have crashed through the banister, head first down to the foyer) and he hit the hallway floor shoulder first, hipbone next, jaw last, the culminating sound like billiard balls after the sledgehammer break.

92

The panic and pain mixed into a blinding cocktail and he used his last bolt of strength to roll sideways. He was eye-level with the doll, the room darkening as he hovered on the edge of consciousness. His vision blurred, the doll becoming two dolls coming for his eyes until he could almost feel their tendril fingers crawling into his skin like insect bites. Pain flared behind his eyeballs, and then he could only squeeze his eyes shut and tremble.

When some time passed and he felt no stabbing and heard no more clicking sounds, he opened his eyes and blinked. There was no sign of the doll. The room was quiet. Empty. He got to his feet and circled the bed, weak through the knees and unsure of what, if anything, he had really seen.

There was a clicking in the hall. He tensed for it.

Alice came around the corner and looked up at him. She was sleepy. She had slept through the whole thing. Probably woke up when he hit the floor.

Conrad rubbed his head as he traipsed through the library and into the bathroom. As if timed with his bladder's release, his heart pounded in slow, heavy thumps that faded only when he had flushed.

He took three Advil and lay back down on the bed. His head began to pound in earnest, and he knew it needed some ice. He was still thinking about going downstairs to fetch some when he drifted back to sleep.

*　　　*　　　*

The next morning Conrad showered, drank four glasses of iced tea, and went to the office. After poking around on Google for forty-five minutes, he read the following excerpt from an article titled, 'Before There Was Teddy: The Evolution of Manikins, Poppets and Other Teaching Icons', originally published by *ON FOOT*, Ohio State University's journal of anthropology.

Not every culture approves of your average toy store doll. Some older customs prevent children from playing with manufactured dolls bearing a human likeness. The Amish, for instance, have long forbidden girls to play with human-resembling caricatures. Many dolls found in the Amish household would not have the same features as, say, Barbie or Ken. Imagine, I suppose, a thing made of cloth and other natural materials. Certainly one would not find dolls with eyes, a three dimensional nose, artificial hair, etc. Such a doll would not have much of a face at all.

The guiding principal here is similar to their disapproval of being photographed, one of biblical origin. Exodus 20:4-6. 'You shall not make for yourself a carved image, or any likeness of anything that is in heaven above, or that is in the earth beneath . . .'

12

If Jo had been home she would have talked some sense into him, told him he was having nightmares, convinced him to go see someone. But she wasn't home and he didn't know when she would be back. He still felt guilty for screaming and hanging up on her, but he was also still hurt by her refusal to come home. What had she said? 'Because I don't feel like it.' Now that was cruel, wasn't it? Unless . . .

What else had she said? 'I'm not feeling so good.' Was it possible, in his quick jump to self-pity, he might have mistaken her words? What if all she really meant was, I'm too sick to fly? I feel like shit?

'So I'm the asshole.'

After completing a short walk around the block, Conrad let the dogs inside, unhooked the leashes and went for the phone. Then he remembered he was supposed to go to Wal-Mart to replace the one he'd busted all to hell.

We came to start our new lives together, he would tell her. *Baby, I love you more than anything and whatever happened out there I won't take no for an answer. You need to come home soon.*

Before something bad happens.

*　　　　*　　　　*

As soon as Conrad had driven the fifteen miles, exited Highway 151, and passed the last dairy farm, he was confronted by the mini-city that was

95

Wal-Mart. The parking lot was vast, hot and full of American nameplates. He'd heard the state's residents bemoaning the retail giant's destructive effect on their small towns on National Public Radio, which, he'd noticed, regularly named the chain as a sponsor. But when Pringles were seventy-eight cents a yard and cordless phones started at $9.23, why shop anywhere else?

'Vote with your dollars, assholes,' he mumbled, yanking a cart from the fossilized greeter. 'Sorry, not you.'

After grabbing the cheapest phone on the shelf, he roamed the DVD new releases, saw nothing worth $13.88. He lost track of time and came back to himself browsing, for no real reason, an aisle of bath towels. He put two ugly green ones in his cart.

Standing in the checkout lane, Conrad fell into a glazed, tabloid-induced stupor until a frog-voiced woman exclaimed, 'How about that, childrens? It's the nice man who moved into our house.'

Conrad turned to see a gaunt woman in her thirties or fifties with gray-streaked black hair and leathery skin pulled so tight around the bulge of her pregnant belly it seemed to drag the corners of her mouth into a pouting brat's frown. She was wearing a large halter-smock and dirty jean shorts. He knew at once she was Leon's Laski's wife, and that he should be polite, but he couldn't stop staring at the tangle of grimy tykes crawling around her legs, swinging from her arms and slapping at her knobby knees.

'I'm Greer Laski, and you're Conrad, right?'

'Oh, hello, Mrs Laski . . .'

There were three of them, ages three to eight (not counting the one in the oven) but it was difficult to tell with their arms raking gum and candy to the floor, the Whiffle ball bat knocking alternately at the cart and a smaller sibling's head. They all had the same genderless cropped haircuts of a cult, and two of them wore identical grass-stained Spiderman pajamas. One fixed him with a drooling, open-mouthed and one-eyed stare, the other eye hidden behind a metal mesh patch hanging by a single strand of dirty medical tape. When she spoke, Mrs Laski's voice came in an accented, babbling run. But what kind of accent? It was more than the usual Wisconsinese his neighbors let slip. This sounded like some unique crossbreeding of shine-drunk Appalachian, Elmer Fudd and Jodi Foster in *Nell*.

'These are Anna Maybelle, Davey and Louis . . .' (massaging her distended belly) '. . . this one's a surprise. How are you settling in? Gosh, we loved that house, we sure do miss it, don't we kids, say hello to Mr Harrison.'

She pronounced it *Miss-tawh Hay-wiss-un*.

'Yes, we're doing fine.' Conrad tried to maintain the veneer of politeness while swiping his check card in the machine.

'Do you want any cash back?' the cashier said.

'No, thank you.'

'Press no.'

He did, then turned back to (what kind of name is Greer?) Mrs Laski. 'How is your new place?'

'Oh, it's hard, ya know. It's really hard, Conrad.' *Rea-wee hawd*. 'With the kids and the movers and ya know how Leon having trouble with crew and his back since the move, but we're doin' okay, aren't we kids, honey stop playing with those batteries, no, Anna Maybelle, no new cereal this

97

week.'

'Okay, then.' Conrad edged out of the line with his single bag in hand.

But Mrs Laski thwarted the getaway by grabbing his shirtsleeve. 'I don't care what anyone says, Conrad, that house is a perfectly good place to raise a family. God watched out for us in our old home just like he's watching out for you now, m'kay? Oh, h'okay, Mommy has to press the button, kids, hold on a second.'

Ah. God is watching us all.

'Yeah, about that, Mrs Laski. Is there something I don't know about our house, your old place? Leon gave me that book and if there is some significance . . . ?'

Mrs Laski's eyes shot up from her pocket book and held him with a hard stare, but it lasted only a second before she was smiling again. 'Leon should have never left that with you. It's a lotta history, ya know, Conrad.' A lot of *hiss-tow-wee*. 'He doesn't like to talk about it, but it's not like we're ashamed of it.'

With her bags in her cart, Mrs Laski dragged the train out of the line and followed Conrad toward the front doors. He knew he could outrun them, but not without appearing insane. One of the kids was now literally clinging to her leg, sitting on her foot so that the woman had to walk in a loping gait. Conrad did an involuntary and quite rude double-take when he saw that one of the boy's hands was—*oh dear God*—missing three fingers and gnarled into a ball of flesh, twin nails growing out of what should have been the first knuckles. On the back of the 'hand' was an Idaho of lumpen black fur.

98

'You can have it back, it's no big deal to me either way,' Conrad said over his shoulder, forgetting he had already torched the album. He shuffled faster past stacks of bulk water softener. Guilt wasn't even a factor now. They were so loud and grubby, it made him feel sick to be in their company.

'Oh, no no, too late for that. The book stays with the house.'

The house? You can have the house!

He realized, tallying it as a group, each child was malformed in some way. *Jesus Christ, is she his wife or his sister*?

'I'm sorry,' he said, feeling sweat leak down his ribs.

'There wasn't no devil at work in there. Lots of lil 'uns made their way into this world thanks to those women.'

'I'm not sure—'

'My family's not cursed. Accidents happen everywhere. We were happy there for a long, long time.'

'Never mind, it's not—'

'Those women were there for each other in hard times. And we all come upon hard times, don't we, from time to time?'

Conrad finally understood, and knew that he had known all along. The women were the lost women and their midwives, broken souls who came to heal . . . and got stuck bearing children . . . like the Laski kids.

'God always gave us more children, and He wouldn't do that in no home that was cursed.'

Something from dinner with the Grums came back to him. Gail and Big John and Steve arguing

99

about how many children the Laskis had.

It's like ten little Indians over there, Steve had said.

Could have been something rare, Gail had said. *Just one of those things.*

'I'm sorry for your loss,' Conrad said, watching the flicker of dark martyrdom in her eyes.

But she recovered quickly. 'No regrets, Conrad.' *No ree-gwetts.* 'And who would trust a hospital any more these days, right? Those places are full of diseases.' Mrs Laski was giggling. 'A hospital! That would be ridiculous!'

Roddy's reference to the doctor. The sketched cross in the yard.

Conrad wanted to slap her face and tell her this wasn't funny. He realized the only things stopping him were the children, staring up at him as if he had joined their traveling circus.

'I have to be—'

'Do you and your wife have any kids yet, Conrad?'

'I'm sorry, I have to get home.' He did not look back as he fled to his car.

'Say goodbye, kids, say bye bye mistah hay-wisson!'

Ten little Indians. Some made it out, some did not.

All of them born in his birthing house.

* * *

The phone had not been docked long enough to hold a charge, but that turned out not to matter. Their conversation was short.

'What's wrong?' He could tell she was crying,

again or still. 'I'm sorry I yelled at you, Baby. That was shitty of me. I just miss you.'

She sniffed. 'I went to the doctor today.'

'Okay.' The house was hot. So hot and humid it made him sway and plop down into one of the chairs at the two top. 'What kind of doctor?'

'It wasn't a surprise. I've known for a while.'

'A while?'

'I'm pregnant.'

13

She was right—it wasn't much of surprise. The rest of the conversation had been a blur. He hoped he'd said at least some of the right things. She had been too tired to go into it. They agreed to keep it a secret for a few more weeks. There was always a chance she would miscarry, and he was ashamed to feel a sliver of hope that she would. No sooner had he thought that than a wild shot of pride and longing he had never imagined filled his heart. He wanted to be a father. This was it. Time to become a man. Do it right, better than Dad.

But that longing was fleeting, too. Something other than Jo's new condition and Mrs Laski's traveling circus was eating him. Something about the timing of her pregnancy did not make sense.

He could see it only one of three ways. Jo was lying and not pregnant, which she would never do. That sort of emotional manipulation was beyond even her. The other possibility was, under the stress of the move and all the shit that had gone on leading up to it, he had forgotten having sex with

101

his wife. That did not seem likely, because men don't forget, ever. The last possibility was that she was pregnant with Jake-the-out-of-work-actor-fuck-buddy's baby.

She claimed they hadn't had sex. But what if they had? What if she had been lying just to gloss it over and move on? He hadn't really wanted to know one way or another before. But now he did. Oh yes, now he needed to know everything.

Oh, this is bad. This is fucked up. How do you ask her if the child is really yours? Without detonating a nuke?

Answer: you don't.

Then, with the out-of-control force of a nightmare, the rest of it clicked into place. Something far worse than deceit or infidelity.

What if he was not the father because there was no father?

What if it was the same with her as with the Boelen's? What if it was something in this new environment? Everywhere he turned he was confronted with pregnancy, eggs, children: he had become surrounded by burgeoning life. There should be nothing frightening about that. It could all be a coincidence.

Unless the house made things this way. Unless everyone who lived here was touched by it.

Unless the house was hungry for more.

14

'It's not only impossible,' Dr Alexis Hobarth said. 'It's fucking impossible. Those animals have been separated, in my care and my care alone, for the past three years.'

'I'm sitting on nine apparently healthy Boelen's eggs, Alex.'

Dr Hobarth was something of a jet-setting playboy in the reptile community. He'd returned Conrad's call while attending the annual National Herpetological Symposium in DC, where he was to deliver a paper on a new subspecies of water monitor his team had discovered on a remote island in Indonesia. So far Conrad had explained the situation with the eggs, but kept his fears about his wife to himself.

'So,' the doctor said, amused, 'what are you doing in Wisconsin, anyway? Are you out of your mind or do you just crave cheese?'

'Alex, it's not important why I'm here. What's important is I have nine eggs in my garage. You told me yourself there was zero chance of fertilization before they reached sexual maturity, at some four years of age and six or seven feet in length. Not only that, she's been eating like a horse since she arrived. You know a gravid female doesn't eat, I don't care how good a keeper you are, and I'm not that good.'

'You have photos?'

'Of the eggs?'

'Yes.'

'No, I don't, as a matter of fact. But I will be

103

happy to email you photos later today.'

'Where are the eggs now?'

'In the garage.'

'You left them with the female?' Hobarth's voice registered concern.

'I'm not an idiot, Alex. They're in vermiculite, sealed in tamper-proof acrylic shoeboxes, holding steady at eighty-eight degrees. Humidity here is high, so I haven't bothered misting them.'

'All right. What do you want me to say?'

'How about, wow, that's a miracle?'

'A miracle? Conrad, please. If anything it's parthenogenesis.'

'What's that?'

'The animal kingdom's version of your virgin birth.'

'I'm not a biologist, Alex.'

'Cases involving insects and plants are well documented. Less so with vertebrates, but it happens with some species of fish, amphibians, and, yes, even reptiles. Every now and then you read about it happening at one of the zoos. A tiger shark couple years back. A komodo dragon just a few months ago. But hold on. Don't get excited. It is possible for a female to lay eggs without the benefit of fertilization, but it is extremely rare with reptiles, and almost impossible to prove because most of our stock comes from the wild, where the female's mating history remains unaccounted for. Even with semi-captives such as our Boelen's, it's dicey because most keepers do not document thoroughly enough to disprove the animals in question have never been put with the opposite sex. But I am not most keepers. I'm the fucking Curator of fucking Herpetology at the fucking San

104

Antonio Zoo.'

'But it's possible? This partho thing, it's a real thing, not some Ripley's Believe It or Not hoax?'

'It's real, but it doesn't make any sense for your animals, or the Boelen's in particular.'

'Why not?'

'Because parthenogenesis occurs only in all or predominately female populations. As with honeybees, when you have a queen and her many drones. Parthenogenesis occurs only when the queen bee, the only female in the hive, dies before reproducing another queen. The male drones panic, or their genetic make-up panics, knowing their future is lost without her. In her place they begin to reproduce, but it is all in vain. They will only bring more males into the hive, and eventually these drones will die, too.'

'How do you know that isn't exactly what happened?'

'Because it's all in the environment, Conrad. Parthenogenesis occurs when environmental conditions are near perfect, when the balance of females to males is less than ideal, or all male. On top that, the Boelen's is such a delicate creature, even in the wild, it's a wonder they reproduce at all. It is why they almost never breed in captivity, let alone accomplish something as rare as this kind of virgin birth. The odds of this happening in a small population of males and females . . . in your, what, your garage? Preposterous, my friend.'

'But, Alex, how would she know there are males in her population? For all she knows, she is alone in the world.'

'Oh, so what you're telling me is, you've never put these animals in a bucket for a soak, never put

105

them in the same bag for transport, never once shared cages, never once left one of them to crawl over another?'

'Not long enough to get their freak on.'

'Conrad, they don't have to get anything on—they just have to understand, to sense that reproduction with the opposite sex is possible. It's like us guys in a bar. We don't even have to be in the bar, or a whorehouse. We can look through the window, smell the perfume wafting out the door. This stuff is in the air. We've known for some time that snakes track pheromones emitted at mating time. Believe me, the snakes know who is or isn't next door, especially when they haven't closed the deal since last spring.'

'Shit,' Conrad said.

'Speaking of, how's your rack these days, chum? Things between you and the missus going all right since the move? You sound a little backed up.'

Conrad ignored the swipe. 'Have I ever lied to you?'

'Well, there's a simple way to prove all this one way or another.'

'Yeah, what's that?'

'Hatch the eggs. We can fingerprint the DNA on the hatchlings. If there's paternal contribution, we'll find it.'

'You can do that now?'

'It's not cheap, but you hatch these Boelen's, the zoo will pay for it.'

'I guess that's something,' Conrad said, dissatisfied but out of ideas.

'You've got eggs? Fine, take care of them. Keep me posted on their development. When they hatch, I'll see that we're published and we'll go to

106

Costa Rica to celebrate.'

Conrad heard chatter in the background and the doctor cleared his throat.

'I'll let you get back to your talk, Alex. Good luck with that monitor paper. Maybe they'll name the thing after you.'

'That is my intention. We've an excellent shot at *Varanus salvator hobarthi*, as is only proper considering I discovered the little beasties.'

'You deserve it, Alex. Sorry I bothered you.'

'Conrad?'

'Yeah?'

'I don't care how it happened. You hatch those eggs, it's a hell of an accomplishment.'

'Thanks, Alex.'

'Dr Hobarth to you, knucklehead.'

Conrad slipped the cordless into his pocket and stared at the eggs in the box. The black, volcanic-looking vermiculite soil was slightly moist and sticky, the eggs leathery, free of fungus, healthy. No sign of movement within, even when he shone a flashlight over the smooth, opaque surface. He wasn't really expecting to see much—it would be another hundred days before they hatched.

If they hatched. Man, that would be something.

He thought about Jo and the life she carried inside of her now. He tried to feel the same welling of pride, but it wasn't the same. Compared to the delicate Boelen's, adding one more child to the six billion souls ravaging the planet seemed trivial. Or maybe it was a proximity thing. The eggs were here, now, under his watchful eye. Jo was in another state, pulling herself away from him with every passing day.

He hoped that when she came home he would

feel that the life within her was his creation, too.

15

By the time Conrad finished their evening walk, he could smell the ozone in the air and the humidity was like a fist of moist cotton balls in his chest. Fat drops fell on his skin, warm as bathwater. Just before he made it home he saw movement out of the corner of his eye and turned to see Gail Grum waving him over.

'One second!' Conrad let the dogs in and darted across the Grums' lawn.

'You made it just in time.' She was laughing when he joined her under the covered porch, where she had established a narrow wicker living room. Gail had to raise her voice above the din of the rain. 'What would you like to drink? I have beer or iced tea.'

'Iced tea. Please.'

When Gail returned with his tea and a Sierra Nevada for herself, another arc of lightning illuminated the gray afternoon haze.

'How's the job hunt?'

'I'm still gainfully unemployed.'

'Oh, goodie. Now that I know you're free you can't say no. Nadia told me how you rescued her from that awful Eddie the other day. Very smooth, Conrad.'

The gist: Gail and Big John were embarking on a road trip through Kentucky and Tennessee. Bourbon distilleries, horseback rides, something involving a canoe. She showed him B&B brochures. The stated purpose was to visit a sister, but Conrad gathered the real motive here was to re-ignite the dying cinders of their middle-aged sex life. One of the stops was named Lovers Last Ranch, for God's sake. Pay Per View, massages, balcony spas . . . yes, Gail had good reason to be excited. She was already out the door, practically vibrating with visions of saddling Big John up for one last ride into the sunset.

'The catch is,' she said, sipping the beer.

The catch was Nadia. She had been 'acting up' all last year. Her freshman 'adventures' at UW Madison had led her down some 'wrong paths' with 'poor choices' in friends and this summer she had 'relapsed' several times.

'Drugs?' Conrad asked, cutting through the quotation marks.

'Not that I know of. But, you know,' Gail frowned, 'Eddie is sort of like a drug, so maybe you could say that.'

'Young love can be that way,' he added, ready to play sage to the hand-wringing parent.

'You know she's pregnant,' Gail said.

'It appears so.'

'Obviously we wouldn't be leaving during this time, but Nadia's very determined to do this all on her own. She insists we go, and John really needs this vacation.'

'Sure, she seems capable.'

Gail finished with her vision of his role for the next ten days, fourteen if they got carried away. Conrad would 'feel free to stay at home', which made sense seeing as how he lived next door, ha ha. But Nadia was not to be trusted with the house. 'One friend at a time . . . no Eddie, no parties, no loud music.' It was to be a strictly pizza and Netflix affair. In addition to keeping one eye on Nadia, Conrad would need to mow the lawn, to water all the plants, check the mail.

'Sure,' he said. 'I need the exercise.'

'Actually, we also need our gutters cleaned. John's worried all this rain's going to start seeping into the basement.'

'I can do that.'

'The important thing is to be present at regular intervals. We'll pay you, of course.'

'I'm home all the time. I wouldn't hear of it.'

Gail touched his arm. 'Just a few hundred dollars. John would insist.'

'Then I won't argue.'

He didn't need the money, of course. But at least he would be assuming some sort of responsibility. Helping the neighbors. Maybe a chance to learn something about the house through Nadia.

Nadia. Pretty little pregnant Nadia.

It depressed him that his new neighbors saw him as closer to their own level of maturity than Nadia's. It suggested he was an adult, which he knew he was, on paper. He just hadn't realized other adults saw him this way, too. He felt too young to be a father, too old to be Nadia's friend.

Stop whining. Have some fun. You're still 'Rad, man!

'I'll be honest, Conrad,' Gail said, the beer having its way with her. 'We like you. And we just don't know anyone else we can trust. Steve and Bailey offered, but if we had someone our age poking around, Nadia would fly off the handle. I think she relates to you. Maybe you can be the cool older brother she never had.'

The older brother. Nice.

'When do you leave?'

'Tomorrow.'

'Whoa—watch out, Kentucky!'

'It's like fate.' Gail leaned in close enough that he could smell the garden and her sweet, beery breath. 'Do you believe in fate, Conrad?'

'I used to believe it was all in my hands. That we made our own choices and there was nothing else.'

Gail nodded. 'And now?'

'I try to keep an open mind.'

* * *

Jo again, back on the horn. 'That's great. It's perfect for you, honey.'

'Really? You're not disappointed?'

'Why would I be?'

'I just thought maybe you'd want me to be out looking for a real job. There are sales jobs in Madison, temp work.'

'Is that what you want to do? Sell advertising?'

'No.'

'So our new neighbors offered you some easy work. Maybe it happened for a reason.'

'Like fate?'

'Sure,' she said. So far she hadn't mentioned the pregnancy. He knew they weren't ready to go into it, maybe not until she came home.

'So the job is good? You're confident this is the right thing?'

'What? Oh, it's good. It's fine. It's not really the kind of job I can see myself in for the next five years.' She snorted, implying the ridiculous.

'Sweetie?'

'Yes?'

'Why do I feel like you've made some decision and haven't told me?'

'Like what?'

'Jo.'

'What?'

'You're so "whatever", like you had another brilliant breakthrough.'

She sighed and he heard the bed squeak like she'd just given up and plopped down to dig in for the inevitable.

'I'm not going to turn this into a whole production,' she said.

'I just don't want you coming to some big decision without me. Don't tell me today it's Detroit and tomorrow it's Amsterdam or—'

Somewhere in the room, a door shut. He heard a faint 'Oh, hey, is this a . . . time?' in the background. The voice sounded neutral, possibly male. There was a muffling sound and he heard his wife say, 'Gimme one second.'

'Who's that?' Conrad said.

The phone unmuffled. 'You know what I think, honey? I think you need to remember I'm just not really there right now.'

'No shit, sweetie.'

'And we might as well get it over with. I'm not going to be there for another five weeks.'

Stay cool, boss. 'Heh heh. Yeah. Please tell me that was a joke.'

'There's a lot going on, for both of us. The move, the house, the job, and your father even though you weren't close and I still think you need to see someone about that, but it's your choice, so okay, and there's everything else. And it's too hard

112

to do it all at once.'

'So . . . ?'

'So, I'm saying, we're not going to do it, not now. We're just not.'

Anger, like whiskey in his belly, flaring out.

'Conrad?'

'I'm coming out,' he said.

'What?'

'To see you.'

'Conrad, no.'

'Why the hell not?'

'Because I don't want you to.'

'Why not?'

'I don't want to say it.'

'Say it, or so help me I will drive there tonight.'

'I can't stand you right now.'

'Nice, Jo. Real nice.'

'I need space.'

'What does that mean?'

She wasn't crying. Not even close. She sounded like a woman he had never met.

'I'm not coming home and I don't want you to come here because I don't want to see you. Do you understand?'

'Ever? What the fuck? Jesus, who's in your room, Johnny Depp? Does he have, a what, a fucking earring, too?'

She didn't say anything for fifteen seconds. Was she trying to make him suffer? Make him go off?

So be it.

'You don't want to see me ever again. You're leaving me, the dogs, the house? And what is this, "I can't do this right now" shit? Are you thinking about having an abortion?'

He'd never even thought of that until just this

second and now it was like a neon sign in his brain—SHE'S GOING TO KILL YOUR BABY—while he stood here in a fucking birthing house. If she did not answer soon he would start screaming and not stop until someone jammed a needle in his arm.

'You bitch—' he started, and then she did scream. No, it was yelling. Like his father speaking at some terrible hoarse volume, controlled and therefore twice as scary.

'You fucking asshole! Are you out of your mind? I'm pregnant with your child! I just moved across the country with you because you decided to buy a house without even asking me! I'm in training for eight weeks, I miss my home, I miss my dogs and, yes, until tonight, I missed you. I can't deal with work and being pregnant and your insecure bullshit about one stupid night that I passed out after talking—TALKING—to your friend. So, no, not now, do you understand?'

'I'm sorry,' he croaked.

'I'll be home in five weeks and then we can worry about whether or not we have the baby, but right now I am trying to follow through on a commitment and I NEED TO GET THROUGH THIS ALONE!'

The same sexless voice said, 'Do you want me to go?'

'No,' she said.

'Who's that—'

'Night, Conrad.' She hung up on him.

*   *   *

So arrived the night that Conrad Harrison learned,

114

to his utter amazement, that there are certain times you don't want to see a young woman's breasts.

As Big John showed him the plants to be watered, the windows to shut when you ran the a/c, and the ladder and tools for the gutter repairs, Conrad felt something was eating the big man— something other than the hope his wife was packing in her Samsonite. Like, for instance, leaving his obviously troubled and not at all unattractive pregnant daughter with an older male he hadn't had time to get to know over bocce and a six-pack.

Conrad did his best to ask questions and nod his head with a vigor that suggested he was memorizing all this just fine, thank you, no need to write it down. The truth was, all of Big John's directions were going in one ear and out the other. He was still obsessing about Jo. Someone had been in her room.

'I want to be clear on the roof access here.' They stopped at the end of the second-floor hall facing the street. Conrad was staring off into space when Big John slapped him on the shoulder. 'You still with me, bud?'

'Yeah, sorry, John. Been a long day.'

'You got that right. Now, when you go out to clean the gutters over the porch, do not attempt to use the ladder from the yard. Because it is *not* long enough, and you will fall and break your neck and then Gail will never let me hear the end of it.'

'Right. No ladder.'

'I don't expect you to do the top gutter—there's only one and I'm pretty sure it's clean—but if you do get a wild hair up your ass, bring the small ladder up here, use the ladder into the attic, open the front-attic window. Using a broom you ought to be able to reach anything on that last stretch of roof, but I repeat. Do *not* crawl outside of the attic. That little patch needs new shingles. Unless you want to do a Greg Louganis into Gail's ferns, stay inside, got it?'

'Of course,' Conrad said.

There was an unlatching sound as the bathroom door opened. Nadia exited wearing a navy blue towel around her waist like a man in a locker room. Her damp blonde hair clung in sticky whorls to her frost-white and drip-drying back. The curves of her wagging hips held the towel low, revealing the dimple above her butt cleavage as she crossed the hall to the linen closet.

Conrad sucked air through his teeth.

She didn't see them standing in the hall until her father barked, 'Nadia, for goodness' sake!'

Nadia did a half-pirouette, covering her breasts with one arm as she looked over her shoulder and scowled, her eyes darting to Conrad and back.

'Daddy, you scared the crap out of me,' she yelped, slipping through her bedroom door at the end of the hall.

Conrad looked away . . . too late. Before the dewy daughter had made her escape, he'd glimpsed one heavy breast squeezed up in the hook of her arm. True, all he spied within the fold was pale flesh (by chance the nipple had been sheltered), but the exposure of the stretch-marked topography of her pregnant belly and milk-laden (*bosom, they were called bosoms or teats back then!*), breasts set off an uncomfortable male charge between father and neighbor.

116

'She thinks she's still living in her damn dorm room,' Big John said.

Conrad kept his eyes averted. He didn't want Big John thinking he was a willing participant in this impromptu peep show.

'They got steers and heifers sharing showers up the school. Can you imagine what that's like?'

'Oh, yeah, they do that now, I guess,' Conrad said, legs literally shaking.

'Well, that's pretty much the whole shootin' match, anyway. Let's go see what Gail's gone and zapped for ya.'

As they moved down the hall, the soapy smell of the girl rode out on a wave of shower steam and settled upon his neck, mingling with the beads of sweat, and he entered the kitchen with a cluster of stubborn girl molecules working its way into his pores.

Gail handed him a plate of angel hair pasta with home-made pesto that burned his sinuses. Conrad ate standing over the kitchen counter while Gail wrote down the emergency phone numbers. He saw Steve Bartholomew's name and another he did not recognize. As he was leaving, Gail gave him at least three more hugs and thanked him.

'No, thank you,' he said, light-headed from the meal, the girl.

'What for, putting you to work?'

'For making me feel at home.'

'Aw.' Gail tilted her head in sympathy. He hadn't meant for it to come out that way. 'You miss her.'

'I don't know what I was thinking letting her go.'

*   *   *

117

Nadia Grum.

MySpace. Her space.

Pink and black frames, looping cursive text for font. Blank spots popped to life while cell phone snapshots of the girl next door looking younger and not yet pregnant filled the screen: with her friends in the woods, standing on a car, on the football field, in her bedroom, sitting on the bed, a bandana on her brow. Hugging various girlfriends, their faces plastered with clown make-up. Nothing gratuitous, nothing revealing, but he was transfixed. The candor with which she displayed herself and the details of her life made him feel like a creep. He learned more about his neighbor in fifteen minutes than he learned about high-school classmates he had known for three years. No wonder parents the world over were terrified.

In a box decorated with flowers and hearts, guitars and guns, her profile:

Name	Nadia Helen Grum
Birthday	1 October 1986
Birthplace	Black Earth, WI
Current location	same
Eyes	blue
Hair	blonde
Height	5' 0"
Weight	120
Zodiac sign	Libra
Status	single

Heritage	Slovakian, Irish, American
Shoes you wore today	my Old Navy flip-flops
Weakness	cheese pizza
Fears	being stuck in a rut
Goal for the year	G.T.F.O.O.H.
McDonald's or Burger King	ugh, neither!
Single or group dates	how about neither, again?
Coffee or cappuccino	coffee
Do you smoke?	not any more, I swear!
Have you been in love?	no
Are you in love now?	see above
Do you want to get married?	what's the point?
Do you believe in yourself?	I better, I must
Pets?	none (we miss you, Jasper!)
Hobbies?	dancing, shooting hoops, shopping
Favorite TV?	*Veronica Mars*, *Entourage*
Favorite books?	*On the Road*, anything by Salinger

How often do you drink?	not enough
Do drugs?	not any more
Dates in the past month?	0
Are you a virgin?	what do you think?
What place would you like to visit?	Seattle
What are you looking for?	truth
Qualities?	dependable, opinionated, fun
Ideal man's style?	I'll settle for sloppy if he's clean
What is your greatest regret?	next question, please
You would like to be remembered?	fondly

Her cliché answers and trumped-up confidence were empty calories, leaving him hungry for more. The most pressing questions—*Who is the father of your baby? How has the pregnancy changed your life? What are you going to do now?*—would have to wait.

Question: *Have you ever been in love?*

Answer: *No.*

He returned again and again to one photo. She was sitting in a slat-backed wooden chair at a small desk in someone's bedroom, her hair pleasantly ruffled as if it had been wet and then slept on. She wore masculine black reading glasses and she was looking up in surprise, her eyes wide and her mouth hanging open, as if the photographer had crept up and caught her in a private act.

HOLLY

If every love needs a home, then theirs was each other. And if every couple needs a home to shelter their love, Holly's mother's house was their sanctuary. Holly's father lived on the other side of town, and he was busy rebuilding his life, building a new brood. Holly was allowed to choose where she lived, and her mother played cool to keep her daughter in her camp. Soon our boy was spending all his time with Holly—including nights, weekends and even the taboo school nights—and together they lived as a new family.

His mother was tired after work and relieved to have him on someone else's watch. Better for her son to be at Holly's than running with boys who didn't have girlfriends and spent their time wrecking cars, stealing CDs and burning cats. He always told his mother the truth—I'm going to Holly's—and then forgot to call home to say he was staying. Nobody seemed to mind.

In her mother's home snuggled up against the foothills of the Rocky Mountains there was a finished basement made up like an apartment for a real adult (kitchenette, living room, full bath, spare room and Holly's cocoon-like bedroom). They lived like a real couple and forgot about school until the alarm went off and they had to commute, sore and feeding each other fruit and listening to The Smiths on the way to class.

The sex had evolved things, but the basement house below the real house was the thing that made it real.

121

They took baths, cooked five course meals, watched movies and became like newlyweds. They dressed alike in shirts and jeans purchased with Holly's mother's credit card. They ate magic mushrooms, smoked good pot, sipped wine. They ate grilled shark, large salads and entertained cleansing fruit diets together. They had small parties with close, chosen friends from school, but they never lasted, the friendships. There wasn't room for anyone else. People grew bored of them, spiteful of their closeness, and drifted away.

Holly always had fresh money in her account. But when they got bored they shoplifted clothing, bedding, lunch, seafood dinners. They walked out on hundred-dollar meals and no one cared enough to stop them. They grew daring in their dalliances, monstrous in their self-absorption, reckless in their search for new thrills.

His grades went down as far as they could go. Hers dropped too, though not enough to alarm her parents. Holly was better at school and talked of college and how they might go to the same one. He did not dwell on the future. Now was all that mattered; it was all he could see. Things were perfect, and he knew she felt the same way. College, no college. He would drive a truck or major in physics or both if that was required to keep them together.

That their separation was already imminent was his denial. That she could thwart it without planning was Holly's.

Sometimes they saw Holly's mom's face on the realtor signs. Holly's mother had the combinations to key boxes to the best homes on the market. They went with her mother to a Sunday afternoon showing and hid in the bathroom. They noticed how the other couples were not much older than they were. They decided it would be more fun to have the whole house to themselves. In her mother's home office they found the filing cabinet and the real estate listings and the combinations.

They took the list of combinations and went to the house that Friday after school. They parked down the street and walked around to make sure no one was inside. They entered before the sun went down. They did not leave until early Sunday morning.

The house was well stocked with fruit, fresh pasta and pre-made sauces, gourmet meats and cheeses and wine. Friday night was a fit of giggles and exploring the house, crashing early in front of the TV. Saturday they slept late, watched movies, made up stories about the owners. The sex was on hold as if they were saving for this night. In the evening, he cooked while Holly turned on the stereo and set the table.

It started gradually, over dinner.

'More wine?' he asked, pouring for her.

'Thank you, darling,' she said with all the proper weight.

'How's your pasta?'

'It's great.' She picked up her fork for the first time.

'Really? Because you're not eating any.'

She set her fork down. He saw that her hands were shaking.It made him nervous that she was nervous.

'We don't have to stay,' he said. 'We could pretend it never happened, go to a movie.'

'What? No, Connie.' She was the only one who

123

ever called him that, before or since. 'If someone comes home we can always say my mom sent us to house-sit.'

'You think they'll believe that?' He had been listening for a garage door clunking to life or the rattle of keys and lock.

Holly smiled. 'So we went to the wrong house. What are they going to do? Arrest us?'

'Maybe. Maybe worse.'

'They're sixty-five.'

'How do you know?'

'I checked them out. He's a retired doctor. She's a teacher, kindergarten. Half-days. The kids are out of college and out of state.'

'You're like a detective now.'

She shrugged and sipped more wine.

'What is it, then? My cooking?'

'I'm sorry. I'm just . . . kinda freaking out,' she said. 'About what's going to happen next year.'

He suddenly saw the whole thing collapsing. Tonight was too much, they'd gone as far as they could go. She had decided to call the whole thing off before she went away to college, before it got too close and too bad.

'Are you having doubts about me, about us?'

'Connie! No. Don't look at me that way.' She ran around and wedged herself between the table and his lap. 'We're perfect,' she said, kissing his neck. 'I just want this to be special. So we never forget.'

'Of course it's special. It's always special.'

'But tonight is different. I want it to be just us.'

'Who else is there?'

'No one, silly. But later, I don't want . . . you don't have to, you know, use anything between us.'

124

He thought about that. Since the beginning he had used condoms. They were smart enough to know that, as often as they 'got beastly' (her term), 97 per cent effective was 3 per cent very likely.

'Really?' he said, not really understanding.

She put her mouth around his ear. 'I want to feel everything. I want you to feel everything.' She pulled her mouth off and smacked him loudly on the cheek. 'It's the natural way to fly, sweetie.'

'Want me to clear the table? It's a nice table.'

'It's not big enough.' She was already walking away. 'Finish your dinner and don't come back here for at least twenty minutes.'

'Where's here again?' he said.

'The big room down the hall. Promise to wait?'

'I promise.'

She went down the long hall past the slate foyer and disappeared into the master suite.

He had always been an imaginative son, and now he imagined all manner of sport and pastime awaiting him in this new space. But he could not see that by following his love into this house he had also set in motion its inevitable murder.

16

Untold hours after falling asleep on top of the covers with Luther and Alice curled at his feet, *Match Point* playing quietly on the bedroom DVD-TV rig, Conrad woke alone to the sound of a baby crying. It was the same choking, newborn *ack-ack-ayyyych* sound from weeks ago, and he knew it was not the movie he'd left on because now there was only the eerie blue screen with the DVD format logo.

He turned on the lamp and looked to their crate beds on the floor, but the dogs weren't there, either. The baby's crying quieted to a tired, tapering sigh and then stopped. Or left. He did not think it was coming from the street or a house next door; it had trailed off the other way, toward the rear of the house.

In its place he heard a scratching, the sound of a garden rake pulling on a thick lawn. There were three methodical scratches and then a pause, three or four more and another pause. The sounds were coming to him from the hall.

If it's another doll I'll just stomp the fucker to pieces, he thought, walking out of the master bedroom. One of the dogs whined. He couldn't tell which, but they usually roamed in tandem. The scratching came again, from the spare bedroom adjacent to the master, the one Nadia'd been in the day he toured the house.

Feeling relieved but still on edge, Conrad shuffled down the dark hall, wishing he'd remembered to buy some nightlights at Wal-Mart.

The door was closed. Conrad pictured his dogs in the room, doggishly wondering how the door had closed behind them. Or maybe they were standing at the window, tails erect, the fur on their napes stiff and bristling at something that had startled them from outside.

Conrad opened the door and patted around for the light switch. He could see their outlines. They were hunched over the floor at the center of the room, backs arched, snouts pressed to the carpet, digging as if he were not even there.

Whatever it was, it had been compelling enough for them to nose the futon aside to get to the floor—he could see its bulky frame in shadow off to one side.

His hand found the switch plate and swept up. Golden light shot through the dusty glass bowl full of dead flies and other winged insects. The dogs looked up at him in surprise, their eyes dilated black orbs, then returned in unison to their buried treasure.

Conrad squinted. The carpet and padding had been peeled back like the skin of an animal, exposing floorboards like ribs.

'Luther! Alice, quit that!' And they did, but they didn't look happy about it.

The hole was jagged from their labors—they had cleared a respectable three-foot circle before he had stopped them. The boards were not the same color as the rest of the floorboards in the library and the hall. These planks were an unnatural shade of chocolate, marbled like steaks. The plum color ran against the grain and was deeper in some places, lighter in others. Near the border of the hole he saw a patch of lighter wood, the natural color of pine.

Then he understood. He wasn't looking at painted wood.

He was looking at a stain.

It looked as though someone had spilled a bucket of brown paint and never bothered to clean it up. No, not paint either. Spilled paint dries in thick, opaque blotches. He could just make out the wood grain beneath the blotches.

A delicate breeze passed through the window he'd opened days ago in a stubborn attempt to

127

cool the house without turning on the a/c. The wind brought with it a smell he could not immediately place. It was musky, like blood only stronger—the scent of a woman's menstruation.

His mind leaped to a shameful memory, to a teen Conrad who had on a whim inspected his girlfriend's panties while she, Holly, was in the shower. He had seen them lying next to her dresser, underneath the jeans she had been wearing less than twenty minutes before. Mistaking them for the same pair she'd been wearing when the rumpus began, he had picked them up and felt the stiffness of the fabric. Not really conscious of his need to know, he had pressed his nose to the brown stain in the crotch and sniffed, then cast them aside with a strange mixture of guilt, sympathy and revulsion. It had lasted less than a second, but the smell remained hidden in whatever part of the male brain that records such things, storing it for some potential future biological imperative. This scent filling the air now wasn't Holly's, but it was from the same place. The same essence.

It felt like a warning.

Or evidence.

He knelt between the dogs and stopped his nose six inches from contact. It had not been such a bad smell then, in Holly's bedroom; just another aspect of her he still found fascinating. But here, in such quantity, in his house, marking the floor like a long forgotten murder scene, the scent sparked in his imagination and

(*Greer Laski and her mutant children all of them deformed born here in the birthing house*)

made him gag.

128

Conrad reeled to his feet and turned away. He coughed, putting a hand on the door to steady himself. When the worst had passed, he rubbed his tee shirt over his face. He was sweating and it suddenly felt twenty degrees hotter in here, even with the summer breeze.

Wanting nothing more than to be out of the room and away from the stain, maybe as far as the couch downstairs for the rest of the night, Conrad opened his mouth to command the dogs out . . . but no words came. His throat locked up and held his breath hostage, silencing him while the baby cried out, louder than before, much too loud, and his chest suffered an invisible blow that sent shockwaves through his heart and lungs. He was sure the baby's coughing panic was coming from his own mouth—it sounded that close.

The dogs jumped back and began barking savagely up at the ceiling. Conrad's spine tingled from his neck to his tailbone. His stomach somersaulted and he swayed on his feet. While the dogs continued gnashing at the air between the three of them, the room jumped another ten degrees in the span of perhaps three seconds and Conrad broke into a hot, slippery sweat. Red blotches in the corners of his eyes, pinholes of black dancing in the air, darkness closing in.

The baby wailed and he was certain that if he did not leave this room, soon, he would die.

But he could not move. His legs and lower back cramped, hunching him into a ball. The futon in the corner snapped open and began to shake, a vague image of a table overlapping the futon and its frame. In flashes he saw the shadow of a long body, the raven-haired sepia woman who was but

129

wasn't Jo, stripped naked and bathed in sweat as he was. Her body shone in the light, and her mouth was open wide, her scar pinched in a crooked snarl as her head thrashed from side to side. Her teeth chopped at the air as if unseen hands were wrestling her down. Her belly was enormous, a shining white globe rivered with blue veins. Below the navel he glimpsed the glistening pelt of her mound and it was with another kind of shame he felt his arousal quicken. Her hips thrust and bucked but she could not escape the invisible hands that pinned her to the table. She slid around its black leather surface and he tried to scream.

Pulses of light scorched his retinas and his jaw popped, trying to pull air into his burning lungs. He could not see the baby, but it was here, crying like it was being jabbed by cold hands and colder metal instruments. Invisible blades jabbed into his ribs, against his temples and shoulders as Conrad and the baby tried to survive some unknowable assault.

The woman on the table howled in agony, sending a mist of spittle up at her invisible assailants before she was slammed down one final time. Having lost the battle for good, she faced him and that is when he realized she had no face. Above her lips peeled over her teeth there was only a formless white slate of flesh.

The barking *ack-ack-ACK* ratcheted up into a primal howl and it hurt his ears, bored into his brains. Luther and Alice were full-on fighting now, gnashing at each other's throats in anger and confusion.

'Help! Help!' Conrad choked, losing consciousness as one of the dogs turned on him.

There was a dull moment when something punctured Conrad's hand, and his mind's eye saw a freshly sharpened pencil stabbing clean through the soft meat between his thumb and forefinger. Then the wound lit up his brain, sending a signal flare of white-hot pain that cleared his vision in an instant. Conrad jerked his hand but it was stuck in something wet, and for a horrible second he was sure the floor had opened up and bit him. He saw a drop of blood, fat and heavy as paraffin in a lava lamp, floating in the air. Luther shook his head from side to side and only then did Conrad realize his dog had bitten him, was still biting him, clamped down on his hand bones and did not want to let go.

Conrad's throat clicked loose and he yelled. Luther cowered on his hindquarters as if a bolt of lightning had just gone off in the front yard. Conrad's hand slipped free and Jackson Pollacked the floor as he drew it back and wrapped it in his sweat-soaked tee shirt. And then the faceless thrashing woman was gone and the table was just a futon and he was here with the dogs, his knees buckling as he fell to the shredded carpet.

'Out! Get out!' This time they obeyed, bolting down the hall. He stood trembling with his hand curled inside the bloody shirt. The pungency that had been in his mouth and down his throat had been replaced by the sweet scent of fresh mowed grass.

He elbowed the light off, pulled the door shut with his good hand and backed away, the sweat all over his body cooling rapidly. He was shivering and very thirsty. He nearly went to fetch his beloved iced tea, but the pain in his hand became

131

real and he hurried to the bathroom before he could bleed to death, freeing the woman on the table to come back for him.

17

Black Earth counted fewer than twenty-eight hundred souls among its population, leaving approximately one tavern, bar, pub, supper club or other drinking establishment for every one hundred or so people. Take away the minors, the recovered, the immobile elders and the infirm, and it should not have been too difficult to find the red-faced Laski.

Conrad started at the top of Main Street and hit them all, seeking the older crowds, the blue-collar guys who came in at five and left a stack of cash for the bartender to chip away at until it was gone.

'You know Leon Laski?' he would ask the bartenders. Most said yes, but he wasn't a regular. 'Tell him Conrad Harrison is looking for him.'

'Whatever you say,' they would say.

Conrad moved on.

On the second afternoon he was at the Decatur Room nursing his fourth Bud longneck, feeling the cool bottle against the hole in his hand—it wasn't really a hole any more; it was, in fact, healing rather quickly—when the former owner of 818 Heritage Street walked in. Same work pants and long sleeves as before, plaster-white dust or paint speckles dotting his hands, neck and ears.

Laski took a Miller from the bartender, an attractive skunk blonde who would not have been out of place at a Def Leppard concert circa 1988. He shared a laugh with a mechanical old man at the bar, then glanced over his shoulder and looked directly at Conrad.

Conrad nodded without smiling.

Laski sighed, wiped his brow with his forearm and ambled to the corner table like he'd rather not. When it was clear Conrad was not going to be the first to speak, Laski set his beer down, magically produced another broken toothpick from his ear and hooked his thumbs through his belt loops.

'You look like a cowboy's been line-dancing with the wrong heifers,' Laski said, chinning at Conrad's hand. 'Trouble on the home front?'

'I spoke to my lawyer today,' Conrad lied.

Laski's smile faltered. 'Oh, can't be all that bad. Maybe we got off on the wrong foot. M'wife . . . she's not been herself lately. Said you was real nice to her the other day over'ta Wally World.'

Conrad smiled unkindly. 'I met the kids. They seem nice.'

Laski took a stool. 'You just gonna sit dare with a red ass or tell me what's on your mind?'

'Take a wild guess.'

Laski leaned in close. 'Your wife pregnant yet?'

Conrad tried not to give it away, but Laski saw what he needed to.

'Probably, what, about six weeks? Right after you moved in it woulda happened, so yeah, about six, maybe eight weeks. Only she just told you, right?' It was pretty goddamned specific to come out of the blue like that. But not impossible to guess. Young couple moves from the city into a four-bedroom house. 'You're trying to remember when was the last time you slipped her the Slim Jim. Because when it happens, it comes fast. All of the sudden you're gonna be a daddy. It's terrifying.'

Conrad finished his beer. Laski sipped, pretending to watch the Brewers on the TV above the bar.

'Okay, Laski. You want to play this game? Let's play this game. I hear things. I see things. Crying sounds. Something is tearing the place apart, opening the floor. You sonofabitch—you bring me this album with a baby tree, a photo full of ugly women, spiders. You want to tell me something? Tell me what happened in my house. I hear there's a lot of *hiss-tow-wee*.'

He didn't remember seeing Laski order them, but two more beers arrived. Conrad swiped one from the table and guzzled.

'Baby tree. That's funny.'

'What?'

'You know, like the placenta tree. Baby tree. Funny way to put it.'

'Placenta? What the fuck does that mean?'

'Old wives' superstition. Not important.'

'Jesus Christ.' Conrad thought about leaving then. He really didn't want to know more. But he had to. 'What happened in the house, Laski?'

'You think it's haunted?' Laski's eyes never left the TV.

'Without question.'

Laski nodded. 'What else?'

Don't tell him about the doll. You want him to think you're fucking nuts?

'I woke up in the middle of the night and heard this clicking sound. Fuck, it was—'

134

Laski cut him off, trying to make light. 'Hey, you think your house is haunted. Wait till you got a family. That's the real horror show.'

'Fuck you, Laski.'

'Aw, don't be like that. You think your house is haunted? Why? Because it's old? I got news for you, kid. A haunting is just history roused from her sleep. Any house can be haunted, even a new one. Know why? Because what makes 'em haunted ain't just in the walls and the floors and the dark rooms at night. It's in us. All the pity and rage and sadness and hot blood we carry around. The house might be where it lives, but the human heart is the key. We run the risk of letting the fair maiden out for one more dance every time we hang our hat.'

'So it's me? You think I'm nuts?'

'I didn't say that. I said what makes 'em haunted ain't *just* in the walls.'

'You think I'm crazy? Bullshit—I wasn't hallucinating the sound of a baby crying any more than I hallucinated my dogs finding a bloodstain under the carpet. We can go back right now—' Conrad was off his stool.

'Sit down.'

'You lying old fuck.' Conrad slapped the table. 'You knew all about it.'

Patrons turned to see what was what.

Laski waved them off. 'Sit down. There, we're just talking now. You're right about the history. It was a birthing house. But haunted? Now let's think about that for a moment. What does that mean? Like in one of those places where the shit gets handed down. Andyville, what was it called?'

'Amityville? Jesus!'

'No, no, listen. This Amityville was, what?

135

Possessed? Some guy murdered his wife and kids up in dare? The Devil? What was the deal on that job?'

'Both, I think. No, it was the son killed his family first. The next one was the husband.'

'Right, so why come I lived dare twenty-six years and never seen boo?'

Conrad had no answer for that.

'You got to keep it together, Conrad. Play by the rules. Use your head.'

'I'm telling you—'

'But let's talk about murder, like one of these movies where the guy chops his wife and kids to bits and leaves a trail of black heart evil all over the house. It's like a coat of paint, this evil. Okay, so dare's dat den. And who cares where it came from. Satan, mankind, don't matter. It happens to good people, because even good people got problems. And problems is what your haunted house feeds on, son. Just like a one of them payday loan stores. So it goes, and sometimes it goes to murder. But if all that evil came from some murderin', what is the opposite of all that?'

'Of murder?'

'Yes, what is the polar opposite of murder?'

'Life.'

'Close. Murder is removing life from this world.' Laski was a professor now. 'Bringing life into this world is . . . ?'

'Birth.'

'Birth. Now let's say dare's a house. A house where not one murder was committed, but birth was committed, and frequently. Hundreds of babies entering the world through this house. Women come and go. Women are drawn to it.

136

Women from all walks of life, from next door, from the next town over, hell, some of them from out of state. And the folks who live dare too, the family. Young ones and old ones. Women on top of women. You got pregnant mothers and children and runaways and strays. Dey come to this house. Why? Because it has magical vibes? Because God has blessed this house?'

'That's what your wife thinks.'

'Excuse me, but fuck m'wife. She's crazier'na badger with a sticka corn up its ass.'

They finished their beers. Conrad had arrived at drunk, and Laski was close behind. The man had begun to philosophize.

Conrad flagged the waitress. 'She said God has blessed this house. It doesn't feel like God blessed this house.'

'And fuck God, too,' Laski said. 'This is about the women.'

'The women in the photo?'

'Some of them. Some others.'

'What happened to them? Something bad happened?'

'Not necessarily. Women give birth and die in hospitals, too, and in greater numbers. A soul for a soul, if ya like. But that's not why dey come. Dey come 'cause the man who lives dare's a doctor. And this is all happening in a time when the nearest hospital, the only real hospital in the northern part of the Midwest for hundreds of miles around, is in Chicago. Later, another one opens in Iowa City or Des Moines, M'waukee. But back den, if you lived in south-west Wisconsin, you had few options outside of the home. These women don't want the Father, Son and Holy

137

Ghost. Dey want the miracle of modern medicine. Dey want their baby to have the best chance at a healthy life. Even the ones who believe God created the world in seven days, comes to life and death, or in this case birth, do dey put their faith in God? No, dey put dare faith in science. Or a midwife. Folk remedies, natural birth, modern medicine. It all comes down to getting the most knowledgeable person in the room when the nipper's slidin' downda chute.'

'This is insane. How can you sit there and tell me this?'

'Ain't telling you a thing a hundred cultures on this earth don't already believe. You're gonna believe what you wanna believe anyway. I can see dat.'

'I might also sue your ass off.'

'You ever see women around babies? Just makes 'em want more babies. Dey can't help it. Da cunnie is a grand mystery to men. What do we know?'

'Tell me what happened.'

'Life. Life's what happened. All this blood splashed on the floor and the walls and the wailing women and the sweat and the pain and the prayer. It's just birth. And what does all this birth do to a house? Your supernatural tales would suggest that death opens a door. And why not? It's a violent act, the spirit leaving the body and all that crap. But birth is violent, too, make no mistake about that. Bringing a new soul into this world makes a helluva racket. Some cultures, dey move the pregnant females away just before birth, or during them menses, figurin' if the evil spirits a comin', might swoop down now when she's got her legs open. I don't know shit about spirits, but I know the Indians got a special teepee for the women. Some folks, like them nutters up in Idaho what got shot in the back by dem Federalis, dey had a birthing shack. Dey were afraid of something besides the government, all right. I don't know about opening no doors, but if dare's doors to be opened, then birth must be one way to open them. Maybe all this ushering of babies into the world could do that.'

'Is that what you believe is happening?' Conrad said. 'The birthing house wants another baby? Are you telling me that's how you kept it . . . happy for the past twenty-six years? Having babies?'

'I'm just a family man,' Laski said, his shit-eating grin revealing yellow teeth.

'Right,' Conrad said. 'And your kids?'

'What about my kids?'

'They're all . . . each one has an abnormality. What happened to them?'

'Bad genes.' Laski went back to watching the game, like they were discussing Ford versus GM.

Bullshit. 'You had more, didn't you? More than the three I saw your wife with.'

'Who tol' you dat?'

'Is it true?'

'You got no idea what you're talking about. You've never been a father.'

'What happened to them? Did they die, or did someone . . . did some*thing* . . . murder them?'

'You know . . .' Laski stood and hooked his beer into his arm, shelling a peanut. 'We were happy dare, once. Good times, bad times. Not so different from any life in any other house.'

'Then why'd you leave?'

139

Laski turned to Conrad, weighing his response. 'My wife, she didn't wanna sell. But we got her for a song. I figured the market was ripe.'

'Fuck you, Laski. What the fuck did you tell me all that for if not to tell me something? You want to confess? Because if something happens to my wife—'

'Yeah, what you gonna do? Move back to California?'

Suddenly the argument was over. Conrad wanted to crawl across the table and smash his bottle over Laski's head.

'My wife is pregnant. I don't know what to do, Leon. I need help.'

Laski looked Conrad in the eye and nodded very slowly, imparting his last and only real piece of advice. 'Listen to the woman of the house. Be a man, but keep your pecker in your pocket unless you're planning on putting it to righteous use. And listen to the woman of the house.'

18

Conrad stood leaning over the bathroom sink with a tube of ointment in his good hand. The problem was, they were both good hands now. The dog bite that had started as a hole requiring sutures was now but a faint red dot, the surrounding tissue pink, clean and dry as paper.

It's healed, he thought. *Damned if it hasn't healed itself up in two days.*

He turned again to the bathroom window facing the backyard, not admitting to himself that he was

140

hoping to see Nadia Grum. He thought he'd seen her there each night since her parents left town, standing still or pacing by the fence. He thought she might be sleepwalking, but eventually she seemed to snap out of it before darting back behind her house.

Twenty minutes later he was dozing on his feet, his face pleasantly cooling against the window, when he saw movement, a shape. It took him another half a minute for his eyes to adjust and see the woman standing in his backyard. Not on the Grum side; this time she had crossed over. She looked up at him and tiredly raised one hand, then turned away slowly.

He lost her for a moment, but she reappeared, walking the flagstone path toward the detached garage at the rear of the property. No, not Nadia. Nadia was blonde as a cocker spaniel, and even in the darkness he could see that this woman had black hair. He might have tried pretending she was Nadia if she had been wearing jeans and a sweatshirt, or even a white nightgown that implied sleepwalking. But the woman who was now headed toward the overgrown vegetable garden at the end of the property wasn't wearing street clothes or pajamas. She was wearing a black dress, the kind that billowed under the waist and fit snuggly above it.

She's crazy, he thought. *One of the locals gone off the radar. She needs help before she wanders into the garden and steps on a rusted rake.*

Conrad trotted down the stairs, leaving a path of lights on as he went. The stove clock read 4.13 a.m. The dogs scrambled out of bed to join him in this new adventure.

But by the time he made it outside and to the edge of the garden, she was gone. He tried to imagine a woman in a long dress scrambling over the six-foot fence bordering the entire back half of the property, but it wasn't working. The late-night numbness lifted all at once and Conrad became frightened all over again. He padded up the flagstone path in bare feet, detouring to the Grum residence on his way home.

He knocked and waited. And knocked and waited.

One last rapping tattoo on the door and then he would give up before someone called the cops. Twenty seconds passed. As he passed their front bay window, he saw a curtain drop and blonde hair on the retreat.

'Nadia?' he whisper-shouted. 'It's just me. Conrad.'

He was still standing there feeling like a peeping Tom when the front door opened. She pushed the screen door with one hand, subconsciously caressing the orb of her belly with the other, leaning out as if she didn't trust the porch with her bare feet. She was squinty-eyed with sleep.

'Hey, Nadia, sorry to bother. Were you just out back?'

'I was sleeping, Conrad.' She became alert mid-yawn. 'Why?'

'I, uh, just wanted to make sure you were okay.'

He noted the small blonde hairs stiffening on the gooseflesh of her upper thighs, just below the hemline of her boxer shorts.

'I'm supposed to be watching the place,' he said. 'Doing some chores—'

'They don't trust me to be alone.'

'Oh, no, it's not—'

'It's fine. I get it.'

He smiled at that. 'Yeah, good night, Nadia. Sorry again.'

As he retreated, she said, 'Conrad?'

'Yeah?'

'Think you could give me a ride tomorrow? Or today, I guess it is.'

'Sure.'

'To Madison?'

'What time?'

'Uhm, like ten? It won't take long, maybe just an hour there and back, maybe fifteen minutes there?'

'No problem.'

'I'll pay for the gas.'

'No, it's the least I can do after scaring you.'

'You didn't scare me.' She gave him a tired smile.

'You don't scare very easily, do you?'

'Not any more.'

*   *   *

He told himself opening the car door for her was more an acknowledgement of her condition than an act of chivalry. Her white hair and whiter skin were glowing in the sun, illuminating the blue veins in her cheek. She wore a knee-length pleated skirt and plaid Tommy wedges, and a snug, navy-colored long-sleeve top. The top slenderized her arms and made her look more pregnant than she had five hours before.

She carried a pink and white Puma sport bag that was either a large purse or small duffel, its

143

contents as much a mystery as their destination.

'Morning,' he said.

'Hey,' she said, sinking into the Volvo.

In the car, her scent. Like she had spilled vanilla extract on her shirt. Made him think of ice cream. Milkshake girl. It was going to be a long ride.

'Thanks for doing this,' she said, doing her lipstick in the visor mirror.

'No problem.'

'Oh, do you know how to get there?'

'You'll have to tell me where we're going once we get near Madison.'

'Right.'

She offered no more details. He figured doctor's visit and wondered if she would want him to come in or wait in the car. Conrad merged from the town's business loop on to the entrance ramp to Highway 151. He locked the cruise control at seventy-two.

'So,' he said, testing the waters. 'I ran into your old neighbors at Wal-Mart the other day. Mrs Laski and her . . . kids. What's up with them, right?'

Nadia nodded without interest.

'Did you know them?'

'I used to sit for them.'

'Really? How was that?'

'I'm glad they moved.'

'Why do you say that?'

'Their kids were difficult.'

'Yeah, I can imagine. They had, what, three? Or more? Because your parents seemed confused—'

'Can we not talk about the Laskis, please?'

'Sure.' *Bingo.*

A small herd of alpacas grazed in a field.

144

Conrad could swear one looked at him as they drove by.

A while later she said, 'Do you miss Los Angeles?'

'I miss the food. In-N-Out burgers. Chicken tacos at Baja Fresh. Not much else.'

'I thought LA was fun?'

'It was, for a while.'

'Why did you choose Wisconsin. You have family here?'

'No. It just seemed to be everything LA wasn't. It's quiet.'

Nadia blew air though her mouth. 'It is quiet.'

A minute passed.

'I don't know why I'm telling you this,' he said. 'But here. Okay, why we left Los Angeles. We're not doing so well, Jo and I. I went back to Chicago a couple months ago. My father died in an accident.'

'Oh, God.'

'No, it's not a big deal. Really.'

Nadia frowned.

'That's not what I mean. I'm sorry he died. But he was never around. He was a stranger to me. I just—anyway. I wish we would have had a chance to do it differently, but he made his choices. But when I got home, a friend of ours was there. With Jo.'

'Were they . . . ?'

'She says no. But I think yes.'

'So that must have sucked royal.'

'Yeah. But the thing is, I wasn't surprised. Or I was, but only for a minute. I kind of knew something was wrong. And I'm no saint myself.'

'What did you do?' Nadia's eyes were very wide.

145

Like maybe she was thinking she'd rather not be in the car with him just now.

'I didn't do anything. Really. But I thought about it. There was a girl I worked with.'

'She was your friend, or you just worked with her?'

The cruise control was holding steady. He steered with the heel of one palm. There were no cars behind, in front, or beside them. The way the wagon pulled them along, it wasn't even driving. It was like being on a ride.

'I thought about it a lot. We came very close to doing something very stupid. But we didn't.'

'Uh-huh.'

'No, Nadia, really. I didn't. I could have. We hung out a little, went for some drinks after work. From the bookstore. We had dinner once and went back to her place, and I know she was interested in me, despite my situation.'

'Was she a total slut?'

'No. She was really normal, I think. I didn't stick around to find out.'

'Does your wife know?'

'I don't know. I don't think so.'

'But?'

'But she knows something.'

'Why didn't you tell her after you caught her and this other guy?'

'I just wanted it to go away. Do-over. Off-setting penalties.'

'What's that, football?'

'Yeah.'

'Nice.'

'I know. It sounds crazy now. But I gave her a choice. Either we stayed and fell apart or we moved and started over.'

'Starting over. Yeah. No, I bet she knows.'

This alarmed him. 'Why do you say that?'

'We're smarter than you think.'

'No, I have known for some time that my wife is smarter than me.'

They ticked off a couple more miles of farmland in a cocoon of comfortable anti-conversation before she said, 'Speaking of starting over, you're taking me to the airport.'

'What?'

'I'm going to stay with some friends in Seattle.'

He looked at the pink Puma bag on the floor. 'Does Mom know?'

'No, and you're not going to tell her, right?'

'Shouldn't I?'

Nadia leaned over, close enough for him to smell the smell of her under the vanilla. 'She would never blame you. She'll say it's typical.'

Conrad pulled off the highway and parked on the shoulder. He turned off the ignition.

'What's wrong?' Nadia sat against the door, facing him.

'You can't just leave,' he said.

'Why not?'

'Because it's not a good time.'

Her flirting confidence had gone sour. 'What's not a good time?'

'Now, before she comes back.' His hands trembled and Nadia's eyebrows formed a V as she leaned against the door. 'All this stuff is happening now. You can't leave.'

'But I am leaving. And why do you care?'

'It's about making things right. At home.'

'You don't even know me. Just because my

147

parents hired you, I don't owe you shit.'

He was glad she asked because he was tired of waiting to say it out loud. 'I think you know. What's going on there.'

'Where?'

'My house. Whatever is in there . . . doesn't want you to leave.' A bolt of pain launched back from his left eyeball and sat there at the base of his skull, pulsing.

'Your house? What are you—'

'I need your help. Maybe together we can figure it out.'

'Figure what out?'

'History. The stuff with the house. If you help me, we could really do something about it.'

She forced a laugh. 'You're out of your mind, dude. I'm going to Seattle.'

He thought it over. 'No, that's not the story.'

Nadia put her hand on the door handle.

'Don't,' he said. 'Please. If you really want to leave, I'll take you to the airport. But think about it.'

'Think about *what*?'

'Nadia. Tell me the truth. Where were you when you got pregnant?'

She stared at him.

'Were you in my house?' He knew he sounded deranged, but he had to know. 'Like that day I bumped into you before we moved in? What were you doing in there?'

'I don't know what you're talking about.'

'Yes, you do.' He was staring at her pregnant belly.

'What makes you think it had anything to do with the house?'

148

'You saw the snakes. Those eggs. That wasn't an accident.'

'Oh my God, don't do this. Don't. What are you—no, don't even. I need to leave.'

'You grew up next door.' Her eyes were starting to well up. 'You're not afraid of me. You're afraid of the house, aren't you? Afraid of what's inside.'

Nadia started shaking. 'Fuck this.' She grabbed the door handle.

Conrad grabbed her by the shoulder and pulled her back. 'How many times did you babysit for the Laskis? Did Leon do something to you? Or did you see something in the house?'

Her lips moved but no words came out.

He softened his grip. 'Jesus, I knew it.'

'Was it Eddie, or Leon Laski? I can help—'

'I don't want your help!' Her voice hurt his ears.

'You want someone's help!' A fleck of spit landed on her neck. 'What the fuck is in Seattle if not someone who's gonna help you? You can't run away, Nadia. It doesn't work.'

Nadia's fist sprang forward and knocked him in the forehead. His head bounced off the driver's side window in a clock-clock. She looked as surprised as he felt.

'Ouch. That hurt, Nadia.' He laughed, reaching for her. 'Calm down.'

She cocked her fist again.

His hand went up. 'Wait, not again, Christ!' She relented. He wiped his eyes. 'How much money do you have on you?'

'Three-fifty.'

'That's not going to get you to Seattle. And if it does, you'll be broke by the time you leave the airport.'

'I told you, I have friends.'

'Oh, did you meet them on MySpace? Are they going to let you sleep on the futon?'

'Drive the car,' she said.

'A thousand dollars.' It just popped out. He hadn't even thought of it.

'You're sick, you know that?'

'I'll finish the chores your mom gave me. Before your folks get home, I'll pay you a thousand dollars. But you have to tell me your story.'

'What story?'

'Everything you know about what happened in the house. After that, you still want to go to Seattle, I'll give you a ride to the airport and I won't tell them anything. Deal?'

She was thinking about it. The money helped, but he didn't think it was all about the money.

'If Eddie finds out—'

'Right,' he said, starting the engine.

'Did you plan this?'

'No.'

'Is this what you did with that girl?'

'What? No. This has nothing to do with sex.'

'So you did have sex with her.'

'No. Nadia, for Christ's sake. I'm scared, okay? I don't know anybody here. My wife's gone. I don't know if she's ever coming back. I just need someone to sit there and tell me I'm not losing my mind. Haven't you ever needed some help like that? Just for a couple days?'

He could see that he had scored a minor point with that one.

'We're just going to talk, right?'

'Just talk.'

'I'm not going to fuck you for money.'

The fact that she could even summon the words in her state sent a nervous quiver running around his stomach. 'I know that, Nadia.'

The car made a U-turn over the grassy median and headed toward Black Earth.

19

Steve Bartholomew was watering his rose bushes and smoking a cigarette when they pulled up. The cigarette dangled like the hose, two limp extensions of the man: one trickling water, the other smoldering fire. Conrad waved obnoxiously.

'Morning, Steve!' *See how routine this is?*

Steve waved back, his hand slowing as Nadia got out of the car.

'Morning.' She waved without turning and headed toward her place.

Steve watched her for a few seconds and went back to his roses. The hose had one of those canisters attached to mix the blue powdered crystals with the water. Steve's roses were yellow and large.

'Nadia.' Conrad gestured toward his front door. 'Don't you want to meet Luther and Alice?'

'We're doing this now?'

'The sooner we're done, the sooner you can leave.'

She followed Conrad inside. He went to the kitchen while Nadia trailed behind, cooing at the dogs in the living room. The dogs fell in love with her, but they fell in love with everybody. Conrad poured two tall glasses of iced tea.

151

Nadia was standing next to the phone when it started ringing. 'Uhm, want me to get that?'

'Sure.' He hoped it was Jo. She could use a little wake-up, even if it cost him.

'Hello?' Nadia said, accepting a glass of iced tea. 'Yeah, he's here.'

He took the phone. 'Hello.'

'Let me guess,' his wife said. 'That's Nadia.'

'Yes, should I introduce you?'

'No.'

'Okay. How are you, Jo?'

'You haven't called.'

'I tried, but you weren't answering. Figured you didn't want to speak with me.'

'Is she standing right there?'

'Yes.'

'Do we have to talk in front of her?'

'I don't know, are we talking?'

She ignored the question. 'I've been ordering some stuff. Did you open them?'

'The boxes? No, not yet.'

'Can you put some stuff together, fix the house up?'

Nadia pointed the front door, mouthing *should I go?*

Conrad shook his head. 'What are you sending again?'

'Furniture, supplies. I want to use the guest room, the one closest to our bedroom. Oh, and rip up that hideous carpet. I want to strip the floors and refinish them.'

'In the guest room?' His headache had returned. A pair of Chinese table tennis champions in his skull, going for the gold.

'Yes, in the baby's room.'

152

'The one next to our bedroom?'

'Why, do you think it should go somewhere else?'

'What?'

'God, are you even listening to me? You sound bad, are you getting sick?'

'No, I'm not, I'm fine.'

'Which one?'

'I'm fine. That's fine. We'll get some walkie-talkies so we can hear her from our bedroom.'

She paused, then spoke with a kindness he hadn't heard in weeks. 'What makes you think it's going to be a girl?'

The house. The house gave it to me, Jo. Don't you see? This is the house's project, not ours. We're just the vessels doing the meat work.

'I don't know. It just feels right.'

She cooed. 'Oh, that's so sweet. I'm kinda missing you.'

'Yeah?'

'I discovered something about being pregnant.'

'What's that?'

'In the morning I don't feel so hot, but at night?' She giggled, a dare.

'Yeah?'

'I usually fall asleep at like eight, like a short nap, and I have these dreams.' She made an unmistakable *mmmmmhhh* sound.

'Are you—'

'And when I wake up, I feel like I just had the most incredible sex.'

'What, like—'

'Last night I had to change my clothes after.'

'Change your clothes.'

She giggled again. 'Think about it.'

153

He got it. 'You're killing me, Jo.'

'Must be the hormones. It's incredible. I wish you were here.'

'Me too.'

He could see her in the hotel room, her swollen belly, all sleepy and writhing in the sheets. Her hand slipping beneath the waist of her panties. He was wracked by a lust that made his knees buckle.

'Too bad Nadia's there. I should let you go.'

Nadia who? 'Wait!'

'Call me later,' his wife said.

'Definitely.'

By the time he had set the phone down his headache was gone. He stood over the sink and drank the iced tea until his erection went away. Why does she do this? He couldn't get her on the phone for a week and now she's got the cord wrapped between her legs? Was it because Nadia was here? Was she staking out turf from four hundred miles away?

He found Nadia in the living \room, on the floor with the dogs.

'I'm hungry,' she said.

'Me too. What're you in the mood for?'

*   *   *

They were seated at opposite ends of the long dining-room table Jo's father had given them as a wedding present. Conrad had made sandwiches, then Nadia napped through a *Monk* marathon. When she woke up, she was hungry again and he cooked penne with Knorr parma rosa sauce. Now he was excited and frightened, and he forced himself to conceal both.

154

'I was only thirteen the first time it happened. I wasn't even doing it for the money. It was just something to do. Same as the older girls I looked up to. My parents insisted I ask for some money for my time. I think I got a dollar an hour.'

'How old were they?'

'Anna Maybelle was six. Davey was a little younger, maybe four or five.'

'So they'd be in their late teens by now?'

'I guess.'

'That can't be right. When I saw them at Wal-Mart, all the kids were young. I think they had the same names, too. Does she have more?'

'She had two then and she was pregnant with another. Then the twins. I don't know how many she has now.'

'Wait, she had three when I saw her. That's like five kids. And twins? Did they move away or something? The ones you were watching?'

'Moved away. They went away. I don't know why.'

'Nobody ever asked? Even with the names? What's that, like naming your dog Rover Two?'

'Maybe I was confused. Hard to say 'cause by the time my parents started to worry, the Laskis were already sorta on their own. They didn't talk to anyone or go out much. I told you, this isn't going to solve anything.'

'Okay. You were thirteen.'

'Right. But I was also, you know, not your average thirteen-year-old. I was . . . like I am now or close enough.' Here she gestured at her breasts and hips as if to say, what I have now is what I had then. 'I guess my parents knew what happens to girls who are that developed and go babysitting.'

'What happens?'

'Either boys crawl through the window and stuff happens or the father who drives you home gets ideas and stuff happens. Either way something that isn't supposed to happen happens. They kept asking me to call every hour or so to check in. They knew Leon and Mrs Laski had a wedding up in Eau Claire. I was gonna be alone for eight hours at the least. I could tell my mom wanted to come and help me. But my dad said no, it would be good for me to handle them alone. And they were going to be right next door. So no big deal. I liked kids. Or I thought I did, until I started babysitting.

'Those kids. I knew they weren't right. Davey was so quiet, he never seemed to care if he was hungry or thirsty, so I had to ask him a lot if he needed anything. Anna Maybelle was different. All she wanted to do was play with her dolls.'

Conrad raised his hand. 'Dolls?'

'Yeah.'

'What kind?'

'That's what I'm telling you. Why, what's wrong?'

'Nothing. Go on.'

'These little home-made dolls. Now those gave me the creeps. They were made of wood. The Laskis didn't have a TV, either, so maybe that was all she had, but still. The dolls were old and dirty from years of playing. Whoever made them forgot to give them a face. But that wasn't so bad. What really bothered me was their hair. It was like human hair, but dry, brittle. I tried to play with Anna Maybelle, and it was hard, but what was I supposed to do? Let the girl sit there alone all night? What's wrong?'

156

Her words had turned him white. 'I'm fine. Don't stop now.'

She frowned at him. 'There must have been four or five of them. Anna Maybelle was busy changing their clothes around, which weren't much more than some beat up house-dress-looking things, also probably handmade. You could see the stitches on them where someone, probably someone's grandma, had sewn them together. Scuzzy little white trash dolls is what they were. She called one Chessie, like Jessie. And I guess I sort of lost myself for a while then because time passed and I was still making this doll walk and talk and doing little voices, but I wasn't playing with her. Anna Maybelle. I was just babbling to myself and making strange noises and making up stories. How Chessie was going to the store and how Chessie was getting her hair done, because it needed some work. I think . . . I did that for a while, a long while. Because when I looked up both Anna Maybelle and Davey weren't playing any more. They were just staring at me, their dumb mouths hanging open.

'Sorry, that's not very nice. But that's how they looked. For a minute it was like the dolls had become more real than the kids. Like the kids were made of wood and the dolls were . . . I was so lost in their voices it took me a few minutes to realize I was the only one talking. When I looked up, the kids weren't moving or saying anything. That just made me mad. Like they were trying to trick me by sitting perfectly still. I had to yell at them to stop staring off into space like that. Those poor kids. They must have thought I was losing it. When I looked up at the clock I thought maybe

157

twenty minutes had gone by. But that was wrong, by a lot.'

'How long were you playing with them?'

'All night.'

'What do you mean, "all night"?'

'The whole night, Conrad. It was eleven thirty when I stopped. We had been in the living room, sitting on the floor since before seven. I know because I remember looking at the grandfather clock when it gonged right before we sat down and I remembered thinking, that thing is loud. But I never heard it again, not once I started playing with the dolls. I didn't hear anything the whole time. As soon as I realized it, my back hurt and I knew. I'd been sitting there all night. In fact, I would bet anything that they didn't move or say a word the whole time. When I imagined myself sitting there for hours, babbling like an idiot, like, yeah, okay, like I was one of them . . . like one of those retarded kids . . . it scared me. I started crying and I blurted it out. "What's wrong with you? What are you doing?" They started crying. I tried to calm them down but they wouldn't come near me. Davey crawled away fast. Anna Maybelle stood up and actually ran away from me. I had to chase them upstairs.

'Then I smelled it. Going up the stairs. Both the kids had crapped their pants. I mean, sure, they weren't right, but they were well past potty training. It happened while I was playing with those ugly little wooden dolls. So I don't know how long, but they were sitting there in their own filth, for hours. I got upstairs and cleaned them up, but they wouldn't even look at me. I felt sick to my stomach that I had lost myself like that.'

'That sounds pretty bad. What did you do?'

'I put them to bed and waited for the Laskis to come home. I tried to convince myself it wasn't possible. But it was. I was hungry, too. Like I hadn't eaten for a week. And my mouth was dry. I was so thirsty. I was dying of thirst.'

She paused, watching him.

He was thinking about iced tea. 'That could have been panic. Don't people always need water when they are in shock or something?'

Nadia drank more water and they sat in silence.

'Is that it?' he asked. 'Did you go back?'

'No. I didn't want to babysit for them again anytime soon. I stayed in my room, went to school, and tried not to think about the dolls. And I did forget about them. But then, very slowly, something changed. I tried to stay away, but eventually I missed them. I had to go back.'

'You felt bad for what happened? You wanted to make it up to the kids?'

'No. I had forgotten all about the kids.'

'I don't understand.'

'I started hearing voices. The same ones I made up, but saying things I never said. They just came to me. They were all different and they weren't mine any more. They were their own voices.'

'The kids?'

'Not the kids. I wasn't missing the kids. After a few weeks, I missed the dolls.'

'What did they say?' But he didn't really want to know.

'Lots of things that didn't make sense. Most of it I forgot as soon as it happened, like waking up from a dream. But one thing I kept hearing in the girl doll's voice. Chessie, the one I played with, the

159

one with the dead straw hair. I heard her in school, in the middle of the day, reading my algebra book. She called out to me in that high voice. *'Come back. Mommy, come back. Doctor gonna kill baby you don't come home soon.'*

20

The following afternoon, Conrad finished mowing the Grums' lawn just before the rain started. He waved at her through the front window and pointed at his house. Nadia nodded and waved— *yeah yeah, I know.*

The afternoon gave way to dusk and she had not come back. He flipped through a couple of Jo's house magazines and debated the wiser of two options—go back to the Grums' and try to get her to open up on her home turf, or call his wife—until he drifted off. He was just about to slide over the cliff when someone started knocking on the door, pounding like they'd been there a while.

When he opened it, Nadia was headed back across the porch.

'Hey, I'm home. Sorry.'

She turned around slowly, clearly disappointed she had not been able to sneak away.

'Sorry. I nodded off. I was beginning to think you were avoiding me,' he said, leaving the door open.

'I need the money.' She followed him inside.

'Have you eaten dinner?'

'No. I'm starving.'

He was sensing a pattern. 'What are you in the

160

mood for?'

'Something with cheese. I'm craving cheese.'

*   *   *

Dinner was a frozen pepperoni pizza and more iced tea. She said sorry, she got really grouchy when she was this hungry. They ate in silence.

When she sighed and leaned back in her chair, Conrad said, 'Better?'

Nadia burped. It was loud and abrupt, a thing she did without embarrassment or excuse. He remembered she was a teenager, or close enough. Before the meal he might have been a piece of furniture. Now that she was sated, she seemed interested in him again.

'How did you meet your wife?'

'Can we maybe talk about the house instead?'

'Who says we're not?'

'What's Jo got to do with the house?'

'You came here for a reason. I figured she was half the reason.'

He walked around and poured them each another glass of iced tea. Nadia was gulping the stuff down as fast as he was, and they were a little wired from it. Good—maybe it would keep her talking.

He set the pitcher between them. 'How's that one go—oh yeah. It's never a good thing when the new woman asks you about the last woman.'

She gulped, dribbling on her chin. 'What did you just say?'

'Something I read.'

'I'm not the new anything.'

'I know.'

161

She glared at him.

'Nadia, relax. I know.'

'Good.' The way she watched him, he reminded himself to watch his words. 'Was she your first love?'

'No.'

'Who was your first?'

Conrad sighed. 'My high-school sweetheart. That ended badly.'

'How bad?'

'How about, I still have nightmares about her, and she was twelve years ago.'

'Tsh. Get over it, dude.'

'You've never been in love.' It was a statement, not a question, but she took it as one.

'Nope.' Without hesitation. 'What, did you ask my mom about me?'

'No.' He grinned and looked away.

'What?'

'I saw your, uh, MySpace thing.'

'My wha—oh. Why?'

He shrugged. 'I was bored.'

'You're a total pervert!'

'Nadia, please.'

'Is that what you do when your wife's away? Surf the web for porn?'

'Porn? Did I miss something on your page?' He laughed.

'You're disgusting,' she said.

'I thought it was nice. I felt like I learned something about you.'

'Like what?'

'That you've never been in love.'

'Creepy . . .'

'So why did you put it up there, then? It's still

162

called the World Wide Web, isn't it?'

'One of my friends made me do it. MySpace is so gay.'

'Why haven't you ever been in love?'

' "In love." God, you sound like my dad.'

'Hey, I don't know. What do kids call it these days?'

'I'm not a kid. And they don't call it anything. Now they just hook up.'

'So why haven't you ever been in love?'

'You can't force it.'

'Well, actually you can, but you shouldn't,' he said.

'What's that mean?'

'You asked about my wife . . . no, that's another long and not very interesting story.'

'Isn't that what we're doing? Telling stories?'

So it was going to be like this. She was not going to open up again until he gave something back. 'Okay. I guess I was still messed up over Holly. When I met Jo I didn't really understand how different we were. I was working in customer service at this software company. She was already in sales, making good money. I was sort of floundering after not finishing college. I was just happy someone wanted me. We started sleeping together. She didn't even want to call it dating at first. Then she got this job offer in Los Angeles, and suddenly it was tearsville, and why didn't I come with her? I didn't have much else going on. I was like . . . you know, I just figured this out after we moved here and Jo went away. I'm the housewife.'

Nadia pushed back her chair and waddled to the couch with the dogs, pulling Alice into her lap

163

while Luther curled at her feet.

He followed her into the living room with the iced tea and struck a Vanna White pose, the pitcher held up next to his smiling face. 'See, I'm the housewife.'

'Housewife.' Nadia shivered a bit dramatically, smiling into her glass as she finished it. He set the pitcher down and sat on the couch opposite her, their bare feet facing each other over the coffee table. 'Why are you the housewife?'

'This is like the 1950s in reverse. You know, when men went to college to get a degree and women went to college to find a husband. I married a smart woman with ambition. The first one who batted her eyes at me. I don't even know what she sees in me now. She's always into her job. She can't relax. I thought I was doing something great here. Buying this house. We moved here, a month later she's out the door. I think I'm having a third-life crisis.'

'Third-life crisis?'

'Haven't you heard that yet? We don't wait until we're forty. Now it's after you've lived a third of your life.'

'I'm about to turn twenty—I wonder what I'm having,' Nadia said, sitting up as if she really wanted know.

'I think you're having a baby.'

They both laughed at that.

'Now she's the one in the big scary business world. What do I do? I cook, clean, ask her about her day. I sulk. My father left me some money, which can only make things worse. I could join the PTA at this point, but I don't have kids. Maybe I was meant to be the stay-at-home dad.'

'Would you really want to?'

'Sure, why not?'

'Most guys around here just wouldn't.'

Conrad drank more tea.

'So what are you going to do?'

'I've got nine Boelen's eggs in my garage.'

'Did you talk to your friend at the zoo?'

'He doesn't believe me.'

'There must be an explanation, right?'

Was she being coy, or was he really that far off base?

'Nadia.' He waited for her to look at him. He drained his glass and spoke very softly. 'Who's the father?'

Her expression was flat. 'What if there is no father?'

'What does that mean?'

'What if it was a miracle, like your snake eggs?'

'You really think so?'

'Please.' She got to her feet and walked to the door.

He followed her. 'Wait, come on. You can't just drop that on me.'

She stopped and faced him. 'Do you really believe it's haunted?'

If she was messing with him, he would seem a fool. If she was testing him, trying to trust him, he needed to tread carefully.

'I don't know,' he said. 'That's why you're here, isn't it?'

'Maybe I'm just fucking with you. Trying to take your money.'

'You can have my money. All of it.'

Nadia shook her head. 'This was a bad idea.'

'What were you doing in the house that day?'

165

'What day?'

'You were in the upstairs room the day I first toured the house with my realtor.'

'No, I wasn't.'

'You don't remember bumping into me in the hall?'

'No.'

'Really? Because the way you looked at me when I was eating dinner at your parents' house, I thought you recognized me.'

'No, that was the first time I ever saw you.'

'Did something happen in the house? To you?'

'It was a mistake. You wouldn't understand.'

He rested one hand on her shoulder. 'Nadia? Hey. You're talking to the housewife, remember? I made a mistake. People make mistakes.'

She kept shaking her head, looking at the wall. He could see she had something to say, but she didn't want to say it tonight.

'My wife is pregnant,' he said.

'Congratulations.'

'Nadia.'

'Con-rad.' Sing-songy, avoiding it.

'I'm not the father.'

'Then I'm sorry. For both of you.' She turned for the door. 'I have to go.'

'The thing is, Nadia . . .'

She was on her way out.

'I wish I was.' His hand fell off her shoulder.

'Good night, Conrad.'

*   *   *

Fifteen minutes later he was in the office, shutting down the computer and heading for bed when the

166

phone startled him.

'Hello.'

'Hey, asshole.'

'Jo?' Shit! He'd promised to call her.

'No, it's Nadia.' Panic and anger in her voice, heavy breathing. 'And this is so not funny.'

His antennae went up. 'What's wrong?'

'I'll call the police, you piece of shit.'

'Why?'

'Is this a game for you two?'

'Who? What game?'

'Who do you people think you are? Did you think I wouldn't figure it out sooner or later?'

'Nadia, slow down.' She was nearly hyperventilating. 'Is someone there? What's wrong?'

'Fucker. I trusted you!'

'Nadia, tell me what happened. Are you hurt?'

'You're such a shitty liar. I know she's there!'

'Who?'

'Your wife!'

'Jo? She's in Detroit.'

'Oh, really,' she scoffed.

'Yes, really.'

A pause on her end, a little hiccup of breath.

'Nadia? What makes you think my wife is here?'

'Your wife's not home?'

'No, I told you that.'

'Conrad?'

'Yes.'

'If your wife's in Detroit . . .'

'Uh-huh.'

'Then who is that woman standing at the window, staring at my house?'

167

21

He was in the office. Walking ten paces around the corner would not only give him a view of the library, it would put him in the center of the room. The house was dead quiet.

'Nadia?' His voice was quieted by extreme force of will. 'Tell me where you are. What do you see?'

'This is such bullshit.'

'I can't see. Tell me, please,' he whispered. The office door was open. If someone were in the library, it would be a short walk around the corner.

She was still crying, but that seemed to be tapering off some. 'She's right there. I can see her in the window. I'm—I'm not doing this!'

The line disconnected.

Conrad opened his mouth but the words caught in his throat.

Count to ten.

Listen.

He couldn't hear anything beyond his own pulse thumping in his ears. He turned toward the open door. He tried to see it before he went to see it. He knew that the library had two windows separating the wall-to-wall bookshelves. The largest window faced the street and was not visible from the Grum residence. The other window faced Nadia's house.

Go look. You must go look.

Where are the dogs?

She must be mistaken. What could she see that would look like a woman?

He had neither the courage to move nor wait in here all night. It occurred to him, too, that if there was someone here and she did come for him, he would be trapped in the office.

He pressed *69, wincing at the beep of each key. The phone rang three times.

'What?' She was annoyed.

He cupped his hand over the mouthpiece. 'Nadia, wait. I'm stuck in the office. Help me.'

'Was she listening to us the whole time? Were you hoping to drag me into some sick game between the two of you?' Nadia sniffed and blew her nose.

Her insistence turned his bowels to water.

'What does she look like?'

'I can see her shape right now. She's tall, with long, dark hair. She's wearing a black dress or long coat.'

'Now?'

'Yes, now!'

'Wait, this is important. Don't hang up.'

'Conrad, is that your wife? That's your wife, right? I won't tell anybody. I don't even know why you're doing this. Just tell me that's your wife.'

He could no longer speak. The line went dead. He closed his eyes, letting his imagination play a cruel game with his mind. The game was called, Which One of These Things Is More Frightening Than The Other? The idea that there was an honest to God ghost in his house, right now, and he was about to see her, his sepia-toned woman sneering from the photo? Or that his wife was home? That Jo had been here all night, watching them?

No, not Jo. It couldn't be Jo. He'd just talked to her earlier today—no, that was yesterday. She could be here. But she wouldn't.

He imagined the other turning away from the window, the one he'd seen in the yard, her scratchy black dress heavy upon her shoulders and wide hips, lurching toward the garage where the eggs—*and the babies, the buried babies, too*—were hidden where the cross used to be. She was pregnant. She had the same dark hair and height and posture as Jo. Her mouth a slanted line with graying lips, her nose—no, she didn't have a nose. The woman bucking on the table didn't have eyes or a nose or anything above the mouth. Would her hair be coarse like the mane of a horse? Like the doll's? He could almost hear her black boots scrape against the wooden floor and—

And then not seeing was worse than seeing, and he moved. The steps to the doorway were slow and enormous, but he made them, turning ninety degrees into the hall, peering into the library, until only the front half was visible. The front window. The shelves of books.

He felt her. Her presence in the room like a scratchy wool blanket draped over his shivering cold body. He could feel her in the room as surely as if she were standing behind him breathing on his neck. He knew this as fact, and now he absolutely had to go all the way.

He took three quick steps, the floorboards creaking as he entered the library. The blood pounded up through him, threatening to blot his vision as it had in the room with the dogs, and he held the phone out to ward off whatever was coming for him. He blinked rapidly, willing the red and black dots clouding his vision to go away.

She was upon him.

She was—

170

The library was empty.

He was blinking, his heart stuck in an elevator ten stories below its natural position. He smelled cloves and something earthen, a sweet spice in the air, but after a few deep breaths that was gone, too.

'She's not my wife,' he said to the room. 'She's someone else. Someone lost.'

Gone. She was gone. It felt wrong, a let-down. He had been hoping for a confirmation, even if it drove him mad. At least he would have known.

He walked to the window, where Nadia claimed to have seen her. He wanted to deny her space, blot her out. He pulled aside the flimsy silk curtain and looked out to the Grums'.

A bedroom window, lights off.

He almost dialed her again, but what would be the point? He would only wind up scaring her worse than he already had. They'd been talking about Jo. Bad things in the house. Scary stories that were bound to have an effect on a girl in her condition.

'Luther! Alice!' His voice was hoarse, but he heard the *whump-ump-ump-ump* as the dogs unloaded from the couch and came trotting to the front stairs and the softer padding as they ran up the deep pile carpet runner to greet him, and for a second he was certain it would not be them, it would be her, come back to finish him.

But it was only the dogs. He bent to pet them, to reassure them and himself. When he stood upright he was face to face with the window, and in its reflection, as if superimposed over his face, a pale woman with black hair stared back at him.

He had been wrong about her face, so very

171

wrong because she had no face before, in the room a few nights ago, but now it seemed, yes, even now her face seemed to be forming itself into something very old and something new. The flat, fish-belly white patch under her hair wrinkled and contorted as he heard the swish of her black dress fanning out behind him. Cool air pulled all around him and her starved ovoid visage filled the glass in jarring increments like a poorly edited film. He glimpsed a line of black stubble high on her head where her brow was filling in even as her stilted footsteps drummed across the floor and she fell upon him, her cold calloused hands wrapping around his neck.

22

Conrad, Luther and Alice slept on the high-school football field three blocks away.

When he had felt her cold hands closing around his neck, he'd screamed like a child and fled the house. The dogs had gone nape-hair wild and barking after him. When they reached the field, the dogs ran in wide circles—it was playtime for them. He'd fallen to the grass and thought about what was ruined now—their fresh start, the new life. Maybe that had all been a false hope, perhaps it was never meant to be.

The sky was so much clearer here than in Los Angeles. Without the smog he could see all the constellations he did not know the names of. He knew that Jo was sleeping now, in Michigan. What he had seen in the house could not be his wife. A ghost, an echo, a reflection. Whatever she was, he had seen the impossible and it sickened him to think she was in the house, had maybe been there all along.

He missed Jo that night more than he could remember missing anyone since Holly, and he would have cried himself to sleep if he had not still been in some form of shock. The night was warm and long, full of half-visions every time he nodded off on the grass with the dogs by his side. He dozed on the football field as the air cooled, and he became aware of the orange tint of his eyelids soon after.

He woke on the field and the dogs were gone.

When he had climbed the steps out of the stadium and made his way down the three blocks to Heritage Street and to his front porch, he found them beating their tails against the door.

They wanted to go home. They had no other choice.

*   *   *

After searching the house (feeling and finding nothing out of place) his fear was cut in half, and the thirty-minute hot shower washed most of the other half away. The yesterdays were becoming like dreams, their contents vanishing as quickly as he could forget them. He left messages with the front desk and on her cell, telling her only that he missed her.

He sat in the office thinking about a job. Thought about becoming a father. Wasn't that a job? There had been an article on Salary.com he'd seen a few months back. Some crack team of industry experts added up the hours and skills and decided stay-at-home moms were worth $131,000 a year. Stay-at-home moms had to be a nurse, a chef, a teacher, a driver, and a nanny all in one. Maybe all he had to do was wait for Jo to have the baby and—snap, just like that—overnight he'd be worth $131,000.

Right now house-sitting was not a job. But he had an obligation.

*   *   *

She answered the door, left it open and walked back into the kitchen while he followed her in.

'There was no one there,' he said. He knew she wouldn't come back if he told the truth. He might have imagined it, he told himself. 'I never saw anyone in the library.'

She ignored this, as well as his assertions that Jo was in Michigan and he was not playing games. What would be the point? He confessed that, yes, he had felt something, but that could have been the fear working on his imagination.

'Maybe there was a . . . presence in the house, but if so, that only proves what I've been telling you all along.'

'What's that?' she said, drinking a peach yogurt concoction from the plastic bottle.

'That I could really use your help.'

'I think I've been telling you all along I don't have any answers.'

Conrad nodded. 'What are you doing for dinner? I can cook something, unless you have plans.'

She set the yogurt down and burped. 'No, I

don't have any plans.'

'You look like you're doing well. Do you need anything for the baby? The, what, the prenatal vitamins?'

'I don't need anything,' she said.

'Everything was fine when you were there, right? I know it got a little personal at the end there, but I thought we had kind of a nice time. Don't give up so easily, Nadia.'

'You think I'm crazy,' she said, flipping through a copy of *US Weekly* with a pregnant starlet on the cover.

'No, I don't.'

'You will.'

'No, I won't.'

'Sooner or later every guy calls me a psycho.'

'That's why you've never been in love?' She closed the magazine. 'You're not psycho, Nadia. I know psycho women, and you're not one of them.'

'Thanks.'

Jesus, could he say anything that didn't make this girl roll her eyes? 'Look, I won't bother you. I'll be making teriyaki bowls later.'

'Maybe,' she'd said. 'But probably not.'

He tried to stare her down but she would not budge. He went to his ace in the hole.

'Five hundred now,' he said, placing the bills on the table. 'Two thousand after.'

She looked at the money. 'After what?'

'After the rest of it. But no more breaks. We don't have much time.'

*   *   *

Nadia was stretched out across the love seat like it

175

was a fainting couch. He hoped the food was a way in, like the money. She'd wolfed down two bowls of sticky rice, with broccoli and thinly sliced filet mignon he'd marinated and grilled for her. He'd eaten one bowl and then gone back to the iced tea. It calmed him to watch her eat.

Feeding her, feeding the baby.

'You really know how to cook,' she said. The dogs huddled around and under her legs. It was what they did when Jo was here and he felt another pang of guilt that this neighbor girl, not their true mistress, was the one keeping them company.

'I'm glad you liked it. There's more if you get hungry again.'

He left the dishes in the kitchen and took a seat on the couch to her right. He was wearing his Sebadoh tee, camo shorts over bare feet. It was too hot for shoes, and he wondered if he looked younger than thirty.

She was wearing holey jeans and a faded green pocket tee shirt, his favorite look on most any girl. Her feet were bare and her toes had been painted iridescent pink, like little pearls. She'd done something home-made to her hair. It was shorter and choppy around the bottom. The bangs were pulled back on the center of her head, leaving the rest of her straight hair hanging squarely around her face. Her pregnancy had moved from a sometime distraction to a sort of Merlin ball that worked the opposite way: he fed by gazing at it, or wishing to gaze into it, to see the future. He looked at the bulge under her shirt and imagined a honeydew melon, a huge scoop of ice cream. Then, like she'd thought of it ten minutes ago and

176

was ready to dump it on him, she told him another story.

'A few times after the time with the dolls, I was attacked in your house.'

'*Attacked* attacked? How? Where?'

'Upstairs. In the guest room.' She nodded up at the ceiling.

'What happened?'

As before, she looked away as she recounted it.

'I was alone, or just with the children. The Laskis were out at the VFW. I made brownies while they sat in front of the fireplace and played with those block things, those thick Legos for dummies. I tried. I really did. But every time I got close to them, they would just stare off into outer space. So I pretended to be with them while I was on the phone with Eddie, then I put them to bed at eight like I was supposed to.'

'You knew Eddie back then?'

'I've been friends with Eddie since I can remember.'

'What kind of friends?'

'Eddie's not important now, not in this story.'

'Okay. So you put the kids to bed.'

'I even read them a story.'

'Which one?'

'*The Tale of Pigling Bland*, I think. One of those little antique books they had that smelled like mold. They didn't fall asleep after I'd read it twice, so finally I just got up and turned off the light and went into the next room to read.'

'What were you reading?'

'Does that matter?'

'I'm a book guy. Just curious.'

'*One Day in the Life of Ivan Denisovich.*'

177

'For school?'

'No.'

'That's a helluva a book for a thirteen-year-old.'

'Not really. The style is very simple. That was part of the point.'

'To capture the voice of the everyman,' he said.

'And to make the story accessible to every man,' she added.

'Jesus. I hadn't even thought of that, and I've read it twice. Did you get that when you were thirteen?'

'I don't know. And, no, it did not give me nightmares, if that's your next question. It wasn't the book.'

'And you're sure no one was here, just the kids?'

'Positive.'

'What time was this?'

'Maybe eight thirty. Does that matter?'

'I don't know.'

'Then shut up and let me finish.'

'Sorry.'

'I think I fell asleep. I mean, I must have, because one minute I was reading and the next minute I was waking up really fast. Like when you have a dream that you're falling and your stomach freaks out and then you wake up right before you hit.'

'I think I had that same dream in this house.'

She rolled her eyes. 'Everybody has that dream. It's like the most common dream you can have, next to flying. I looked it up.'

'Excuse me.' *Smarty pants*. 'Go on.'

She settled into the memory, zoning out with her hand stroking Alice behind the ears. 'So I'm falling, I wake up, and the room is blurry and kind of dark. I can see shapes in the room with me. There are at least three of them. They're big, like farmers. Big rough women in heavy coats or dresses. All in gray wool or black. They are standing in the corner, watching me. It's the *zeks*, I thought. From the book. But not like I really thought they had come from the book. It was just a name that popped into my head. I knew these were something else.'

'*Zeks*,' he said. 'The prisoners in the labor camp.'

'Right. The name just stuck in my head. I can't see their faces because everything is blurry but I can smell some chemicals and it makes me panic like I need to get out of the house and maybe that's why they're here, to get me out. I try to get up from the chair and ask them what's wrong but I can't move. The *zeks* are moving in a circle, surrounding me. And I guess this is when I realize it's me. Everything that's wrong here is me. I'm the thing they're staring at.

'They start to close in, tightening the circle. It looks like they're holding hands but I can't tell for sure. They seem to float toward me instead of walking. I can't hear or see their feet. I can't lift my head. The closer they get the more gray they are. Like animal skin beneath the fur. Finally, when they are almost on top of me, I can see their faces but there are no faces. Everything above the shirts is gray. Flat, like smooth stone. I'm so out of it I'm more curious than frightened, but something inside me is saying this is bad and getting worse. My body is trying to . . . my mind is understanding that my body wants to jerk away or get up but it's like my body is thinking of it, not my mind. My

179

mind is just watching.

'When they lean over me and their arms are coming down at me I know they are touching me. I can't feel the arms or hands but they are too close not to be touching me. I'm numb. Then I got scared. Because if they're doing something to me, shouldn't I be able to feel it?'

She paused and looked down at her hands as if wanting to make sure they were still attached to her arms. 'You're not going to believe me with the rest of this.'

'I believe you now. Why wouldn't I believe the rest?'

'The next part is where Eddie stops believing me. Like I'm telling him this for his entertainment or some shit and he gets to choose what parts he likes and what parts are stupid. But he doesn't get to choose. You don't get to choose.'

He nodded. 'I promise.'

'One of the *zeks* touches my forehead. Her hand is right above my eyes even though I can't move my head to look up. She stands beside me while the other two women are crouched in front of me. All I can see is the room in front of me at about waist level and a little bit above. The tops of the heads are smooth and gray like the rest of their heads and faces. Then they all jump back, because suddenly someone else *was* there. They all moved back and stood in the corner, like they were afraid of this other one.'

'What other one?'

'I don't know. I couldn't see. He was taller, thinner.'

'It was a man?'

'I don't know. I couldn't see him. He was

180

wearing black like the others and his face was covered, like one of those women in the Middle East. Maybe it was a woman. I don't know—but she was big.'

'Jesus, do you think it was—'

'I don't know!'

'Okay. Calm down.'

Nadia rubbed her eyes before continuing. 'The other one was in charge. She, he. It took over. She leaned over in front of me and started pulling in bursts while her other hand is squeezing something, maybe pressing me down. And then, very faintly, for the first time I begin to feel something.

'I can feel something hard inside me, like my thighbone or my back, and it's being pulled like the handle of a stuck refrigerator door. I'm scared of what it might be and what they're doing. I think if there is something bad inside of me I want her to get it out. That doesn't make any sense, I know. But for some reason I still trusted them. A part of me feels the same way you do at the dentist. It's my fault I have a cavity. The dentist is the guy who's been working on your teeth for years. It's not pleasant, but you know he's right. You have to let him work. It was like that.

'Then two things happen at the same time. I hear a voice in my head and it's my voice but it's not me talking. It's telling me *no, don't let them do it, don't let them do it, you have to stop them*, and it's getting louder. It's me shouting at myself to stop whatever they are doing. The second thing that happens is I start to feel pain. It comes slowly like it's real far away. Like a train. I visualize it as a train and I can barely see the light on the front,

181

but it's coming, and the light is the pain. The closer it comes the bigger and brighter the light becomes and the more it hurts and I know when it gets here it's going to be unbearable. I can't stop the train. I don't know why it's coming but it is.

'The one kneeling in front of me bobs her head like she sees something she likes and the me inside of me starts shouting *no stop stop stop get away get up and get away* and finally the pain wakes me up because it's so close now I can see the blackness behind the light and it feels like someone is burning me from the inside out, and it makes my body jerk and then I *have* to move. The more I move the more it hurts. And the more it hurts the more scared I am. She starts pulling again and I can feel the arms in front of me, and maybe something like hands inside of me. I'd never had anything inside of me, not *inside of me* . . . not then, and so I can't be sure, but I'm pretty sure she's inside me and she wants to take me apart in there. *You'll never be put back together again!* the voice screams at me. *Once it comes out you can never put it back in!*

'Then the worst thing happens. All three of the *zeks* in the corner snap their heads up all at once. For the first time I can see their eyes. Their eyes are marbles, black like a newborn's eyes. I'm still waiting for them to smother me or tear me apart when she rakes her arms down over me and the pain explodes inside me and the blood, so much blood, it's black like ink comes out and covers her arms and her face. The ones in the corner run from the room but she stays a minute longer, speaking in a voice that is either mumbled or in another language, I can't understand her, but it's a prayer she saying over me, I think. And then she is gone. The pain is so bad the dark room is gone and everything is white and I can't think or see or move, it's obliterating me the pain is so incredible. It's beyond me, it's impossible to describe because I wasn't there any more and it felt clean. Like it was washing them all away, the *zeks* can't hurt me, and she can't be inside me any more because the pain and the white is too strong for them. And that's it. Then it was over.'

Conrad swallowed audibly. 'Did you wake up?'

'I was awake. I had been awake the whole time.'

'I don't get it.'

'It just ended. The white and the pain faded and when it was gone I was alone on the bed. I went to check on the kids. They were lying in bed with their eyes open, staring at the ceiling. They looked like they were dead.'

'Jesus, did they see them, too?'

'I don't know. They wouldn't talk. I asked them if they were okay, but they just sat there and I couldn't deal with it, so I turned out the light and went downstairs. The Laskis came in laughing. They were too drunk to walk and Mrs Laski left her purse at the place, so I said forget it, pay me later, and I left.'

'Did you tell anyone? Besides Eddie?'

'No. Not then. The next day Leon came over and gave me seven dollars, asked me how the kids were. I said they had a hard time falling asleep. I think he knew, though, because I was still kind of shaken up and he said something like, "I know it ain't easy putting them down, but that's the way it goes around here, so thank you." Something like that.'

183

'I'm not sure . . .' Conrad began, then stopped. She was like someone with an alibi and doesn't care who believes her because she was certain of the truth. 'Nadia. If you felt fine after, how can you say it was real?'

'Why are you making me do this?'

'Am I making you do anything, Nadia? Really? Because it seems to me you keep coming back, you keep telling me these things.'

'The *zeks*—those gray women—they were real. They took my baby away.'

'Who—'

'I'd never been with a man. But I knew I was pregnant. And someone else, those *zeks*, whatever they were, they were judging me. When they saw I was unfit, they decided they didn't want me to have the baby. So they took it.'

She was a scared kid. She was confused. She's still fucked up about it. Something had happened, but not this. She was wrong, had to be.

'I told you, you don't get to choose what to believe.'

'Then explain it to me, because I don't see how.'

'It took me a long time to understand. It was real, but it didn't happen to me. Not then. Not that night.'

He realized she was crying.

'I was seeing myself, later, like I am now. I saw myself pregnant, and now I am. I saw what would happen if I got pregnant . . .' she was near to sobbing '. . . and I didn't deserve this baby.'

'Oh, no, Nadia. No.' He went around the table and sat beside her, resisting the urge to hug her. He held her hand. 'Don't think that.'

She looked around the room. 'Now do you

184

understand? Why I don't want to be here?'

'Nothing is going to hurt you here.'

'It doesn't matter. You couldn't stop it. If they want to take it, they will.'

'Did you tell your mother? Anybody?'

'Not my mom. Eddie didn't believe me.' She fell into his shoulder and cried. He didn't know what to say, so he held her there for a few minutes until she slowed down and caught her breath. 'What if I don't deserve it?' she said.

'Why wouldn't you deserve it?'

'Because I'm not married. I don't know how to take care of it.'

'That doesn't matter,' he said without hesitation. She wasn't teasing him now. This was real. He still didn't understand, but he was glad she let him in. 'Whatever it takes. I'll help you.'

23

He was back in high school, aware that he hadn't been there for years. He was the older self but also the boy he had been. He was wandering through the halls looking for her. He found her in the cafeteria, sitting on a crackled brown leather couch in the corner. The lunchroom had been half-transformed into someone's house, a house party. He waded through the other students, ignoring them as he pressed forward, thinking of what he would say to her. He knew he had to get it right. Had to say the right thing or else he would scare her away.

When he arrived she looked up at him. She had

185

the same flawless young face, all wide glowing cheeks and semi-flat nose.

Holly. Holy Girl.

He wiped his hands on his jeans. He was a mess, the older version. Wanted to hide this version. She wasn't supposed to see him this way.

'Holly,' he said.

'Shhhsh. Don't say anything,' she said in a whisper. 'She'll hear us.'

Conrad thought of Jo, a stab of guilt pressing into his belly. He turned around and the cafeteria behind him was a black wall. A terrifying black edifice. His fault it was here. He'd brought it with him, let her down. Had to save her. His heart slammed as Holly turned and her face changed—

He snapped awake in bed, in the house, blinking into the dark. He felt the blackness with him, in the room. He dared not sit up or move. If he did, it would come to the bed and devour him, end everything.

His eyes adjusted to the dark and still he saw only different shades of black against black. The curtains over the window. The open closet a funnel of black going blacker. The wooden sleigh bed curling like a wave at his feet. A blanket draped over the sleigh frame.

A shadow moved.

He did not move so much as his eyeballs.

At the foot of the bed, there was a body standing over him. She was tall. Not moving. She was watching something, looking down. Tall enough to be his wife.

Not real, he told himself.

Maybe she came home early.

Could not open his mouth to ask her anything.

Impossible to act. The terror so great he thought he was dying while she loomed over him, staring down, willing his heart to stop.

Not real, he kept thinking. She's not real. Not real, not—

She moved.

Or maybe she had been moving all along. For he saw now that her arms were rocking back and forth, slowly. Holding something in her arms, her head tilting forward, her face and eyes invisible while she looked down at the bundle in her arms.

'Behbee,' she whispered. Her voice hoarse, deep. 'Ohmmma save the behbeeee.'

It was a full minute later, another interminable minute of watching her arms rocking, when she turned. Her body moved stiffly with grief away from him, out of the bedroom.

No footsteps in the hall. He felt rather than heard her departure and only then did he breathe. The bed shook as the tremors rippled through him. He almost began to cry, but he was afraid to make a sound.

There is another woman in this house. She wants something, and she's growing bolder.

*   *   *

The next morning, Conrad found more packages on the porch. It was not the first batch, but it was the big one. He hauled them in with the others and opened them all, a summer Christmas he had been avoiding. All the invoices were made out to Joanna Harrison. The boxes disgorged drapes with zoo animals on them, rustic wooden shelving units that looked more like Lincoln Logs than furniture, and

187

a designer trashcan designed to keep baby shit off your fingers when disposing of diapers. But it was this final item that kicked off the project and got him going full-tilt.

'Okay, kids,' he said to the dogs, opening a cold beer and thinking he was overdue for a good old-fashioned drunk. 'Let's do this.'

Using a painter's razor, he slit the plastic manifest and inspected the packing slip from the largest box. TOTAL: $2845. He sucked at his beer. The invoice was the yellow copy torn from a generic three-layer pad. At the top, the pressed ink stamp read

Karl Stobbe Carpentry
Wisconsin's Finest
Amish Carpentry & Woodcrafts

He arranged the contents in an exploded view across the living room floor, taking extra care to keep the dogs from running off with the sanded pegs and support beams.

There were no instructions, and Mr Karl Stobbe, fine craftsman that he was, had not left a phone number or web address on the invoice. Conrad knew the usual stereotypes about the Amish—most were in Pennsylvania but plenty had settled in Ohio and Wisconsin, too—living without telephones. Maybe Stobbe was the real deal. Conrad stared at the contents for almost half an hour before he packed it all up and carried the box upstairs.

He set the kit in the library, tuned the radio to NPR's classical station, and began ripping up the carpet. Avoiding the stain on the floor as best he could, he pulled staples from the wood and chipped away the dried, stuck padding. He dragged the mess to the garbage cans on the side of the house. He returned to the fridge for more beer three times—he was sweating the stuff out as fast as he could drink it—and lost himself in honest labor.

He swept the floor, scraped paint and then used Jo's Ryobi belt sander to strip the wood of blood and blood dust in an attempt to restore its natural color. He swept the floor again and when he saw that the stain was not going to go away without replacing some of the boards, he decided, to hell with it, let's keep the blood and spill some paint. He did not stop to eat and eventually he forgot about the beer.

When he ran out of paint he returned to the porch and unwrapped the pallet. She had ordered gallons of the stuff delivered from the local hardware store a week ago. Quality, custom-mixed latex in peach, lavender and sea green. A gender-neutral palette, very progressive. Finished with the floors, he started on the walls. He inhaled sweet fumes and remembered moving to new apartments with his mother. New beginnings. He was a man who loved beginnings. The way he left a job before giving it time really to learn something new and get promoted. The way he had started a new screenplay before finishing the old one. The way you met a girl and had no idea what comes next. The way he avoided cleaning up the old mess. Moving. Always a fresh start, never a permanent home.

He brought in the throw rug she had sent a week ago, the one with the sailboat braving indigo waves under gold stars and a smiling silver moon. It took Conrad the rest of the night to peg and glue the oak slats in place, set the natural fiber bed pad in the tiny fortress center to the room so that the moonlight would catch it the way

(the house showed him)

he saw it in his head, and sweep everything clean once again. He brought in the lamp she had chosen, an ivory-colored ceramic beast with lion's feet at the base and winged shoulders above, a safari motif on the shade. When everything was in its place, he sat on the floor and stared at the crib, alone in a transformed room the dogs still would not enter. In the dark with the lights off and the moon on the soft carpet, ashamed.

The crib was the thing. Even empty it changed everything. Made the future real, a thing to hold on to.

He fell asleep on the floor beside the crib and awoke hours later in his bed. She came to him before dawn, as if preparing the room had been an act of penance and she were his reward.

*   *   *

He was in high school again. Some event setting up and waiting to be played out. He felt like a king. His friends were all there with him, the best ones from the days when they were all kings. He was wearing his favorite pair of Adidas basketball shoes, the orange and blue Knicks colors, his Ewings. He felt unstoppable. A cool can of regular Budweiser in his hand. He was glad to be back with the Budweiser, the choice of kings and Beastie Boys back in 1989.

190

It was the buoyant feeling of prom night, of having an infinite life ahead of you and the right girl by your side. Then his friends were calling to him—let's get out of here, dude. But he wanted to stay. Holly standing over him, where they'd left off the night before.

Holly was neither as tall and formidable as Jo nor as short and full as Nadia. She had the build of a cyclist. Her legs were sculpted and thick through the thighs and calves, her ass as firm as two volleyballs. He smiled into her waist as she leaned against him. Her smell was familiar and somehow also new, the smell of jasmine blossoms and another herb, nettles perhaps. The little new age bohemian even then, before it had become fashionable to go natural in high school. He remembered her thing with iced tea.

She pressed her weight fully against his lap, pinning him to the couch. Her wheat-thick hair was soft against his cheeks and over his face. Her skin was cool and smooth. He heard himself whispering in her ear, 'missed you so much . . . missed you so much . . .' over and over, stuck in the lingo of the adolescent and unafraid to plead with her.

Under her rocking movement and warmth and sweet spicy scent, his body responded and he tried to lift her up but her thighs were iron-clad, holding him down. Her hand closed against his crotch and squeezed. Her hand was cool, her grip exquisite. Her breath childlike, scented with milk.

He raised his hands to touch her neck and breasts and hips, but his fingers kept slipping through her hair. She was all hair and gossamer cloth, a shifting wisp he could not grasp.

191

She leaned back and maneuvered him inside. He sighed in surprise at how she was wet but somehow cool, even down there. She warmed with him inside and fell heavily back down upon him as her hips pushed forward and back, rolling, the fullness of her bush—different, thicker than he remembered—scraping his waist and the tops of his thighs. The physical sensation brought him another level closer to consciousness and she fucked him this way for a minute longer. The whole experience was a reminder of some recurring dream he had come to expect but never taken this far.

But thinking it was a dream always killed the dream and so he tried to deny himself further awareness.

She rode him, bringing him closer in a hurry and then paused, adjusted herself on top of him, grunting in anger and all at once he was awake, at home, in his marital bed. Fear like electrified water shot through his legs and snapped his back straight, but her hands pinned his arms to his sides and her full breasts pressed against his chest. The fear amplified the sensations—good and bad—tenfold.

He tried to see her face but her head was down, monitoring the point where they met, a triangle of black that opened and closed with a wet slapping sound he found erotic and disgusting. She gained substance before his eyes. Her dark form shifted from the ethereal to the clumsy and mechanical, driven by something other than love or even lust.

He struggled beneath her. She yanked his wrists up and planted his palms against her breasts, which were heavy and sheathed in white lace. They

192

were fuller than he remembered, and her entire front was wet, hot with her sweat. He thought her injured; he thought of accidents and blood.

She moaned, winding him tighter. His mind bounced between fear and escape for another thirty seconds while inside her the muscles contracted and pulled. Her walls closed in. To this tension she added a rocking movement, forward and back, repeating the dual motion until he lost control. The sensation conjured a rope with twelve knots at six-inch intervals pulling out of him from his legs and spine through his cock, each knot detonating white flashes of blinding pleasure in his reptilian brain. Only when she was climbing away from him like a spider in the dark did he hear himself screaming.

She scurried out the door with one last fretful moan and her feet padded staccato-like down the hall.

Footsteps. This time he heard her footsteps.

Or thought he did.

Conrad sprang forward and heard his lower lumbar pop in at least three places. He tried to stand and was greeted by pins and needles from the waist down. He fell back into bed, his penis still lost in its own delirious spasm. Muscles shot, cold and shivering wet with her residue, he felt like a freshly shucked oyster, soon to be eaten.

'Why are you doing this to me?' he shouted, trying to laugh after.

No one answered. He sat on the bed listening, turning it over in his head, until he had nearly convinced himself it was another bad dream or a hallucination.

In the morning he thought of Nadia. Nadia had been here before. She even said she did not remember being here the day he bumped into her while Roddy was downstairs having a smoke. But she was just a kid. Would she really come to him in the middle of the night? Not likely.

The only other possibility—that it had been Jo, that she was watching him, toying with him—was so ridiculous that he convinced himself all over again it was a dream. He was lonely, sex-deprived. He had been through a bad couple of months. He might be having a nervous breakdown. It wasn't real. It was only a—

It was like before. When he had woken up on the floor of the bathroom. The skin of his penis was chaffed, stinging and sore in the right places. What did that leave? A nocturnal emission? Fucking the pillows?

Probably. Yes, definitely.

But when he lifted the plastic cup of warmed-over tea from the nightstand to his nose, he could smell her. He remembered feeling the warm blood on her breasts. Then he saw the evidence. Not blood. In the morning light his fingers were chalky, dry, crackly white. He put two in his mouth without thinking and the texture was brittle, sweet. You don't remember, but you know.

A mother's milk.

'So what've you been up to?' he said, filling his coffee cup from the Bunn machine in the Grums' kitchen. The coffee was thick, as if it had been sitting all morning, the way he liked it. Nadia was sitting on one of the stools at the kitchen island, flipping through the paper, sipping from a Winnie-the-Pooh mug and pretending he wasn't there. 'You feeling all right? Nadia?'

'Sleeping a lot. I feel like shit.'

Her flannel shirt and shorts clung to her plump curves and he searched her body for something that would affirm his suspicions—a scar, a line, the coarser hairs at the tops of her thighs—something to jar his foggy memory of the flesh he had cupped and caressed some thirty-six hours before.

'Everything okay with the baby? Did you call your doctor?'

She winced but did not look up from her paper. 'I can handle it.'

'Your parents would want me to ask. When are they due back, anyway?'

'Four or five days.'

'I'm behind on my chores.'

'I got the mail,' Nadia said, the sarcasm blatant. She slipped off her stool and went around the corner to the living room.

Conrad sipped his coffee. This didn't fit. She was not acting in any way clever or seductive. If she was playing games and sneaking into his house at night, she was one messed up girl. He went into the living room. Nadia was tucked under an orange

Ralph Lauren blanket. He could see the little man on the horse near her feet. She unpaused the DVR.

'What's on?'

'*March of the Penguins*.'

He looked at the TV. Hundreds of the fat little birds were huddled together while the frozen wind whipped around them. Close-ups of the birds squatting on their eggs on the ice. It looked impossible.

He said, 'If I was a penguin I would leave. Go to Mexico.'

'Don't be an ass. This is amazing.'

'What part is amazing?'

'All of it.'

He watched their fat bodies hunker down, a community under the dark wind. They appeared miserable.

'What part do you like best?' he said.

'They share responsibility. They take turns until the baby is hatched.'

'Is that the one—'

'Shut up.'

He shut up and watched the penguins tough it out. Morgan Freeman explained how, when the mothers are away getting more food, the fathers take over and sit on the eggs. The fathers did their best, but sometimes they fucked up and the eggs rolled away and died. The mothers returned with food to feed the fathers, and they traded places. Sometimes, when one of the mothers returns and finds out her egg has died, she tries to steal another mother's egg. But the community won't let her. She is grief-stricken, inconsolable and ostracized.

'That's so sad,' Nadia said, sniffing.

He watched the broken egg on the ice, the little dead bird inside. 'What happens when the mother goes away and doesn't come back? What does the father do with the egg then? Find another mother, or just take care of it on his own?'

'I don't know,' she said, looking up at him with glassy eyes. 'What happens?'

He was still formulating his answer when the phone rang. She looked away, wiping her eyes. After three rings he said, 'What if it's Mom and Dad?'

'Knock yourself out.'

Conrad went to the kitchen. 'Grum residence.'

'Yeah, where's Nadia?' The guy on the other end sounded startled, out of breath. His was the panting of a wired, anxious little man.

'Who's calling?'

Nadia padded in and poured orange juice. The carton said NO PULP! 50% More Calcium!

'I said who's calling, please?'

'Chuh!' The spitting sound of incredulity. 'Who's this, the neighbor guy?'

'My name is Conrad.'

'Where is she?'

'If you tell me who's calling, I'll see if she's home.'

'Eddie. I know she's there.'

'Okay, Eddie, please hold.'

Conrad held the phone out. Nadia shook her head slowly.

Conrad experienced a ridiculous, eleventh-grade thrill. 'I'm sorry, Eddie, she is unavailable. Can I take a message?'

'She won't talk to me?'

'She's not available, Eddie. Would you like me to tell her you called, or is there some other message?'

Eddie breathed into the phone. 'Are you f-f-fucking her now?'

Conrad resisted the urge to laugh. The boy's emotionally induced stutter induced pity and he did not want to be cruel. Well, not in front of her.

'You know, Eddie, I realize at your age that must be the most important thing in the world. But girls don't like it when boys talk out of school. So what do you say, guy, think you can rise above it?'

Nadia frowned and Conrad made a 'chill, it's under control' wave of his hand.

'Oh, you f-f-fucker,' Eddie moaned. 'Y-y-you are! And if you aren't, you're t-t-tryin' to! You f-f-fuckin' asshole!'

Something banged in the background and Conrad pulled the phone away from his ear. 'Hey, hey. That kind of language is uncalled for. Now it's none of my business, Eddie, but if you two aren't exactly best friends these days, this temper of yours might be part of the problem, you know what I'm sayin'? If she wants to talk with you, she'll call. Personally, I'll advise her not to, but she's a big girl. She can make up her own mind.'

Eddie's breathing filled the line before he cranked up again. 'PUT NADIA ON THE PHONE, YOU MOTHERFUCKER!' Sans stutter. 'I'LL FUCKING KILL YOU IF YOU DON'T PUT HER ON THE PHONE!'

Nadia reached for the phone, but Conrad waved her off. He wanted to own this little shit now. Reach through the phone and break his skinny red neck.

A repeated banging sound on Eddie's side.

'Eddie?' Conrad said. 'You want to stop pounding your fist into your trailer wall for a minute?' The pounding stopped. 'You're taking out your frustrations on your wall because it's that cheap wood paneling they put in doublewides like yours. That's right, I know where you live. You make a threat like that, normally it's none of my business. But the Grums hired me to watch out for their things while they're away and Nadia happens to be one of those things. So for a few more days, guess what, it is my business.'

'Asshole, asshole, asshole—'

'Now I want to give you a piece of advice. Are you listening? Eddie, are you listening?'

'Yes!'

'Good. Now, when you make a threat. The first thing you have to do is stay calm. Because when you sound like a hysterical little bitch, no one takes you seriously. The person you're yelling at thinks, no, this guy sounds like a girl, he's just blowing off steam, he ain't gonna do anything. Are you with me, Eddie?'

'Yes.'

'Rule number two. Make sure you know something about the person you're threatening. This is very important because the last thing you want to do is make a threat you can't deliver on. Now, I haven't exactly kept my fighting weight over the years, but I'm capable, Eddie. Last asshole who threatened me, in front of my wife? Well, I plumb went sideways, Eddie. Put his head through a window at Ruth's Chris in Westwood. Paramedics had to pull glass out of his neck. Why do you think I had to leave LA? The stress, Eddie.'

This was fiction, of course. But it seemed to be working. Eddie was silent. Nadia watched him with her arms crossed.

'B-b-bullshit.'

'Now see, you just skipped ahead to rule number three, Eddie. You gave yourself away by hesitating. And you never hesitate when you make a threat. It's too late—the other guy knows he's got you.'

'You can't threaten me! I'll call the cops!'

'Yes, you call the cops, Eddie. File a report if you like. Do whatever makes you feel like a man, Eddie, so long as you stay away from Nadia. Because here's what will happen. Are you listening? If you come around here again, if you drive by and maybe decide to poke your nose into the Grums' house or make any more threatening phone calls or do anything other than mind your own sad business, I will come to your house and I will beat you silly with a cinder block. I'll drop it on your chest, Eddie. I will leave you bleeding and alone, unable to jerk off with your two broken arms. Now, is that what you want?'

Eddie was crying. It couldn't be from this speech, either. There was a lot more behind it. Most likely a broken heart. Conrad's stomach lurched.

'Let me know you understand what I'm telling you, Eddie.'

'C-C-Can I please! S-S-s-speak with Nadia?'

Unbelievable. The kid had crossed over from stupid to pathetic and brought stupid with him along the way.

'Eddie, give it up. The girl is gone. Gone gone gone. Now please, for everyone's sake, go away.'

'She's a whore! Tell the whore that the father of her—'

Nadia reached for the phone and Conrad clicked off.

'Sorry, he had to go.'

She yanked the phone away. 'Asshole!'

'What? Are you telling me you still like this creep?'

'You don't know him!'

'What's to know?'

She stormed upstairs. Conrad stood in the kitchen and finished his coffee, staring at the IN USE light on the phone's cradle. The light was off. Unless she was using a cell, she did not call Eddie back.

Time to go. He'd done enough work for one day.

* * *

He went to Dick's and bought some groceries. More iced tea and one of those sun tea bottles to brew it on the deck. He paused in front of the newsstand and flipped through baby magazines. Threw three in the cart for Nadia. He paid for his groceries and drove around front to wait for them to be loaded—they had a number system and you just sat there while the kid in the apron filled your trunk. No tips allowed.

The front door was unlocked. He made a mental note to start locking it. He was halfway to the kitchen when he noticed the blood and shattered glass on the floor. The frames were broken, three of Jo's matching mirrors from the front living room destroyed. Leading out of the

201

glass shards, the paw prints.

When had he last seen the dogs? Had he fed them this morning? He could not remember.

'Alice! Luther!'

He ran yelling their names as he searched the house, at once hoping and fearing that the perpetrator was still in the house.

25

His dogs were bleeding, and had been bleeding for some time judging by the paw prints and smudges and stripes of blood on the floors, walls and couch. He ran calling their names into the dining room and made a U-turn into the front parlor. The TV room. The kitchen.

No dogs.

Conrad's pulse went off the chart. If something has happened to my dogs, he thought, if someone hurt my first and only real babies, I will simply run amok.

He'd hung the mirrors high on the walls. No way the dogs jumped up and dragged them down—and why would they? Someone was here, broke them, and left the dogs to cut themselves. Or worse. Someone—*Eddie! That little fucking shit, Eddie!*—broke in and went fucking nuts and maybe there was a struggle. Maybe the dogs attacked him and he had pulled the mirrors down, scaring them before—

When he had checked the entire first floor, he circled back to the front stairway.

'Alice, Luther! Daddy's home!'

He stopped halfway up the stairs and listened. Was that . . . ? Yes, familiar whining. He pounded up the stairs and lurched into the library bent over at a forty-five-degree angle, head turning like a cop in a police drama. The library was clear.

The upstairs felt wrong. You learned to sense where your dogs were at all times and the upstairs felt empty.

The master bedroom was also empty.

'Alice! Luther! Come on, babies!'

A sound like rocks falling on hollow walls— *whock-whock-whock!*

The basement.

Jesus, he hadn't even thought of the basement. He had been meaning to take the broom down and give the whole works a good spring-cleaning and refill the water softener system with salt pellets while he was at it, but, like most things he had been meaning to do, he had forgotten.

He took the front stairs two at a time, rounded the foyer and careened back into the kitchen, yanked the basement open and tripped over her.

Alice had been at the door, scraping her paws on the wooden steps and the door. His feet caught on her legs and he tripped, then skated down two more steps, his hand snapping the rail as he slammed down tailbone first, lost his wind, and slid down the six remaining stairs until his feet stopped against the foundation wall and sprawled him on the landing.

He saw more blood on the door above him and trailing from her as Alice came down after him.

She's on her feet, how bad can it be?

And where is Luther?

Alice's claws scratched his chest and legs as he

stood and sucked in the first, pained breath, getting his wind back. He inspected her through watery eyes. He couldn't see a wound that required immediate attention, but she was shaking, her bristly brindle coat bunching up more in confusion than in pain. Maybe anger for being banished to the basement.

Then he saw her ear. The seam where the ear connected to her head was gaping pink and white tissue like a second, smaller mouth. Pat-pat-pat went the blood on the floor, but it wasn't flowing, so that was something.

'Okay, baby, calm down, calm down. Where's Luther?' Like she could tell him.

Conrad ducked under the ventilation ducts and wooden crossbeams in the basement proper, peeking around makeshift walls and unfinished rooms. There weren't many hiding places. He charged forward, knocking into the water heater and doorframes. The only closed room was Laski's abandoned workshop: a wall of pegboard, a plywood bench set upon four by fours, scraps of indoor-outdoor carpet. No blood.

There was another, deeper space left of the shop's entrance, with a separate light. Conrad flailed for the beaded string hanging below the bulb. *Cha-chink*.

Luther wasn't in here. There was still the backyard. On the way to the short wooden door that opened to the backyard, he stopped and pivoted, heading back to the one place he hadn't checked.

In the basement at the front of the house was a smaller space, lower to the ground, where the furnace was tucked behind the stone support wall under the fireplace and chimney. At the very front of that, in the deepest recess where the foundation floor became a pile of dirt and cast aside rocks, the ground sloped up as if reaching toward some forgotten cellar door or coal chute.

Conrad crouched, shimmied forth, and found his dog.

Luther was huddled in the corner, hopping gecko-like from one front paw to the other as if the ground were too hot to stand on. He was staring at the wall, like the teacher had called him a bad boy and sent him to stand in the corner.

'Luther? Luther!'

When Luther turned, the dog's eyes were two pinpoints of gleaming white, his black and white cow spots shivering. The dog had been intent on something on the stone foundation wall. Now he looked confused, and Conrad's skin crawled. He took a step and Luther growled. It broke his heart and worried him all over, but he needed to get past the dog's fear and tend to the wounds, if there were any.

Conrad came in fast but steady, speaking in his gentlest voice, 'It's me, Luther, it's okay, good dog . . .'

Luther lashed out in a snapping bark that missed Conrad's hand (the one that had just finished healing) by inches. Conrad scooped up his dog and crouch-dragged him backward, and it was like dancing in a cave with a wet seal. Finally they were clear and Luther stopped fighting and then it was a half-blind spree up the stairs into the kitchen.

He spent half a roll of paper towels trying to staunch the flow before he realized the dogs, in

205

their agitated state, were going to bleed out before he got them under control.

Compared to Alice, Luther looked as if he'd attempted to tightrope walk a fence barbed with concertina wire. Luther's legs and paws were cut in at least six places. The front of his chest just below the throat was a coin purse, and Alice's ear was still hanging halfway off her narrow marbled head like so much furry lunchmeat.

Conrad snatched the keys from the kitchen table, scooped Luther up and bolted for the car. He left the front door wide open and Alice did not need to be told to follow.

He opened the rear driver's side door with one hand and spilled Luther into the backseat; Alice brought up the rear. Then he was behind the wheel, weaving up the street, the blood spattering on the seats and doors and windows and up to the passenger visor as the dogs jumped from backseat to front and back again. He yelled at them to calm down as he blew through the first stop sign and floored it past the Kwik-Trip. He had gone a mile up the old Highway 151 business loop before he realized he didn't even know where the vet kept offices, or if the town even had one.

She answered the door dressed in jeans and a faded Abercrombie tee, and for once his eyes did not settle on her belly. Her face went pale when she saw the blood.

'My dogs are hurt. Can you take us to the vet?' For one agonizing moment he saw the hesitation, that moment of distrust even the best neighbors have before they decide to jump into the scene of impending tragedy. 'Please help me, Nadia.'

God love her, she nodded quickly and followed

him.

'You drive while I try to get them under control.'

'Oh, shit!' She saw the inside of the car.

'Yeah. Come on, I don't know where the vet is.'

Nadia stared at the stick shift.

'It's just dog blood,' he said. 'Move!'

'I can't drive stick!'

'Just put in second and pop the clutch when I say go.'

The car rolled down hill a ways. 'Go!'

Nadia popped the clutch. The Volvo sputtered . . . then shot down Heritage Street. Conrad crawled in back and tried to still his pets. By the time they reached the small farmhouse on the outskirts of town—it didn't even have a sign, just a wooden figure of a horse next to the mailbox— Alice had her nose out the window like she was enjoying a Sunday drive. Luther was in Conrad's lap, heavy with a kind of gulping motion sickness, eyes droopy.

'Easy, boy. Easy.'

*   *   *

Fifteen minutes after his wife phoned from the front desk, Dr Michael Troxler came in from the field wearing a pair of muddy wellingtons and Oshkosh overalls over a bright madras shirt. He had a streak of mud on the wire-framed glasses standing over thick gray moustaches. Dr Troxler was at least seventy years old, reeked of manure and moved like an aging linebacker who could still open-field tackle an errant calf.

'What do we have here, young man?' Troxler bent to scratch Luther's head.

'My dogs are cut up,' Conrad said, fighting the urge to *scream hurry up you old goat-fucker*! 'I think she's got just the ear cut, but Luther here is gonna bleed to death if we don't do something soon.'

'Okey-doke. Folla me.'

The examining room smelled of alfalfa and medicine. Conrad shot Nadia an evil look—*are you kidding me?*

'He bite?' Troxler had his back to the table, sorting bottles and syringes until he found the right combo.

'No. He's a good dog.'

'Get him up on the table and hold him. I'm gonna stick him pretty good.'

Conrad didn't know what he'd expected, maybe some doggy version of *ER* with IVs, latex gloves and scrubs. But Troxler didn't even bother to wash his hands. He just pulled Luther's hackles up with one huge mitt and rammed a large needle into the fold.

'That's not gonna knock him out, but keep a watch on him cause he might feel like falling over. And we don't wanna drop ya, do we buddy?' Troxler patted Luther on the head.

Conrad swayed on his feet as Troxler used a thimble and needle large enough to hook marlin to thread black cord through the many holes and slashes in Luther's legs and undercarriage.

'This breed's rambunctious, got to use the thick stuff.'

When he'd finished with Luther, Troxler said 'Next', and wound his pointer finger in a loop. Conrad set Luther on the barn-dirty floor and Nadia held Luther steady while Conrad heaved Alice up. Alice's turn came and went much faster, having just the one deep cut in her ear.

When he had finished with the sutures and was dabbing the outside of the wound with more gauze soaked in Betadine, the purple solution staining the doctor's thick fingers a morgue yellow, Troxler said, 'They fight like this often?'

Conrad became the defensive parent. 'They don't fight. I think they knocked some mirrors off the walls or something. There was a lot of broken glass when I came home.'

'They get into all kinds of mischief, don't they?'

'Yes. They do.'

'That'll do 'er.'

Despite his earlier misgivings, Conrad felt like hugging the lumbering veterinarian. Even without the usual shaving and sterilizing, all the bleeding had stopped. And the old man's calm through it all had helped.

Nadia led the dogs to the car while Conrad settled up with Mrs Troxler. At the front desk, he thanked the doctor profusely and offered to clean up the blood on the floor.

'Just get them critters home and make sure they drink some water when they come out of their stupor. The one lost some blood, and he's gonna be slow for a couple days. You bring 'em both back in ten days we'll pull the sutures out.'

Mrs Troxler was filling out an invoice. 'What's your name, young man?'

'Conrad Harrison. What do I owe you?' As she tallied the work he patted his pockets. 'Oh, hell. I was so worked up before we left the house, I didn't bring anything with me.'

'No trouble, dear. Bring it by anytime,' Mrs Troxler said. 'And tell your wife goodbye for us.'

'She's not—. Thank you. I will.'

When they were halfway to the house, Conrad said, 'Do you have any money?'

'Twenty bucks or so.' The car jerked as Nadia fought with the stick.

'Stop here.'

Nadia wheeled into the Kwik-Trip. 'What for?'

'I need a drink.'

*   *   *

Conrad was on the TV room floor, leaning against the wall, the remaining half of the Budweiser twelve-pack between his legs. He felt like he'd just passed some test and the beer might as well have been iced tea for all the buzz it gave him. Nadia was sitting crossways on the couch, the dogs sleeping soundly at her feet, as Troxler had promised. Nadia's suspicions and weariness of their ordeal seemed to have vanished. She was smiling more, talking him through it, helping him cool off.

'God, look at them,' he said. 'No idea it happened.'

'We saved them, didn't we?' Nadia said.

'Yeah, we did. I don't know what I would have done without you.'

'When you came to my house you looked like someone died.'

'I thought they were goners. Just fucked.'

'Oh, you're okay now, girl.' Nadia kissed Alice on the nose. 'You're not fucked.'

'I don't know what I . . . I wouldn't make it without them.'

'They're like your children, huh?'

210

'You have no idea how much.'

'I might,' she said. 'Some day soon, I just might.'

'Yeah, you might.' Conrad sighed, watching Luther. 'I'll tell you this. The woman from the rescue shelter found him tied to a street post on La Cienega when he was seven months old. Ribs like a xylophone, mange, broken leg. He was terrified of the endless honking taxis and banging trash trucks. You could tie a steak to the stop sign, he still wouldn't walk down a loud street.'

'Oh, Luther, you just can't stay out of trouble, can you?' Luther snored. 'So, you just found him at the pound?'

'No, no. It was a bit more than that. It took us six weeks to adopt him. This rescue group, Mighty Mutts. Run by a veterinarian, total non-profit. They don't mess around. They put us through a lot of waiting, came to our home, made us fill out a ton of forms. I kept calling, pleading my case. Jo was against it at first. She can't stand the hair on her clothes, if you can believe that. But I knew. I never wanted anything so bad as I wanted that dog. He's my boy.'

'Why'd it take so long?'

'The rescue people know. Dog bonds with his master. People will give up a dog like it's a hobby. A bag of garbage. You give him up it breaks his heart and he rarely gets over it. Lot of dogs walking around out there, nervous wrecks, all faith in life shattered. Some turn mean. But the ones that do get over it, they never forget. They love you like you have never been loved.'

Nadia watched him drink. He knew he was getting dopey-eyed, slurring a little.

'Luther never really got over his fear of walking,

211

and he was destroying the house with the separation anxiety. People said medicate him, but that's not right. He was only a year old. We tried herbal supplements, more toys, a litter box, pads on the floor, short trips to the front porch, forcing him, letting him take his time. Jo said get rid of him. I told her she could leave anytime she wanted. Finally the rescue group said get another dog. Jo and I fought about that. A lot. We adopted Alice, who didn't have any fear. She helped Luther get over it in one day. He wouldn't leave her side, followed her right down the street.'

'So you saved two dogs' lives.'

'Best thing we ever did. Sometimes I think they are better than us.'

'You and your wife?'

'People. Better than people.'

They sat quietly for a minute. Nadia said, 'She couldn't have kids? Before, when you got the dogs?'

'I don't know that she ever wanted them.'

'But you did.'

'I never avoided it . . . I think it's better not to plan too much. You take what life gives you.'

'But eventually you need a plan,' she said.

'Like Seattle?'

'Hey now,' she said, scolding him. 'Unless you have a better one, Seattle it is.'

It came out light, but then she paused like she'd just realized what she'd said and she became very still. He'd never seen her look so scared.

'Nadia.' Conrad smiled and wagged his beer and set it down before rising from the floor. 'I want to show you something.'

Nadia followed him up the front stairs.

'Watch your step,' he said as much to himself as to Nadia. 'This banister is a hundred and forty years old.'

When they reached the guest room, he pushed the door open and pulled the switch on the safari lamp. Warm light filled the room, floating a halo over the crib.

'What do you think?' he said.

'Oh, Conrad. This is very nice. Did you do this by yourself?'

'Yes. You really like it?'

'It's more real than any room in the house.'

He liked that. 'Nadia?'

She turned and faced him in the doorway.

'We didn't . . . we were not together in any way. Not for months before we moved here, and we haven't been since. What she carries inside her, it did not come from me.'

'Come on. Don't say that.'

'It's the truth.'

'I'm sorry.'

'But I'm more worried about you,' he said, pulling at her shirt with two fingers. 'I told you I would help you.'

'Conrad. You're a nice guy. But I'm leaving soon.'

'You don't have to.'

'Yes, I do. And she's coming home, eventually.'

'There's another guy out there, in her room. I heard him. I don't think she is coming home. And maybe I don't want her to.'

Nadia shook her head slowly.

'Something is happening inside this house,' he said. 'And we are a part of it. Maybe fate. I don't care. I want to take care of you. I can't stop

213

thinking about taking care of you.'

He leaned forward, his breath beery and loose. She stared up at him, unmoving. He kissed her on the mouth. Her lips hung open, undecided. Then her tongue pushed in first and he swooned, literally. She pushed him back against the wall, holding him up.

'You're kinda drunk,' she said.

'But I know what I know,' he said.

'And you're exhausted. Come on.'

She led him into the bedroom. She was so small in front of him. He could look right over her blonde hair and he wished he had the strength to lift her up and set her down on the bed, but he was too tanked to be gallant.

'Here.' She turned him sideways and he leaned over to kiss her again. She put one palm against his chest and pushed gently.

'My dogs.' He flopped on the bed, clothes and all. 'We can't leave them down there.'

'I'll watch them.'

'Promise?'

'Yes.' She turned off the light. 'I promise.'

'Nadia,' he said in the dark.

'What?'

'Don't leave me alone here. I won't make it without you.'

She lingered a minute, and he passed out before he could hear her walk away.

HOLLY

If you ask men when they are happiest, their first and rather unimaginative answer is usually something along the lines of, *right after I come*. And that is a peaceful time. All the fighting and working and wooing and pleading are past; the lucky man has been satisfied and done his best for her, and now the siren has him down. Time to drift and recharge and meet the world another day, which fills us up with more longing, anger and madness until we start all over again.

But remember I said happiest, not most peaceful. If someone were to ask me when I am happiest—have you guessed this by now? That our boy is me, that his story is my story? Of course you have, for you are a very bright girl who only happens to be a little lost, as he, as I, once was lost—I would answer, not at the end, when it has been done, but at the beginning. The moment when you know it is going to happen, and you have the whole event, in all its twists and turns and tests and mystery lying directly on the path ahead. And here I should add I am not speaking of sex, or not only of sex, though it was sex that taught me this. How I am most alive when I am standing on the precipice of the next beginning.

Consider the steamed lobster and melted butter and tenderloin and home-made bread are set before you by a kind waitress and you have not eaten all day. Consider iced tea with mint, its tall glass dewy with waiting for you to finish mowing the lawn on a hot July afternoon, that first bite as it washes over your scorched, panting tongue. The way the lighted Christmas tree looks when you come downstairs in padded feet to see all those gleaming boxes and ribbons and bows. The puppy whining in its crate that was put on this earth to be your best friend for the rest of his life, whether you prove him worthy or not. The smell of your crisp white Stan Smiths on the first day of school and how that fertile green emblem is going to telegraph to that one girl in the hallway exactly what you cannot find words to say, that you could have gotten any current style in the store but you are cool enough to have gone classic, old school, and this might be the year you become her boyfriend. That is what any good beginning does— takes you back to the moment when it was the first time, when it was all new, when you had nothing but new experiences in front of you and it was all magic.

Of all the beginnings, this night, in these strangers' home, though I could not know it then, I was standing on the precipice of the last and only true magic I would know until I found this house.

It was to be a miracle. What other miracles are there but beginnings? It is being born. And if birth is a miracle, it is a shame we cannot remember it. Because this I remember, and, in some ways, it was the moment I began to live.

Which is to say, also, that it was the beginning of my death.

When my twenty minutes were up, I made my way down the hall, passing family photographs I did not linger over. My mind was focused and relaxed, but I locked the front door just in case.

When I reached the door at the end of the hall I

saw the orange flicker of light. Candles. I should tell you now, in case you're wondering what was so special about this night, that though we had made love and the other kind, that fast, quickie sex perhaps two or three hundred times, we had never made love in the light. Whatever position we found ourselves entangled in, however raw our hunger was expressed, as dirty as we spoke to each other (we had covered a lot of ground, as I said before), it had always taken place under cover of darkness. As a child of divorce and possibly some madness on her mother's side, Holly had suffered from anorexia before she came to our junior high school. I was told, though she didn't like to speak of it, that she had to be institutionalized for a period of four months. Since the first day I saw her in the halls when we were fourteen, she always had the body of a young woman: curves, breasts, thighs a bit chunky, though she would slap me to hear that now. Her butt was what you would call a bubble butt and the rest of her had a perfectly healthy weight and shape. I don't know if she ever accepted this new version of herself, but I know she trusted me when I told her I liked her body this way better than the other way, the one I could only imagine. If she still heard the voice in her mind that said, *You're too fat, lose some weight, because no one, especially Daddy, will love you this way until they are afraid of you*, she was not listening to that voice now, tonight, as I entered the bedroom.

I understood immediately that she had not been preparing herself with lotions, creams and lingerie for the past twenty minutes. Nor had she showered or primped. It was the candles, dozens of them or

217

perhaps a hundred that had taken her twenty minutes to light. Had she delivered them earlier or found some stash in the house? I do not know. They were on the night tables, the headboard, the dressers, the leather trunk at the foot of the bed, the window sills. I say that like I was studying the décor, but that is absurd—my eyes went the only place they could go, directly to her.

She had stripped the bed and remade it with only one layer, a fresh fitted sheet of sky-blue Egyptian cotton, five-hundred-thread count. I know this because for months after I searched for the exact texture and weight of that sheet. She had two pillows behind her head, and all was bare.

She was stretched across it diagonally, so that she faced me upon entering, the tips of her toes pointing at me like two hands in prayer. She smiled at me with a slow, involuntary widening at the corners of her mouth, her lips spaced just so. One arm was up under her head, her hand buried somewhere in the thick fan of her hair, which hung loosely and combed out over her shoulders to the tops of her breasts. Her other arm was at her side, her hand resting flat on her belly somewhere between navel and the lowest rung of her ribcage. She was the color of honey. Her eyes, normally wide with daring, were now low and glistening like an addict's, so that she was looking down at me even though it was I who stood above her, moving closer to the foot of the bed as I removed my zippered sweatshirt, the tee shirt under, and kicked off my jeans.

Now is where you will ask me to skip ahead to the outcome, but I'm afraid I cannot do that. What seems like sparing you the details is to rob myself

218

of the better understanding that comes with telling the thing the way it happened, and some details matter more than others. So cover your ears if you don't appreciate what I am about to say, but understand that to me, to the seventeen-year-old me and the man I have become, these seemingly tawdry details matter. They matter very much.

My Holy Girl, she let me look at her.

She consented to my inspection, so I stood there, now in my loose boxer shorts, the pink Oxford ones she had stolen for me at the outlet mall, and I studied her. It was not so easy as head to toe or toe to head or anything like that. I would watch her chest for signs of heartbeat until I saw it, the skin over her breastbone literally pulsing, perspiring. I remember sitting beside her looking down and noticing for the first time her tiny purple dots where the hair follicles on her calves had been traumatized from her last shave. I saw the curve of her toes, thick and characterless. The balls of muscle on the inside of her knees were shiny in the firelight of the room.

No doubt I said things that were juvenile and ill equipped. 'I can't believe how beautiful you are' and 'you're a goddess sent here for me' and 'don't move, just wait, I want to memorize you for all time' and all those things you will laugh at now, but I meant them, and they were true. When I said she was a goddess, I understood that she held a power over my soul, and that if she were to command me to end my life with her at that moment, I surely would have. I believed in her the way one comes to believe in any other god, a work of genius, a fact of life, that song. The horizons revolved around her soul and her soul was the sun.

Holly Bauerman was love incarnate.

Her heart was strong and rapid, so different from her expression, which remained languid like her pose. I traced her breasts with the speed of a tortoise traversing a desert, I marveled at the pebbled brownness of areoles, the network of veins, the fine blonde hairs sprouting around them. I'd looked at them a hundred times before, but I had never *seen* them. At my touch she tensed and told me my fingers burned. As I traced her belly and hips I let my fingers rest on the stretch marks, those clues to her history like white tiger stripes in miniature.

I suppose this watching went on for hours, but it could have been minutes. Each moment was condensed and stretched out like a rubber band as time elasticized. When at last I could not resist I drew my two middle fingers from her calf behind her knee and up her thigh in a slow arc until they brushed against the lips of her sex (she called it her chi-chi, which at the time sounded to me like a toy poodle but now recalls something more accurate, the *chi*, or life force, in Eastern philosophy) and they came away instantly wet in a way that shocked me. She had remained so calm, I did not realize what had been going on inside of her. I looked down, of course I did, and watched my fingers exploring her, trying not to gasp as I saw not only the color and quantity of her desire but the markings we were making on the sheet. I confess that my adolescent mind did not understand fully what was happening at first. I worried for a moment she had lost control and truly wet the bed. She reacted to my touch by reaching out for me—*Enough is enough*, she said

220

without so many words. *Come to me now*.

But I could not, yet. I needed to understand, to create, to wallow. I let my fingers roam back to that spot and around and inside and over her hips and thighs and back inside until she was covered in her own salty sweetness and on the verge of her first of this night's orgasms, and only then did I lose all thought and sit upright to allow her to pull my shorts off.

I felt clumsy on top of her and we slid against each other, searching for the right angles. The prospect of feeling all of her made it like the first time again. The heat of her soft belly flesh pressed against me as her hand encircled me and slid down, and in the confusion I assumed I was inside.

She was staring at me, wide-eyed with desperation and patience. That she had planned this and wanted me without protection, that when she said she loved me like no one else and would always love me, filled me with the power and purpose of a righteous man.

'I want to be with you forever,' she said, whispering to me, watching me as I watched her. 'I want to love you forever. Can I love you forever? Will you promise me there will never be anyone else and that we can have each other and be like this forever?'

'Yes.'

'Do you love me?'

'More than anything. I love you.'

We spoke fast, repeating these declarations until they became vows.

I moved against her and slid into her and up against her and out again, over her triangle and to her navel. I was shaking all over and she cradled

221

my head in the back of her hand, pulling me down, moving her hips up against me. Without guilt or thought I cried out in actual pain and shuddered as the pulses of my ejaculate made us comically wet and still we had not done the 'it' part of it.

'I'm sorry, I'm sorry . . .' I was mortified.

'Shush, no, it's beautiful,' she said, kissing me. 'This is only the beginning.'

I felt her hands reaching for me, or pulling on me to keep me up. This latter, if it was her intention, was not necessary. At seventeen and coming down from one of the most powerful climaxes of my life, I had lost nothing. In a way it was better, for now I could start again and do it for her.

'This is what I want,' she whispered. I waited for an explanation while her hand circled between us, on me and then elsewhere. 'I want you, I want all of you. Inside me. I want you forever. I want to have your baby.' Her eyes glowed as she said it again, making sure I understood the words she had never spoken, not even in jest. 'I want to have your baby.'

I lifted myself off of her so that perhaps twelve inches of space remained between our bodies and I watched as, eyes closed, her breath coming in gulps, she gathered the threads of my semen and applied them to her sex with a repetitive motion that was somehow repulsive and graceful. I did not understand. Just know that, whatever distortions you are tempted to assign my recollection, don't make the mistake of thinking she was putting on a show for my benefit. Though it was the most erotic act I have ever witnessed, it was also without thought, instinctual. Her hands moved as if she

222

were not in control, efficiently cleaning up the mess like the sweep of that woman's hand in the paper towel commercial, only more primal, the way one imagines our ancestors weaving reeds. Each sweep of her palm gathered whatever fluid it could find, and then smoothed it over the cusp of her belly and further, down into the place God intended. She pressed her fingers into herself, rubbing herself until she was bucking against me.

I watched. I kissed her. I watched.

What did I know, at seventeen? She could have been performing some secret act only women learn when they have sought counsel to help them conceive. I certainly did not know that this was an act no woman, including my wife, would ever perform in my presence again. I knew only that this was it, the greatest proof my girl could offer that she loved me, that when she said forever she meant forever. Because, when you think about it, what is more risky to a teenaged girl than getting pregnant? What commitment is more long term than having your child, knowing she will likely be ostracized for it?

On another, more selfish side, my ego soared. What so many women understandably find repulsive—this thick, bleach-smelling substance—Holly was devouring to a place so much more dangerous than her mouth. I watched her hands do their work until her muscles clenched and pulled my seed deeper within her, and I understood the degree to which I had misjudged her love for me, how all-encompassing it had become, and that our future was sealed, that we would forever be us. I understood I would never, ever be alone again in this world.

Whatever you think happiness is, whatever you think it really means to be safe and secure and loved, I can tell you this. It is never more present in us than when we have coveted and loved and risked everything to claim another, and having done so found our equal, having reached the mutual understanding that we want the same thing, and that the thing we want is nothing. *Nothing*. Not money not fame not cars not houses not artistic greatness not even children, nothing except the person we are mated to, lost and found. This ecstatic mental state so perfectly in tune with our physical design is our home, the only real home we are given a chance to find in this life, the place we are lost, found, safe, forgiven, remade and forged into better men, the home we are forever trying to get back to, the one true birthing house.

When she had become almost frantic and I could bear observing her from a distance no more, I pulled her hands away and pushed myself inside her again, and this time I stayed.

We stayed this way for more than seven hours. I keep telling you it was not about the sex, but now it was the sex and nothing else. I know that I came inside her three more times, and she every time with me, pulling me deeper. The candles burned to their foundations before we drifted off to sleep.

Are you sleeping now? Is my voice soothing, or does it frighten you? If you want me stop, that is okay, too. Not every story needs to be heard to be understood. But I think you have heard this story before, or at the very least have felt it growing between us. That is why I'm telling you now—so that you will know everything about me, so that nothing will grow between us.

When you wake up, in the end, we will be together.

That is all that matters now.

26

It was a beginning, and he was a man who loved beginnings more than middles or endings.

He told himself he was being foolish. He told himself he was being a fucking idiot. He told himself that his wife was smart, beautiful, decent, forgiving, working to preserve their new hope in the ongoing experiment that was their marriage, and most of all that she was pregnant with his child.

Or a child.

But every child needs a home. He'd given Luther a home. Then Alice. It wasn't enough. He needed the other half. Wasn't that what the Bible said? Eve was the rib, and you missed her forever. Except, in this age of MBA wives and husbands who were good at cooking and cleaning and wringing their hands but not even handy enough to change a pipe under the sink, Conrad knew he was the rib. Jo, his host body, was her own strong woman and she was pulling away.

Nadia Grum was here. Half a family, waiting for the right man.

He had admitted that he wanted her. Wanted her, but wanted what of her? Not sex, or not only sex, because he was if anything painfully aware of her condition and the preposterous nature of their situation. Sex was a distant thing if it was there at all. In its place, something unnamable, and more powerful.

Oh yes, he could see how a sane man might decide it was time to seek counsel in the form of one's doctor, one's wife, one's family. But Jo was his only family, and like a man running from the avalanche of emotional debt but not yet bankrupt of pride, he chose to leave Jo out of it. To call his wife and inform her of his experiences, his utter emotional fucked-uppedness, would be an Armageddon, what the marriage shrinks called a relationship-ending event. No, whatever the end turned out to be, he would determine the course on his own. He knew that seeking advice would not change his wishes. Because the real horror is that when you're busy ruining your life, self-awareness doesn't stop you.

Sweating out the beer in their new cotton sheets, thinking of her one story below, he could see all these things, but he was powerless to them. And to one more thing.

The house.

Something had happened here, maybe several somethings involving life and death and the things that slip through the cracks in between. Something had been born here and it lived here still. He did not have all the pieces, but he felt it. He felt the will of the place working on him every time he returned home and it was not going away. It was, in fact, getting stronger. It had broken the mirrors, out of anger. Angry that he was next door with her, or that they hadn't been here, where they were supposed to be, tending to business. He wanted to know it. He wanted to touch the ghost, if that's what it was, maybe even help it. Her. He was terrified, repulsed, and drawn to it as he was drawn to the girl and the destruction she would bring down. And never mind Dr Alexis Hobarth, the animal sage, and his scientific explanations for what was, in effect, a miracle birth. He wasn't religious, but he wanted to be faithful, to find something deserving of faith, even if it cost him his marriage. Maybe this house would offer such an article. And maybe this thing inside him, driving him, was but a quaint strain of madness. And if so, so what? Wasn't love like that? An excuse to go mad, just for a little while? Who didn't wish for that? A padded room to protect you while you flipped out, a chamber where your most vile stench will be expelled and ventilated, a darkened theater to project your dreams on to the willing patrons of your all-too-human freak show.

A house to call a home.

*　　　*　　　*

She slept on the couch that night, and stayed with him for the next sixty hours. The incident with the dogs had put them together and unlocked a hidden need to abandon reality, together. He supposed she was interested in more than money for a plane ticket. Maybe not a father for her unborn child, maybe not yet.

But if circumstances made it possible, the next days made it real. What was once a hidden thought, a phrase tinted with flirting, a lingering question, now became a tactile sensation, the electric of the boundary pushed.

There were no long conversations or weeping

227

confessions. They did not make love physically.

Instead, theirs was a time of domestic gestures and offerings. The bump of the hip while he cooked over the stove. The looking out the window saying nothing, seeing how it felt to stand side by side. Once, when he had come down from a shower dressed in a clean shirt, she squinted and plucked lint from his shoulder. It was a small thing done like she'd done it a hundred times before, almost simian in its normalcy, but it was a statement. The female claiming a small right. After seeing the baby's room prepared that way in the warm light, she moved through the house no longer a guest, but a new resident.

They woke late the next morning. She was at the refrigerator, searching, grumpy.

He understood what to do. 'Stay here. I'll be right back.'

Into the bloody car to fetch real groceries. He spent three hundred dollars on good food and fell in love with feeding her. He prepared omelets with mushrooms and tomatoes, flipping them in the pan like a pro while she watched. Hash browns he'd shredded himself. Buttered toast. Fresh juice. What else did she like?

The stint as a prep cook in college came back. He cooked three meals a day. She would sit and watch him move around the kitchen. Never seen a man cook, she said, fascinated. He put things together she'd never eaten: Thai green curry and miso soup, green chile stew with warm tortillas, London broil with twice-baked potatoes and asparagus sautéed in olive oil. Salmon filets, sweet beets, mesclun greens with walnuts and Michigan cherries and crumbled blue cheese. Dozens of rolls and a loaf of home-made bread from the wedding present breadmaker. Cheesecake, pound cake, pecan pie and strawberry ice cream. Her appetite was astonishing. She ate for two, then three and sometimes four. She smiled the most after finishing a meal.

She helped him change the bandages around the dogs' legs. He could not be sure, but it seemed that the cuts were healing almost despite the sutures. The dogs no longer limped or slept all day. They acted like they had never been wounded. He was reminded of the quick healing in his hand, but he did not dwell on the idea that had struck him since he first moved in.

This is a healing place, and we are healing.

They lounged, watched movies, soap operas. He hadn't seen *Days of Our Lives* since high school, when Holly had forced him to watch it with her after school. Usually he would indulge her for half an hour, then get restless, horny, until Holly caved in and they had sex. Holly. They had been the craziest couple in high school—or the only real one. Watching TV with Nadia was different. It was a way to be together without doing anything. It was safe. Nadia said her feet hurt and he rubbed them from the other end of the couch until she fell asleep in the late afternoon.

The clock ceased to matter. They stayed up late, woke early, napped. They played Scrabble through the afternoon thunderstorms and she surprised him by beating him two out of three.

She slept on the couch even when he offered her the upstairs bed, insisting he would behave and stay in another room. She refused. On the second day he came down to find her lying still like one of

229

Laski's kids. He sat on the couch next to her and she sat up suddenly, startled, then pressed her mouth to his. He tasted her morning breath and she pulled his hair. They pushed against each other's mouths for fifteen minutes without anything else. He somehow knew to keep his hands down, and that was better. She moaned when they kissed, and he stopped, thinking her crying again. But she wasn't. Nervous, excited, don't want to talk about it. He couldn't remember if Jo had ever been so moved by a kiss. Nadia would kiss him that way for ten minutes, then push away. She would disappear into the bath for half an hour and resurface wearing his old tees and boxers. She came down one time in his Sebadoh and he thought that was perfect.

The dogs were warm to her, but he sensed they knew. He would catch them looking at him and he would think, *They know. They know she is not Jo and something is wrong with this picture.*

The second night he could not sleep and he went to her on the couch. She was sleeping. He sat next to her on the couch and watched her. He placed a hand on her swollen belly—she must be seven months now—and she woke to his touch. He did not pull his hand away and she left it there, looking up at him. I'm falling for this whole deal, he thought. The woman and everything inside her and what it will cost. When she sat up he said sorry, but she said it was okay, she just had to pee.

When she returned she held the blanket open for him and the morning passed in a cocoon of unmoving, unsleeping silence. Two bodies learning something before their brains could catch up.

He was dozing spoon-to-spoon when she said, 'I
230

don't know why, but I feel safe with you.'

'You are.'

She sighed heavily with contentment, and he felt now was the time to ask.

'Nadia,' he whispered.

'Mh-hm.'

'Is that why you tried to run away? Because you weren't safe with Eddie?'

'Yes.'

'He is the father.'

'Yes.'

'Was it here? In this house?'

A minute passed before she answered. 'The Laskis moved out over a year ago. The house was empty last fall and winter. Eddie and I . . . we had nowhere else to go. I'd spent so much time here growing up, it felt almost normal, like I deserved to be here. We spent the afternoons hiding out in the rooms, drinking wine, smoking cigarettes. For a while we were both happy, but kinda out of control. But then it happened, and my parents would not allow us to see each other again. Eddie was always wild, but he got mean after that. How did you know?'

'It just makes sense. The house wants life.'

'Does it? Because sometimes I feel like it doesn't want me here.'

'Why would you think that?'

'I dunno. Maybe because I've always been an intruder.'

'No.'

'It's true. First I was the babysitter. Mrs Laski was always suspicious of me, and I saw the way Mr Laski looked at me.'

'You are beautiful enough to halt birds in flight.

231

Can you blame them?'

'Then I was with Eddie, when no one owned the house, and I became pregnant. I was never really frightened here, not during those afternoons, but I always knew I was breaking the rules. I always felt like I was angering her somehow.'

He did not think to clarify whether if by 'her' Nadia meant Mrs Laski, the house itself or someone else.

'I thought about getting rid of it. Eddie asked me to. But I kept putting it off and putting it off. And then one day I didn't care what anybody else wanted. It was like the time I was baby-sitting, when the *zeks* came for me. I'd already lost it once, and I couldn't go through that again. This baby is my baby, but now I am an intruder again.'

'You're not. I invited you in.'

'But I am not the woman of the house.'

'Is that something you heard from Laski?'

'I don't remember. It just feels that way.'

'Well, it's my house now. And I want you to stay.'

He kissed her neck, fell asleep in her hair.

*   *   *

On the third morning he woke to find her in the kitchen banging around, looking for a pot. He made her peaches and cream oatmeal and he could tell something was gnawing at her.

'What's on your mind, Ms Grum?'

'I'm antsy,' she said. 'I need to get out and do something.'

'Yeah, sure.' He nodded and looked outside. It was sunny, with a light breeze coming through the front screen door. 'You wanna go for a walk?'

'Actually,' she said with a shining fear in her eye. 'I think I need to go home. Just for a few hours.'

He didn't ask for what. He went to her and kissed her. This seemed to calm her momentarily. She gave in, sucked at his tongue for a minute, then giggled and ducked away from him. Back to grumpy.

'You shouldn't be doing that.'

'Why not?'

'Because it's getting too easy.'

'Too easy?'

'Comfortable. We'll forget ourselves.'

'That's a good thing.'

'Not if we get caught.'

'I'm not afraid,' he said. 'Let's get caught.'

'No one knows, Conrad.'

He smiled. There was something to know.

'Are you for real? Is this—are you sure you want this?'

'Not a few hours,' he said. 'One.'

'Promise you won't change your mind?'

He kissed her. She started to cry and he heard himself speaking before he'd even made the decision.

'I'll call Jo. I'll tell her—'

'No!'

'—the truth.'

'No.'

'Nadia. We have nothing to be ashamed of. This stuff happens. If we're honest about what we want, they will understand. Not right away, but I'm not afraid.'

She smiled through her tears.

'Come right back.'

But he was afraid, and he did feel guilty.

He sat for a while at the kitchen two-top with the phone in his hand. It seemed so natural when she was here, but now, trying to shape his . . . no, not plan, it wasn't even a plan yet . . . desires into a thing his wife would understand, he was terrified. There would be no understanding, only screaming.

Rage, accusations, pain.

Get it over with. Come clean. Because this situation here, right now, is untenable.

He dialed Jo's room. No one answered. He dialed her mobile, got voicemail. She could be out. She could be ignoring his calls. She could be with That Fucker Jake. She could be studying.

'God damn you, Jo. God damn you for leaving me,' he said. 'If your father had died, I would never have left you. Never. Just remember this was your choice. Leaving me alone here in this house was your choice.'

The robotic woman asked him if he wanted to replay his message, or rerecord it. He clicked off and dropped the phone.

His hands were shaking. He went to the cupboard and removed a bottle of Jim Beam. He drank it straight and warm from a plastic tumbler, punishing himself and blotting her out for a little while longer.

*   *   *

He slept late and woke to the sound of knocking. He got out of bed and felt every stair on the way

234

down. His emotions were blunted. He had found himself drunk so quickly he had never got round to calling Nadia to see why she hadn't come back. He vaguely recalled wishing she never would, then crying because she hadn't. His father had made an appearance at some point, and after that it was just black. Now his synapses felt as if they had been coated with maple syrup and then set on fire. When he opened the front door in his boxers and morning half-wood, she was just standing there wet-faced.

'What's wrong?'

'I didn't mean to,' she said. She was holding a small red cell phone away from her body like it was a bloody knife.

'Didn't mean to?'

'Promise you'll help me.'

He pulled her in and shut the door. She grabbed him and squeezed hard, her belly pushing into his waist like the head of a ten-year-old between them.

She looked up, her chin digging into his chest. 'Eddie's dead,' she said. 'I think I killed him.'

27

'He probably deserved it,' he blurted before clapping his mouth shut.

'I didn't mean to, I didn't mean to . . .' She kept saying it and she didn't sound defensive so much as stunned. She was hiccupping and shaking all over.

Conrad moved her into the living room. 'I'm sorry. Here, it's fine it's fine sit down. I'll be right back.'

He went to the kitchen and poured her a coffee left over from the previous morning's pot, added a wallop of Brennan's Irish Cream and speed dialed one minute on the microwave. He went over it in his head. It didn't take very long or help much. Conrad had been home for the past three days and nights, with her. She'd left for a night and now what? Now Eddie was dead? How? Was someone else involved? Nadia wouldn't kill Eddie, really, would she? She was pregnant, for God's sake, and she clearly had feelings for the boy.

Poor kid.

Nadia, not Eddie.

Well, maybe him, too, but maybe not. Maybe Eddie had been asking for it. Maybe Eddie accidentally set his meth lab on fire and got stuck charring in the blaze.

She was sitting on the couch, her shoulders bunched up to her ears like she had just been rear-ended by a full-size SUV, her face still pale from the impact.

'Here. Go slowly and take deep breaths until you're ready to tell me.'

She accepted the mug and just stared at it. It looked like an oil slick with the Irish in it.

'I don't know whuh-whuh-what happened. I left my cell phone at home, otherwise I would of-huh-huh heard sooner.'

'Heard what?'

'The phone. He called like thirty times. But he didn't say anything. Until last night. He left a mess-oh, God. No, I can't . . .' She was crying again.

'Okay. Hold on. Breathe. That's it. Breathe.'

She recovered a bit. 'He left a message. On that?' He was pointing at her cell phone.

'He's been going crazy this whole time. For weeks. He had this . . . this *plan* for us. He promised to take care of us.'

'What did the message say?'

'I can't listen to it again.' She dropped the cell phone.

Conrad picked it up, flipped it open. 'How do I listen?'

'It's in my address book, under voicemail.'

Conrad opened her address book, scrolled down through a dozen names, selected voicemail and pressed call.

A voice said, 'Please enter your password.'

'What's your password?'

'Two-one-two-one.'

He entered the numbers. The voice said she had one saved message. He pressed one.

At first there was only heavy breathing, but he recognized it as Eddie's near hyperventilation. Same as from the last time they had spoken. Something slammed loudly and Conrad pulled his ear away for a moment. Then Eddie started screaming.

'God damn you, how can you do this to me? To the fucking baby! Why are you hiding from me? You want me to leave you alone? I'm not good enough? Is that it, you fucking whore bitch! Fuck you, fuck you, fuck you—'

Conrad shook his head. The kid was having an absolute tantrum. Nadia turned away and gagged. Conrad reached out for her, but she jerked away.

'—fuck you, fine, fucking fine, if this is what you want, you got it, bitch,' Eddie's voicemail

237

continued. 'You made this mess, you clean it up. I'm leaving this whole shitty deal, right now. You ready? You ready, Nadia? Suck on this!'

There was a deafening bang. Conrad was pretty sure it was a gunshot. Then a clatter, as if the phone had been dropped. After ten seconds of silence, coming from some distance away from the phone, there was only a low moaning sound. It was sickening, something that could not be faked, and it went on and on. Finally the time allotted for messages expired.

Conrad closed the phone. 'Jesus.'

'I killed him,' Nadia said.

'No, you didn't. We don't even know for sure if—'

'He shot himself! I know he's dead!'

'Nadia—'

'I knew he was going to do this! Don't you see? I could have gone over sooner. I could have talked to him. He was going crazy for three days!'

'It's not your fault.'

'You don't understand, you can't . . . Eddie's fragile. I almost asked you to come with me, but I thought that would only make him worse.'

Conrad held her by the arms, gently but firmly.

'Nadia. Calm down. What did the police say?'

She reared back. 'The police?'

'Nine-one-one?'

'I didn't call the police! Are you crazy?'

'Who did you call?'

'Nobody. He's still there.'

'Where?'

'At his house!'

She hung her head in her hands and cried, chugging hard. Anger rose up inside him. They

238

were supposed to be sorting things out and making a plan, not dealing with Eddie's problems. Now she was a wreck. Eddie was dead. I'm in over my head here, he thought. Way over.

'Nadia, we have to call the police.'

'No!'

'No?'

'You have to go there with me!'

'No. What good could that possibly—'

'Maybe he's not dead.'

'Explain that.'

'What if he's just hurt? Maybe he's alive and needs help!'

'If you're worried about that, if you thought he was alive, why didn't you call for help?'

She squeezed her eyes shut and then opened them, grabbed the coffee and threw it at the wall. The mug shattered above the TV and dripped down to the floor.

'I'm asking for help now!' She got up and ran for the door.

He caught her on the porch, held her by the arm. 'Nadia, wait. Stop. Just stop.' Conrad looked across the street and thought he saw a shape in the Bartholomews' window. 'Don't make a scene of this or you are on your own, do you hear me? I will go with you and we are calling the police when we get there, so you better get your story straight. Can you do that? Can you be calm now?'

She nodded.

'Stay here. I'll get dressed.'

He ran upstairs and pulled on a pair of shorts. His flip-flops. Brush the teeth—fuck it, later. When he came back she was standing beside the Volvo. Steve Bartholomew stepped out his front

239

door and crossed his lawn, heading directly toward them.

'Get in the car,' Conrad said under his breath. 'Morning, Steve!'

They slipped in and Steve raised one hand to wave them back. The car was still splashed with dusty dog blood. Conrad turned the motor over, stomped on the juice and made the Volvo work. In the rearview mirror, Steve was standing on the sidewalk, hands on his hips.

'Where's Eddie live?'

'You said you knew.'

'On the phone? Nadia, I was bluffing. Wait. He actually lives in a trailer?'

'Yes.'

'Oh.'

Lucky guess, huh, 'Rad?

*   *   *

Eddie lived in Dewey, a forlorn hamlet of starter homes some seven miles south of Black Earth. They took 151 toward Dubuque and followed county road XX east until they came to the only stop sign. Next to that, *Welcome to Dewey, Pop. 784.*

'There some sort of state law says if a town can support just one business it's got to be a Kwik-Trip?'

Nadia ignored his attempt at levity. A small stone Lutheran church stood catty-corner. A post office. 'Where now?'

'Go straight.'

They passed an abandoned tin car wash and they were heading out of town again.

240

'Turn left up there.' She pointed to a fork in the road that led them past a babyshit-brown entrance gate proclaiming Valley Village Court, *Where Wisconsin Families Settle Down!*

They entered the trailer park proper and Conrad let the Volvo troll. There was a slight dip in the road, but he did not see anything resembling a valley or a village, just a shotgun smattering of turtle boxes no person should ever call home. Nadia pointed to a reddish-brown unit with a blackface jockey statue in the yard and a mailbox marked 64 *The Kellogs*.

'Eddie Kellog?'

'Park here,' she said.

'I'm guessing no relation to the cereal dynasty?'

Nadia shot him a nasty look and he turned off the car. She reached for the door and he held her back.

'Hold on. What are we walking into?' She stared at him. 'Nadia, his parents? Where are they?'

'His mom lives at his aunt's house in Iowa City.'

'He lives alone?'

'For now, yes.'

'Where's Dad?'

'He lives in Milwaukee.'

'Neighbors, friends? Anyone else who might pop by while we're in there staring at the body?'

When he said 'body' she bit the heel of her hand.

'You sure? Eddie has no friends? Because I see a lot of cars.'

'No one here likes him.'

'Let's go.'

They stepped out into the hot sunlight. Going to be another scorcher—not a good day to decompose. He hoped it wasn't going to be bad. Conrad had never seen a dead body before—his father didn't count, because Conrad had fled the hospital room after that last breath, signed the papers and never looked back. He needed to remain calm, keep an eye on Nadia. She might break down again—and, if so, fine. He could deal with her. But they could not afford for both of them to lose their shit. They reached the porch.

'Should we knock?' Conrad whispered.

'Won't do any good.' She opened the door for him and he entered.

The lights were on. Eddie's home was . . . decent. Brushed cotton sofa and matching armchair, a large television and handsome black audio appliances stacked beneath. The breakfast nook looked like granite, a bowl of tangerines on top. Short pearl carpet, very clean. It all looked like someone had poured their home equity into the interior instead of just moving to a better town, a better life.

'Is it always this clean?'

She nodded. 'Eddie's a bit of a neatnik.'

Conrad moved down the hall. He smelled fresh laundry and looked inside a closet with shuttered doors. A stack of white tees and black cargo pants were folded on top of the over-and-under laundry unit.

'Did Eddie have a job at The Gap?' he said.

'What?'

'Never mind. This the bedroom?'

She nodded and he guessed she wasn't going to leave her post in the kitchen.

Conrad grabbed the knob, realized he was leaving prints and wiped it with the hem of his tee

242

shirt. He took another breath, gripped the knob through his shirt and opened the door.

More white carpeting, cheap IKEA-type furniture, a desk with a black Dell PC on top. The monitor was a flatscreen and large. Next to the desk: simple pine bookcases lined with junior college textbooks and *Ultimate Fighting* DVDs, first-person shooter games, a new Xbox console tucked inside a storage unit below the desk. The bedding was all black and military crisp. Conrad saw no blood or sign of a struggle. If Eddie was here, the kid was folded into the closet.

This whole deal was starting to feel like a set-up.

Conrad backed out of the room and looked at Nadia. She was hugging herself, pacing a square into the kitchen floor.

'Are you sure he was calling from home? Nadia?'

She looked up. 'He's not . . . ?'

Conrad shook his head.

She stomped down the hall. She pointed to the bed and a small animal noise rose up within her as she lunged forward and ripped the bedding off revealing clean white sheets.

'Well?'

'The blood . . . he shot himself. You heard the message! This is impossible. Someone took him away.'

'How do you know he wasn't trying to trap you?'

'He wouldn't do that. Someone knows. Someone cleaned it all up!'

She went to the bathroom, looking behind the door.

'What makes you think he was in bed?' Conrad

243

said.

For all he knew, they were both playing with him. But why? What could he possibly have that they wanted?

'He always called me from bed. There's nowhere else to go in here.'

She came back. 'Did you check the closet?'

Conrad went to the closet. Somewhere outside a screen door creaked and latched. He listened for footsteps coming up the walk. He heard none. He stared at the cheap aluminum closet doors with their fake shutters and waited for a sound, a clue. Maybe Eddie was going to jump out and brain him with a sawed-off baseball bat. He felt strangely calm. You could sense when you were trespassing in front of a watchful eye. This clean little home felt empty. Conrad's hand worked with its own curious will, the metal door folded out. Aside from clothes hanging in color-coordinated groups, the closet was empty.

No, it wasn't.

There was a suitcase on the floor, a big one, open and full of folded clothes, like the laundry in the hall. A *Time Out—Seattle* city guide. Planning to follow her to Seattle?

He heard a click.

Time to get her talking, she's been lying to you, boss.

Conrad stood. 'Nadia—'

Eddie was taller than he remembered. His hair was better, recently cut, neat over the ears. He had her in a chokehold. A blue-black gun with a wooden grip was pressed to her abdomen and shaking, stabbing at the outermost bulge of her belly. The boy was shaking, too, eyes roadmap red.

244

A large square Band Aid was stuck to one side of his forehead, a maroon bullseye.

Jesus, he's a lousy shot.

'Where's your big money now, fuckface?'

The kid was as quiet as . . . something pretty quiet, Conrad thought, trying to come up with a casual response to the situation.

'Hi, Eddie.'

'You're in my house, fuckface,' Eddie said.

Was this the kid's only name for unwanted guests? Couldn't he do any better . . .

'I'm sorry, Eddie, don't worry about him—' Nadia started to say.

'Shut up!'

Conrad tried to breathe deeply without showing it. Jesus, it was hot in here. 'What money, Eddie?'

'I thought you could help us,' Nadia said. She was trying to signal him with her eyes. 'He can help us, Eddie.'

'Absolutely, Eddie, just hold on a sec,' Conrad said.

'You hold on, asshole, you just hold on.' A little too cool for Conrad's liking. The stutter was taking a time out, apparently. 'You think you can buy it?'

'What?' Conrad heard the words, but he did not understand.

'You can't buy it. I won't let you take my baby.'

Nadia yelped. Eddie was jabbing her with the gun. Jabbing her right in the—wait a minute. Was she in on this? Had she tried to trick him?

'Eddie, don't!' Nadia was being too loud. She was—

The gun.

The gun was everything. Look away. Show no fear.

245

Conrad forced himself to look into the kid's eyes, but his eyes kept going back to her. Nadia was as white as the carpet. Her cheek twitched violently. Eddie's mouth hung open like he was being held hostage, too. Saliva dripped from his lower lip and fell past the gun, hitting the floor with a soft *pat*.

The gun . . .

Conrad reached out. 'Eddie, we were worried—'

The gun exploded.

28

When the gun went off in the hot confines of the trailer's hall, Nadia fell to the floor in a limp heap. Eddie's snarl froze and then he just looked surprised. Conrad flinched from the pop, covered his head and yelled, 'Don't!'

When he opened his eyes she was bleeding from just below her equatorial center, maybe Tanzania on the globe of her belly. Eddie was staring at her like some fourth party had pulled the trigger, like he was the other victim.

'I-I-I'm sorry,' Eddie said.

'You little fuck,' Conrad said.

The kid's remorse evaporated as soon as Conrad stepped forward and reached for the gun. Eddie went ape shit, screaming into the bathroom. Conrad shoved very hard and the trigger-happy suitor fired another shot into the wall before tripping over the toilet and slamming against the half-open sliding shower door, which rattled at an astonishing volume but did not shatter. Eddie's gun hand slapped the wall, Eddie slipped and Conrad leaped on top, his senses on full alert. He punched down, missed. Aimed for the neck, punched down, missed. Sweat-greased and hyped through the roof, Eddie slid beneath Conrad, spun out and yanked the towel rack out of the wall as he rebounded up and dashed past Conrad, careening off the wall and directly into the door, closing them both into the bathroom. He fumbled at the knob, but already Conrad had a ball of Eddie's shirt in one fist. Conrad yanked Eddie back and turned to the side. Eddie pivoted wildly, lost his balance, whirled past like they were swing dancing. Eddie's feet tripped on the edge of the tub and he began to go face first between the sliding shower door and the backsplash, directly into the tub. Conrad was still holding his shirt like a bronc rider and for one long second Eddie hovered over the tub, bent forward, the horse halting before going over the edge of a cliff. Conrad realized he was losing his balance, too, and he did not want to land on top of Eddie in the tub with a gun between them. He jerked his arm back once, bringing Eddie nearly vertical again, then kicked him in the ass as hard as he could, releasing the shirt at the last minute. Eddie's spine arched with whiplash and his hands flew out on instinct, trying to brace his fall. His right hand—the one holding the gun—hit the soap cradle, bent inward at the wrist, and the gun bucked. The shot went high on the right side of Eddie's forehead and exited his ear, spraying maroon and gray sludge over the grout and the bottle of Pert Plus to his left.

Conrad flinched back over the sink and covered his face. His ankle twisted and his knees gave out.

He sat there on the shag throw rug, staring at Eddie's twitching legs until they stopped. Another minute seemed to pass before he realized what had happened. He stood up. Eddie was face down, his neck askew. Something shiny and white dangled from his ear . . . and it was the rest of his ear. Conrad was only slightly relieved he did not have to look into the boy's eyes.

His first coherent thought was, *Thank God it wasn't me.*

His second was, *It's his fault. I didn't shoot him.*

And last but not least, *It happened in the shower. Easier to clean up.*

He was reaching for a towel when he remembered Nadia.

Jesus Shitting Christ she's pregnant and shot.

He turned away, closed the bathroom door, and crouched next to her in the hall. Nadia's foot pedaled the air and banged against the wall of the trailer a couple times, found purchase, and pushed her shoulders against the opposite wall until she was stuck and partially folded, her eyes rolling back and around, searching while her mouth puckered and emitted 'nnnya-nnnyaa-nnnyaa' sounds.

Conrad pulled her shoulders off the wall until she was lying flat on her back. It seemed important to get her straight. Her shirt was red from the waistline up to her breasts and sopping wet. His vision became foggy. Eyes watering up as if the wind were blowing invisible particles into them.

'I'm here, girl. Okay, we're going to be fine . . .'

He didn't know this would be fine. He ran back to the bathroom and—*don't look! don't look at that problem in the shower, not yet, not now!*—grabbed

248

two yellow and white striped beach towels off the rack, spun to the sink. Was he supposed to wet one first? No—soak up the blood. The medicine cabinet was open and he saw a tin of Band Aids and some Preparation H.

He crouched and pressed a towel into her abdomen.

Nadia screamed and kicked.

'Hold still, hold still!' He sounded too loud, so he repeated it softer until she blinked and saw him, twisting against the pain, trying to get away. She beat her head against the floor and clenched her teeth, staring through him, and he knew she was angry on top of the pain. Was he to blame for this, after all? Probably, in some way.

Three gunshots. Someone must've heard. The police will be here soon.

He felt the towel dampening beneath his hand and lifted it to make sure he was pressing in the right spot. Her shirt was up, revealing white skin gone grainy and smeared. He couldn't see the wound's exact location yet. There was too much blood. He inspected her hips. Jesus Christ, where was it?

'Be still. Nadia, be still!' The blood was pooling in her belly button. 'Oh God . . .'

Nadia was whimpering. So much for the hope she was in shock. Shock would be a blessing. 'Burns, it burns,' she whimpered.

He put his finger to her navel and she screamed, jerking toward him. When she came up, his finger slipped under the flap of skin at the ring of her belly button until he was certain he was poking her in the guts.

Nadia howled and stretched herself taut as a

piano wire. He snatched his hand away and fresh blood poured out.

'I know, I know! Stop moving!' Amazingly, she swung her hand around and clutched his forearm, her grip fierce. That was something, wasn't it?

'Easy, easy, I have to stop it.'

She gritted her teeth.

Conrad wadded the end of the second towel to a conical point and pushed it in. She opened her mouth to unleash another scream and nothing came out. Her circuits overloaded as her face went ash-gray and her breath locked up. She blinked through tears for a long silent spell. When it broke, the hot gust of her sour breath poured over him without a sound. Then she started panting, everything on autopilot.

Now she was in shock.

He had pushed the towel under the flap of skin. It went sideways, a tear in her outer fabric. He lifted the towel again and fresh blood flowed once more, but not before he saw that the core of her navel was intact. The bullet had not gone in. It had gone across shallowly, sideways through her belly flesh, entering at the navel and exiting three inches closer to her hip. It was possible that the curvature of her belly had prevented Eddie from getting a direct shot, and in doing so saved the child. Her skin under the blood was stained gray with either gunpowder or the first bruising. Underneath the ripped exit wound he saw yellow fatty tissue made pink with her blood.

No sirens. What are you waiting for, asshole?

The saner voice in his head screamed at him to call an ambulance and get the girl to a hospital. Yet he hesitated. This wasn't his fault, but there would be many questions. What made Eddie go off? What had you two been doing before this happened? How could you let this happen to our daughter? Our grandchild? Gail and John would rush home. Nadia would make the news. Jo would never return, or kill him when she did.

They would blame him. Tell the truth—you shot Eddie, didn't you? You wanted him out of the picture. Well, now he's out of the picture!

'Oh fuck, oh fuck . . .' Panic was setting in.

Wait. The phone. Eddie killed himself. His suicide note was on Nadia's phone!

Fine. Let Eddie be Eddie. But Nadia needs an ambulance—now.

But still he hesitated. Needed to get his story straight. He couldn't think it through, and the longer he sat there the more frightened he became. He just wanted to go home. The sane voice was losing the battle, being drowned out with each passing second by another voice, the one that had been there as his hand healed from the dog bite and been there still as the dogs themselves healed.

This is a healing place.

Was this what it wanted? The house and the things connected to the house? To make life out of life?

He imagined it was so.

*　　　*　　　*

He parked behind the garage and carried her up the backyard, over the deck, into the house. He had to set her down in the kitchen to catch his breath and she almost fell down, but he caught

251

her. After more screaming and coughing, he got her up the stairs and into bed, carrying her like a bride. It took another twenty minutes to stop the bleeding, and he held the towel on her, offering her water she could not swallow without coughing and shaking and reopening the wound.

He went through the motions of doctors he'd seen on TV, in films. He cleaned and semi-sealed the borders of the bullet-torn flesh with Neosporin before applying butterfly bandages from the first aid kit they'd moved from Los Angeles. He cleaned, dabbed and staunched it with more ointment and clean gauze, taping her waist all the way around with more of Luther's flex-bandage. It held. Outside, the wound was the shape of a question mark. Whatever the damage on the inside, it would have to take care of itself.

Finally, half an hour later, her breathing slowed and she whimpered one last time before dozing off. She was tougher than he would have guessed, maybe tough enough to have made it in Seattle. A granite slab of guilt pressed down on him. That he had pushed Eddie to do this to her; that she was here at all.

He held her hand and thought about the baby inside. The life between them they had discussed only in vague questions and long silent stares now seemed enormous, everything. A bullet had grazed its soft thin shell and what was inside was now a little hero.

This is a healing place. If she does not get better in a day or two, I will take her to a doctor.

He didn't think anyone had seen them come home.

*   *   *

The afternoon and evening passed. Conrad awoke just before dawn with a pounding headache, convinced this was the day the Grums were coming home. He counted back, ticking off days that had become a frightening blur, until he realized Nadia's parents were not due for two or three more days. Perhaps.

He did not call to alert them to Nadia's condition, and she had not asked him to before the double-dose of Tylenol PM took her under for the night. He'd also slipped her two of Alice and Luther's Baytril tablets, a broad-spectrum antibiotic he knew from working with Dr Hobarth to be mild and safe for human consumption. She did not question the pills—she was just out.

The Doctor. You're playing Doctor.

He did not answer the phone when it had rang just before midnight. He doubted Jo would call so late. He had no idea what he would have said to his wife, and did not have the energy to pretend everything was fine.

Early the next morning there was a knock at the door. By the time he'd gotten up and pulled the curtain aside, they had gone. If they had found Eddie, the police would have come in a car, or three. He saw no police cars. Another UPS shipment from Jo? He did not see or hear a truck. Still, he remained at the window, waiting for Steve Bartholomew or the mailman or someone to reappear in his front yard, looking up at the second story, pointing an accusing finger. No one materialized and he did not linger.

Through the morning Nadia was in and out of

253

it, but stable. The wound had reddened, puffed, cracked and seeped blood, and he changed her bandages. The bleeding had stopped. He brought her orange juice. Nadia swallowed more Baytril but did not speak. She fell into a long afternoon nap. He stretched out and lay beside her, careful not to disturb her.

Twenty-four hours had passed since Eddie went Eddie on them.

The second time the doorbell rang, he was awake and assumed his post at the window. It was nearly dark. No cop cars. Just as he dropped the curtain aside, he saw a figure step back in the yard and look up. Conrad could not make out a face. Might be Steve Bartholomew, their trusty neighbor. He dimly recalled how just a few weeks ago he'd thought Steve was the kind of man with whom he might strike up an easy friendship. Maybe be more than just neighbors, borrowing each other's tools and drinking beer during the annual neighborhood water-balloon fight in the street on the Fourth of July. But that window of opportunity had passed.

The figure on his lawn paced like a tiger in the zoo, peering into the front parlor windows, searching for an opening. The tiger planted his hands on his hips.

Conrad whispered into the curtain. 'Go home or pounce, buddy.'

The figure disappeared and Conrad lost the line of sight through the thick leaves of his one-hundred-and-forty-year-old maple tree. He relaxed.

Dong-dong-dong! The doorbell.

'Fuck.'

Nadia stirred in the bed. 'What's going on?' She squinted at him in the dark, her hair matted, eyes crusty with sleep. 'Are my parents home?'

'Nothing, it's fine. Stay there.'

The doorbell rang again, setting the dogs off.

Conrad slipped out of the bedroom. He left the lights off as he padded to the door—no use backlighting himself before he knew who was there. He stopped and grabbed a knife from the block on the kitchen counter. It could be the police. He left the knife in the kitchen and headed for the door.

29

Conrad flipped the porch light on, casting their visitor in a yellow spotlight. The guy had his back to the front door, but it was obvious from the buzzed flat-top and hunter-gatherer posture it was Steve Bartholomew.

'Hey, Steve, what's up?' Conrad stepped out and pulled the door shut before the dogs could escape and Steve could move in.

Steve turned. 'Conrad. Did I wake you up?'

'Yeah, as a matter of fact.'

'Oh, are you sick?' Conrad realized he hadn't showered in some forty-eight hours.

'My dogs are beat up, Steve-O,' he said, going on the offensive. 'I came home to smashed mirrors and bleeding dogs, and it wasn't easy finding a vet in this little conclave of ours, so I apologize if I haven't been exactly out and about.'

Steve frowned. 'Your dogs?'

'You saw Nadia and I leave the other day, right? She helped me get them to the vet. Thirty-six stitches in Luther's legs. Alice almost lost an ear.'

'What happened?'

'I have no idea, Steve. Dogs can be dogs.'

'How's your wife? She come home yet?'

'No, she hasn't.'

'I'm sorry. Sounds like you got them fixed up. Speaking of fix up, how's your little job next door going?'

For a minute Conrad was so sure Steve knew about Nadia he forgot about the work he was supposed to be doing at the Grum residence.

'Yeah, how 'bout that?' he said, stalling for time. Did that mean the Grums had called Steve, maybe poking around after they couldn't reach Nadia at home? Or had he seen something suspicious? 'Seems like every time I get around to pulling the ladder out it rains.'

'Anything I can help you with? We're expecting John and Gail, what, tomorrow?'

'Day after or the next. And no thanks. I'll manage.'

Conrad yawned. *Beat it, Steve-O.*

'Hope John and Gail had a good time. They deserve a break. These kids'll wear you out.' Steve grinned without pleasure. 'I know Jesse's keeping me awake more nights than not.'

'Jesse's your daughter?'

'Yes.'

'You said she's up at UW Madison?'

'Virginia Tech. School's fine, but these kids. These kids.'

'How's that?' Conrad didn't know if this was going somewhere or just small talk.

'I didn't like the boys she was hanging around with here in town. Wastrels, the lot of them. Only now, she's calling her mother every night. "Mommy, Josh is being a jerk. Mommy, Josh said it's normal to see other girls in college." You see where this is going.'

'Actually, I'm not sure—'

'I ever get my hands on this sapling Josh who's been sticking it to my daughter? He even thinks about coming to my house for one of his booty calls? I'll drive him down to the limestone quarry and only one of us is coming back.'

Conrad flinched. Steve was suddenly too close and smiling too widely.

'So, where's Nadia hiding?'

It came out so quickly that Conrad heard, where you hiding Nadia? But of course that was silly. If Steve really—

'She's not at your place, is she?' Steve glanced over Conrad's shoulder.

Conrad scoffed. 'No. Maybe she's out with friends?'

'What about Eddie? He been around?'

'She said he was calling her, trying to put the band back together. But I didn't get the impression they were exactly hot and heavy these days. I tried, but she told me to mind my own business, Steve.'

'Her parents are not going to be happy, Conrad.'

'She's twenty. It's not like she's a minor. Can't ground her, can they?'

Easy, 'Rad. This whole show is dry kindling and you're throwing lit matches.

'She's nineteen, and pregnant,' Steve said. 'And you obviously don't have children.'

257

'Nope, not yet.'

'Uh-huh. Well, if you ever want to, you might do well to tell Nadia to get her ass home before Big John returns. I've seen the man bend rebar with his bare hands.'

'Jesus.'

'Imagine what he'd do to your neck.'

'Eddie's neck,' Conrad corrected.

Steve nodded. *I know, and you know I know.*

'Good luck with your chores, Mr Harrison.'

'Night, Steve-O.'

Conrad went to the liquor cabinet and poured three fingers of warm silver rum. It tasted like rubbing alcohol and burned for five minutes while he checked the doors front and back, locking everything twice.

* * *

The night of Steve's visit, she began to feed herself and he watched her from the reading chair he had pulled into the room. He knew the big talk had arrived, and he waited for her to go first. Her voice was strong and clear, almost professional.

'I feel much better now. But I think I should see how bad it is.' She reached for the bandage.

'No, no, don't. It's superficial, but it needs more time to close up.' He patted her hand. 'I was very worried about you. You're lucky Eddie was a bad shot.'

'Did you call my parents?'

'No. Should I have?'

She licked her lips. 'Where's Eddie?'

'You don't remember?'

She just stared at him. He considered what to

258

tell her. If she knew the truth, she would probably panic and ask him to call the police. And she might never forgive him.

'It was bad, Nadia. I wasn't thinking straight. I was worried about you.'

'Did he run away?'

'No.'

'What happened?'

'There was a fight. He had the gun in his hand. I didn't . . .' He couldn't finish.

'Is he dead?'

'Yes.'

'You just left him there?' She didn't sound angry, just stunned.

'I had to take care of you first. I should have called an ambulance, but I didn't want it to . . . we were there, but it was Eddie's fault.'

She was crying soundlessly.

'Tell me what to do,' he said. 'I'll do whatever you want me to do.'

Nadia closed her eyes.

'He left his suicide note on your phone, Nadia. He shot himself in the head on your voicemail. You thought he was dead.' She squeezed her eyes together. 'We tried to help. Now he is. Dead. I'm sorry.'

After a long while, as if trying it out, she said, 'We were never there.'

'I think that is the best way. Don't you?'

'Will you leave me alone now?'

'I don't think—'

'I need to be alone.'

He stood in the baby's room and listened to her crying through the wall.

259

Later the same night, after she woke up and he fetched her another glass of water, she seemed to have improved physically but lost something mentally. She was drained, sinking into this quicksand he had accumulated for her.

'Do you have a plan?' she said.

'I'm working on it.'

'Someone's going to find him, if they haven't already.'

'You said he lives alone,' Conrad said. 'Right?'

'How long has he . . .' She could not finish.

'A day and a half,' Conrad said. 'If they found him, they'd be here by now. We need to get our story straight.'

'Our story? Are we going to jail? Are they going to take my baby?'

'Hey, hey. Easy. I would never allow that.'

She was crying again, without even changing her expression. This frightened him more than if she had been sobbing.

'Nadia, we can do this. If you still want me, I will see it through to the end.'

'Your wife is pregnant. Don't act like a hero when all you want is to throw your life away, too.' She coughed. 'My parents are coming home in two days and then this shit is going to be the next local scandal. If you want to help me, it's time to make it real.'

'I'm trying,' he said. 'I will.'

'Maybe I'm being punished. Do you think I'm one of them, too? One of the women who runs away but keeps coming back?'

'Like the women in the photo?' he said.

'Like the women with nowhere else to go.'

'No.' But it had crossed his mind.

'Do you think if we stay—' she coughed '—it can be different this time?'

'Yes.'

'What about Eddie?'

'Eddie let you down. I will never let you down.'

He held her, and watched her cry until she fell asleep.

*   *   *

When he woke later he had no idea if it was the same night or the next night, but it was still very much night. The room was pitch-black. Nadia was sitting up in bed, staring at the wall. She was speaking to someone. Repeating something.

'. . . a young girl's heart', he heard her say.

Conrad turned on a lamp. 'What? Nadia?'

Nothing in her expression had changed, but her eyes were different. Flat. Dead. And when she spoke, her voice came out the same way, as if under someone or something else's influence. The voice was jilted, old and sore.

'Thread through a needle cannot mend a young girl's heart.'

30

Conrad moved around the bed to be in front of her, to see if she could see him. She stared right through him. She was flesh and bones—alive, but not aware.

261

'What does that mean, Nadia?'

'Thread through a needle cannot mend a young girl's heart.'

She had not blinked. Her eyes were watery, their pupils big as nickels.

'Nadia, can you hear me?'

She did not respond.

'What happened? Is there someone here in the house?'

Nothing.

'Is there something in the house?'

He moved from the bed to the chair, afraid to be close to her.

'Nadia, what thread through a needle? What's that?'

Her head rotated slowly, stiffly, her chin tucked and her eyes averted. It was not her voice that answered. Her words came awkwardly, her sentences strung out.

'Try take ohmma bay-bay way.'

'Who?' He went rigid in his chair. 'Who took all your baby away?'

'Man.'

'Man? What man?' He heard Roddy's voice in his head, the reference to 'the good doctor'. 'Do you mean the doctor? The doctor who lived here?'

'Was no docca no mine what he say.'

'Who was he?'

'First he take all-ma mothers and women runsaway. Then she growed up and he took the insides away. Then he bury'm others and took 'em behbee away.'

Conrad saw sketches of the house, the unsmiling women on the porch. His scalp began to crawl. He sat up straight and seriously considered bolting

262

from the room, the house. But he couldn't just leave her here.

'Who are you? Where's Nadia?'

'Runsaway.'

'Nadia ran away?'

'Nah-dee run . . . away.'

'I don't understand. Nadia, are you Nadia, or are you telling Nadia to run away?'

'All-ma.'

'All ma? All mothers? Are you someone's mother?'

'All-ma not runsaway. All-ma *stay*.'

Then he understood. Not all-ma. Alma. A name. Someone named Alma was speaking through Nadia. Where had he heard this before? Something from the past week. Then he knew. The woman in the room. She had been rocking her arms. *Ohhmma take care of behbee* . . .

Oh. Holy. Fuck. This was not right.

'You are Alma? Alma, what about Nadia?'

'Nah-dee not fit. Nah-dee betray.'

'What? Why—how did Nadia betray Alma?'

'All-mommas give a life . . . if she wan haff a life.'

'Why?'

'To haff a life she must gif a life. Life . . . circle begins and end on-on-on same ssss-sphere. In betwee the juuur-nee from one side t'other, circle provides. For we each owes a life.'

'No.' He did not like the sound of that, or any of it. She sounded like Greer Laski, like an idiot child. 'Nadia must stay. Alma *cannot* stay.'

'Once long time house full of womans and behbees. But long time now circle . . . circle of this houses belong only t'Alma.'

263

'This house belongs to me,' he said. 'And I don't want you to stay, Alma. I want Nadia to stay.' But he was too shaken to say this with any real force or conviction.

'Alma not runsaway.' Her lips were trembling, sneering. 'Alma stay.'

'Why?'

'Alma tur . . .'

'What?'

'Alma turn.'

'Alma turn for what?'

Alma—Nadia—looked up at him, her lips pulled back in a sickening and false grin. 'Docca no! Alma behbee no take away,' she said. 'Docca never never never taken Alma behbee away!'

Her eyes were black, murderous. Her hand lifted slowly from her side and hovered in the air between them. He leaned back. She reached out until her fingertips began to tickle his throat.

Conrad slapped her face. It had been building inside and then his hand just moved. Immediately Nadia and the thing inside her recoiled, started blinking and coughing, and then she was crying. Softly, then louder, then softly.

'Nadia? Nadia, wake up. Wake up, wake up—'

'Chessie behbee mine,' the girl croaked in Alma's voice. Then her voice changed through her next words, reverting to Nadia's softer tone. 'No one, no, I won't let them take my baby away.'

'I know, it's okay, Nadia, we're okay,' he said. Nadia was back, shivering all over, cold when he put his hands on her arms. Maybe it was a nightmare. Maybe she had been talking in her sleep. But he didn't believe that. He had an idea who Alma was. He'd seen her before.

Touched her . . .

He held her until her breathing slowed and she slumped over, going limp in his arms. He rested her back on the pillows. He was too stunned to think through their situation, and eventually he gave up the fight and fell asleep.

It was not restful or lasting.

*   *   *

'Conrad. Conrad, wake up!' She was hissing like an old woman.

'Uhn . . . hm.'

'Someone's here.'

'Uh-uh.' He had been so far down, where there are no dreams at all. He just wanted to sleep forever. 'Is jus' Steve . . . took care him.'

She shook him hard. 'Conrad! Someone was here.'

He came around again. 'At the door?'

'No.' Nadia clutched the skin over his ribs, pinching into him. 'She was here. Not sixty seconds ago. In the room. Standing at the foot of the bed.'

'Nadia, don't.' Now he was awake. He sat up and faced her in the dark and saw the whites of her eyes. She made a tiny whining sound, like Alice when she was waiting to be let out into the backyard. 'You were dreaming. I didn't hear anything.'

'No. Conrad, no.' He could feel the dry heat of her breath on his ear. 'Same as the one in the window. She was tall, with dark black hair. She was wearing black clothes and her skin was white. When she moved—oh, God. She just stood there staring at me. I could—oh, Jesus, I heard her neck cracking in the dark.'

Conrad swallowed. 'How long?'

'She was there when I opened my eyes. I've been frozen waiting for her to leave for almost an hour.'

'Did you see her leave?'

'Yes.'

'Did you hear her leave?'

'No.'

'If you didn't hear her . . . her footsteps . . . she's not real, is she?'

Nadia pointed to the foot of the bed. 'There.'

He could not see past the frame where their feet had piled up the blankets, kicking them off in the heat. He sat forward on his knees, one hand lingering on the girl as he focused on the shape. A low, guttural sound rose from the end of the bed, followed by two, then three faint *clicks* on the wood floor.

'No—' Conrad lunged forward. 'Leave us alone!'

Nadia turned the switch on the lamp and screamed.

The dark shape lunged up, then scrabbled back, growling. Conrad fell on to his stomach. Alice barked at the two of them, as startled as they were. Nadia scrambled out of bed and fell to the floor. Alice panicked and fled the room.

'Stop it!' Conrad said. 'It's just Alice.' The adrenaline washed away, leaving a tired anger behind. 'Fuck.'

'I can't take this.' Her knees were tucked into her chest, one leg sideways. Sitting in the corner, she appeared at that moment like an ugly, misbehaving child and he barely suppressed the urge to smack her again for scaring him.

'God damn it, Nadia.'

'I saw her.'

'You had a bad dream.' He forced himself to lower his voice, lest he raise Steve Bartholomew again. 'You thought you saw something, and you did. My dog, Alice, who is now scared shitless on top of being cut to hell. So please. Before the police decide to lock us both up.'

But Nadia was still shaking her head. 'No. There was a woman.'

Conrad stared at her, telling himself that there must be another explanation, even though he knew it was a lie.

'I'm sorry. Get back in bed. I need to check your bandages.'

'You don't believe me?'

'It doesn't matter—'

'Then what the fuck is that?' Her arm shot out, pointing.

'What? I don't—'

He walked to the doorway.

It was lying on the floor, center to the doorframe as if it had been delivered. Of course he recognized it; it had come from his kitchen. He picked up the knife. It was the long serrated one, the thin blade that came to an almost needle-like point made for cutting fish. Tied to the handle was a thin yellow ribbon laced through a scrap of yellow paper.

On the yellow paper, in a fine and femininely looped script, four words in black ink . . .

other mother must go

31

'It's your wife,' Nadia said. 'She came home. I need to leave.'

He was still holding the knife, reading the four words over and over. Jo's handwriting? He didn't think so, but it still made him feel sick just holding it. He set the knife on the dresser, wishing for it to disappear. Nadia had gotten to her feet and was bent over in pain. He knew that if she had the strength she would have bolted.

'Don't do that.' He rushed to her side and tried to maneuver her back into bed. 'Not in the middle of the night. Let's think about this.'

'I need to go home.' But she sat down, winced, and leaned back into the bank of pillows he was arranging for her.

'It's not Jo,' he said. 'Why would Jo do this?'

'What do you mean, why? Because she's trying to send us a message? Because she's crazy? How should I know, she's your wife!'

'No, no. Jo is not the kind of woman to play tricks. I'm not saying she doesn't have a temper. And, yes, if she saw us here, if she came home and found us . . . convalescing together, she would be upset. She would be very fucking upset.'

'Oh my God. Are you trying to make me lose my shit? This is so wrong. Please take me home.'

'I'm just saying, Jo wouldn't be creeping around at night, watching us. She would be screaming her head off. And the dogs. No way would she be able to get within half a block of the house without the dogs going wild. They haven't seen her in a month.

No. Uh-uh. It's not Jo. This is something else.'

Nadia gathered herself up, trying to maintain. 'When was the last time you talked to her?'

'Just yester—' It seemed like yesterday, but the last time they had actually spoken was at least three . . . no, at least four or five days ago, before the incident with the dogs and the mirrors.

'Jesus,' he said, rubbing his eyes. 'I can't believe this.'

'What?'

'I don't remember the last time I talked to my wife.'

'So, there you go. Michigan is like twelve hours by car and an hour by plane. She could have come home, maybe seen something strange and decided to wait and see. She could be watching us right now, Conrad!'

'Don't panic,' he said. 'You're going to hurt yourself.'

'Don't tell me what to do,' she said, hiccupping.

'Nadia, it's not Jo. Where would she be staying? The Dairyland Motel up the street? This isn't some murder mystery with stakeouts and the jealous wife. That's crazy.'

'Are you sure? Because it sort of feels like it.'

'I know her. Trust me.'

'Maybe you're not telling me everything.'

'Nadia, for all I know you put the knife there.'

'What? Why would I do that? How would I even—'

'You were talking in your sleep. Completely out of it.' He dared not tell her about the 'conversation' he had with Alma. For one, he was trying not to believe it had actually happened. For another, telling Nadia she had been invaded by a spirit that wanted her to 'give a life to have a life' would only confirm her worst nightmares and send her jumping out the window.

'So, what are you saying? You think I'm a total psycho now?'

'No. Just . . . maybe we don't know everything we're doing here.'

'How do I know you weren't the one who brought the knife back? And how would I know where you keep your knives, anyway?

Conrad frowned, not at all appreciating having the tables turned. 'You think I'm part of this? I'm trying to help you, not scare you away.' He grabbed the knife off the dresser. 'For all we know, Laski's wife's gone off the deep end and come back to scare both of us. Now, she was fucking nuts.'

'Mrs Laski is not a tall woman with black hair. Your wife is.'

He had no response for that. He headed for the door.

'Where are you going?'

'To search the house.'

'No way. You cannot leave me here.'

'Nadia, I specifically remember locking the doors, twice. If someone broke in, I'll know.'

'What if she didn't break in?' she said.

'What do you mean?'

'Just what I said. What if it's . . . her?'

He knew, but he didn't want the girl to believe it, too. 'I didn't see anyone in the library.'

She watched him. 'You're lying. You've seen her, too.'

'If it was her, then you don't have to worry.'

'Why not?'

'I have to say it now? Okay, because she's a ghost.'

'A ghost,' Nadia said.

'Sure, why not? And who cares, because what can a ghost do?'

'I don't know,' Nadia said. 'This one seems to have written a note and dropped a knife on the floor.'

She said this almost flippantly, but the notion rocked him. Alma had taken control of Nadia long enough to speak in her tongue. Could she have come back and sent the girl to fetch the knife? To write a note? Warning herself—Nadia, the other mother—to go away?

If they stayed another night, would Alma command Nadia to take her own life? Or his?

He rubbed his eyes, hard. 'I have to check the house.'

'You better come back soon.'

'I will. I promise, no one's going to hurt you.'

He moved around the stairs, through the library. 'Alice, Luther,' he called. 'Come on, doggies.'

The sound of their nails clicking on the wooden floor echoed softly up the butler stairs. He paused in the back hall, listening. Somewhere a door creaked. He thought that must have been Nadia, deciding she would be safer with the bedroom door closed.

*   *   *

All three doors were locked.

The dogs were on the couch. Alice raised her head when he entered the room, giving him that *Are you going to feed me now?* look. Luther yawned

271

and stretched his back, producing a disturbingly human-sounding fart. If they were still in the living room, what was with the clicking? Had they walked into the kitchen, then gone back to the couch?

He left the dogs and set the knife down on the kitchen table, glancing at the note one last time. He went to the fridge and poured a tall glass of iced tea, letting it drip down the hollow of his throat while he stood over the sink.

The knife was just about the worst kind of unsettling. He did not believe Jo had gone that far off the rails. But another part of him, the part that had read enough detective novels to question motive, wondered if it wasn't possible. The enraged wife thing was an obvious angle. The problem was, it didn't feel like Jo.

What if it was you?

What if you've lost your mind for this girl and the stress and killing that kid and all the loneliness has finally driven you to the point where you know not what you do in your sleep? How about that, 'Rad?

This possibility bit into him like a viper, poisoning all confidence that he was doing the right thing by trying to manage the situation alone.

What have I done? What am I about to do?

No, you wouldn't be standing here thinking about it if you were that far gone.

But you do need help. Quit fucking around and call someone.

He needed to talk to Jo. He picked up the phone and tried to develop an explanation, a cover story to hide the panic.

Just tell her—

'Aw, shit.' He sat down hard on one of the chairs

at the two-top. All at once he was out of gas. As long as he covered his tracks, there would be no relief. The whole secrecy routine was eating his guts. He needed to end this before someone else got hurt.

He made himself the same promise all over again. If she answered, he would tell her everything. Ask for her help. Be honest. Let her panic and scream at him if that's what it took, but he would come clean.

'You put your fate in her hands and cut Nadia loose and start over. With or without Jo, you start over like a man.'

He dialed before he could change his mind. The line buzzed. Four, five times. Conrad's knee did a little jig and he tried to smother it with his free hand. Seven, eight. The oven clock read 2.12 a.m.

A throat rattled wetly. 'Har-ugh. Uh-huh?' The guy sounded like he'd been drinking Jack and cokes all night.

'Ah,' Conrad searched for the words. Was it the same guy as before? That voice had been softer. It didn't seem like the same guy, but . . .

'Hello?' the guy said forcefully, waking up.

'I'm sorry,' Conrad said. 'I'm looking for my wife.'

'What?'

'My wife. Joanna Harrison.'

'Nope.'

'What do you mean, "nope"? She's not there?'

'Nope.'

'Where is she?'

'Why would I care?'

'This is room three-four-one-eight?'

'I guess so.'

'Who are you?'

'I'm tired,' the guy said. 'Look. I just moved in. Your wife was, what, here on training?'

'Yes. This is her room.'

'Not any more.'

'Did you know her? You one of her friends? Classmates?'

'Don't think so. They told me some woman from the last class left for a condition. Medical purposes, whatever.'

'Medical purposes? What the fuck does that mean?'

'I don't know.'

'She's gone? She left training?'

'Look, I didn't get a name. I just started the new round of classes. And I have to be up in three hours, so good luck, ace.'

The phone sounded like the guy was trying to bury it under the mattress.

'Wait!' Conrad said.

'Yeah?'

'You see her leave? She leave anything behind? Come on, I'm her husband. Help me out here.'

'They just said this woman had to leave training early. It happens.'

'Who said that? What's this medical shit?'

'Davidson, the training instructor. There's a few of them, so I don't know if she was in the same group. Hey, it could have been a rumor. I don't know. I asked if she got fired or couldn't take the pressure or what. They said no, she had a medical thing. Hey, you think they were just saying that? You get that with a lot of these sales things. Fucking corporate. I really don't wanna do eight weeks if the program is shit. I'm here to make

274

money, you know what I'm saying.'

It wasn't really a question, and Conrad wasn't really paying attention. He was too busy imagining bad things. Jo in a hospital somewhere, for Christ knows what. Or she's on her way home. Or already here. Watching.

'Fuck. Oh, fuck.'

'Hey, take it easy, bro. You want me to call someone, have the company get in touch with you?'

'Yeah, you think?' Conrad hung up.

He dialed her cell. Her voice crisp and professional, asking him to leave a message.

'Jo? Sweetie? It's me. Where are you? I'm sorry I yelled. Why won't you pick up? Some guy answered in your room. Please, please call me as soon as you get this. I'll keep trying. Why haven't you called me back? I love you.'

He clicked off and lunged out of his chair to check the windows—

He never made it.

Before he had taken two steps, he noticed that the door to the basement was ajar, a faint glow emanating from below. He knew damn well he had closed the door and turned off the overhead shop lights after finding Luther down there.

'Conrad!' Nadia said, startling him from upstairs. 'Who are you talking to?'

'No one. Stay there. I'll be right up!'

He grabbed a flashlight from the junk drawer and tromped down the stairs. By the time he remembered this was the sort of expedition you'd want to take with two dogs by your side, it was too late.

In the basement he found what he was looking

for all along.

*   *   *

The air was moist with the scents of lime and mold. The basement was something between a crawlspace and a real basement. And yet there were signs the space had not been written off as uninhabitable. If one used one's imagination, as Conrad did now, wagging the flashlight around, one could see where a man (doctor) with a load of guests (patients) might find the cooler, peaceful depths of the house suitable for short periods of recuperation (torture).

It might have been a place to heal.

Or a temporary morgue.

The non-perimeter walls were covered with cheap walnut paneling, most of it bulging with moisture and splitting at the seams. The carpet was newer, but the cement beneath it might have been easier to clean, to disinfect. And what of this, the trough-like groove in the cement floor running out of the south-east room into the center drain? Was that routine flood protection, a gutter for water from a burst pipe or heavy rain? Or was it something else? Like, say, a place to wash the really bad ones down?

Conrad pulled the chain on the bulb hanging in the basement's main 'room', and turned three hundred and sixty-five degrees, wiping cobwebs real and imagined from his face as he went.

He tried the shop first. This room had the newer electrics and a wall switch and the fluorescent bulbs were on. He felt better having the extra light behind him while he worked up the

276

courage to check the last room, the place where he'd found Luther sliced up and cowering. The shop was empty.

He aimed the flashlight at the boiler room, swinging it in wide arcs over the stone walls and the sloping dirt mound under his front porch. The flashlight's beam narrowed with each step, leaving more darkness in its wake. One of those dull *whumping* boiler noises would have been enough to send him running in a blind panic, but all was quiet.

Had the dog been interested in this spot on the floor, or the wall? Enough to cut himself to ribbons trying to get in? Conrad looked for blood or teeth marks—anything that would confirm a dog's persistent interest. The image of Luther gnashing his teeth on solid rock conjured the same kind of eerie screech you hear when the class asshole rakes his fingernails across the chalkboard, and Conrad cringed, stepping away.

The thought wasn't out of his head for two seconds when he heard another sound, equally electrifying.

'*Aaayyy-ay-ay-aaaaack!*' Just as before, the baby's cry wormed its way into his head and fried his nerves. It paused, hitching in fits and starts, and then rose again in that same choking, raspy cry. The shop lights went out, leaving him with only the flashlight to illuminate his way.

Oh Baby, oh Baby, what the fuck is happening in this place?

It was an awful sound, but something in the urgency took hold of him and this time he heard it for what it had been all along—a cry for help.

'Okay, okay, it's okay,' he babbled, moving out

277

of the corner. 'You want help? Okay, are you hungry? Are you hurt?'

His hand shot out and flipped the switch. The lights flickered once and fell dark. In this half-second that lit the room like a distant lightning flash and left retinal echoes even as the room was plunged back into pitch-blackness, he saw a shape darting from the corner of his eye. He tried to track its movement, but it was gone. Two steps later his kneecap rammed into one of the workbench's legs and he bit down on his lip to keep from shouting.

The anger came back with the pain and he brought the flashlight up quickly. But now the infant's wail had been muted, perhaps by his clumsy and clattering response. His breath became ragged, the beam moving in erratic swaths before it slowed and fell at last on the swaddled bundle resting on the workbench. A tremor ran the length of the beam even as it shrank, the diameter of its spotlight closing down until it was shining from less than eighteen inches above this tiny package. He held the beam still and everything under its cone became the world.

He was aware that something larger than his own fear was at work here, and that he was powerless to stop himself, forced to watch the rest happen as if to someone else.

Under the beam a dirty hand appeared and patted the soft fabric grayed with the indifferent passage of time. The beam swept from one end to the other until it found an opening and the dirty hand peeled back the layers with the grace of a florist stripping petals from a dried rose. With nothing left to stop its progress, the beam shone

278

deeper, revealing the face of a doll burnished and painted with all the color and detail of a proud toy-maker whose principal calling is to animate what can never be. All the maker's love was evident in the way the thin strands of hair had been combed and made glossy over the tiny painted brows and suggestion of a nose. The beam stilled over this creation and for a lingering moment the illusion achieved its goal; its beholder regarded the doll with some reluctant swell of his heart and returned the smile. And then his heart broke. The only hope for a lasting art vanished as all life's likeness fell away, revealing black holes where once were eyes, tiny blackened nubs of teeth, and the decaying, bird-like ribs, spine and pelvis of a newborn.

32

If it was a sin to keep a woman not his wife in the marriage bed, then it was also a sin to leave the child in that dark forgotten corner of the basement.

As he climbed the stairs with the bundle in his arms, that which weighed no more than the balsa model airplanes he and Dad had labored over on those endless summer nights of which you can never grasp the fleeting nature until you have grown sad beyond your years, he thought of death. Not only how it seemed to prefer the young and unprotected, but how you can see it every day all around you and never understand it until you are holding it in your arms.

How death was final, yes. But also how something lived on, trying to communicate with the living. How, too, it was all the sickening secrets revealing themselves, finding depths you did not know you possessed, giving birth to some new you both loathed and welcomed.

Someone wanted him to know her secret. In delivering hers, she had forced his own to the surface. He had been chosen to share it because she knew, somehow, that her secret was safe with him. That he would understand. That she might rouse his empathy to an act of faith.

He placed the bundle the only respectful place he knew, a place it would be safe until the rest of it had played out. Setting the swaddling on the natural fiber pad inside the crib, he pulled the blanket over the older, rotted cloth. He would return when she had made clear the rest of her wishes.

He left the safari lamp on, fearing he would not again be able to make the approach in the dark, and shut the door.

He had to deal with Nadia first. Something here was testing them. Something had brought them together, and he would need her to go all the way with him. Their survival required a different confession.

He went to her and rested his tired body next to hers on the bed.

'Did you see anything?' she said, breaking the ringing silence in his ears.

He nodded.

'Was someone here?'

'Someone was here,' he said, closing his eyes. 'We don't have much time.'

'Conrad. I want to go home.'

'I know.'

'Can we go now? Why can't we go now?'

'Listen,' he said, inching close to her on the bed, taking one of her dry hands in his. 'I have never told anyone what I am about to tell you. I think you need to see how we got here. Me to this house. You in this room, with me.'

If she could see his face, she would not have been able to stay, the pain be damned. He was grinning like a child fascinated by some enormous and just-grasped scheme: the sound of his mother's car arriving in the driveway at midnight, the orbit of the planets, conception at the cellular level.

'What happened?'

He leaned over and kissed the exposed white space just below the wound.

'Conrad?'

'Her name was Holly. You remind me of her. Sometimes, when you are with me, it's like she never went away, Nadia. And that's strange, I guess, but it's beautiful, too.'

His heart filled with something beyond blood as he remembered her face, her eyes full of hope and trust.

'No one knows what we did, Holly and me. No one knows anything about it.'

Nadia's grip tightened around his fingers. 'Did you hurt her?'

'What we did was, we made a baby.'

HOLLY

That night in the house we had entered as children and left as something else; we exchanged much more than cells and fluids and the physical particles that transmit. We created a third entity that depended on the two of us, a spirit that was made of the part of myself I had willingly abandoned inside her, and she in me. Having given this, we were never whole again, together or apart. This is something else I say without the benefit of sarcasm. There are days when I wish we had died there before it ended, but end it did.

Eventually we dressed, packed up the candles, remade the bed and cleaned our dinner plates. We folded our single blue sheet and took it with us out the door, locking everything up the way we had found it. The sheet was Holly's idea, after I suggested we wash it.

'No,' she said with territorial authority. 'They can't have this one. This one we keep.'

Later we would refer to it as 'our night' or 'the night' but we never discussed what had passed between us.

We both knew she was pregnant.

We never talked about what we had wished for. The words, the promises, the vows. They were there. But we could not square them with the rest of our seventeen-year-old lives. The secret we carried was about to blow up and we had no way of knowing how much destruction it would leave behind. We wanted to prepare, I think, but we

282

didn't know how or where to begin.

Like everything else that had been our secret—the long walks at night, the shoplifting, the drugs, the sleepovers—we wanted the conception of our child to remain ours and ours alone. To tell our parents, our friends, would somehow diminish it.

Of course we were terrified.

Looking back, I still believe that if some twist of fate had dropped a million dollars in our laps, killed off our parents or in some other catastrophic way destroyed the rest of the world for us, we would have made it. We would have emerged stunned but ultimately glad, free to live out the secret life we had made together.

How did it finally end?

I thought that would be the hard part. But now that the rest has been told I find that everything that came before was the pain. Seeing myself with her has always been the hard part. The end is easy. The end, unlike Holly and the five years I knew her and loved her, is not alive. The end is easy because it has no life, no soul. It is easy to tell because it is death.

When Holly's mother found out her daughter was pregnant and that we wanted to have the baby and make a go of the life we had imagined together, she was almost freakishly supportive. But there was the other half. Holly begged her mother not to, but eventually Mrs Bauerman had to tell Mr Bauerman.

Mr Bauerman had more money and therefore more power, and he did not take it well. He sent Holly away.

To a private school? A town? Another country?

I searched for two years. When I would not stay

283

away from her father's house, he had me arrested. I wrote letters, talked with lawyers and worked on Mrs Bauerman until I was a weeping, vengeful menace that even she had to turn her back on. The family moved to be with her, or so her friends told me.

Eventually my mother wore me down. She said she would support me as long as it took, but I had to let go.

The reason I quit was pretty simple, actually.

I realized, reading some book or another at three in the morning on my mother's threadbare sofa, that if Holly really wanted to see me, she would have found a way to write or call. She had done neither. I knew that whatever she had gone through to get to the point where she didn't want to see me or talk to me had also killed her. Everything between us had been real. But whatever forces her father had marshaled, whatever people or doctors or hospitals he brought in to dissolve her wishes and render her speechless, whatever world she lived in now, well, they were stronger.

I was just a kid. I tried to be a man, but in the end I was just a kid.

You think of them living somewhere with some other guy. Maybe he is an executive, or owns his own company. You see them standing on a porch, holding hands. Your love is now a woman and your unborn child is now a son. He's ten. He rides a skateboard. He needs a haircut. You think you will be upset by this, but you are wrong. Seeing this would make you happy, because then you would know.

I never knew where she went, or if she kept my

284

child. That is the sucking black hole of it. I never knew. I let go, but you never let go.

I moved, worked, tried college a few times, and then my mother died. I never saw my father, but someone told me later that he had been there, at her funeral. He went back to his life and the last time I saw him he was burned and dying of a stroke in Chicago.

He was a coward. He failed. He ran away. I never ran away. I won't ever run away. Because if the world can take my child and my family, is it not possible that same world can deliver me another?

This is why I chose this house. This is why I am here. Now I have found you, Nadia. I have been dying since that night. But I'm here to take care of you.

This is a beginning.

I understand why you are crying, but you should stop that now, Nadia. And trying to pull away. Now that you know my story, you must understand why I will never, never let you leave.

33

He waited in the silent room for her response, a judgment. Now that it had been told, a stab of regret went through him. What had he done? What must she think of him now? Telling her had been like going back there with Holly, a little bit. Okay, a lot. He could not really be sure what he had said and what he had seen only in his head. When another minute of silence passed, he suspected she had fallen asleep. Then a violent, full-body twitch seemed to confirm this, but no. She was awake. Whatever she'd heard, she'd heard enough.

'Conrad, I'm sorry.'

'What for?'

'For you.' Her voice had changed yet again. Or maybe he had been hearing Holly's high voice and forgotten Nadia's flatter tone. 'But I don't think we should do this. I want . . . I need to talk to my mom.' She hitched a few times. He could hear the tears running down her cheeks, patting the pillow.

He coughed. 'Aren't we a little past parents now?'

'We can talk to them. They're going to find out, anyway.' She paused, and he let his silence tell her what he thought about that idea. 'I'm hurt. Maybe when things calm down—'

'The baby is home, where he should be. And as long as we take care of the baby we'll be safe.'

'But—'

'We need to make amends and do it right this time, Nadia. There is no other way.'

He counted seventeen heartbeats before she said, 'What did you find downstairs?'

'We're being tested. But we're going to be good now.'

'Tell me. I know you saw something. It's making you confused.'

He grabbed her hand and squeezed. 'We're healing. This is a new life between us. This life. And this life between us.' He rested his other hand at the top of her belly to see that she understood. She stared at him, eyes glassy. 'I just want to be a good father. Will you let me?'

She rolled over on her side, her back to him.

He slid under the blanket and pressed against her. His left arm fell over her hip, his fingers spread in a fan, the palm resting on her soft belly above the wound. She tensed.

'I'll take care of you,' he said.

Her breathing slowed.

'You can choose,' he whispered in her ear. 'Who is the father of your child.'

She did not answer and he had to fight the sleep pulling him down.

'Tell me.'

'You.'

Later, early in the morning, Conrad dreamed of three gray women cloaked in black. They bowed their heads when they entered the room, following orders from another, darker presence that lorded over the proceedings. In the dream he felt the bed shift as the *zeks* carried her away to a place he was not allowed. He tried to scream but his muscles were frozen by her cool shape enveloping and pressing him to the bed until it was safe to let go.

When he woke just past noon the room was bright and Nadia was gone.

34

'When was the last time you spoke to her?' Gail Grum was placing souvenir bottles of barbecue sauce on the table in a neat little row, already sensing the need to restore order.

He made a face of recollection, and his face was convincing, because he did not know. Conrad had spent yesterday—the long day that followed the morning Nadia had vanished—catching up on chores, cleaning the gutters he had neglected for the past ten days. He had called Jo half a dozen times, but still she was not answering. He thought of calling the police, but that would open a line of questions he was not prepared to answer. Having Nadia or Jo by his side would give him someone to lean on when the questions came down—inviting more on his own was unthinkable. He waited for the phone to ring all night, and he could not remember sleeping. He had been frantically washing dishes and sweeping the floor when he realized the sun was rising. He had seen their car arrive just after noon, and went to greet them with the news.

Now, sitting in the kitchen with Gail while Big John unpacked the car, Conrad was not as nervous as he had imagined he would be. He was concerned, even frightened. But he had no answers, and acted as such.

'Last time I spoke with her? Hard to say, Gail. I think . . . today's Wednesday?'

'It's Friday, Conrad. Are you all right? You look like hell.'

Did she suspect him of something? Or was this just part of the deal when you've come home to find your daughter missing?

'Oh, I guess I'm not, Gail. I meant to call, but I didn't want to worry you.' Gail tensed. 'It's Jo. She's left the training grounds. They don't know where she is. A man mentioned health issues.'

'Jesus!' Gail put one shaky hand to her cheek. 'She's missing?'

'She could be home any day now. Or not. We, uhm, we've been fighting.'

288

'Have you called someone? Friends? Family?'

'I appreciate your concern, Gail. But let me worry about that. I don't want to burden you two on top of this other thing.'

'Other thing?'

'Nadia. I didn't really think she's missing, you know. I mean, she was still talking to Eddie. I heard her on the phone a few times. She didn't share her plans with me.'

'Nadia doesn't make plans. That's the whole problem.'

'She's a smart kid, though. Tough. We had some nice conversations.'

Gail frowned. 'Conrad. I'm sorry. I'm still a little lagged from the trip. But is there something you're not telling me?'

'What do you mean?'

'Did she go to a friend's and ask you not to tell us? I understand—I encouraged her to talk to you, in fact. But it's not like her not to call or leave a note, even when we're fighting.'

'As I said, I was a bit wrapped up in my own problems. But that's not the whole truth, Gail. Nadia told me she was planning on running away. She asked me to drive her to the airport.'

'Running—the airport!' Gail had forgotten about the barbecue sauce.

'I know, hold on. I talked her out of it at the time. But she said she wanted to go to Seattle.'

'Who does she know in Seattle?'

'I was going to ask you. I thought maybe you had family there.'

Gail dropped into a chair at the kitchen table and dropped her face into her hands. 'Our family. Is in *Wisconsin*!'

289

'What's wrong?'

Conrad jumped at the father's voice. Big John Grum was standing at the kitchen's entrance.

'Nadia's run away again,' Gail said, bursting into tears. 'Welcome home.'

'I'm sorry.' Conrad placed the check for four hundred dollars on the table. 'I didn't do enough to deserve this. Let me know if I can help.'

Gail was still staring at the check when Big John patted Conrad on the back and walked him out.

* * *

He was headed for the grocery store with visions of iced tea waterfalls in his head when a new thought nearly drove him off the road.

There is a dead baby in my house.

Inside, he ran past the dogs, up the stairs and into the guest room. Sickened by the thought of the lifeless, skeletal form—and by the spell that had caused him to leave it there—he flung the door open and latched on to the rails of the newly assembled crib.

The crib was empty.

He forgot about going to the store, about food, about sustaining the illusion of normalcy. He simply walked down the stairs and fell on to the couch. His heart beat faster and harder. He considered the angles, finding no solace. Either he was imagining things or the house was haunted— and those could be two extensions of the same phenomenon. Whether the house contained spirits, other environmental conditions acting upon his perceptions, or his mind was simply playing tricks on him was at this point a discussion

290

for academics. People who were not involved. They boiled down to the same thing—he could no longer trust his eyes, ears or thoughts. Not while under this roof.

Still, he tried. The answer was in here somewhere. He was missing something, something vital. A ghost was something perceived. He needed evidence.

Time was running out. He could run. Just put the dogs in the car and drive away. Withdraw his inheritance and disappear to Canada. Would she follow him to a cabin in the woods? Would she emerge from his nightmares under any roof, not just this one?

No, he had to stay because he had to know. And because one of them would need a father.

If the tiny skeleton had been real (as real as the knife, the note) and his house was not haunted, then someone had been here. Someone could be here still, alive. Fucking with him. Jo? Whoever did this had to be insane, a broken soul gone way, way over to the other side of everyday criminal behavior. The sounds, the visions of the woman in the house, the absolute inhumanity required to exhume and deliver a dead child into another man's home? That wasn't Jo. He did not believe his wife insane.

I got news for you, kid, Leon Laski had said. *A haunting is just history roused from her sleep. Any house can be haunted, even a new one. Know why? Because what makes 'em haunted ain't just in the walls and the floors and the dark rooms at night. It's in us. All the pity and rage and sadness and hot blood we carry around. The house might be where it lives, but the human heart is the key. We run the risk of letting the fair maiden out for one more dance every time we hang our hat.*

So it's me? You think I'm nuts? Conrad had responded.

I didn't say that. I said what makes 'em haunted ain't just in the walls. Which led him back where he started. As much as he wanted to, he no longer understood his own motivations, and that was a circular thought best left unexamined.

Listen to the woman of the house. Be a man, but keep your pecker in your pocket unless you're planning on putting it to righteous use. And listen to the woman of the house.

Maybe he was losing his mind. And maybe before losing his mind the void in his marriage and the lust in his heart had set the rest of it in motion. He'd been caught trying to put his pecker to use. The events of the past few weeks had been a lot of things, but none of them were righteous.

Suppose Laski's fair maiden *was* real. Had he meant the woman of this house? Alma? Was he to stay and learn what she wanted? She had obviously come back for her child, or a child. Was he to remain and do her bidding, to deliver her another? Was that righteous?

Or had Laski been selling a simpler wisdom, some marriage survival tip about deferring to the wife? Maybe in this version Jo was the fair maiden. Mrs Laski had spoken of this blessed house, and how God always provided her with more children—despite their lost ones. Was Leon Laski blind to the rest? Or did he just know the secret to keeping the ghosts at bay? Refrain from original sin and do right by your creator, except when your wife starts cooing for another child to keep her

292

warm on those cold winter nights?

Maybe the fair maiden was both. Maybe Jo and Alma were two sides of the same coin. Maybe Alma was using Jo to show him a version of herself he would recognize, and one day embrace.

He was willing to be righteous, to embrace the woman of the house.

But first she had to come back.

He waited for all of the women to come back, but mostly he waited for her.

*   *   *

He moved to the bedroom, then the library. This was the place he had first seen her. This was the nexus of the house, the seat of her longing.

He sat. He waited through the evening and into the night.

His back ached. His legs were stiff. He was dizzy from lack of food. He wanted a glass of iced tea, it seemed, more than he had ever wanted anything in his life. But he dared not go for it. That would require a trip to the kitchen, and anything could happen while he was away. She might show herself.

Worse, despite his thirst, he needed to take a piss. As soon as the thought was there, it would not go away. He needed to go now.

He glanced at the window where her reflection had been, and stole away from the library. It was only a few short steps to the bathroom, and he flicked the light on as he entered. He sighed over the bowl, and flushed. He turned back to the door, but the window facing the backyard caught his eye, and he stopped.

How many nights had it been since he'd seen his

fair maiden out back, walking that path to the garden? The night he'd run outside, and wound up on Nadia's porch? He could not remember, but by the time he stopped trying he was already there, at the window, looking out. He cupped his hands around his eyes, but the yard was dark and he couldn't see with the glare from the light. He backed up and flicked the switch off, then moved back to the window.

His nose touched the cool glass. He squinted.

After what could have been no more than thirty seconds, his eyes adjusted to the night and he began to make out shapes. The walnut tree. The bushy pines off to the left. The slope of grass riding down like an ocean swell. The garage, with only the faint red glow. His snakes! Christ—he hadn't checked the Boelen's or the eggs for days now. But he could not go out there tonight. He needed to be here for her. First thing tomorrow, then. His eyes walked back up the path and were almost to the deck directly below when he saw movement. A shape.

It was tall, rigid, halfway down the path. His eyes dilated. It leaned forward, pitching itself at an odd angle as a young tree bows to the wind. It took a step. Then another. It was moving slowly, almost plodding along, leaning forward the way a mule goes strapped to the plow in deep soil.

She was dragging something on the ground.

A burst of clicking ratcheted up the stairs and Conrad whirled away from the window, his top teeth biting over his bottom lip, drawing blood.

Alice and Luther were standing on the carpeted landing, staring at him.

'Jesus Christ,' he said, exhaling. They were

294

hungry. They had heard him flush and decided he was awake. 'God damned dogs.'

He turned back to the window, but after a full minute of squinting and standing on his toes to peer down, there was no sign it. Of her.

I was imagining it.

He returned to the library and sat. The dogs stepped around him, whining and sniffing for food. He patted them reassuringly and sat down.

'Soon. Soon.'

Scenting the foul spirit he carried, they gave him one last confused look and returned to the kitchen. He heard them scratching at the door, knocking open cabinets for something to satisfy their empty bellies, and his own growled in sympathy. After several minutes, they *click-click-clicked* their way back to the living room to lie in waiting on the couch. His eyelids grew heavy and he fought to stay awake.

He drifted off and fell to his side, curled fetal on the floor. Hours—or perhaps just very long minutes—passed. He doze-dreamed of the dogs feeding. Heard their frenzy as the bag was ripped. The tinkling of the kibbles spilling, impossibly, into their bowls. Were they feeding, or was someone feeding them? There was a long silence. He lost track once more, and slept on.

It was still dark when he woke again, this time to the sound of water running. He listened with his eyes closed, trying to trace the flow through the pipes, to understand from where the water was flowing, and to what end. The flow stopped. The sound of dripping—*plop plop plop*—continued for a few seconds and then ceased. The woman was crying. Soft sobs that ebbed and flowed over the

295

course of minutes that stretched on and on. Definitely not the child this time. This was a mother grieving as only a mother can.

She was in another room. She had come for him, and she wanted him to come to her, to find her. She wanted him to understand.

In the hot night a controlled panic entered his bloodstream, propelling him to his feet. His legs were throbbing, and he grabbed a bookshelf to steady himself. The blood fell down and he almost blacked out.

Water. She was in the bathroom, then. He walked out of the library, into the rear hall toward the bathroom. His feet shuffled on the carpeted landing, swishing.

A dim glow was visible under the bathroom door, which was open a hand's width. Hadn't he left it wide open only hours before? He went to it and pressed his palm to the old wood. He pushed the door open.

The woman in the tub was sitting upright, hunched over. Her long black hair draped in strings over her shoulders and breasts, on to her knees. She was not moving. Her hands and arms were dirty and he saw the maroon crusts around the shores of her fingernails. She was no longer crying, and he saw no intake of breath.

The bath was shallow, its water a pink cloud.

She lifted her head and stared at him.

Her eyes were also black and deeply set in a pale countenance. The mouth appeared as a seam, the scar above running from her top lip to her thin nose, then opened, revealing small teeth. She was dreadfully beautiful. The eyebrows were thicker, grown nearly together and her eyes were devoid of color or emotion. He could feel her weight, her bone structure, her hardened flesh in his mind as surely as if he were holding her in his arms.

His words were hushed. 'What do you want?'

'There's no one here. It's just me.' Her voice was raw. 'There's no one here.'

He moved closer, weightless with fear. He knelt beside her, looked into her eyes, the dark circles around them. Her metallic scent enveloped him.

'What have you done?'

Her eyes were full of death. This lifeless creature could not be his wife.

'Our baby is dead. I'm waiting for it to come out.'

35

But of course it was Jo. At last she had returned.

He waited in the bedroom for her to finish her . . . bath. He sat on the bed and tried to figure when, exactly, she had come home. At first he had assumed she arrived an hour or so ago, come in, fed the dogs, then gone straight to the tub. But that just didn't feel right.

The bath drained and the shower started. The dogs waited for their mistress outside the door, ignoring him as she rinsed and scrubbed and rinsed. He could hear her sobs through the spray. He had never seen her this upset. He knew he was responsible for half of it.

'Where were you?' she had asked in the tub, in that dead voice, staring at him with colossal disappointment.

'The house. The house is haunted,' he said.

She blinked at him. 'Get out.'

He stared at her hands. The dried blood under her nails. 'I don't understand what—'

'Leave me alone.'

He left her, shaken by the change in her eyes, her body.

He was sitting on the bed trying to understand what was so different when he felt rather than heard her return. He stood and turned around. She was standing in the doorway, staring at him with that same faraway look on her face.

'Oh, Jo, Baby,' he said. He walked up and tried to hug her, but she jolted at his touch and blinked furiously.

'I've been in hell all week,' she said, moving away. He saw the bulge of the pad in her panties just before she drew her pajamas up to her waist and let the elastic snap. She pulled back the covers. She hesitated, smelling the sheets.

'I'm sorry. I let the dogs sleep with me. Haven't changed the bedding since you left.'

He stood there useless as she stripped the bed and went to the linen closet. While she was away, he replayed that answer in his head—*I've been in hell all week*. Did that mean she had started to miscarry a week ago? Did it really take that long? Or by 'hell' did she mean her general state of mind while not being able to reach her husband? Something about the timing felt wrong.

It's your wife, Nadia had said. *She came home. I need to leave.*

Was it possible Jo had been here?

No. Not for three days. He'd searched the house.

But one day earlier? He'd seen someone in the yard.

Jo came back carrying fresh sheets and Conrad studied her. Something more was off. She was no longer wounded, just tired.

'What?' she looked confused, suspicious.

'Are you sure we shouldn't be at the hospital right now?'

'I've been to the hospital.' She moved around him, tucking everything in. 'You would have known that if you'd answered the phone.'

'I was worried about you. I wanted to help—'

'Help? You're in no shape to help anyone.'

'But tell me again. When did you come home?'

'After I left the hospital.'

'When did you fly home? Did you rent a car?'

'I . . .' Her eyes glazed over. She thought about it too long. 'When I left the hospital.'

Conrad's scalp began to crawl. *She's talking like a goddamned robot again.*

'What did the doctor say?'

When he said 'doctor' she flinched, and not subtly. He took a step toward the bed.

'Jo? What did the doctor say?'

She flinched again. She stared at him, unsmiling.

'He wasn't much of a docca,' she said.

'A what? Did you say—'

Jo blinked, rubbed her eyes. 'Don't come to bed until you're clean.' She looked away, then abruptly crawled into bed and turned off the lamp.

Conrad could not bring himself to stand there looking at her in the dark.

But there are few states of mind a hot shower cannot improve, and as the water washed away his

299

stale sweat and he dug into his scalp to clean under his fingernails, a frisson passed from his stomach to his toes, forcing a comical sigh from his mouth. She had been through a miscarriage. She was bound to be a little off kilter. What was important was she was home. There would be a talk. Perhaps a reckoning. She had been through something awful. Like Nadia. But now Nadia was gone and this was better. It was proper.

But what about the baby? Was it really gone?

He returned to the bedroom and watched her sleeping, thinking of the first night they had finished unpacking. How he'd been so content, so confident their new life together had finally begun. What if the past six weeks were just an interlude? What if this was the real beginning?

He sank into the clean sheets, offering a prayer as he slipped into darkness.

Please don't take her, too.

*   *   *

His first thought upon waking was, *Mother's home*.

No. Mother was long gone, and father, too. Jo. Jo was home.

But not in bed. The smell of frying bacon permeated the entire upper floor, with coffee underneath.

It was after eleven. He could not remember his last meal. His stomach growled as he pulled his shorts over his underwear. It would be horrible at first, but they would talk through it. They would talk and talk until the air was clear between them and then they would discuss the next steps. Maybe he would look for a job. She could stay home and

300

heal. They could try again. He brushed and rinsed his mouth, dug a tee shirt out of the dryer. He slipped into his brick-red sandals (the ones he would never be able to wear again because they reminded him of the blood) and trotted down the servants' stairs to join her in the kitchen.

The bacon was black and smoking in the pan. The kitchen smelled like death and his stomach clenched.

'Jo?' He kept his voice at a normal pitch and busied himself by shutting off the stove and wiping up the grease spatters all around the pan. She liked her bacon crispy, but this was pushing it. 'Jo? Where are you, Baby?'

Predictably, the dogs came running in. He dropped some of the charred stuff into their radar range and they snatched it out the air and swallowed without chewing. He looked out the window over the sink. She wasn't in the backyard. He saw the garage. What had he seen last night, from the bathroom window? A shadow? A tree bowing to the wind? After finding Jo in the tub, it seemed insignificant. Luther sprang from the floor and shoved Conrad in the back.

'Where is she, huh? Where's Mommy?' he said, throwing the dogs more shriveled black carbon. He tossed the pan into the bin. He unhooked the trash bag and carried it to the front door and stopped, the bag swinging in his hand.

He glanced out the front window. Jo was standing next to the mailbox. Talking to Steve Bartholomew, good ol' Steve-O. Well well. She stood stiffly with her arms crossed over her chest, hair pulled back. Tee shirt, pink sweat pants, no shoes. Like she went out for the mail and got

301

waylaid by the curious neighbor. The bacon had been burning; she had been out there longer than she had expected.

Steve-O was doing all the talking and Jo was just staring at him, looking as stiff and tired as she had before bed. Steve-O looked grave, but that might not mean anything. He always looked pissed off unless he was guffawing at his own jokes and pouring wine down his throat. *Maybe she's just tired. Doesn't mean Steve-O's giving her a minute-by-minute surveillance report.* Steve jerked a thumb toward the Grum house.

Conrad's heart stopped and then beat double-time, sending a branch of pain into his shoulder. Gail Grum was with them, standing to Steve-O's right and slightly behind him. The skin around her eyes was visibly red from twenty-five feet away.

'Here we go.' The trash bag was slippery in his palm, the plastic sliding through his fingers as he yanked the door open and stepped out.

All three turned to look at him.

'Morning,' he said, pacing off the path from the porch to the trash cans on the side of the house.

'Conrad,' Steve said.

'Morning?' Gail said, looking sharply at Jo.

His wife didn't say anything. She just sort of squint-smiled at him.

Conrad dropped the trash in and replaced the lid. He stopped halfway up the walk and looked at Jo. 'Do you want me to shut off the stove, sweetie?'

She did not respond for half a minute.

'Jo? The bacon?'

She jumped. 'Oh, yes, please.'

Shit, she is a wreck.

Steve and Gail waited, watching him like they wanted him to go back inside so they could finish their chat.

He walked across the lawn to join them, completing their square. 'No word yet from Nadia, huh?'

'No.' Gail looked worse up close. Her hair was uncombed and her usually gleaming smile had been supplanted by a tight, lipless grimace.

'This business,' Steve-O said. 'It's not sounding too good, Conrad.'

Jo shifted her weight and looked at him like she was merely an observer, not yet fully a member of the drama. Even though she knew nothing, she seemed too . . . not relaxed, that was too generous a word . . . but unconcerned.

Suddenly Gail dropped her fist from her mouth and made a small, eeking sound. 'I have to tell you, Conrad, I have a bad feeling about this. I've spoken to the police!'

'Okay,' he said, hoping it came off as calm. 'That's wise. What did they say?'

'Eddie is dead, Conrad.'

'What?' Conrad said, genuinely shocked. Not by the fact, but by the knowledge. It was out. Now things were going to get really fucking hairy. *Watch your step, 'Rad.* 'How?'

Steve shot Gail a look before elaborating. 'Dale Stuart, his floor manager at Menard's, called yesterday when Eddie hadn't shown up two days in a row for work.'

'What happened? What about Nadia?'

'Eddie's wounds are indicating a possible suicide, though the police aren't revealing much yet. As for Nadia, Big John went with Sheriff

303

Testwuide. They're looking for her now. In four counties.'

The air inside the square absorbed the charges coming from each, becoming electric. None of them had all the pieces, but each of them suspected something was off. If he let it continue this way, waiting for them to add up their suspicions, they would turn it all on him in one great zap.

'Jesus. That's awful. What can I do?'

'What did she say, Conrad?' Gail was as close to blasting off. 'She must have said something! I know you know something!'

'Conrad?' Jo prompted, suddenly coming to life for the first time. 'Do you know something about Nadia leaving town? Did she say something about leaving this, who is it, this Eddie?'

Why was she chiming in now? Where was she getting this bit about Nadia leaving town? He stared at her. He did not think he had mentioned Nadia trying to leave town—not to Jo. He frowned at his wife. Jo nodded, just a little marriage nod, the kind so small only a spouse can recognize it. *Go on, tell them about Eddie*, the nod said.

If you say so.

Conrad looked back to Gail. 'Did Nadia leave her cell phone at your house, at home, I mean?'

'Her cell phone,' Gail repeated, blinking. 'I don't know. Why?'

'There was a message from Eddie,' Conrad said. 'He was screaming. He said he was going to kill himself. We heard a shot.'

'Oh, my God . . .' Gail tottered back on her heels. Steve took her by the arm and bore down on Conrad.

304

'A shot!' Steve said. 'When was this? Are you sure?'

'Oh my,' Jo said, which really wasn't something she had ever said before.

'It was three days ago,' he said. 'And I'm sure because Nadia played it for me. Eddie had been calling her all the time, screaming and crying and begging her not to leave, telling her to get out of his life, threatening to hurt her if she left without him.'

Gail moaned again.

Steve made a fist. 'Jesus! Why didn't you mention this the other day, Conrad? Why didn't you call for help?'

'I was trying to help her, Steve. I told her we should call the police, and she panicked. She said Eddie liked to play with guns and she didn't want to get him into more trouble, because she was his only friend. She said he pulled shit like this all the time, trying to scare her, manipulate her. I told her she was crazy and she better stay the hell away from him. I made her promise, in fact, not to talk to him.'

'Not good enough, Harrison. You're an adult. You don't play around with guns. You call the fucking police!'

'God damn it, Steve, I tried! Nadia said she was going to run away. She said if I called the police or you, or you, Gail, she would leave town and never come back. We argued. She cried about it. I thought we had reached a deal. She promised to stay away from Eddie and not go anywhere without me, and I promised to back off.' Jesus, he was really feeling it now! Could even feel Jo beside him, nodding, encouraging him—yes yes, more

305

more! 'Maybe you shouldn't have left your pregnant daughter alone, Gail. I'm very sorry, but obviously you—none of us—had any idea what a fucking basket case this father of her child turned out to be.'

'You lied,' Steve said. His voice was quiet.

'She must have run away, Steve,' Conrad said. 'Nadia was with me. We heard the shot. He couldn't have hurt her . . .'

Gail was sobbing.

Steve was staring at Conrad like he wanted to throttle him.

'Oh, I don't feel so well,' Jo said.

They all looked at her. She really was pale. She staggered back, just like Gail had a moment ago. She turned around in a slow circle and vomited into the grass. It was mostly orange juice.

Gail looked up at the sky and wailed. 'What is happening to me?'

'Oh, for Chrissakes go home,' Steve said, disgusted. 'Take care of your wife.'

'I'm sorry,' Conrad said.

'And stay by the phone, pal,' Steve said over his shoulder, walking Gail back to her house. 'The police are going to have questions, very soon. Count on it!'

Conrad followed Jo, who was trotting into the house.

*　　　*　　　*

Jo was in the downstairs bathroom, vomiting again. He knocked and spoke through the door.

'Jo, can you let me in? Do you need a doctor?'

'No,' she said, choking. 'No doctor.'

306

He backed away from the bathroom door and walked back into the kitchen. He was still shaking when he reached the refrigerator and popped his first beer. The beer went down like he'd just held it over the drain until the foam dribbled out.

'Fucking Nadia,' he said, looking out the window to the backyard.

'What was that?' Jo said, coming up behind him.

He turned, surprised by the change in her voice. She had her hair back in a band, her face splashed wet and pinker, more like herself. She was patting her brow with a hand towel. The sick woman from the lawn party had been replaced.

'Is this normal?' he said.

'Normal?'

'You look better, if that's possible.'

'I feel like I just woke up. What's all the fuss about with Nadia?'

'She was just a dumb kid.' He dropped the empty into the sink and popped another.

'Conrad. We need to talk.'

'No shit.' He turned to face his wife. She was scaring him, and he didn't like that. He was pretty sure she was hiding something, too.

'Did something happen between you and that girl?'

'Tell me about the baby, Jo.'

'You weren't there. You have no idea what I went through.'

'You left me. You told me to stay home.'

'That's not fair. You're hiding something. If our neighbors can see it, how obvious do you think it is to me?'

'You're not going to tell me what happened to our child?'

307

'Not until you tell me what went on in this house.'

'What went on in this house,' he repeated, tasting the words. 'Yes, that's one way to phrase it. Another way is, what is still going on in this house? Still another is, what has always been going on this house, what is going to happen next in this house?'

'Was that a threat? I don't fucking believe you.'

'You should believe me.'

'Don't even speak until you're ready to be honest with me. And then you better tuck yourself in, mister, because we are in for a very long haul with this little experiment.'

She was angry. So very angry. But beneath that he saw fear, too. Good. Let her be afraid, a little. She deserved it. Coming home and giving him this shit.

'You are a piece of work, you know that. I found this house for us. I gave this "little experiment" everything from day one, and what do you do? You move out of state, for what? For some job. For some money. You treat me like a walking hard-on while you're away. You disappear, I can't reach you, some douche bag in your room, hanging around like the gay sidekick on a bad sitcom. Did you convert him? Or was it Jake? Did you let him fuck you, Jo? You know what? I hope you did. I hope someone got laid while you were away, because it wasn't me, and it seems to me like you really could have used a good fuck in the past three months.'

Patches of red crawled out of her shirt and up her neck. She wheezed, holding the back of the chair like she was going to keel over.

'Right,' he said, going for his third beer.

'How. Fucking. Dare. You!'

'You already said that, Jo.' He had seen this conversation play out before in his head so many times it was almost a memory.

Her lips quivered. 'Who are you that you have so much black rage inside you?'

'Hey, Baby,' he said, affecting a sort of jive-ass tone. Rollo on *Sanford and Son*. 'You knew what kind of cat I was when we got hitched.' He thrust his hips back and forth, fucking the air between them.

She slapped him across the mouth, lit up his whole face. He tasted blood.

'I am two seconds away from calling the police on you,' she said. 'What did you do to that girl?'

'I told her to get a life.'

'What did you do to that girl?'

'I told her to get the fuck out of Dodge.'

'What did you do to that girl!'

He sighed. His wife was standing ramrod straight, tears running down her cheeks.

'Just tell me the truth,' she said, her voice hoarse. 'I might hate you, but I'll at least respect you for it.'

'Tell me,' he said, a nasty smile curling his lips. 'Did you lose it, or did you throw it away? Or was it Jake's? You know, I'm glad you lost it. Now I don't have to raise the little fuck and wonder every day if he's mine or if he belongs to the talentless asshole who fucked my wife while I was burying my father.'

Something in her broke. The fight was gone. His tall wife was sitting on the floor, head buried in her knees, sobbing. He knew that if he wanted to, for the first time in their history, he could punish her.

He could win. He could reach in and grab her emotions like apples from a tub of cold water and take them out one by one and smash them on the sidewalk. But she was already crushed.

After a time she said, 'I've never been unfaithful to you. Never. Jake was too drunk to drive. He never even made a pass at me, you fucking asshole.'

She sobbed, and in her sobs he found her ugly. He pitied her then.

'Joanna,' he said, his voice soothing, eerily normal. 'I'm sorry. This has been the worst three months of my life. I want you to understand, okay?'

She looked up. Her face was turning gray again.

'The truth is. I tried like hell to seduce her. I did. I was not myself, but that's no excuse. How I got here, it's . . . leaving Los Angeles was something we both wanted and needed, but something else triggered it. Maybe my father dying. I don't know. When I was seventeen my girlfriend Holly got pregnant. I loved her in ways you will never let me love you. I wanted her to have the baby. She did too. We were going to make it. We almost made it. But her father. Jesus, our fathers. It's always our fathers. I'm tired of blaming him. It's my turn now, isn't it?'

Jo wasn't crying. She was just staring at the wall, stunned.

'She disappeared. I could have a son walking around out there in Portland, or Austin, or Denver. Or a daughter. I would have loved either one, but I never found out. Then I met you. And we have been drifting for so long, Jo. I don't think you wanted to have a child. But it's all I ever wanted. It's all I want. I thought this house would change things. It was supposed to be our new start. I should have told you about Holly. But remember what you said about your cut in salary, how I really didn't want to know? Well, this was like that. You didn't want to know. I thought as long as we made a new life of our own, it didn't matter. It was past. If you had been here right after we moved. I don't know. I'd like to think I would have been happy with you. I would really like to believe that everything would have . . . *healed itself* . . . if you had never left. Can you understand that?'

Jo swallowed, raising herself on coltish legs. 'I'm, uhm, glad you're finally talking to me, Conrad. But I think . . . I really need you to tell me now. What did you do with Nadia?'

'It's not Nadia. I mean, you can't understand what this house does to you, Jo. Leon Laski. He knows. He tried to tell me. These women keep coming back. It was a birthing house, Baby. It wants to be one again. If you stay, you will have another child. That's what it wants. That's what we want, isn't it?'

'Wait, are you telling me you tried to get into Nadia's pants because the house wanted you to?'

The anger was gone. He was excited. It felt so good to tell the truth. Now he just had to make her see.

'Baby, that's a very small piece of something much larger. Listen, do you think it's a coincidence you got pregnant so soon after we moved here? Huh? No, of course not. It happened in this house. And I know what you're thinking, but listen. The women in the photo—shit, you haven't seen the photo! Why did I burn—it doesn't matter. It's a

311

healing place. You should have seen my hand. And the dogs! The dogs were all cut up from the broken mirrors. She was here, the woman in the house is trying to get out—'

'What mirrors?' Jo shouted. 'The dogs are fine, Conrad. Please stop saying these things. You—'

'No, I know, they're fine now. Listen. This is how it works. God, why didn't I see this before? You were pregnant . . . then you left . . . and then you lost the baby. Don't you see? Here, look—'

'Stop!'

'What?'

'Can't you hear yourself?'

'No, listen, this is going to work. I'm ready to be a father.'

'No, you're not.'

'But I am.'

'Conrad, listen to me.'

'I'm—'

'I was pregnant before we left Los Angeles!'

He gaped at her.

'I knew right before we left. When you came home and saw Jake there, I knew what you were thinking. But you just shut down. I wanted you to have time to grieve, but not like that. I thought it would be too much. You weren't ready. I wanted to be sure we could get through this. The way you were holding your father's money over my head, buying this house. It wasn't like you. We were supposed to do all these things together. Everything together.'

'You were pregnant before?'

'Yes.'

'But you didn't tell me?'

'I'm not pregnant now. You need to see

somebody, Conrad. Oh, I knew—'

'But the snakes.'

'What snakes?'

'The Boelen's pythons. Shadow dropped nine eggs.'

'You bought more snakes? Why?'

'Because they are beautiful. I wanted to invest in something, and I had the money to do something I had always wanted to do.'

'This was your surprise project in the garage?'

'Yes.'

'Why didn't you just tell me?'

'You thought they were stupid. You told me to grow up. But I knew. I knew they would help us one day.'

'I'm not sure how keeping snakes helps us.'

'She laid nine eggs, Jo. A virgin birth. The house wants life.'

'Stop saying that.'

'It's true.'

'Maybe so.' Jo's face had taken on a vacant stare, after seeing his fervor. Her words became disconnected. 'But I don't like all these secrets. I think I should go.'

She turned her back to him.

'None of this would have happened if you stayed here,' he said. 'Don't you see that?'

'It wouldn't have changed anything.'

'It's okay, Baby. It's past. You're home now. We can do it again.'

She walked to the kitchen entrance. 'The neighbors are waiting for their daughter to return.'

'Jo, wait. She said she wanted to run away. I admitted I tried to seduce her. But I didn't, and I don't want her now. I want a family. I want you.

313

Why would I confess all this and lie about the rest?'

'I don't know who you are or who we've become.'

'I'm the father of your child.'

'There is no child.' She disappeared around the corner, into the living room. 'There is no child.'

But she didn't sound certain of that, either.

36

He was hungry.

After days of feeding that girl soup and sitting in the library waiting for the walls to open up, he was salivating, ravenous, his thoughts honed to a single goal: food. He searched the cupboards and in the empty spaces he conjured grilled T-bones smothered in sautéed mushrooms and peppercorn sauce, bowls of creamed spinach, piles of hot garlic cheese biscuits, salad drowning in Italian dressing and chocolate ice cream by the bucket.

He grabbed the car keys and looped around into the TV room.

'I'm going to the store. Do you want anything?'

Jo was sitting on the couch, petting Alice, staring at the TV. The TV was off.

'The store,' she said.

'Look, we're not thinking clearly. You've been through a lot. I haven't eaten a decent meal in days. So here's what we're going to do. I'm going to make you a lunch you'll never forget. We'll eat, we'll rest. Then we'll talk. I promise, we'll do whatever you think is right.'

'What will I do?' She said this to the blank TV.

'We just need to eat first. You look pale, Baby.'

He turned and headed for the door.

'Tell me about the snakes again,' she said.

He stopped, came back.

'The snakes? I'm blind with hunger, Baby.'

'Where are you keeping them?'

'I told you they're in the garage. I'll show you the eggs later, after we eat. I don't want you disturbing them now. If the temperature drops even a few degrees, it can damage the embryos. And then it's bye-bye ninety grand.'

'Oh.'

'I'll be right back.'

He drove fast and the store was only half a mile away. Inside, he filled the shopping cart with seventy-nine dollars' worth of food, yanking steaks from the cooler like a bear pawing salmon from a stream. He dumped potatoes into the child seat without a bag. They fell to the floor and he grabbed more, throwing asparagus and cauliflower in with them. Bananas. She needed potassium. He raced to the other end of the store. Three kinds of cheese. Milk. Frozen corn, peas, okra. Okra? Fuck, why not okra? A Mrs Smith's blueberry pie, Breyer's vanilla bean. He was in the checkout line when he remembered the wine. Once they had some food in them, the wine would grease the wheels for the rest

'One second,' he told the kid in the apron punching the register.

The liquor aisle was ten feet away. He searched labels and tried to remember what kind she liked. White, he knew that much, but there was no such thing as white wine. There was Pinot Grigio,

315

Chardonnay, Sauvignon Blanc. He had always bought whatever was on sale, but now he wanted to get it right. For her. All the labels had kangaroos and dogs and moose on them. What the fuck was going on here? Had some genius in marketing realized we see ourselves as cute little cartoon animals like kids with cereal boxes? He reached for something with a koala bear on it and changed his mind, tipping the bottle off the shelf. His arm shot out and the koala bear smashed on the floor, sending a geyser of sour juice up his leg.

'Fuck!' He jumped back, crunching glass under his red sandals. Gashed his big toe. 'Jesus Christ.'

'It's no problem,' the kid in the apron said, coming round to help. 'Just watch your step so you don't cut yourself.'

'I'm sorry,' Conrad said. 'I'm just trying to find the right one.'

Something in his eyes made the kid stop and look at him.

'I'm sorry. My wife is not well. Can you help me?'

'Sure, yeah, it's no problem. What are you looking for?'

'White wine. Just any white wine. But a good one.'

'Maybe this one? It's pretty popular.' The kid pointed to a large bottle with a gorilla on the label. The price tag said $14.99.

'Sure, that's fine. Great.' Conrad reached for the broken glass.

'Just leave it.'

'You sure?'

'It's not a problem.'

'I appreciate it. My wife just got home from a

long trip. I'm kind of in a hurry, you know?'

Not much time now. She could be ovulating.

'Sure. Totally.'

He almost turned the car around when he realized he had forgotten the charcoal briquettes —then he remembered they owned a gas grill.

He made it home twenty minutes after he'd left. He felt like he was walking on air. His stomach had shriveled into a tennis-ball-sized knot. It was going to take another fifty minutes to prepare the meal, but it would be worth the wait. She would appreciate it.

He was halfway across the front porch when the door opened and Jo popped out, her rental car keys in one hand and a small backpack in the other. It was her old forest-green L.L. Bean from grad school, the one she used to pack an extra bra and panties in when she stayed the night at his crummy little apartment. Panties in the pack. God, she had been beautiful. And wild, too. Now she looked pale, haggard.

'Where you going?' he said, standing five feet in front of her.

She jumped slightly. 'Oh, you're back.'

'I have food.' He held out the bags for her to see. 'Some steaks, wine. You need to eat, Baby.'

'No, right, that sounds good.' She looked over his shoulder, up the street.

'Where are you going?' He thought of all the acceptable answers: to return the rental, to refill my prescription, to lend Gail a cup of sugar.

'Oh, I just don't feel like myself.'

'Obviously.' He looked at her hand holding the strap slung over her shoulder. 'What do you need? Do you need a *doctor*?'

Again, on that one word she flinched.

'No!' She blinked, and he waited. Then, in a calmer but still pleading voice she said, 'I'm not myself, Conrad. Ever since I came home I don't feel like myself. Please . . .'

He took a step closer.

'We should work this out together, Jo. Until they find Nadia. It's dangerous out there.'

'I never felt like myself here,' she said absently. 'That's why I went away.'

Conrad waited.

She continued to present her case. 'I'm not mad at you any more, honest. I'd just feel better if I got some rest. I can't sleep here.'

'Oh, you're not mad. Okay. Good. 'Cause when I saw you come out with your bag over your shoulder, I thought . . . I know I dumped a lot of this crap on you. You must have come home and thought I'd lost my shit here without you.'

She was breathing hard, and worse, trying to not to.

He stepped back and cocked his head to one side. 'I understand, Jo.'

'What?' She tried to smile.

'I understand how you feel. But the bag gave you away.'

She stopped smiling. Her eyes went to his hands, to the bags he was holding.

'That's your overnight bag. You aren't planning on ever coming back, are you?'

'Conrad. Please.'

He saw her think it through, weighing her odds. 'Nope. Not this way. Maybe out the back, but out here you don't stand a chance.'

She slumped, letting her backpack fall from her

318

shoulder.

He reset the groceries in his grip and took another step forward.

She ducked, clutched the strap, swinging wide and up. The sound of nylon against his head was a dull *whap*, but he felt like he'd been hit with a sack of grain.

'Ah, sonofabitch—' He staggered into the siding.

Jo darted forward, all six feet of her waist-high. He kicked his leg out and surprised both of them by connecting with her neck. It was like kicking an iron pole, felt like he broke three toes. Jo fell down, coughing, then she was on her hands and knees scrabbling about on the porch like one of the dogs in a way he might have found funny if some last remaining sane part of him did not recognize she was still his wife.

'Stop it,' he hissed, disgusted. 'Do you want the neighbors to see this?'

'Stay away from me,' she coughed, pulling herself up, rubbing her throat. 'Stay away from me, you piece of shit.'

'You're not leaving,' he said, idly swinging the bag with the wine bottle. 'Just turn around and go back inside so we can talk.'

She looked past him again, looking for a way around. Then all the fight was gone and she was just standing there.

'I didn't mean to hurt you,' he said. 'I'm sorry.'

She nodded, rubbing her neck. 'Fine. You win.'

She took a breath, looked next door and kicked for his balls. She missed, but connected with his thigh and wheeled, darting back into the house, knocking the door open as she blew into the kitchen.

He dropped the groceries on the floor and missed her shirt by inches as she fled out the back door. He pounded down the wooden steps to the yard, glancing wild-eyed over the fence to see if Gail and Big John were getting an eyeful, and took the deck in three giant strides.

She was making a beeline for the—

(birthing shack)

—garage. He realized that in all the years he had never seen her run. It was something to watch, all that woman pumping her arms like a track star. She didn't look back.

She can't make the fence, he thought gleefully, *and the garage is locked. She's fenced in!*

'Jo, don't!' he yelled, closing the distance.

She was twenty feet from the garage. Closing. Long legs, thighs shuddering like a thoroughbred. Fifteen feet. Ten feet from a nasty surprise—the door was locked. He saw the rest, how it would play out. It was like it was scripted. As if he had made it all up and now it had come to life. He could see the beats forming on paper the way he used to write them.

The WIFE, an attractive brunette in her early 30s SLAMS into the warehouse door, YANKING to no avail. Her HUSBAND, disheveled in a handsome, dopey way, gives chase.

She WHEELS, her eyes as black and large as a doe's, then back to the door, KICKING as if her life depended on it. Which of course it does.

                    HUSBAND
          Baby, stop, just please stop!

                     WIFE
                  (shrieking)
              Stay away from me!
     CLOSE ON: her SHAKING hand, clutching
        the doorknob. It won't budge.

                    HUSBAND
          (deranged; paying homage)
       The dingo ate ma' bayyyyyy-beee!

The door would not open. She would be forced to
turn and fight him on the lawn. The scene would
end badly. How could it not? That was the rule of
conflict, the stuff of good drama.

But this wasn't scripted and, instead of finding
the door locked, she hit it hard with one shoulder
and banged it open.

He jogged across the rest of the lawn, mindful
of that first step before the door. No way was she
strong enough to break the padlock.

*Someone must have left it unlocked. And it wasn't
me.*

The garage was dark inside—not even red.
What happened to the heat lamps? He heard
fumbling sounds, a shovel falling to the floor as he
pounced over the two steps down and he was
inside, landing on the carpet. The sliding garage
doors were shut and he could see her moving past
the cages, searching for the handle.

They were trapped.

He found the light switch. The overhead Vita-
Lites flickered and cold white filled the room.

                      321

Jo turned, chest heaving, hair in her face.

'This is stupid. I'm not going to hurt you,' he said.

Jo's eyes shot to something on the other side of the cages. Her face contorted and the room was silent.

'Jo?'

Her scream erupted, an inhuman sound. He looked around, her screams fanning out as he tried to understand what, besides her stupid husband, was upsetting her so. She sounded like she was being impaled.

He saw the cages. He saw the snakes, black and sleek. One stretched out across the branches he'd built into the walls of its home. Another, lower, coiled like a fire hose, its head resting at the center of the nest it had made of its own body.

He saw the incubator smashed on the floor, the black vermiculite soil spread out in wet clumps, the leathery eggs destroyed, their slug-like contents oozed and congealed on the floor.

Somebody had sabotaged the eggs.

Oh, fuckers. Murderous motherfucking whores!

Jo was still screaming.

He turned away from Shadow's ruined clutch. His eyes roamed across the cages and higher, to the corner of the garage where the hooks had been bolted into the wooden ceiling beams, the rubber hooks for hanging bicycles.

A yard of cord came down stretched taut. There the hands were bound by the same black rope. The arms, stretched until the shoulders had dislocated, were bruised all the way down and into the milk-white skin of her naked torso. Can't see shouldn't see don't want to see the face cover your eyes

322

don't let her see you with the black eyes. Her breasts were full, engorged. Not black eyes. Black around her head. She was blindfolded, and later, when he had time to process such things, he would realize that had been an act of mercy.

Nadia's belly bulged, and the gash ran from under her breastplate to the pubis. Her intestines were strewn about, leaving what he could only assume to be her womb, ovaries and the rest of her organs spread between her knees, the tops of which touched the blood-soaked floor. Her legs were tucked behind her, the feet like the hands, bound and swollen purple.

He was walking in it. He saw his red sandals merge with the blood congealed and so thick the skin broke like the top of a Jell-O mold. To one side lay one of the stainless-steel gaffs for handling the serpents. It was caked with blood and more of her grue.

Our Eden.

Nadia's mouth hung open, her teeth exposed. His mind short-circuited and he knew that he needed to stop the screaming but he could not move. It wasn't only that she was here and cut this way. A deeper part of him was not surprised to find her here at all. It was more the problem of how could it *be*, her insides all torn out like that, strung in this tableau pose, when she had seemed so alive just a short while ago and now he could still hear her screaming, screaming for the baby that had been so callously removed before its due date.

37

As her screams wound down and became whimpers and then one long chain of suffering breaths, he used the garden shears to cut the rope. The body slumped cruelly on to its face. He used the dirty plastic tarp to cover her naked back and buttocks. He knew that she deserved better, but there wasn't time for any of that now. Whatever fate had befallen Nadia Grum was irreversible.

His wife was here. Alive.

Jo was on her feet, swaying. Her face was wet with tears and mucus. Her eyes were wide from shock and red, her skin gaunt. Her entire body was under siege, the cords in her neck like cables on a suspension bridge as the earth quaked and threatened to tear her asunder. Her teeth were literally clacking. He understood the next few minutes—maybe seconds—would determine the rest of their lives and possibly end one or both of them.

He took a step toward her with his palms up, and she jerked back, slamming into the metal garage door with a nerve-jangling clatter. He stopped, but left his hands up high. He did not realize he was crying until he spoke.

'Jo, I did not do this. Please, don't run away. I swear to you, on the lives of our dogs, on my mother's soul. I did not hurt this girl. This is the first time I have seen her since she was alive in our house two days ago. I am begging you to believe me one last time. I did not hurt this girl. I did not do this.'

He was not sure she could even hear him. The way her eyes were roving around, he suspected she might be hearing him but not seeing him.

'Joanna? Joanna Harrison. Joanna Keene,' he said, using her maiden name. 'I did not do this. A monster did this. I'm not a monster.'

But did he know that for sure? The past weeks were a blur of nightmares and strange changes. Someone had brought the knife into the bedroom. Nadia had been talking in another woman's voice. Alma's voice. But she couldn't have done this to herself—this required brute strength. Was it possible Alma had taken him over, moved him to act upon her cruel justice?

No, he would not accept that. He stepped forward, reaching for her.

'Stay away from me. You stay away!'

He kept his hands at his sides. She began to shuffle sideways but could not bring herself to abandon the hard surface of the metal door against her back. She moved on shaking legs, inching across the garage, her eyes hot and accusing.

'I won't hurt you. Please don't go. I won't ever make you do anything again, but please listen to me before you run away.'

She had reached the end of the wall and found herself in another corner. Rushing past him on either side would require passing within arm's reach. It appeared to be a risk she was not ready to take.

'Someone else was here. The mirrors. She came in and broke them like she didn't want to be seen. She left a knife outside the bedroom door, Jo. She wanted Nadia to run away. She said it was her turn

325

to be a mother. Alma! She said her name was Alma. I've seen her. She keeps coming back for the babies. I don't understand what's happening here, but you have to believe me, Jo. I didn't do this. I didn't do this!'

Her eyes locked on him. 'K-K-killed her. You killed her. You're s-s-sick, a sick man. Don't move or I will tell on you. I will tell them what you did.'

She snatched a scrap of fence lumber from the floor. A plank of treated green pine perhaps three feet long and sharp at one end.

His legs buckled and he sat down hard on the floor. *Show no aggression, only compliance. It's your only chance.*

'See? I'm not. I won't do anything.'

She lunged from the corner and stabbed the wood at him as she ran by him, up the steps, out the door.

She's going, she ran away, she's going now, she's gone gone gone forever now—forever—

—unless you stop her.

No. Let her go. It didn't work.

And you're going to be in Hell eternal unless you make it work.

He was out of plans, but he went after her just the same.

38

When he stepped into the backyard the sky had turned from blue to a darkening gray slate. He walked until he could no longer stand his thoughts—*what is she doing, who is she calling,*

326

where will she go—and then broke into a run.

He had crossed the deck and hooked around the back porch, halting when he saw movement down low. For an insane second, and they were all insane now, he thought the house was swallowing her alive. Her feet were kicking and shoving against the porch boards as her body was pulled through the dog door.

Then he understood that she had no other way in but to crawl through. He could hear the dogs barking inside, but it was a hollow sound, buried behind the walls.

He ran forward as her bare feet disappeared and the little plastic flap's magnet snicked into place. He tried the knob and indeed it was locked.

The gate. Why hadn't she used the gate to let herself out so she could run to the car, drive to the nearest police station or hospital? Was she going for the dogs, or a weapon?

He yanked the bolt on the gate and the wood screeched as it swung inward. He ran past the garbage cans around the side of the house. He slowed in case the neighbors had one eye out the window. He was relieved to find no one in the front yard, no patrol cars arriving with strobing lights to take him way.

The insulation. You insulated the garage to keep the snakes warm. No wonder everything was normal on the block; they couldn't hear her scream. Yes, and you couldn't hear Nadia screaming either, could you? How convenient. You were the one who ordered the garage insulated, just before you lured the girl next door into your twisted fantasy.

Stop it! Stop that shit right now!

He came through the front door. The dogs were

327

barking from the basement. Jo was bent over the kitchen sink, retching herself empty. Again. He closed the door behind him and she turned around, snatching the same long serrated knife from the counter. The note that said 'other mother must go' was gone. Her face was pale, her mouth dripping water and a yellow trail of bile. Some of it stuck in clumps in her once beautiful hair.

See what you have done? Turned your beautiful wife into a monster.

'Jo, stop this. Someone's going to get hurt.'

She stabbed the knife out like a spear. 'Don't fucking move!'

'I'm not!' He stopped behind the threshold. 'Your fingerprints are all over it now.'

Her expression changed. Some new wave of disgust that he would try to implicate her. She lashed out with the knife twice more, but she was too far back to cut him.

'What are you doing? Will you at least tell me that?'

'Stay away from me!'

The dogs whined from the basement.

'You had to crawl through the dog door, Jo. Do you think I actually remembered to lock up before I chased you into the yard? And who put the dogs in the basement? Don't be crazy. Someone was here. They could be here now.'

She opened the basement door. The dogs scrambled out, and he knelt before they could get a handle on the menace building between mistress and master. They might sense danger, smell blood and take up sides. If they did, he had no doubt whose they would choose. Between his six-foot wife and the hundred pounds of street mutt, he wouldn't live to see his way into a jail cell.

He reached for them. 'Alice, Luther, it's okay now, come here—'

'Don't touch them!'

The dogs jumped and pushed off her like she was holding Snausages instead of a knife.

'God damn it, put that down, you're going to cut them,' he said, stepping in.

She came at him with the knife waist-high, jousting. He sucked in his breath and leaned back on his heels. The knife swooped at his chest and the blade glanced off the doorframe. He fell forward and she brought it back. He thought she was breaking for the stairs, but her arm went forward once more and she put the blade into his belly as if she were trying to stop his fall. She jerked back and the knife was standing out of him like diving board.

'See!' she said, staring at the knife in him.

The pain going in was like a punch, and then it was hot, searing him. Conrad hissed, glancing down. It was off to one side, but it was in more than halfway. There was very little blood.

'Okay, it's okay,' he said, reaching for the knife. But when he touched the handle the burning shot through his guts and made it impossible to move.

'Oh my God,' she said.

'Baby, I can't . . . walk.'

Her face was a mask of horror and shock, and then neither. She remained still, a dead calm descending over her, into her. Her features slackened, became blank. She wasn't crying, he noticed. Not even breathing hard now.

The dogs whined, sniffing something new, and then backed away, growling at her. Conrad stared

329

at his dogs, their dogs. They had never been afraid of her before.

Jo's eyes had gone cold, dead-black as they had been in the tub. As they were in the photo from a century past. He remembered the figure in the backyard, dragging something on the ground. He remembered how confused she had been about coming home, how out of it she had been until after she left house to talk with the neighbors. The change that had come over her then, as if something was leaving her. She had vomited in the yard. How she'd come out of the bathroom a changed woman. Ever since she had come home, this duality had been inside her. One woman fighting the other. The red crusts under her fingernails were not from her miscarriage. Now, too late, he finally understood what had happened to Nadia.

Jo had come home, and Alma had found a new home.

'Jo . . . ?' He coughed, and the tightening of his abdominals seared him all over again. 'Aw, no, Jo . . .'

She walked forward in three halting steps, her movements stilted. Her hand was steady and she placed it on the handle.

'Comes,' she said, her voice grown much older and much colder. 'Comes the time Nah-dee join the red hair of fire.'

'You didn't,' he said. 'Please say you—'

'Alma turn.'

'Jo . . .'

'Alma git rid Connie's lil' whore . . . now Connie be righteous father.'

She was smiling. Mother of God, this monster

330

inside of his wife was smiling. He waited, pleading with her, searching for the woman he had known.

She looked into his eyes, into his soul.

He inhaled long and slow for one last attempt to reach her. The pain was glorious. Her face was inches from his mouth.

'Joanna come back!'

'Noooo . . .' Alma's voice cracked, and he could swear then that she was still there, fighting this thing inside of her until the one that wanted to keep him alive lost the battle to the one that wished him dead.

And that was his mistake, because Alma did not wish him dead.

Alma wanted a father for her behbee.

'I won't tell—' he began.

Jo blinked. His wife saw him for the monster she thought he was.

'Murderer,' she said and twisted the knife once, ruining something inside, then yanked it free. Blood poured, wetting his pants.

He screamed but no sound escaped his lips.

'Oh my,' his wife whispered, backing away from him. She was still holding the knife as her eyes rolled back in her head and she turned away and stumbled up the butler stairs. The dogs followed close on her heels.

'Don't leave,' he said, dribbling pink spittle.

The pain was enormous, a star. He was on fire from his knees to his throat. Urine leaked out, hot against his leg. He didn't want to die here. Not like this. Not at all. Not alone. He wanted to be with her. He knew he'd been bad, but she could help him die. She could do that. And though it blinded him, when he focused and bit through his cheek, he found that he could move after all.

He began to climb the stairs. He could hear her stomping through the library. With the dogs in tow, thudding on the floorboards.

She screamed. Once hard and sharp, followed by a second scream that went off like an air raid siren.

He was halfway up when the second scream froze him on the landing. Even in his dizzy, searing state he was certain the first scream had not been his wife's. Jo's was the second, the one that was still going in a great winding wail.

The first scream belonged to someone else.

'Aw, no,' he moaned. 'Nah, nah . . .'

The dogs began barking furiously and he lunged up, taking the six remaining stairs in two steps, snapping the handrail free of the wall as he hit the second floor and tripped, sprawling in his blood.

Claws scrabbling on wood. Jo struggling, fighting Alma. More barking.

A hoarse, animal voice. 'Get out of my house!'

'Leave me alone!' his wife shrieked.

'Alma save the behbeeeee!' she screamed.

The thump and crash of dead weight hitting the floor.

He was on his feet again, halfway down the hall. He could see across the library into the slit of the other doorframe where she danced, into the hall where the black maple banister curled all the way around.

The dogs have gone into a bloodlust. They're attacking her.

He loped, his guts boiling. Seconds stretched into minutes.

'Jo! I'm coming.'

332

His shoulder hit a shelf, knocking books to the floor.

Through the doorframe on the other side he saw a flash of gray skin. The curl of black cloth. The dogs jumping, gnashing. Jo's pink sweatpants kicking out. The whole mass twisting, flashing out of view.

Falling . . .

'Jo!'

He made it across the library but the dogs were pulling and pushing her in a frenzy. He had time to see the knife on the floor and her arm yanked back—

'Justin Gundry Justin Gundry,' the darker voice screamed.

—as she slipped from between the dogs and he lunged, his fingers missing her shirt by inches as she fell over. He reached out but his hips connected with the banister and stopped him from going down with her.

He was stuck watching, their eyes meeting for the last time as she arced back, her long body bowing as she tilted head first, sliding down in some gymnast's move gone awry. For the next few feet she seemed to hover like that, sliding down in perfect balance, the banister pressed into the small of her back like a fulcrum while her body made up its mind which way to go. Gravity chose for her. Her upper body was where all the weight lived and it sunk first.

The dogs raced after her down the stairs, but even they could not stop her momentum as she back-flipped head first over the banister and dropped the remaining ten feet on to the wood floor. He heard her neck. It was the sound of a sapling birch cracking in winter. Her body folded over itself and she came to rest looking up at him.

The dogs went to her immediately, whining and licking her arms and neck and face.

He stood motionless at the top of the stairs, then fell to his knees, peering through the spindles under the elbow of the banister. He watched the stain spread through the crotch of her pink sweatpants, her body releasing what it no longer needed.

But for the sound of the dogs lapping at her skin, the house was quiet.

'I'm comee, Baby,' he said, his speech slurred. 'I'm onna be with you.'

He was light, floating down the stairway to meet her. Would she be cold? Would she tell him what to do when he got there?

He watched through the spindles under the banister, looking back and low now as he descended, until, tilting his head sideways, he could just make out the top of her head, her hair fanned out behind her.

The final slide down to the floor was painful, but the pain kept him awake a while longer. When he reached the foyer he collapsed, and the pain sharpened as if the blade were still in him, twisting and carving out the important parts, burning him in a fever that left him wet and chilled until all he could think of was that witch in that movie, melting.

Now he lay in the foyer, looking up at the stairway, counting spindles under the banister until he forgot how to count. Now he lay here thinking of his father. Now he lay here waiting to die.

His dogs came around once, sniffing him,

whining, and then ran off. Time passed. He hadn't seen them for a long time. He hoped they would be able to escape. Find a new home.

The bleeding worsened for a spell and then slowed to a trickle. He wanted to die next to her. But even this was not enough to carry him further. He was stuck on the floor, and his head fell sideways so that she would be the last thing he would see. He reached a hand out. He wanted to touch her before she became cold.

'Jo . . . Baby.' He could feel the words but not hear the sound of them.

He stared at her. The fact of her death brought its full weight on him, and he would have endured this pain burning him inside every day for a hundred years if doing so would bring her back. He was shivering. He shut his eyes for a moment, then opened them one more time.

Jo's hair moved over the floor.

He blinked, forcing his eyes to stay open.

Her body tensed almost imperceptibly. He watched, fascinated, certain that he had imagined it. A minute passed. Then her spine jerked, arching her off the floor, and her neck began to crack as her head swiveled. She rolled to one side and took hold of her leg, pulling it like a dead weight log across the floor.

She sat up.

Oh, thank God. Jo . . .

She grunted, and got to her knees. She fixed upon him with her black eyes and smiled. Her teeth were red and broken and she was drooling blood on to her shirt. When she stood above him another of her bones popped. Her lip was split open along her ancient scar, and her mouth curled inward with her first inhalation, twitching like an epileptic's. When she coughed her blood rained down on him. He was still trying to scream when she leaned over, scooped him up like a doll, and began to climb the stairs.

39

He was nothing.

He was a blank slate of consciousness. The night was full upon him and he could no longer see or hear. A freezing cold enveloped him, seeped into every fiber, every pore, until his bones became ice. Something responding to his need was entering his body now, and she had a need of her own. His deadened perceptions were being fed, ignited by the smallest sparks of memory. He tried to name his thoughts with words but clasped only sliding images both fundamental and meaningless. At last he succumbed and let her thoughts flow into him. They wrapped around the tent poles of his imagination and stalled the heavy canvas of enshrouding death to stage a play, filling the tent with objects and performers to weave the history he had been hiding from since the night he burned the album.

The first objects came in a blur, things between words and images.

Candle.

Sky.   Stone.

                    Garden.

                            Wet.

Gray.

                                                    Doll.
                                   Mother.

Doctor.
It's as if someone has screamed this particular
word in his mind, and in doing so left an exploding
pain behind his eyes. His eyes open now, seeing a
world unlike this one and yet eerily familiar, for it
is at once artificial and historic, a private vision
granted in sepia. While he is still not sure where or
when he is—or even *who* he is—he understands,
slowly but with gathering force, that she has made
it this way for him. She is constructing a way for
him to share her mind, transporting him back
through time a century or more, using a muted
palate and jumping, impossible Super 8 home
movie-like segments to help him to bear witness.

He is in one of the smaller bedrooms of the
birthing house, standing before a mirror. He
knows he is here, but he does not see himself in
the mirror. The reflection staring back at him
belongs to a girl. She is four or five years old, thin,
with blonde hair the gold of honey, a yellow ribbon
laced through the gold in a bow. She is wearing a
black dress that falls to her ankles, and small
pointed leather shoes. She watches him, confused.
She is saddened by something just beyond the
reach of their shared thoughts.

Then he understands. His eyes are now her
eyes. He is with her, a guest or a prisoner, he does
not yet know.

Behind him—behind her—there is a heavy
knock on a wooden door.

'Come now, Alma.' The voice is deep.

At this intrusion, the girl in the mirror startles

337

and turns, her hard shoes clocking on the wood floors as she runs from the room. The floors of the house tilt beneath him and the front stairs become a blur as the vertigo returns. He loses sight.

The Doctor. Again this word that is more than a word, a formidable presence that cloaks her every thought like a god. It is all he hears in the blackness, and perhaps it *is* the blackness. He feels as if he is holding his breath for a long time.

When the sun sends streaks of peach and gold over his eyes, he opens them again and sees a large hand holding her hand, feels its heavy grip.

The Doctor's hand.

The Doctor is pulling her along the worn path in the backyard. Conrad, what is left of Conrad and what has now become child Alma, is filled with her emotions—fear, hope, the oblique sadness. They are walking over the wet green grass of the magical place, the once forested land the Doctor calls in his tall strong voice *Our Eden*, where the slope of the land rides like the ocean swell down lower to the garden and, off to one side, the place he thinks of as his garage but which she knows only as the forbidden place.

Speaking either to herself or to him, her voice comes to him again.

That is where he takes the Others like Mother when they are near their time.

His instinct is to speak, but no sooner does the thought emerge than her much stronger thoughts clamp down on him from inside.

No. Do not speak. Mind what he say, and mind what he do.

He falls deeper into her, becoming only a spectator.

They have stopped near the iron-gated garden where the raspberry branches and grape vines curl and form a lush green wall, and the Doctor's hand releases her hand as he removes his black hat and places it against his broad chest, nodding at her with his sad gray eyes. He is hard-faced, with rosy cheeks and a rough black beard. There are red lines in his eyes and tight creases around his brow and grim mouth, and she is reminded that he harbors an intensity that can change from love to wrath in a blink of those sad gray eyes. She is hoping to do it right, always hoping to do it right for him. The April rain has come and the air is cool, cooling and wetting her dress as she kneels at his side while he says the words he says here. She can hear his heavy breath hitching through the words. She feels ashamed that she is not crying too, but she cannot bring the tears to flow as he invites her to the prayer he gives over the small cross planted before them:

Aye, Lord above us the fallen
Accept our humble offerings and bless us
In His wisdom and the sacrificial blood
Of our fallen family
We shall bear this burden of the innocents
Lost
And give thanks for the life He brings
To our blessed house
Our place of commune and husbandry
To rehabilitate and shepherd the mothers
Daughters of Eve, the All Mother, all
Though we welcome them into our blessed shelter
And warm them by our hearth in their time of
    need

Forgive us, Dear Lord, our humanly trespass
Know thy heart remains true though these hands
Sworn to heal and serve
Remain yet frail and prone to the sin of temptation
We are committed to His path
Forever and ever
Amen

He realizes he can do more than see; he also feels what she feels. His chest aches for her, with her now, as her throat tightens and her little voice emits this one word, understanding at last who has been buried here. It is not another lil'un from one of the Other Mothers.

—Mother

Alma's cry pierces the morning. She is trying to pull away from the Doctor, but he will not release her small hand.

—Do not cry for Mother, Alma

The Doctor's voice cracks but does not break.

—Be still

Alma is sobbing and swatting at the Doctor as he shushes her repeatedly, and unspools his lesson.

—This is our burden. This is our light and our darkness and our duty. To have a life we must give a life, for life is a circle that begins and ends along the same sphere. In between the journey from one side to the other, the circle provides, and for that we each of us owe a life. The wool that keeps you warm at night is of the sheep, the roof over our home of the forest, the blood in your veins of your mother. On top of the circle is our Lord, and He commands us to take when we are in need, to give when our time has come. Mother's time has come, and she is home now, Alma.

Alma does not understand the circle now, but the time is coming when she will understand all.

The world cuts. He sees only blackness.

*   *   *

Then, as if she has blinked, as if the camera shutter has been reopened, they are back in the house and the Doctor—Mother called him Dr Justin Gundry—is calling her name from the front parlor where he sits near the hearth. The angles of the room jog as Alma comes, allowing his embrace, for that is all that remains to warm her since the end of the cold cold winter when Mother went away. Alma knows Mother was the biggest and most beautiful woman in the house and the Doctor's favorite. Alma knows this because she saw the love in his eyes and the gifts he brought Mother when he returned from his travels to and fro a place he calls Redruth, the place he learned his first calling as a mason, where he learned to build a house on a God-proper stone foundation with his healing hands. Alma calls him Docca Gunree, but only sometimes, for her words are few and seldom heard. Docca Gunree has built a fire and now he offers her the doll Mother made for her.

Playing with the doll is a way to bring Mother back, for a little while.

But already Docca Gunree is rising and Alma pretends not to notice as he puts away his glass and takes her hand and leads her down into the basement. Here among the stone foundations and the cool floor are the beds. Alma is crying, but one quick jerk of her hand is enough to silence her.

341

She crawls as bidden into one of the cots he has arranged next to the empty bassinets. Docca Gunree pats her head and pushes the doll into her arms before turning back to climb the stairs. Alma makes the connection once again with the doll, recalling how playing with the doll is like singing the song Mother sang for her, back when Mother rocked Alma in her arms and said what a big strong girl Alma was going to be some day. Back when Mother promised she would watch over Alma, always.

Mother is here now in spirit, warming her from inside, even though Alma knows Mother has gone away. Mother reminds Alma that she is a very brave girl and that one day Alma shall have a room of her own. Alma dreams of Mother's voice in all its clarity and sweetness, and when Mother sings it is better than any feeling Alma knows.

> *Sleep the dream sleep o' sweet child*
> *Mother is here*
> *when the sun she rises and when she sets*
> *Mother is your home, the only home Alma needs*
> *remember Mother lives forever, forever in Alma's*
>   *heart*
> *remember every day, o' sweet child*
> *no tears for me does child Alma shed*
> *thread through a needle cannot mend a young*
>   *girl's heart*
> *Mother is here o' sweet child Alma even when*
> *thread through a needle cannot mend a young*
>   *girl's heart*

When next she opens her eyes, the basement of the house is full of Other Mothers who are not

Mother, coming and going before Alma can learn their names. The women of the house, sturdy pale women in black dresses and boots and caps or bonnets, are growing in number, too, but they are always busy tending the lil'uns in the bassinets while Docca Gunree works long days and late into the night to perform the Lord's work. At night, Alma can hear Docca Gunree's voice through the floor and the hearth-stone walls warmed by the fire all the way down to her bed. Sometimes the women of the house talk of the day with him, and sometimes, Alma knows, he talks only to himself and the spirits he carries inside.

—More of the menfolk lost in battle

—Filling the house faster than we can take them

—They call it the Great War

—Some of them don't wish to see them behbees, rather to leave 'em behind

—This is a healing place, we shall continue the Lord's work

—'Tisn't time in the day for me to take care of any of them, let alone dote on her

—But Justin, Dr Gundry, have you considered, sir

—What will I do? What can I do? I promised her mother

—She must learn to take care of herself if she wishes to remain in this house

*   *   *

Comes the night Alma wakes to screams. A commotion tramples above her head, shaking the floors and echoing down through the rock foundation. It is the middle of the night and the

343

basement is so dark as to be black, but Alma knows the way and she scampers from her bed, up the stairs, passing the lil'uns in their bassinets who have begun to cry.

Upstairs she becomes entangled in a procession of the women of the house led by Docca Gunree, who is pushing a new Other Mother Alma does not recognize in a wooden chair with wheels. The Other Mother in the chair is thin and her eyes are ringed with black. She is the one screaming and in her lap is a blanket soaked in blood. The procession flows through the front parlor, into the kitchen, and out the back door to the yard, down the worn path to the forbidden place. Alma follows unnoticed until they reach the door and then she is shut out.

She takes up her position by the window, trying once again to peer inside to see how Docca Gunree makes behbees from the Other Mothers. The night grows long and Alma grows frightened by the screams that do not end. When woman of the house Martha Marsten finally rips the door open and crying flees back to the house, Alma chases after her.

Inside, Martha collapses into a chair beside the fire and clutches Alma to her bosom and sobs into her hair.

—He says it has turned, the healing power has turned, but it is him what's turned, turned to the drink and playing God

Alma tries to comfort Martha but she is scared, trembling.

—His hands, I saw his hands, so much blood on his hands, heaven help us, Alma

Later, when the women of the house return, the

344

Other Mother does not come with them, nor her child, and Alma never sees her again. She understands the Other Mother and her lil'un have gone to be with Mother, that now they are also doing the Lord's work.

When Docca Gunree returns, the women of the house step away from him and disappear into the corners, leaving him to drink beside the fire. When his tired grey eyes fall on Alma it is as if he has never seen her before. He tilts his head and blinks. Slowly, a recognition fills his eyes and he sneers at her, showing Alma a naked hatred she has not seen on any face.

—You carry the eyes of your mother

Alma's eyes brighten at the mention of Mother.

—She understood sometimes a woman must give a life to have a life

Alma is too frightened to speak or move.

—Your mother gave a life to have a life, for you to have a brother

This is the first Alma has heard of a brother.

—But these are cold times and the Lord cannot always provide for so many mouths

Alma thinks of the women feeding the lil'uns in their bassinets.

—He took your mother away from us, and he had to be sent away

Alma blinks at Docca Gunree.

—It is inviting evil to keep the lil'uns who bring death upon their arrival

Alma does not understand, but she is more frightened than ever by the strange light in Docca Gunree's eyes. She turns and walks slowly down the stairs to the basement, crawling into her cool cot, pulling the single wool blanket over her

345

shivering body.

*   *   *

When she awakens later he is standing over her bed. He is a huge figure dressed in black, his suspenders dangling at his sides, his enormous head leaning over her, his body swaying. Alma can smell the medicine coming from his open mouth from more than four feet away. She closes her eyes and pretends to sleep as he looks her over.

*   *   *

When he awakens next within her she is on the floor, deep in the basement, digging at the mortar around a rock the size of a small pig. She is using a steel trowel of some sort, patiently scraping at the chalky dust, humming as it falls away in a hissing cascade.

*   *   *

She is standing before the mirror again, in the guest room upstairs. But now the little girl is as tall and lithe as a willow, and her once golden hair has taken on the wash of brown that goes unnoticed until it is much too late. Her black dress is different, a handover from one of the other women of the house.

Mother has been gone four winters now, she says to no one.

She turns from the mirror and begins to wander, following the women of the house here and there, but when she attempts to help string clothes from

346

the line over the path outside of the kitchen, woman of the house Big Helen shoos Alma away.

She wanders into the basement and looks over the lil'uns in bassinets, counting how there are only three now out of twelve, and she knows that since the Great War has ended there are fewer and fewer Other Mothers and therefore less work to share. Alma knows that the women of the house wish her away now, and she must be careful not to upset the order lest he shoo her out of the house for good. She walks silently, in many ways already a ghost, into the deep corner of the basement and uses her thin but strong fingers to remove the piggy from the wall to open her lair.

Inside, she clutches her doll and dreams of Mother.

* * *

When she awakens next her body is sore all over from curling upon itself in the tiny space which grows smaller with each year. She is shivering and when she places a hand on the rock wall she knows the fire upstairs has gone out and that she has slept through supper again. She pushes the piggy loose and crawls out, her large feet cold upon the basement floor. She climbs the stairs in search of sustenance. In the kitchen she finds a pot of cold soup and a scrap of hard bread, which she breaks. Alma carries her bowl to the front parlor and prepares to load the fire, but a thump from upstairs startles her. She thinks perhaps the fire is still burning in the belly stove upstairs and she carries her bowl up, up and into the library.

The fire in the library is also cold. Alma hears

the thumping sound again and forgets her soup and eats only one more bite of the hard bread before she turns to the room Mother made so pretty. Alma walks down the hall and around the black wooden banister at the front stairs for the patrons. Alma hears a woman in Mother's room and her heart jumps as a rabbit. Though she knows it cannot be possible, for a moment she dares hope it is Mother come home and that the weeping sounds are Mother crying tears of happiness.

Alma opens the door and sees three women of the house who have grown cold to her standing in the corner, heads bowed to the leather table in the center of the room with candles burning from every sill. The Other Mother on the table is tall and her lustrous black hair is strong, but she is not Mother. The Other Mother on the table is crying in soft rhythms and sweating all over her stripped bare body. Even though the winter is deep on the house, the room is very warm and full of the woman scents Alma knows from the house but stronger than ever before.

Docca Gunree is kneeling before the Other Mother in her time of need and his glasses are almost falling off his large red nose. His thick black hair and gray-streaked beard are oily and dripping from his labors as he speaks in mumbled commands. The Other Mother screams louder in three short peaks and then begins to howl. None of the women in the corner turn to see Alma, and Docca Gunree is concentrating so that he is unaware Alma has entered.

—the Lord has blessed Our Eden

Alma draws near, called to the table as if she might at last understand an important piece of

Mother's history. Docca Gunree's face turns red as he pulls and shifts his black boots and becomes impatient the way Alma has seen Farmer Mitchell with the foals in spring in the field beyond Black Earth. The howl goes on for minutes and Alma must cover her ears it hurts so much until Docca Gunree jumps back and the streams of black spatter his arms and face. As if by magic the behbee is in his arms and the women of the house run from the room. Alma thinks of the doll the way the Other Mother's legs collapse. Docca Gunree pays them no mind as he takes the tiny behbee in his rough hands. Alma thinks the lil'un needs a bath so that he—Alma cannot see to know if he is a boy or a girl, but she knows he is a boy—can be swaddled and set in one of the bassinets to await the women of the house come to feed him. Alma's heart hurts when he cries, which are somehow small and very loud in the hot room.

—forgive us dear Lord our humanly trespass

Alma sees the blue cord that runs from the lil'un's belly to the unseen dark between the Other Mother's legs and Alma follows it up and back down, marveling at the connection. Docca Gunree's other hand moves with the silver blade over the lil'un's small round belly and he cuts and cuts. Alma sees the cord and Docca Gunree shakes his head, fighting something inside of him Alma cannot see, and Docca Gunree curses, weeping as his large hand moves.

The world cuts. But the world does not cut away.

Already the cord is wrapped around the neck and Docca Gunree is pulling until the small crying sounds gurgle and stop. Alma does not know how she knows, but at last she knows about all the behbees Docca Gunree has made and how though he says sometimes a woman must give a life to have a life, *this is his choice, not His choice.*

Alma falls back on her bare feet and bumps against the wall.

Docca Gunree's face turns to her and his tears are flowing with the sweat and the black down his cheeks. His tongue pushes over his cracked lips. The Other Mother is not moving or screaming any longer and Docca Gunree's red eyes are seeing into Alma until he knows what she has seen, what she knows. She screams and runs back and around and down the front stairs and deeper into the house, into her secret hiding place grown cold. Alma pulls the piggy in place and flattens her body against the wool blanket and holds the doll Mother made for her close to her chest and closes her eyes as tight as she can. She is careful not to sing but she knows the words and Mother's sweet voice is here in the dark and her warm breath is on Alma's cheek. She pushes away the memory of Docca Gunree's face and the black and the little face and lips when he stopped and cut—

Sleep the dream sleep o' sweet child
Mother is here
when the sun she rises and when she sets
Mother is your home, the only home Alma needs
remember Mother lives forever, forever in Alma's
  heart
remember every day, o' sweet child
no tears for me does child Alma shed
thread through a needle cannot mend a young
  girl's heart

350

*Mother is here o' sweet child Alma even when
thread through a needle cannot mend a young
   girl's heart*

—and through the song Alma is with Mother
and no longer frightened, even when his boots
come thudding down the stairs and over the floor
and the piggy is loose and the cold comes in and
his hot wet hands are pulling her out. Even when
he is tearing her dress on the piggy and lifting
Alma high and throwing her down on the bed and
screaming over her and pressing his wet lips and
the salt penny blood and black beard against her
young skin and his heavy hands are scratching are
touching are shaking Alma for the first time in
many months as he will again for many nights in
the next six winters which are for Alma the longest
seasons.

              *   *   *

She is standing before the mirror. Alma. She
stands bare before the tall glass and marvels at her
body, the strange power she feels building within.
Her legs are equine, rippling with sinew and whiter
than snow. Her hips are as dinner plates, sliding
beneath her flesh as she twists. Her breasts are
heavy in her hands, and she traces the mysterious
blue lines pulsing beneath the surface like rivers
flowing to the wide rose circles, one larger than
the other, each aching with a dull throb she
encourages and fears. Beneath her waist is thick
delta that has grown as luminously black as the
strands falling below her shoulders. She places one
palm over the cusp of her belly and closes her eyes.

She thinks by now she should be able to feel the lil'un inside, but his pulse continues to elude her fingertips. All the things Dr Justin Gundry has done to her. Alma knows she has given a life, but she does not have a life. Not yet. Or perhaps, as she heard one of the last remaining women of the house comment late one evening last winter, the things he has done have already ruint her. Perhaps she cannot make life. Was a time this thought brought tears to her eyes, but that time has passed. Alma fears not this fate. She does not know her age, but she knows she is a woman. She knows that Mother was correct. Alma has grown big and strong, and at last she is prepared to take a life to have a life.

Downstairs the Other Mother with red hair of fire is singing her gayest song, as she has been singing for the past three months since her arrival, since Dr Justin Gundry gave her the lil'un. Dr Justin Gundry has grown old and feeble, but his spirits appear to lighten in this new Other Mother's presence. Though the Other Mother with red hair of fire sings, her voice is not sweet like Mother's. Alma knows the night is coming, and soon.

*   *   *

Alma is standing over the bassinet where the lil'un with red hair sleeps. She awakens at the sight of her, her shining black infant's eyes searching in the dark. Alma extends a finger and she clutches it with a stubby but firm grip. She blinks up at her, and Alma loses herself in singing to her.

She is still singing when the Other Mother with

red hair of fire enters with the oil lamp and begins shrieking.

—Away, away from my child, Justin make her go away

* * *

Alma is standing on the porch feeling the snow blow in. The Other Mother with red hair of fire is shouting but Alma cannot hear her words. She is staring at the Doctor, who cannot bring his red eyes to meet hers. At last he pulls his new bride inside and leaves Alma standing in the cold.

* * *

Alma is pacing in the woods, stomping through snow that covers her ankles as she rakes her hands through the winter air, clutching and snapping at branches. Her shrieks echo through the dell and no one is here to answer.

—mother mother mother mother mother

Inside her, he feels the color of her mounting rage and knows it is a blackness without end.

* * *

When Alma returns the house is silent, dark, sleeping. She moves through the front parlor, up the servants' stairs, into the library. She walks on soft bare feet and opens the door to the Doctor's quarters. He is sleeping deeply, the sour perfume of his medicine hanging in the air. Alma closes the door and retreats. She walks back around the black maple banister to the delivery room where some of the Other Mothers gave a life, that which has now become the nursery.

The Other Mother with red hair of fire is sitting in the rocking chair, head bowed, with her back to Alma. The lil'un coos in the night before returning to her feeding. The lil'un is still suckling when Alma brings the blade through her mother's throat.

*   *   *

In the basement, Alma removes the piggy and places the swaddling child in her lair, making a nest of the wool blanket, adding another to ensure her warmth until she is able to return.

—I shall call you Chesapeake, from the place Mother was born

The child with red hair stares up at Alma, reaching for her finger.

—Sleep the dream sleep, Chessie, until Mother returns

*   *   *

Alma's arms are burning. She has grown strong, but the Other Mother grows heavier with each step. The path to the forbidden place stretches out into the frozen night, and the snow is streaked red with each lumbering step. She leans forward, pulling as a mule pulls the plow through deep soil. Inside the forbidden place is a table and Alma rests the body there. Above is a rope dangling from one of the beams. Alma loops the rope around the wrists and neck and pulls. She knows the ground is too hard for digging, but tomorrow

354

she will have to dig no matter the weather. For she knows the secrets the Doctor keeps and what bones wait under the cross in the yard. For many years he has kept these hidden from the rest of their growing society outside of the house in Black Earth. Alma knows there are men of the law who would come if she sent word and the Doctor would hang for his crimes, as the red hair of fire now hangs for hers. But she knows too that exposure would bring the house from under them and Alma would be lost without a home for Chessie. Worse, the people of the growing society would perhaps spread their judgment and take her Chessie away.

She closes the door and washes her hands in the snow.

Inside she warms herself by the fire. Her hands are stiff, and she moves them over the flames. Her work this night is not finished.

* * *

Alma stands in the hall, in the doorway facing the sleeping Doctor.

—Comes the time

He is slow to stir and so she makes her voice stronger, undeniable.

—Justin Gundry comes the time to join Mother

Her voice, after so many seasons of silence, mutes Doctor Justin Gundry with a fear he has not known, but already he is rising from his bed. He is on his feet quickly, then hesitating, unsteady. Alma is forced to bring the silver blade to use sooner than planned, but she is not yet concerned. He lunges. Alma has grown tall and strong but the old Doctor is stronger. In the struggle that ensues

355

between the master quarters and the hall where the black maple banister curves all the way around, Alma is pushed back even as she employs a life of hatred and rock-hard strength to plunge the knife into his belly and up, up, under the breastplate. He gasps, spewing spittle in her face. She rolls him aside calling his name over and over to place her judgment and for Mother.

—Justin Gundry Justin Gundry Justin Gundry

Justin Gundry the mortally wounded falls, but not before clutching his orphaned child Alma to tumble with him. Together they descend to the main floor foyer and the sound of Alma's neck is as loud and small as a sapling birch in winter. He is on top of her, her hand still clutching the handle of the blade, the point of which the fall has driven into his spine. As he breathes his last, his gray eyes bore down and Alma releases the knife to take him by the throat. She crushes the bones under the flesh until his gray eyes run to black and rupture as he passes from this life into that which lies beyond.

In the deep of the house the child called Chesapeake cries out for its mother, for any mother, to mend her young heart.

Alma rolls the Doctor off her. She cannot feel beneath her waist, but she can move her arms. She claws at the floor and begins to drag herself to her lil'un. Her cries echo all around her, and she cannot find the way down. She uses the last of her strength to lift her head, straining like a serpent there upon the floor, until the cords stand out and flex and the last splintered bone severs under the pressure and there is no more pain.

Alma's body abandons its functions even as her spirit, this indomitable inside of her, lashes out for the new life it has always desired, staining the floors and walls and stones as it joins the Other Mothers who have given a life to have a life.

Child Chesapeake's cries go unanswered. She perishes in the stone walls that hide their secrets until another Great War passes and the new people of faith come bearing hope for a new life. Only then are the Daughters of Eve, the All Mother, awakened, ready to usher in new Life and Its unending need into the birthing house.

The world cuts.

40

Time became once again a thing he could sense, and the room smelled of medicine. He was warm, floating in a womb of weightlessness, surrounded by dim sounds and occasionally rocked as in a crib. He regained physical sensations of soft cotton wrapping his naked body, but still he remained heavy with sleep.

He was too weak to rise but in the darkened room there was warm flesh and the pressure in his mouth. When the cool button slipped between his teeth at first he resisted, but his hunger was stronger and so he fed. During the feedings he experienced the last of the visions that weaved her history, and he came to understand that he had been feeding this way all through the long long night.

The last he remembered was the fight, and chasing his wife up the stairs so that he could apologize to her. There were flashes of her fall

357

that came after, but nothing beyond the stairs. He knew that he was missing an important detail from the very end, but whenever he tried to remember his wife's face it escaped him. When the pain in his stomach flared up like an umbilicus of fire, she would come again, hovering over him, feeding him, filling him up as he had filled her during the lonely nights. He did not know how much he had healed, but he felt better after, full of her.

The pain was still a fire inside of him, but he was driven from bed by the need to know. He looked under the moist cloth around his waist and saw the purple-black thread where she had sewn him up. He was able to walk, slowly, and he moved down the stairs over the better portion of an hour. He shuffled around the main floor and checked every room. He looked behind the doors in the bathroom and the kitchen pantry and in the foyer. When the dogs began to follow him he stopped to feed them and nearly fainted bending over the bowls.

He went down the stairs into the basement. He shone the flashlight on the stone foundation walls and stood in the spot where Luther had been growling and bleeding. He stared at the foundation and traced the stones with his eyes until they fell upon the one that was loose. He was too weak to remove the stone to see what lay inside, but he need not bother. He already knew what secrets the little piggy kept.

If there had been any doubt, it vanished. Not doubt that he had lost his mind, for he knew that he had. He had fallen prey to loneliness and delusions brought on by guilt and the emotional, if not completely physical infidelity with Nadia. But if any doubt remained that Alma had been real, as real as his wife, this before him ended all such doubt.

A single loosened stone. He had not noticed it when he searched before. But his dog Luther had noticed it, and knew something inside these stone walls was not right. He was for a moment, but only for a moment, relieved at the sight of it now. Because it allowed that he was not a murderer. He knew he had lost track of time—the time between Nadia leaving his bed and Jo discovering her in the garage—but he had never believed he was a true savage, a killer.

But he was guilty.

What had Laski said about hauntings?

It happens to good people, because even good people got problems. And problems is what your haunted house feeds on, son. Just like a one of them payday loan stores. So it goes, and sometimes it goes to murder.

Conrad knew that he was responsible. Alma may have performed the ritual removal of Nadia's unborn, but what had given birth to Alma? Had he not fed Alma as he had fed Nadia? As surely as the girl's pregnancy and hopes were fed by his domestic duties in the kitchen, so too was Alma fed by his yearning, his desire to be a father. From his first days under her roof, he had left the door open for her return.

She had always been here, but now she was loose, reclaiming her place among the living and breathing.

He had to do something about that.

He exited the basement through the wooden door to the yard. The night was cool and he

359

walked slowly down the path toward Our Eden.

He stopped when he reached the grave. The dirt was fresh, bulging obscenely above the grass. A small cross made of sticks had been set on top, tied with string, just as the Doctor had taught her more than a century before.

He was about to start digging when self-preservation kicked in again.

The Grums. The police. They would have scoured Eddie's trailer. They could have evidence linking him to the crime scene by now.

No, the authorities would have been here, and he would have come back to life in a hospital, or a cell. The yard would look like the site of an archeological dig, and the neighbors would be lining up with torches to burn the house to the ground.

Not yet, but they would be here soon.

He said a prayer asking for her forgiveness and turned away from the dirt. He walked in agony back up the path, over the deck, and up the stairs into the house. As he focused on each step, wincing at the fire of his wounds reopening, some trunk in his mind unlocked itself and asked the final question.

For the first time since coming back to life, he wondered if his wife was here too or in some other place, with Nadia.

41

When he reached the kitchen he saw that the living room was blinking with red and white light. His skin crawled and his heart tripped. The blood began to pool at his waist, soaking the bandages anew. He moved forward, swaying, and clutched the mantle in the living room to keep from fainting. There were no sirens yet, but through the front window, through the gauzy curtains, he could see the cars parked in front of the Grums'. The lights on top were sliding in flat rows, greetings from an alien craft.

He closed his eyes.

They knew you were lying, and they are coming for you tonight.

Another siren squelched, and then a woman screamed from the front lawn.

I'm sorry, Gail. I'm so sorry.

Elsewhere his dogs began to moan, and he knew they were not upset about what was coming, but what was already here.

42

He turned away from the windows and the red lights. The dogs were standing in the foyer where Jo had come to rest, whining with their tails tucked low. He heard footsteps above and the dogs began to bay. With his neck arched back he could see directly up the stairway and under the black maple banister to the master bedroom hallway.

Her pale legs moved under a swishing dirty hemline, her bare foot turning away from the posts as she entered the bedroom.

'Stay,' he bid them, taking the stairs.

And, as he went up to meet the author of his resurrection, they did.

THREAD

As he climbed the stairs he felt like a dead man reborn.

He had come back, but as what? His skin felt porous and his feet light, as if he were already a ghost, all spirit ready to flee the flesh. But this notion was brief and with his next step obliterated by the stabbing pain in his torn belly and the warm blood that still trickled from his near-fatal wound. In a panic he reached for his chest and found his heart beating strong, audible in the silence of his ascent. He had survived, and now he wanted to live, no matter the cost. Beyond that, he knew only that the house was dark and he was finally going to meet her with clarity and purpose. He focused on the stairs one at a time, moving slowly, absorbed in every detail even as one fated moment slid away to make room for the next.

This is my house. These are my feet. See them climbing the stairs. See them carrying me to where at last my love will be revealed. For whatever she has become, she is the final product of my love. I will go to her, and I am going to her with a heart only she can mend.

Seven stairs, eight.

Nine.

Tonight I go to her. Tonight I go to be a man. To do man's work.

Oh yes, I'm still alive.

Here at the top of the stairs are the walls and the floorboards stained with the tears of childbirth. Life has emerged through this house and life has passed out of it. There is a crack in the floor and it is the crack of the world, the house's hot canal, forever giving birth. From the home we are born and to the home we return. All that lies between is the hearth and the dying embers of the fire that once burned inside.

Tonight we will feel warm again, together. One last time.

When he entered the bedroom it was as if he had stepped back in time with Holly. They were intruders in a home they had claimed as their own, owners by the rights granted new love. Candles burned from nightstands and dressers and ledges and window sills. She had remembered their night, and made it so that he would remember. She wanted to please him. And so that even in the dark of night he could see her clearly. He stood on the threshold of the master bedroom and studied her as she lay in waiting on the bed. She was his Holly girl on the night she had conceived his lost child, weeping for what they had done. But he didn't want to go back to the pain and the loss, only forward.

With that wish, to his relief, Holly was gone.

In her place was Nadia, the curve of her milky white belly glowing, a shy smile on her lips. But he had never loved Nadia, not this way. Not with the

363

depths of knowledge and sorrow the house had unlocked in him. Their common history and shared suffering. He had never known love such as this, because his love was always shifting. You love one with an intensity that can kill, and then she goes away and another comes to take her place. You grow full of love and then lose it and you shrivel and die, and then you awaken. The heart has needs and the heart needs the body. You change, adapt, and find love again. It is survival. This one you wed and declare the one, the final, the ultimate. But she dies too, and yet you survive. Your love survives because your love needs a home.

Eventually there is the last love, and then only death.

Nadia was dead. As soon as he accepted that without deception, Nadia was no longer the woman on his bed.

In her place was a long form, the full six feet of her, the womanly sway of her curves. The second chance that could not be. His departed wife, Joanna. The candles flickered as a summer breeze lifted the curtains and she glowed in the dim light the way he had always dreamed her waiting for him in this house. The way he'd imagined her the night after the unpacking, when he'd thought he was bedding his wife and managed only to awaken a much older presence in the house. He let himself study her as long as it lasted, but summer was ending and what wind blew through the window was now cool as the breath of autumn. The imagination has power but the heart has more, and when his heart desired the final truth it was granted.

All his expectations slipped away and he saw her.

His woman in the back row, the one who scowled because she was not like the others. Alma reborn, at first ethereal and later, after feeding on him, corporeal.

Daughter of Eve, the All Mother, cruel as Mother Nature Herself.

Alma.

Leon had done his best by her, but his best had not been enough to keep the fair maiden at bay. She had taken her toll on the Laski children—a maiming here, a stillborn there—and eventually driven his shattering clan from the house. If *Our Eden* had once been blessed with life, then its history of darkly human deeds had spawned Alma, and its healing power now came at a cost. A cost tallied not by God or nature but by the goddess who still resided here. She had waited until she could wait no more, until she found one who shared her pain, then gambled on his need, his tired lust. Perhaps God or Dr Hobarth's debunked theory of parthenogenesis had been responsible for Shadow's miracle clutch of python eggs. But God's had not been the vengeful hand at work in his wife's demise, in the gruesome termination of Nadia and her unborn. Alma, who had suffered God and man's wrath too long, had long grown tired of the miracle of life. Alma desired only the miracle of her life, a miracle that produced life for her.

He understood now that she would keep exacting her pound of flesh until she was given one to call her own. If fate had delivered him to her, his longing opened the door for her. Each taking new life from their darkest couplings. She had fed on him, then Nadia, and finally Jo. Alma had fed until she was finally strong enough to claim Jo and finish her work. Tonight she had offered him one last glimpse of the other mothers—Holly, Nadia, Jo—and one final choice.

The ghosts of women past, or the flesh of the ghost incarnate.

He chose Alma.

She was raven-haired and tall and her pose was stiff, her arms and legs resting in the parallel lines of a corpse on the autopsy table. Her skin was not gray—that had been a trick of the light. She was white. Startlingly so from lack of sun and loss of life and blood. Her back bowed proudly and her breasts were large and round, with wide rose tips. Her nipples were stiff and, though she made no attempt to cover herself, she was shivering. Her sex was full and black, the color of her love. With his eyes he traced the curve of her hips, the familiar lines of the woman she had been.

He knew this body well, this body she had taken. What was once illusion was now a cold and cruel reality. The skin and hair and the rest of her shell was Jo, but the spirit, everything that was the soul inside and staring back at him, was Alma. In this house she had lived for a century and he only a summer, but to each it remained the only home they'd ever known.

Husband and wife, until death do us part.

Outside these walls, the car doors began to slam and the voices became a chorus of shouts and orders barked. Their footsteps pounded over the porch boards, shaking the front of the house.

Conrad ignored them as his clothes fell to the

366

floor in a whisper. When he lay down beside her his heart beat stronger, and he was not surprised to feel his arousal quickening toward the familiar. He thought of murder and revenge and blood gushing between his fingers as they sank into her neck to end the thing that had taken Jo and Nadia and the other mother with the red hair of fire and her child, but Alma stalled all such dreams when she rolled to one side and pressed her cold shape against him. He saw stars under clenched eyelids until she pried his fingers loose from the bedding, and her touch was a welcome balm.

When he looked into her eyes and saw himself reflected in the black liquid pools, his fear began to ebb. She had saved him when he no longer deserved saving, when all others had abandoned him. She was offering him forgiveness.

He pulled her tightly against him, wishing to make her warm. To know that she was alive too. He wanted to stay with her forever. As if to prove her vitality and further allay his fears, her limbs stirred and claimed him, rolling him onto his back to sit astride his hips. Her lips were firm and he saw the fissure scar above as he kissed her there upon her healing. He tasted her cool tongue warming, warming even now, pushing into his mouth at the same moment that he pushed past her slick opening and deeper, to the end.

She pulled away before he could taste her breath, or know that she was breathing at all. But her chest expanded as she began to rock, wetting his lap, and their hearts began to beat in unison. He felt one last spike of the blackness, the fear and lust and hunger for violent revenge, certain that none of this would last and that he would die here, alone.

His thoughts swung between two choices, as they had for all men.

Love and death.

Life and murder.

An end and a beginning.

The front door burst open with a thunderous crash and the men were shouting his name, ordering him to come out, to reveal his sin. The voices fanned out through the house and the dogs sang as they set upon the interlopers.

She took his hands, folding them in prayer. She held him until her warmth spread through his fingers but he clung to the darkness, the grief, the anger.

His fingers crawled over her breasts and along her throat and she moaned, reading his intention as if reading his mind.

Without slowing she opened his palms and slid them down, lower, lower, placing them flat against her belly, showing him his work, holding his new world inside her body until he could feel what was to come, what he had never felt before, that which he had been searching for since it had been stolen from him years and years ago, when he was seventeen.

The men with guns beat a heavy drum up the stairs.

Any second now, in a sliver of time, a span within which life might blossom or be smothered, the law would fall on them and its weight and judgment would be mighty. Knowing this, he entertained visions of cold courtrooms and colder prison cells, of foster parents for the dogs and endless grief for the parents, of earth tilled for

368

burial and graves wreathed with flowers, all of them strands of a future flowing from this human contest to go on.

But those were only visions, realities yet to be born. Until they cast him inexorably toward such a fate, he refused to allow them shelter. For at last his home was full, its hearth so very warm.

Inside her womb he felt the affirmation of his power to create, the other side of the darkness, his only purpose in this world, his final beginning.

The stirring within, its tiny beating heart.

Soon she would be a mother, and he a father.

Acknowledgments

If any first-time novelist and his first-born ever received a warmer welcome to the delivery room, this author is unaware of them. To my agent and friend Scott Miller, and the entire team at Trident Media Group, your faith changed my life. To my publisher, David Shelley, you are a gentleman whose passion continues to astonish. Thank you for introducing me to the UK, and for your interest in the house. Nikola, Thalia, Nathalie, the two Emmas, Richard, Simon and everyone else at Sphere—you are all multi-talented saints and I owe you many pints.

To the citizens of the real Black Earth, please forgive my geographical liberties and warped perceptions. I know this ain't your town, but the name was too appropriate to resist.